A PLUME BOOK

OTHERWORLD SECRETS

KELLEY ARMSTRONG is the number one *New York Times* bestselling author of the Otherworld series, as well as the young adult trilogy Darkest Powers, the Darkness Rising trilogy, and the Nadia Stafford series. She lives in rural Ontario, Canada.

OTHERWORLD SECRETS

MORE THRILLING OTHERWORLD TALES

KELLEY ARMSTRONG

A PLUME BOOK

PLUME
An imprint of Penguin Random House LLC
375 Hudson Street
New York, New York 10014

Originally published in Canada by Random House, 2015
First Plume printing 2016

Some of the stories in *Otherworld Secrets* have been published
online or in obscure collections.

❚❚ REGISTERED TRADEMARK—MARCA REGISTRADA

LIBRARY OF CONGRESS CATALOGING-IN-PUBLICATION DATA
has been applied for.

ISBN 978-0-45-229835-4

Printed in the United States of America
1   3   5   7   9   10   8   6   4   2

CONTENTS

LIFE AFTER THEFT

PROLOGUE

*S*haron Avery settled her large frame into a chair on Fredrick Birkan's rooftop deck and gazed down the mountainside at Lake Geneva. How much money did one need to own a house in the Swiss Alps? Enough that she was quickly recalculating the price of the goods she was about to offer Birkan.

Birkan came out the French door and handed her a glass of wine and then set a plate of cheeses on the patio table. He made the requisite small talk. She replied by rote. Idle chatter really wasn't her thing, but Birkan was the kind of man who'd dismiss her as a crass American if she got right down to business.

Finally, he broached the subject himself, swirling his wine before saying, ever so casually, "I took a chance inviting you to my home, Ms. Avery. You are a stranger to me and I do not usually invite strangers here. But I made a rare exception, based on your excellent professional reputation."

That was a lie. According to her sources, he said the same thing to every potential new business associate, to make them feel both honored and obliged to live up to his expectations. And, she presumed, so he could show off his estate—a don't-fuck-with-me display of his wealth and power in the supernatural community.

"I will admit," Birkan continued, "when you first contacted me, I thought it was a joke. The item you offered . . . well, it is not exactly easy to obtain."

"I wouldn't offer it to you if it was," she said. "That would be an insult to the quality of your collection."

He nodded, pleased. "Yet you believe you can obtain it? While you have a sterling reputation, I am told it is impossible, even for a master thief."

"True, but I've come into some information that will make it much easier. And I have a particular thief in mind. One whose reputation surpasses even my own."

She reached into her briefcase and passed him a file folder. As he read the first page, his brows shot up.

"Karl Marsten? The werewolf?"

"Is that a problem?"

"He is notoriously difficult to hire. I have tried myself and have not even been able to arrange a meeting with him."

"I can get you one."

Birkan tapped the folder. "So he has not truly retired?"

Avery smiled. "Oh, he says he has. But I believe we can persuade him to take one last job."

ONE

As I edited the piece on chupacabra sightings, I sipped my decaf coffee and ignored the disapproving looks from the sales director. A week ago, she had informed me—complete with Web links—that even decaf contained caffeine and I was endangering the life of my unborn child. I'd pointed out that I'd drunk decaf all through my pregnancy with Nita, whereupon she'd made some snide comment about my daughter's high activity levels. I ignored that. Nita had a werewolf and a chaos half-demon for parents—one couldn't expect her to sit quietly for long.

I returned my attention to the article, written by an intern who apparently had managed to get through college without learning the difference between "there," "their," and "they're." I had only myself to blame, given that I'd hired him. I'm now the editor at *True News*, which would be far more impressive if I hadn't been promoted during a downsizing, when they'd decided I could handle the position while still being lead reporter. But it's a miracle we're open at all—*World Weekly News* stopped publishing years ago when the Internet began fulfilling the public's appetite for "Proof of Elvis on Mars!" stories.

When my phone rang, I answered with, "Hope Adams." My brother, Joel, laughed and said, "You guys can't afford call display?"

"No, I can't afford the two seconds it takes to look at it. I'm rewriting an intern's piece and lamenting the state of the modern education system. Which makes me feel very old."

"Maybe so, but I'll join you in that lament. I just hired two MBAs who don't know how to write a proper business letter. Which segues nicely into the reason for my call. Good employees are hard to find, and when you do find one, you do everything in your power to keep him. I need you to talk to your husband."

"I thought Karl was working out well."

"Better than well. I had three guys working on a security plan for weeks, and they couldn't meet the specs. In two days, Karl had it done. The client was ecstatic."

"Okay . . ."

"Then I put him on this project protecting something called the Anatolian Hoard. It's supposedly cursed, so figured he'd get a kick out of it, given what you do for a living."

"So what happened?"

Silence. Then, "He didn't tell you? He quit."

"What?"

"I gave him the project yesterday morning. He started work on it. Then, after lunch, he tells me he wanted to go back into sales. I tried to talk him out of it, but you know your husband. I may be his boss, but with Karl that's a technicality. Which is where you come in. Will you talk to him? Please?"

When I married Karl, I knew exactly what he was. Not just a werewolf, but a jewel thief. Hell, I'd met him because I'd been hired to foil one of his museum heists. So there were no illusions. And the fact that he retired from the life six months ago has nothing to do with me. In fact, if I had my way, he'd still be stealing jewels, because that's his life—it's how he's lived since his father died when he was fifteen. More important, it's how he works off the nastier instincts that come with being a werewolf. Instead of chasing human prey, he chases the glittering variety, getting his adrenaline rush from that.

Nobody understands the importance of that sublimation better than me, as a half-demon who craves the same rush.

Karl had begun talking about retiring when Nita was born. He'd been shot in the head a couple of days before her birth, while I'd been taken captive, our unborn daughter held as "ransom" to get my father's—Lucifer's—attention. All that had nothing to do with Karl's profession, but it still put things in perspective, and he'd wanted to make changes, starting by quitting the life.

I'd convinced him there was no point. He took only a few jobs a year, all out of country, and it would be years before Nita started asking questions. Then we'd started working on having another baby, and he'd barely broached the subject of quitting again when we had an . . . incident. It was at a Pack Meet. The youngest Pack member, Noah, had asked Karl to show him a few tricks, because he was taking law enforcement in college, so he was curious. Karl obliged. Nita watched. Then we returned home to discover her luggage contained two books, a stuffed animal, and a necklace that she'd stolen from the Danvers twins.

Nita had been very proud of herself, regaling her father with the story as best a three-year-old can tell one. She'd gotten a long talk about the notion of private property and a trip back to Stonehaven to return the items with apologies. The twins had been very impressed and made her show them how she'd done it—getting the books and toy from a high shelf and the jewelry from around Kate's neck. Elena and Jeremy had been amused. Clayton was not. But one person was even more appalled than Clay: Karl. When we got home Sunday night, he'd called my brother to see if his long-standing offer of employment still stood.

TWO

*A*fter Joel's call, I packed in my editing early and headed out to find Karl and Nita.

After Nita was born, we'd moved from a condo to a house . . . the sort of home that befits two people with very healthy bank accounts. Not some obscenely tacky modern mansion—that isn't Karl's style or mine. It's an early twentieth-century two-story on an acre of land, backing onto a ravine. The money went into the location—a neighborhood dating back almost to the time my dad's family landed on the *Mayflower*. And by "dad," I mean Will Adams, the man who raised me, not my biological father. Dad's family may be old, but compared with Lucifer's, they're strictly new blood.

Given the time, Karl and Nita would be at the park. Karl worked only part-time for Joel, doing as much as possible from home, because he was the primary caregiver for our daughter. As he says, there's only a brief window before kids go off to school, and it's an experience he's never going to get again.

Even from the parking lot, I could see my husband. In a sea of au pairs, nannies, and mothers, the only man stuck out. Not that Karl wouldn't stick out anyway. He's fifty-six, but werewolves age slowly, so he looks more like a forty-year-old guy in prime condition: six feet tall, well built, wavy black hair barely touched with silver, and a face that belongs on the silver screen. Of course, being married to him, I could be biased, but the looks he got from the other caregivers said I was not.

As Karl watched Nita on the climbers, a couple of the twenty-something nannies stood nearby, trying to catch his attention and failing miserably. When Karl switches on the charm, he's undeniable, which is why he'd made a good salesman. Yet it really is a switch, and when it's off, that's a hint: leave him alone or you'll wish you had.

When he saw me, that somber expression broke into a smile and he turned . . . just as Nita attempted to leap across three bars. I yelped a warning, but Karl was already in flight, catching her as deftly as if he'd never taken his eyes off her, which he hadn't, not completely.

"Oh, your nanny's here," one of the women said, adding, "Finally," with a look that told me I really shouldn't force my poor boss to—God forbid—take care of his own child.

As for why she presumed I was the nanny, let's just say that every other woman of color in that playground was caring for someone else's kids. My mother is Indo-American, and being half-demon means I get my looks from her. That's when Nita spotted me and let out a whoop of "Mommy!" diving from Karl's arms. I scooped her up as Karl came over and kissed me, and the nannies decided they really ought to get back to, you know, actually watching the kids they were being paid to watch.

"Mommy, Mommy, Mommy," Nita sang as she hugged me tight enough to inhibit breathing. "Did you see me jump?"

"I saw you nearly *fall*."

"Daddy caught me."

"Daddy won't always be there to catch you," I said, ignoring the look on Karl's face that said he damned well would be. "You need to be more careful. Or you'll take a tumble and—"

"Break my arm," she said, giggling. "Kate broke her arm. I want to break mine."

"No, you do not."

"I never broke a bone. I want to."

"To see what it's like? I'll tell you. It hurts."

She shrugged, as if this was inconsequential compared with the thrill of a new experience, and I cursed Lucifer for that. When Nita was born, my demon father said she would inherit some of my chaos hunger, making it more manageable for me. Which it is, but it's left my daughter with a thirst for adventure that keeps us very, very busy. This is as bad as it will get, though, and if pressed I'll admit that's not such a horrible thing, and it's not entirely the fault of *my* genes. If I were too worried, I certainly wouldn't be having a second child.

"Park done, Daddy." Nita twisted in my arms and launched herself back at her father. "Ice cream time."

"I believe ice cream is on Tuesdays," he said. "Today is Thursday."

"Mommy's having a baby. She needs ice cream. My book says so. Milk and cheese and ice cream for . . ." Her face screwed up.

"Calcium," I said.

"Calcium!" she said, screeching the word like she'd found a new toy. "Calcium, calcium, calcium. Mommy needs calcium. Mommy needs ice cream."

"You're right," Karl said. "So we'll buy Mommy some. You and I will sit and watch—"

"No! Daddy watch. Mommy and Nita eat. Need calcium, calcium, calcium!" She wriggled down, saying, "Slide!" and then took off for one last ride, running and singing at the top of her lungs.

"She's such a deeply unhappy child," Karl said. "I don't know where we went wrong."

I laughed. Nita does have a temper—no idea where *that* came from—but the best word to describe our daughter is *exuberant*. I watched her run off, black curls streaming behind her. If the nannies were surprised she was my daughter, they needed glasses. Her big blue eyes are Karl's, but otherwise she has my hair, my features, and skin only a shade lighter. Also, sadly, she has inherited her mother's size, meaning we've just barely gotten out of the infants' section.

Karl took my hand, entwining it in his as we walked. When we first started dating—after two years of being friends—he'd have no more held my hand in public than he'd have worn brown shoes with black trousers. I won't say marriage and kids have mellowed him, but they've calmed something in his core. It is the realization of a goal he never allowed himself to even acknowledge. He had a stable life now—with territory and family—and public displays of affection declared that this was his choice and he was happy with it.

His hand tightened around mine. "I'd ask if you got done early, but I know that never happens. Was it work you could bring home?"

I nodded.

"Excellent timing. Nita goes for her nap after we get back home."

"Giving me a quiet hour to work?"

He met my smile with one of his own. "Not exactly what I had in mind, but you can certainly *try* to work during it. I'd be rather disappointed if you managed, though."

I laughed. I was tempted to let the job conversation wait until after sex. Four months pregnant meant I was into my favorite stage of the process, where I'm past the morning sickness, far from waddling, and enjoying the surge of hormones that make sex even better than usual, which is saying a lot.

It helps that I have a partner who very enthusiastically takes advantage of my libido upswing. Having a three-year-old, though, means scant private time. If I got the chance for an hour alone with my husband, I really did not want to spend it having a discussion that might turn into a fight. Sadly, I wouldn't be able to push this conversation out of my mind enough to focus on sex.

As we were walking back to the house, I told Karl that we needed to talk first. Then I put Nita down for her nap, which is easier than one might think. She actually embraces the rest time, even reminding us if we forget it. She can feel her batteries running low and wants the recharge.

When I came out of her room, Karl had made tea.

"I came home early because Joel called," I said as I settled onto the sofa.

Karl was at the bar, getting a water from the fridge. At my words, he stiffened, just a little. He uncapped a Perrier, his back still to me.

"I was going to tell you," he said.

"I should hope so."

"I planned to do it after dinner," he said as he turned to meet my eyes. "Last night, we were preoccupied with Nita bumping her head, and this morning I didn't want to hit you with it as you were heading to work."

"Okay. I'd still rather not have heard it from my brother, but let's move on. You *liked* the security work, Karl. Liked it a hell of a lot more than sales. Designing and debugging security systems is right up your alley."

He'd been standing in front of the bar, listening. Now he came over and sat in the chair across from me. He fingered the bottle and stared out the back window, and as I watched him, turned away from me to hide his expression.

At home, Karl doesn't dull his edges—he just keeps them covered. Working as a salesman, though, doesn't just dull those edges—it smashes them and leaves him a little bit broken. It was killing me to watch it happen.

Worse, I had to *feel* it happen. As a chaos half-demon, I get a direct line to other people's chaos. My powers may have weakened along with my hunger, but when my husband is struggling, I feel every twitch and roil of it.

I got to my feet and walked to the patio doors and out onto the back deck. Karl followed, leaving the door open so we could hear Nita's bell. We refuse to put a lock on our bedroom door for privacy, so we put a bell over hers. We tell her it's her princess bell, so we know when the princess is awake and her loyal servants can be ready.

I waited until he was outside. Then I turned to face him. "Tell me what I can do to make you quit sales."

"Hope . . ."

"I know this isn't about me. It's about you, and what you want for your family, for your kids. You want to be able to tell them what you do for a living and have them be proud of you. But you know what, Karl? You being miserable in a job isn't going to make them proud."

"It isn't about them being proud of me. It's about having *some-thing* to tell them. I don't want my children to grow up with lies. The sales job is a temporary measure while I figure out what I want."

"How about the security work that you just quit?"

He eased back. "I had a reason."

"You researched the Anatolian Hoard, saw the Eye of Pldans, and knew if you designed the plans to secure it, you'd be tempted to breach them yourself. To steal it."

He looked up sharply.

"What?" I said. "I'm your wife. I hope I could figure out at least one plausible reason why you quit after being given that specific job. I looked up the Hoard. It contains the Eye of Pldans. A jeweled amulet with a diamond center. In the human world, they say it's cursed. But in the supernatural world, it's believed to convey the power of fire to anyone with demon blood. In other words, for a half-demon, it adds a bonus power. That means that while it's valuable to humans, it's even more valuable on the supernatural black market."

He was quiet for a minute. Then he said, "I put out a few feelers to see if anyone was looking to buy it. I told myself that was part of the research. A security system must protect against the super-natural powers of potential thieves."

"Yes, and you can't steal it even if you wanted to. It's historically significant. That violates your agreement with Clayton."

"True, but the buyer I uncovered isn't a supernatural. He's a Turkish national who plans to return it to his government, the rightful owners."

"Meaning you could get the thrill plus the payday of a heist, and even Clay would admit it wasn't a bad thing."

"Not really my priority."

"But still, win-win, right?"

"Except for the part where I betray my brother-in-law's trust. And betray my own decision to retire, a mere six months after making it."

I lowered myself into a deck chair. "I just want you to be happy, Karl."

"I am."

I met his gaze. "Chaos half-demon, remember? I can tell when you're unsettled."

"Unsettled, yes. Not unhappy. Am I as happy as I was three months ago, when you told me you were pregnant again? No. Am I happier than I was before I met you? Absolutely. The worst days since you came into my life are better than the best days that came before it, Hope." He paused. "Except for when I was shot in the head while you were kidnapped by your psycho ex. That wins for worst day ever."

I laughed in spite of myself.

He continued. "But other than that, I'm much happier now. Also, being shot in the head makes a man rethink his life. I didn't want to die and have you lie to our child about what her father did for a living. Perhaps that shouldn't have crossed my mind. But it did. It still does. I want to be able to look our children in the eye when I answer that question."

"Getting a legit job doesn't mean you need to *stop* being a thief."

"Try to have it all?" He shook his head. "I spent fifty years thinking only of myself. I've had enough of that to last a lifetime. I'm only struggling a little because this is a period of transition. And it's not as if I plan to give up every bit of adventure in my life and settle into a desk job. I have Pack missions, and I have inter-racial council investigations with you."

He pulled another chair over to sit in front of me. "I'll feed my own chaos cravings with those, and I'll find a better position, and everything will be fine." He leaned back in his seat. "By the way, the answer is four."

"To what question?"

"How many kids I want. I know we keep going back and forth. Three, maybe four, no, three . . ."

"So we're done talking about the security job?"

"You want me happy. I've picked a topic that makes me much happier." He rose, picked me up, and put me on the railing, his hands on my hips as he moved closer. "You've said it's up to me, and I keep waffling, which is highly uncharacteristic. But I've never felt it *should* be my choice. Yes, I know, you've said you don't care, but you're still the one who has to go through a nine-month pregnancy and childbirth. Yet I have decided that since you've given me the choice, and I believe I've proven that I'll take on my share of the postpartum responsibilities . . ."

"*More* than your share."

"Then if you *are* giving me the option, I need to be honest and say four. I would like four children." His hands slid under my skirt and over my hips. "Yes?"

"I said it was your choice."

"I'd still like to hear you say it." He tugged my panties down and I lifted my hips to help.

"Yes, Karl, I'd like four kids, too. You realize you can't start on number three now, right?"

He chuckled. "I can practice."

"Uh-huh. You like that, don't you? Particularly when I'm already knocked up."

His nose wrinkled. "I wouldn't put it that way."

"Knocked up? Oh, hell, yeah." I leaned back a little on the railing. "You like having kids. You like working on making kids. But you also really like this part."

I eased my dress up over the bump it concealed. His hands slid up to that, fingers running over it as a smug smile played on his lips.

I chuckled. "You like that, and you like it even more when it's big enough that everyone can see what you've done."

"That would be positively Paleolithic of me."

"Yep."

His fingers dropped back to my legs and eased down my inner thighs, but his gaze stayed fixed on that bump, the smile growing, just a little.

"Very pleased with yourself," I said, arching back as he slid a finger into me.

"Never. Any man can make babies. Most, anyway."

"True."

"Of course . . ." Another finger, working expertly, as I closed my eyes and moaned. "If I was overly pleased with myself, I would have good cause."

"Would you?"

"Impregnating a woman is no great accomplishment. How-ever . . ."

He paused here for more wonderful finger-work. I responded with more appreciative moaning. With his free hand, he undid the buttons on the front of my dress. His hand roamed up my stomach, pausing at my belly, and then continued to my bra, flicking open the front clasp.

"However . . ." he continued. "A brilliant and beautiful woman who agrees to have my babies . . ." He cupped my breast with his free hand and teased one nipple. "Who, furthermore, agrees to have as many as I want . . ." His lips came toward mine. "That is, I believe, cause for me to be very pleased with myself."

He kissed me and I wrapped my hands around his neck and returned it. Then I pulled back, my hands dropping to undo his belt.

"That's . . . not entirely true," I said.

"No?"

I opened his button, pulled down the zipper, and reached inside. "I wouldn't say I'm *willing* to have your babies. I believe the word"—I moved my lips to his ear and whispered—"is *eager.* Very, very eager."

He let out a growl, grabbed my hips, and pushed into me.

THREE

A week passed, and I was once again editing my intern's latest piece when my phone rang. I heard Joel's voice, there was a moment of déjà vu, and I was so distracted by it that when he said, "Someone stole the Eye of Pldans," the first words out of my mouth were, "Karl didn't . . ." Luckily, I caught myself in time and finished with, ". . . work on that project."

"Um, yeah, sis. That's what we discussed last week. Baby brain?"

"No, I thought we talked about the Anatolian Hoard last week."

"Right. Well, the Eye is the crown jewel of the Hoard, so to speak. I'm calling to see if he can help me figure out what went wrong. He has a knack for this, and I'm . . ." His voice lowered. "I'm in trouble, Hope."

"The client isn't holding you responsible, is he?"

"*She*. The necklace is insured, of course, and we don't owe anything except a refund, but it's a black mark on the firm, and considering we only branched into security work a year ago, it's a huge blow to our credibility. I don't want Karl to get the jewel back or anything . . ."

He trailed off, as if hoping this was exactly what I'd suggest. My family isn't stupid. They'd never asked a single question about Karl's "import-export business." My other brother investigated Karl's finances, but only to make sure he actually had money and wasn't a gold digger. As for Karl's former occupation? My entire family was completely uninterested. The messed-up baby had found her feet at last—a career, a loving husband, now children. I'm happy, so details don't matter.

I doubt my family suspects the truth about Karl's past. They just think it might not be . . . squeaky-clean.

"Retrieving stolen goods really isn't Karl's forte," I said, which is absolutely true.

"Can he look at the plans, then? Show me where we went wrong?"

I suspected Joel's real goal was to get Karl back on that team. *See how fast you figured that out? We need you, Karl. No one else can do this.* Which would be great, if Karl were the kind of guy who needed his ego pumped with flattery.

"You know, he does have this amazing piece of technology called a cell phone," I said. "Better yet, he's going to be at your office later, because he, you know, works for you. You can talk to him about this directly, Joel. Really. He doesn't bite."

"He doesn't listen, either. Not to me. He just humors me because I'm signing his paychecks."

"You're his boss. You need to establish dominance."

"You're laughing at me right now, aren't you?"

"Never," I said, biting my cheek.

"Yeah, yeah. I have about as much chance of 'establishing dominance' with Karl as I do of winning an argument with Mom. I know my limits. Just talk to him, okay?"

I sighed and agreed.

That evening, we were on the back deck again, this time watching Nita run through a makeshift obstacle course Karl had set up for her.

"No," Karl said when I told him about Joel's request.

"Okay."

"And . . ." he prompted.

I shrugged. "Okay."

"You're not going to argue?"

"Would it help?"

He shook his head.

"Then no, I'm not going to argue. I've made my point as strongly as I can, and you've made yours. Pushing veers dangerously close to nagging. You're an adult. I can try to make you happy, but ultimately, I can't force it on you."

His lips twitched in a smile. "You can always try, though possibly not in the way you're suggesting."

I sipped my tea. "I will . . . after Nita goes to bed."

He chuckled and settled into his chair. He didn't ask if I was serious. Withholding sex because I wasn't happy with him fit my definition of the old adage about cutting off your nose to spite your face.

We sat for a few minutes, watching Nita wear herself out for bedtime. Then he said, "It means a lot to Joel, doesn't it?"

I didn't answer. He knew it already.

Karl shifted forward. "I would like to help, Hope, but I don't . . . I know your family suspects I have a shady history. They look past it for your sake. But there's a limit. Showing Joel exactly how thieves circumvented his security passes that limit. It raises questions that I'd rather not raise."

"Okay."

He shifted again. "He doesn't need me to look at those plans. He can hire an expert. He just wants to woo me back to security work."

"Okay."

"If you really want me to . . ."

"Nope, not falling in that trap. You make up your own mind."

"Then the answer is no."

"Okay."

He sighed and slumped back in his seat to brood some more on the matter.

The next afternoon, I got another call. This one was from Paige, leader of the interracial council.

"Hey," I said as I answered. "I was just going to call you. Hold on." I took my phone out onto the office balcony. "There, privacy. I was going to see if you had any missions for me. Preferably the type custom-made for a chaos demon. I'd like to get some credits logged before I'm too pregnant to be chasing down leads and bad guys."

"I . . . might," she said. "But right now . . ."

"You have something else in mind. Something important and troubling."

A strained chuckle. "I didn't think your power worked over the phone."

"It doesn't. I can just tell this is a call you'd rather not make. What's up?"

"The Eye of Pldans."

I cursed under my breath. "Karl didn't do it."

"A very valuable artifact with a supernatural history has been stolen in Philadelphia. That would have me wondering already, Hope. But apparently the company guarding it is owned by your brother. And it's the company Karl has been working for . . . in the security design division."

"Right. And the fact that my brother's firm is responsible for the necklace means Karl sure as hell wouldn't steal it."

She didn't respond to that. Paige and her husband run a law and private investigation firm dedicated to helping supernaturals in need. She's never going to understand Karl, and she's given up trying.

"Put it another way," I said. "What if *I* owned that company? Would Karl steal the necklace then?"

"No, of course not."

"Betraying my brother would hurt me. Yes, Karl did work in Joel's security unit. Yes, he was given the job of designing security for the Anatolian Hoard. But as soon as he found out what it was, he went back to sales, because he's determined to go straight and didn't want to be tempted."

"All right." She didn't sound convinced, but before I could argue further, she said, "I just wanted to warn you that it's out there on the grapevine. The Eye of Pldans is gone, and Karl Marsten stole it. That's not merely a rumor or conjecture. It's being spread as undeniable fact. Elena is eventually going to hear about it."

I sighed. "Meaning we need to get ahead of that. Okay. Thanks." I was about to wind down the call when I thought of something. "Wait. Karl did some research before he dropped the security job. He said the guy looking to buy it was a Turkish national who wanted to repatriate it. But if the story is on the supernatural grapevine, I'm guessing someone else got it."

"No, the buyer *is* a Turkish national. Fredrick Birkan. Who is also a half-demon collector and most assuredly is not repatriating it."

"Not when it's rumored to give a second power to half-demons." I paused and then cursed. "Karl's been set up."

"What?"

"A valuable artifact with a supernatural history has been stolen in Philadelphia. The security company hired to protect it is the one Karl works for. And the most obvious buyer had a cover story about repatriating the Eye, which means Karl could have justifiably stolen it."

Silence.

"Which he did not," I said.

"I'm not trying to cause trouble, Hope. It just seems—"

"—too obvious. Which is the point. Under those circumstances, particularly with someone intentionally spreading the story, no one is going to believe Karl *didn't* do it. No one except me. So I guess I have an investigation after all—prove my husband didn't renege on his retirement and steal this."

FOUR

$\mathscr{I}$ had to warn Karl before Elena contacted him. I called as soon as I got off the phone. When he didn't pick up, I waited ten minutes before trying again. Then I took off. Karl was supposed to be at home with Nita, and while I tried not to worry, he'd just been set up to take the blame for a major supernatural jewel heist. I had reason to be concerned.

I rang again as I pulled into the lane . . . and heard Karl's ring tone through the open windows, with no one answering. I raced inside fast enough that I almost forgot the alarm. It's a custom-designed system, the best Karl could dream up, because, as he'd discovered three years ago, his reputation alone didn't protect his family against supernatural thugs with guns.

The fact I had to disarm it should mean everything was fine. I could see his phone, left on the side table where he often set it down. I wasn't picking up any chaos twinges. He'd probably taken Nita out for a walk or a bike ride.

I was telling myself to relax when tendrils of chaos slid through the open back windows. At one time, even if that chaos meant my family was in danger, I'd have lapped it up. That was the hell of my demon hunger. Even when it meant someone I loved was in danger, I was like a crack addict getting a long-overdue fix. Then Nita came, and I lost just enough of that hunger that while I still paused, unable to resist an initial rush of "Damn, that's good stuff," it only lasted a split second. Then I was racing toward the back door, my gun in hand.

A scream cut through the yard. My child's scream. Any lingering trace of that chaos buzz evaporated. I yanked open the back door and—

"Daddy! Do it again! Again, again, again!"

A splash and another scream. No, not a scream. A squeal of delight. Karl and Nita were in the pool. That was the chaos I'd picked up. Happy chaos. I stood in the doorway, letting it wash over me as I smiled.

My daughter has brought so much into my life, but this is one of the most treasured gifts, and one reason we never rein in her exuberance. Joyful chaos is such a rare thing. And I get to enjoy it almost every day of my life. It's like finding the one glittering diamond in a heap of razor-sharp glass.

When Karl's phone rang again, I took out mine to see if I'd butt-dialed. I hadn't. I walked to his phone, saw the caller's name, and groaned. Then I answered, not waiting for a hello because I knew I wasn't going to get one.

"Yes," I said, "a valuable supernatural relic has been stolen on Karl's territory. Yes, it was being guarded by the company he works for. No, he did not do it. Yes, I know rumor says otherwise. No, Karl didn't break his vow—not the one about going straight or the one about promising you he wouldn't steal anything of archeological significance. And, by the way, Clayton, shouldn't Elena be making this call?"

"She's busy."

"I can't imagine she'd ask you to handle this."

"She's *very* busy, Hope," Clay said, a warning growl in his voice telling me not to pursue it. Luckily, the great thing about not actually being a Pack member is that I can ignore protocol.

"So you went behind Elena's back—"

"When I say she's busy, I don't mean she's making dinner for the twins. I mean she's dealing with a problem, one big enough that, yes, I'm going to handle this without telling her."

"Is it Malcolm?" I asked, my voice softening.

"The Eye of Pldans—"

"—was not stolen by Karl. Any other time, I'd be the first person to suspect him of this, and you know it. He's quit the life."

"Or so he tells you."

"I'm the one who doesn't want him giving it up because I don't think he'll be happy without it."

"He'd be fine without it. He's just too damned selfish—"

"Enough."

"I know you don't want to hear that, Hope, but it's the truth. I'm not saying he doesn't care about you and Nita. I'm saying he cares enough to pretend he's given up thieving. But he's sure as hell not going to do it. I've known Karl for thirty years—"

"And you've hated him for all thirty of them, which means you might know him, but you don't know him very well. At all. You just aren't interested. To you, I'm just a messed-up half-demon chick with a bad-boy complex—"

"I don't think . . . All right, I did. I don't anymore. But I still believe the fact that you're married to him and he's the father of your children means you're going to cut him some slack, not look all that hard and see him for what he really is."

"Huh. You know, I've heard that before. But they were talking about you and Elena."

He gave a soft growl. "That's—"

"Elena knows exactly what you are. No illusions. Same with me and Karl. My husband is an egotistical, arrogant thief and a were-wolf with a brutal reputation, which he earned. But if he tells me he quit the life, then he quit the life. And I'd stake my own reputation—and my pride—on shouting that from the rooftops. But I'll save my breath and focus my energy on a more productive show of support—*proving* he didn't do it."

"Fine. Do that. Elena doesn't need this shit. Not now."

"And I'll ask again, is it Malcolm?"

"Elena will be calling a Pack Meet to discuss it. Make sure Karl's there."

"I always do. Would you like me to come up and take the twins out with Nita? This doesn't sound like the kind of Meet where you'll want kids around."

"It's not, but Elena would like you at the meeting too. Vanessa's coming to look after the kids. She says she'll take them to the range and teach them to shoot." He paused. "I think she's kidding."

I smiled. "Hopefully. But I can leave Nita at my mom's if—"

"Bring her. Kate's been asking when she's coming up again. Apparently, she has baby name ideas, and she's decided Nita is the one to give them to."

"Oh, Nita has already chosen her name for the baby: Rainbow."

Silence. Then, "And if it's a boy?"

"Rainbow."

That got a soft chuckle. "Okay."

"Believe me, we have no intention of letting our three-year-old name our child. But tell Kate yes, Nita will be there and—"

The screen door flew open with a screech of "Kate!" Nita had overheard me on her way in. She raced across the floor, water spraying everywhere, a river forming behind her.

"Nita, no!" I said. "You'll slip—"

She was already beside me, chanting, "Kate, Kate, Kate," while jumping for the phone. There's a mild case of hero worship here. Nita adores Logan too—he's teaching her to read. But Kate is, well, a *girl*—one who can teach her all kinds of special girlie stuff, like how to climb trees and then cannonball off them into the pond behind Stonehaven.

"It's not Kate," I said. "It's her daddy."

Nita yanked on my pant leg with "Kate! Want to talk to Kate. Wish her *Happy Birthday*!" She singsonged the last two words as loudly as she could.

"You called and wished them both Happy Birthday two weeks ago . . . on their actual birthday."

A voice in the background said, "Is that Nita?" It was Kate, her werewolf-sharp hearing apparently picking up my daughter's screeches.

"Who else?" Clay said to his daughter.

Kate's chuckle sounded remarkably like her father's. She's almost as much of a handful as Nita—always on the go, usually up to trouble—but for Nita she finds a well of gravitas and patience that surprises everyone.

"Let me talk to her," Kate said. Then, after Clay handed her the phone, "Hope?"

"Hey, Kate."

"Kate!" Nita crowed. "Kate, Kate, Kate!"

"I'll pass you over before she yanks off my leg. When you're done, just tell her it's nap time. She likes her naps."

"Your kid is weird."

"I know. She gets it from her dad."

Kate laughed, and I passed the phone over and headed outside to fill Karl in.

To say Karl was not happy would be an understatement. Someone had besmirched his professional reputation by framing him for a job. Worse, they'd publicly damaged his integrity by claiming he'd taken that job after telling his contacts he'd retired. Yes, there is honor among thieves. Or, in their own way, honorable thieves. Karl had spent a lifetime building a reputation as a man whose word could be trusted, a rare thing in his line of work. Now someone apparently had "proved" otherwise, and it didn't matter if he no longer needed that reputation. In fact, it was worse coming after he'd retired—a black mark at the end of a career, reversing the legacy he'd left.

Personally, I was a whole lot more concerned about the damage this did to his position with the Pack. There'd been a time when he would have brushed that off. Hell, there'd been a time when part of him would have said, *Hmm, maybe I'll get lucky and they'll kick me out* . . . He'd stayed in the Pack because I wanted it for him. But it was different now, with Nita and another child on the way. The Pack is "his" side of the family, and our children need that as much as they need my side. Moreover, they need the protection the Pack offers. So, yes, while he didn't think this jeopardized his position, he wanted the matter cleared up.

Karl and I were up half the night planning our investigation. Lots of questions to answer, starting with why Karl had been framed and ending with whodunit.

We knew who the buyer was: this Fredrick Birkan. Had he framed Karl? That didn't make any sense. It must have been the thief. Was he someone with a grudge against Karl? Or someone who merely hoped to blame him for the crime? Whatever the motivation, we had a mystery to solve and a false accusation to clear.

FIVE

*T*he next morning, we dropped off Nita at my mom's. Then Karl met with Joel and the security team, having agreed to look over the plans.

At one o'clock, I joined him at the scene of the crime. Joel didn't question Karl bringing me along—my journalism gave me an investigator's eye. But Karl also wanted me there for my chaos detector.

The Anatolian Hoard had been rented to a woman by the name of Melinda Fitzwilliams. Actually, Lady Fitzwilliams. Apparently she'd married into the name and Joel said she insisted on using it. It's Philadelphia—we get some of that, as I well know from my days as a debutante.

The Hoard's owner hired it out for events—a private exhibit to liven up your next charity gathering. The necklace was supposed to have been worn by Lady Fitzwilliams. Joel's men had brought it to her house and secured it in the safe they'd installed specifically for this purpose. It had disappeared from there.

The only chaos vibes and thoughts I picked up from Lady Fitzwilliams were the ones that said she was dreadfully worried about the effect this whole nasty business would have on her sterling reputation. Also, she thought Karl was hot. Thoughts like *what is a man like that doing with a little chit like her* thrummed with the anger and angst of a woman whose own husband had —according to our research—recently left her for a twenty-three-year-old.

Lady Fitzwilliams took us to where she kept her safes—in a panic room they'd installed after a neighborhood home invasion a few years ago.

"Who had access to this room?" Karl asked.

"Only my family."

"Does anyone on staff know the code?" I asked. "For cleaning or checking the alarms?"

"Of course. The room does need to be aired out weekly, and I like the emergency water replaced every month."

"Who does that?" I asked.

"The housekeeper. She has the code posted in her instruction book."

"Which she keeps . . .?"

"In the kitchen."

"Is it secured?"

"The book? I wouldn't know."

In other words, this "secure" room was about as secure as my college dorm, where my roommate would pass out keys to everyone she knew in case they needed a place to crash.

There were three safes in the panic room, because, apparently, Lady Fitzwilliams had a lot of things she considered valuable. One held papers. Another contained jewels and other tangible treasures. The third had been installed specifically for the Anatolian Hoard, to comply with the owner's requirements. Karl examined it at length and then said, "There are two ways of opening this: with the combination or a stick of dynamite. Possibly multiple sticks."

When I glanced over, he gave a small shake of his head, which meant he couldn't open it either.

"Which means obviously the thief had the code," Joel said.

"Yes," Karl said.

Joel looked at Lady Fitzwilliams, who squawked and said, "*You* have the code. Your men installed it."

"No, you reset the code," Joel said, "as per our instructions. My man showed you how and then he waited in the hall."

She deflated. "Oh. Yes. That's right."

"Who had access to *that* code?" I asked.

"Only me."

"Did you write it down anywhere?"

"Of course," she said, bristling. "With my Internet passwords."

"Is *that* secure?" *And please don't tell me they're in the house-keeper's book.*

"It's in my bedroom wall safe."

That led to further questioning about who had access to *that* safe, at which point the woman declared, with absolute conviction, that only she did. Well, as far as she knew. But her sons might. And maybe her ex-husband. She'd been meaning to change the code after he'd left . . . However, none of those three people had been in the house between the time the Hoard arrived and the time the necklace was discovered missing.

The most likely answer, then, was that someone on staff had it, because God knows she'd probably written her wall-safe code somewhere else, too. Which meant, as we'd suspected already, it was an inside job.

When we were done in the panic room, Lady Fitzwilliams didn't realize I stayed behind as Karl diverted her with the smiles and personal attention that had charmed many jewels off wealthy and lonely women. Alone in the panic room, I focused on picking up leftover chaos. I can catch visions of past trouble, but it's always been an unreliable power, becoming even more so after Nita's birth. Given that we also had no reason to suspect anyone had been hurt in the robbery, it wasn't surprising that I caught nothing. I rejoined them in the parlor.

We started by questioning the young man who'd served as security— Joel's firm having advised a round-the-clock guard for the house while the Hoard was there. Lady Fitzwilliams had insisted on hiring the person she usually used, because he was the grandson of her butler. Yes, there were so many flaws in this security "plan" I could have stolen the Eye myself.

Joel's staff had come up with a sound concept on paper, but they hadn't factored human fallibility into the equation. He needed to contractually insist that the client follow his instructions to the letter or it voided his responsibility.

The young guard—Miguel—put out some serious chaos vibes. But the thoughts I picked up were only, *Holy shit, they think I did it and now I'll lose my job and my girlfriend will dump me and I won't be able to pay off my bike and . . .* In other words, scared rather than guilty.

We continued interviewing household staff. Lady Fitzwilliams lived alone and yet maintained a butler, housekeeper, maid, and cook. Does that seem wasteful? Maybe, but it was her money to waste, and if she was paying the wages of four people for what was probably light work, I saw no problem with that.

When we got to the maid, I picked up stronger chaos vibes. Not worried for herself, but for someone else. I couldn't tell who. I'm not a mind reader. I can only pick up fully formed mental sentences strumming with fear or anxiety or anger. Usually, though, chaotic thoughts are more a jumble of words, tangled in free-flowing thought. That's what I got from the maid.

During the interview, I turned my sympathy on full blast. If Karl's questions had even the slightest edge, I reworded them. When she mentioned she'd gone to Zumba class the day of the theft, I professed an interest in learning and derailed the conversation for a few minutes, getting her to relax. After she left, I slipped out to use the bathroom, and on my way back, she appeared and motioned for me to follow her outdoors.

I caught up with her behind the pool house.

"Miguel didn't do it," she said. "I know everyone's going to think he did, but he's not like that. I've known him for years—my mom used to be the housekeeper here, and Lady Fitzwilliams would let Miguel and me come swimming when we were little. He's not one of those guys who sees all this and thinks the rich people owe him. He appreciates what she's done for him. He'd never steal from her."

"Then who would?"

She nibbled her lip and looked toward the house.

"Theresa . . ." I said. "The best way you can help Miguel is by giving us another suspect."

"She lied," Theresa blurted. "Not on purpose. Well, yes, on purpose, I guess, but not to get Miguel in trouble."

"To protect someone else."

She nodded. "She doesn't think he did it, but . . ." The girl looked back toward the house. Then she straightened her shoulders. "I'd never do anything to hurt her, either, but if he did this, then *he's* hurting her, and she doesn't deserve that."

"What did she lie about?"

"She said her sons weren't here that day. But Bradley was. He's also the one who recommended your brother's firm."

Gotcha.

SIX

We took Nita home for a few hours after that. By eight, she was back at my mom's, and Karl and I were preparing for our night mission.

Come midnight, we were outside a crack house, waiting near Bradley Fitzwilliams's car. As for how we knew where he'd be, well, presuming he'd just made some serious bank off the Eye, he'd be flush and looking to spend it. So we'd run extensive background checks, figured out his bad habits, and cleverly deduced which one he'd be pursuing and exactly where he'd pursue it.

I'm lying. That's far too much effort. We knew where Bradley was because we'd swung by his office tower, located the parking spot with his name on it, confirmed that the vehicle matched his DMV records, and attached a GPS. What we *had* done for research on Bradley Fitzwilliams suggested he wasn't the sort to stay home on a Friday night, which meant tracking his signal and lying in wait. Apparently, outside a crack house.

When we saw someone approaching, I slid into the shadows. Once I was sure it was him—alone—I stepped out with, "Um, excuse me . . ."

The female voice got his attention. He turned, but all he could see was a figure in the shadows, the long, curly hair and voice telling him I was female, my tiny size screaming *nonthreatening* or, yes, possibly *drugged-out waif.*

As soon as he took a step toward me, Karl pounced.

I let out a shriek and tore off. Karl had insisted on that—no matter how deeply I'd been hiding in those shadows, he wanted it to seem as if I'd had nothing to do with the attack, on the off chance I ever met Bradley again.

A few minutes later, I was slipping into the backseat with Karl. Bradley Fitzwilliams was in his driver's seat, blindfolded and hand-cuffed to the door handle. Over the next two minutes, he ran the full gamut from "You'll pay for this, you crackhead scum" to "You want my wallet, take my wallet" to "I'll give you my PIN codes, too." Karl hadn't laid a finger on him—just sat back and waited in silence.

"What do you want?" Bradley asked finally.

"The Eye of Pldans would be nice." Karl spoke with a German accent. He doesn't like disguises—he says they make thieves over-confident and sloppy. Instead, he kept out of view and saved the disguise for his voice.

"I-I don't have . . . I mean, I don't know what you're talking about."

Karl said nothing. He waited until Bradley, now visibly sweat-ing, said, "Hello? Are you still there?" Then he pressed cold metal to the back of Bradley's neck, and from the yelp the guy gave, he'd need a change of underwear.

"Okay, okay," Bradley blurted. "It wasn't my fault. I was set up. I hold parties, you know? Big parties, lots of people. Important people. So this guy contacts me and says he wants to be my new supplier and offers me all the favors I need for my next bash, free of charge. Coke, smack, girls. I say sure. Seems legit, right? Businesses do that all the time, offer freebies to get new clients."

Karl said nothing.

"So I have the party, and the next day I'm out walking my dog and these guys show up with a bill. A huge bill. I laugh, thinking it's a joke, and they kill my dog. My *dog*. Right in front of me. They say I have a week to pay or I'm next. When I tell them I need more time, they give me an option. Somehow they know my mom throws parties of her own—very different ones—and she likes to rent stuff. Museum-type stuff. They want me to tell her about this Hoard thing and get her to rent it, and then get this certain company to protect it. Then I had to steal the necklace. *Steal* it. Like I'm some kind of common criminal."

Says the guy who just spent his evening in a crack house.

"But I didn't have a choice," he continued. "And, well, it wasn't exactly hard work. Mom's always looking for new shit to rent for her shindigs. She doesn't know anything about security, so she trusted my advice. And taking it was easy. I know where Mom keeps her codes, and she's never going to suspect me."

Which is why she'd lied about him not visiting the house? No, I suspected Lady Fitzwilliams knew exactly who'd stolen the necklace and had decided she'd rather pay the insurance fee than turn in her son.

"Where is the necklace now?" Karl asked.

"I, uh, gave it to some guy—"

Karl pressed the cold metal into Bradley's neck, making the guy twitch.

"That's all I know! He didn't give me a name or anything. I can describe him, but I'm not sure how that will help."

"Contact information."

"Wh-what?"

"How did you contact him?"

"Right. Yes. That's right. They gave me a phone number. I'm sure it's just a— What do you guys call them? Burner phones? Is that enough?"

"It better be," Karl said, and withdrew the handcuff key from Bradley's neck.

Someone had gone to a lot of trouble to set Karl up. This job had been orchestrated right from the point of bringing the Anatolian Hoard to Philadelphia, through Lady Fitzwilliams. Getting a confession from Bradley Fitzwilliams didn't help as much as it might seem it would. If we turned him in, those who thought Karl did it would simply think Karl had set up Bradley. And it didn't resolve the issue of *why* he'd been set up.

I spent the next week trying to identify the middleman. That was frustrating, because we knew the identity of the buyer, and it was tempting to just attack the problem from that end. Except Fredrick Birkan lived in Switzerland, making it a whole lot harder to waylay *him* in a dark alley. And considering he was a very wealthy supernatural with underworld connections? Waylaying him definitely wasn't the answer.

So I was digging, using all my connections, and coming up empty. Thursday night, I was in the kitchen, taking a break, tidying up as I waited for a pan of brownies to cool. Karl was in the living room, Nita on his lap, dressed in her pajamas and curled up listening to a bedtime story.

When Karl's phone rang, he didn't even take it out to have a look.

"Phone, Daddy!" Nita sang.

"It can wait. I want to see how the story ends."

The call went to voice mail. And seconds later, it rang again.

"Phone, Daddy. Phone, phone, phone!"

"Just answer," I called. "I'll bring the brownies while they're warm and you can take a story break."

"Brownies!" Nita said, and then slapped her hand over her mouth as Karl answered his phone.

She launched herself off his lap and was halfway to the kitchen when Karl growled, "Where did you get this number?" and she stopped short, looking back in alarm.

I hurried in and scooped her up as Karl waved an apology and took the phone call outside.

"Daddy's *mad*," Nita said.

"No, he's annoyed. Mad sounds more like this." I imitated Karl's voice with a deeper growl and more snap, and Nita giggled.

"An-noyed," she said as I handed her a warm brownie. "Daddy is an-noyed. Like mad. But not as bad." She tilted her head, hearing the rhyme, then grinned and said it in a singsong, "Like mad, but not as bad. An-noyed. Daddy is annoyed."

"Daddy is indeed annoyed," Karl said as he came back inside.

"Who was it?" Nita asked.

"Just boring old work."

She wrinkled her nose. "Work's not boring. Work is fun."

Karl hesitated, just a second, before snatching the rest of her brownie and making her squeal.

"Mommy will get you a new one," he said, "and we'll finish the story."

"Why is work boring?" she asked.

"I didn't mean that. I'm just, as you said, annoyed."

"Mommy's work's not boring. Mommy likes her work. I'll like my work. I'm going to make up stories. Just like Mommy."

Karl gave a soft laugh at that. I didn't argue. I write for a supermarket tabloid. Despite the name, there's not a lot of truth in our news.

"I'm going to make up stories. Right now." Nita bounced over to where they'd left the book and slapped it closed. "I'm going to make a new ending."

"That sounds like a fine idea," Karl said, and went over to sit with her.

I put Nita to bed and came out to find Karl in the same chair, staring out the window. When he heard me, he gave a start and rose, saying, "I was going to make you tea."

"Later. Sit. Talk." I took a seat. "That wasn't work, was it?"

He glanced toward the stairs. I got up and motioned him outside. When we were seated out there, he said, "It was one of my former clients. An important one."

"Who was not happy when you quit."

He made a noise, as if to say none of them had been happy. Which was true. He'd handled the matter professionally, finishing his current jobs and informing everyone of his plans. He had, however, closed down all methods of contact, making it very clear that he was done.

"So he found your number and called to say he's heard you're back in business."

Another noise deep in his throat.

"He's pissed because you didn't tell him. And he's not a man you want to piss off."

Karl shifted in his seat and the noise he made now was an unmistakable growl. This was why he'd been so careful about how he shut down his business. It was more than mere professionalism—it was protection, for him and us.

"Is there any chance he'd—"

"No," he said sharply. "When you and I got together, I cleaned out my contact book of anyone who might come after you if they were angry with me."

"I know. I was asking if there's any chance he'd make things difficult for you, in some way. I know you're extremely careful, but he did find your personal number."

"The majority of my former clients could not do that. He's one of the rare exceptions. If he ever tried to cause serious trouble, I have blackmail material."

Which meant the man could cause some trouble, just not Karl's definition of "serious."

"Has there been anyone else?" I asked, softening my voice.

He was quiet for a moment. Then he said, "Benicio called yesterday."

I winced. Benicio Cortez is Paige's father-in-law . . . and CEO of the most powerful Cabal in the country. Considering that Cabals are often called the corporate mafia of the supernatural world, this *really* was not a man you wanted to piss off. Karl had developed a good business relationship with Benicio, which had even translated into a semi-personal relationship, possibly because he is rather fond of my mother.

"And . . ." I prompted.

"As you know, we'd been discussing a job before I decided to quit. I offered to complete it, but he declined. He's heard about the Eye, and he called to express his disappointment that I would reverse my retirement decision without notifying him."

"Mmm, yeah. That's not good."

"He's giving me the benefit of the doubt—for now—but . . ."

"The number of 'displeased parties' is adding up, meaning we need to move faster on clearing your name. I just can't get anywhere with what Bradley gave me."

"Nor can I."

"Well . . ." I eased back into the deck chair. "You've always wanted to take me to Switzerland."

"On vacation. This is not a vacation."

"It could be, for a day or two. And I won't be able to travel in a few months. Plus, I was just telling Paige last week that I'd love a chaos-fix mission while I'm still able to take one."

He said nothing.

"Or you can go to Switzerland yourself," I said.

A long minute of silence. "I would rather go with you. However, I've been careful to keep you out of my business, and I'm reluctant to change that."

"This is an investigation, not a heist. And the sooner we settle this, the sooner we don't have to worry that some past client is going to do more than 'express his disappointment.' So far, you have a powerful client, the Pack, the interracial council, and the Cortez Cabal all thinking you lied about retiring. Let's fix this before it gets worse."

SEVEN

*S*aturday morning we were driving through the Alps, Lake Geneva glistening in the morning sun as Karl told me about the city where we'd be staying—Lausanne.

"It also has world-class shopping," he said.

"Uh-huh."

"If we get through this business quickly, I'll take you."

"I saw something at the airport about castles. Find me a castle and then I'll let you take me shopping."

He sighed. Shopping really isn't my thing. Karl is the clothes-horse in this relationship. In fact, I suspect it was his impeccable taste that started winning my mother to his side. Even if he didn't turn out to be the man for me, at least he might teach me some fashion sense. God knows, she'd failed there. Both my brothers used to make the annual best-dressed-bachelors lists and my sister still routinely graces the society pages. I would get the occasional picture, too . . . under a "Crimes of Fashion" caption.

Whatever it takes to know the difference between a dress that looks good on a rack and one that looks good on me, I lack it. Karl picks out my clothing now. It makes him happy and, admittedly, it's nice to walk through a door and turn heads without an accompanying look of horror. He also chooses Nita's clothes, sparing her any undue trauma.

"You do realize that anything we buy won't fit me in a few months," I said.

"I was thinking jackets for fall," he said. "And accessories. Switzerland definitely is the place for watches."

"And chocolate."

His lips twitched. "Yes, and chocolate. We'll find you—"

His phone rang. He hit the answer button on the rental car's Bluetooth system.

"Hello," said a man's voice in an accent I couldn't place. "You have arrived in Switzerland?"

"Yes . . ." Karl said carefully.

"I trust you had a good flight. Long?"

I mouthed, "Hotel," and Karl nodded. Because our flight arrived in the morning, Karl had tried to book our hotel for last night. That hadn't been possible, but he'd been told they'd make every effort to ensure our room was ready by ten today.

"Very long," Karl said. "Our room is ready, then?"

"I have no idea, Mr. Marsten. But if it is not, you may join me for lunch. That is why I was calling. To extend the invitation."

Marsten. Karl wasn't traveling under his real name.

"Who is this?" he said.

"Fredrick Birkan. I believe you came to Switzerland to see me. I had hoped to track your flight, but it seems you used different aliases for both that and your car rental. I did, however, have the one for the car rental. I told the agency I was your host here and arranging a surprise welcome party. They were kind enough to telephone me when you picked up the vehicle."

Karl glowered but only said, calmly, "Lunch, then?"

"Yes. Let me send you my address."

Karl decided not to tell Birkan that I would be joining them for lunch . . . or that I'd joined him on this trip at all. He didn't insist I stay at the hotel, either. One, he knew better. Two, given that Birkan obviously had some of his aliases, Karl wasn't taking a chance on leaving his pregnant wife alone. Better to keep me close and let me do my job—scouting for trouble before and during his meeting with Birkan.

That meant sneaking me onto the estate . . . past cameras, a stone wall, and a roving guard. We figured out the guard's route then found the right location, and Karl helped me over the wall. From there, I darted behind the main house to check it out before Karl arrived.

It wasn't exactly the mansion I expected from a guy who could offer a half million to steal a necklace. It was a relatively modest spread of maybe three thousand feet. As with our house, the value was in the location. According to Karl, Switzerland was one of the most expensive locales in the world. A place like this, with acreage, really was a mansion.

I scouted outside first. It was a gorgeous September day and the household staff had opened every window. I listened through those for any hint that Birkan was preparing to meet Karl's arrival with a hail of gunfire. Karl would have rolled his eyes at the suggestion. We'd researched Birkan enough to know he wasn't a thug. He was, like most of the collectors Karl dealt with—and like Karl himself—a dangerous man, but one who prided himself on being civilized.

I heard Birkan giving his staff instructions for lunch and nothing suggesting a trap. I also heard him talking to his guards—one on patrol, one in the house, and the third stationed at the gate. He warned them there was going to be a werewolf thief in the house. Don't make any sudden moves. Don't get in his face. And keep a very close eye on all valuables.

This was no more than I'd expect, and I texted it all to Karl. Then I moved to someplace where I could watch his arrival.

He drove up exactly on time. The guard let him through the gates. Birkan met him at the front door, and they were exchanging greetings when a second car rolled into the lane.

"That would be Ms. Sharon Avery," Birkan said. "She obtained the Eye for me and has asked to join us for lunch. She is quite a fan of yours, Mr. Marsten."

Karl watched the car park. A woman got out. Middle-aged. Large enough in stature that, if it wasn't for her dress, I'd have mistaken her for a man from this distance.

As she greeted Birkan and Karl, I hunted for chaos vibes, but picked up only mild anxiety from Karl, as he tried to figure out the situation. I slipped off to my next spot—where I could eavesdrop on their lunch.

*L*unch was well under way, and no one had said a word about the Eye. That would be rude. They dined on veal cutlets with wild mushrooms and rösti. As I nibbled a dry protein bar, washed down with a bottle of water, I reminded myself that Karl had promised raclette for dinner.

Only when dessert came out did Birkan say, "I presume you would like to see the jewel that brought you so far?"

I could hear the shrug in Karl's voice. "The Eye doesn't interest me. Being set up does."

A pause, and it was obvious Birkan had expected the chance to show off his prize. After a moment, Karl decided to play nice and said, "All right. I wouldn't mind seeing it."

Birkan sent the guard to fetch the necklace. Karl feigned half-hearted interest in the Eye. Then he said, "It's a nice-enough piece, but again, what interests me is how it got here. And why I'm being blamed for that."

"It was Ms. Avery's idea. I say so, not to deflect blame, but to give her full credit. People say there is nothing she cannot procure, and now I see why."

"And what exactly is it that you're trying to procure?" Karl asked. "Not the Eye, obviously. That was merely the bait."

Birkan chuckled. "Excellent deduction. Yes. I wouldn't have needed Ms. Avery to get the Eye of Pldans. It is a fake. Real jewels, of course, but no actual supernatural power. I tested it, to be sure. A good story. Nothing more. I'll resell—at a profit, naturally—but the purpose of stealing it was to lure you here."

"There are ways to contact me."

"Only if I want to hear you tell me to go to hell. No, there isn't a price I could set that would have brought you running, once you'd chosen to retire. I needed more. I needed blackmail."

"I believe the word you're looking for is *extortion*."

"Ah, yes. Thank you. I went to school in America, but that is, as you might guess, many years ago. I stand corrected. Extortion it is. Or perhaps more of a hostage taking. I have seized your reputation. You must render me a service to get it back."

"Accusing a thief of stealing is hardly smearing my reputation. All you've done is get my attention. And not in a good way."

I swore I heard the smirk in Birkan's voice as he said, "But now that I have your attention, I believe I can *make* it very good—for both of us."

"You've caused trouble with my Pack. You've caused trouble for my wife's family. However, neither situation is dire enough to persuade me to do anything for you. I will resolve this on my own."

"I'm sorry. Again, I misspoke. By 'good,' I meant profitable. I will ensure your name is cleared of this theft . . . in addition to a very generous payment, one that will ensure you can indeed retire, in comfort."

"I already have, and I hardly think clearing my name of a theft by having me *steal* something else establishes the fact that I've retired."

"But you did. Now you've been lured out for one last job. One irresistible job that no one will blame you for taking: stealing the Eteocypriot grimoire."

Karl snorted. We'd both heard of the Eteocypriot grimoire—a legendary spell book written in a long-extinct language. One of a kind. Absolutely priceless. Benicio Cortez had tried to hire Karl a few years ago to steal it for five million. Karl did the research . . . and turned him down.

"That grimoire is untouchable," Karl said. "It is protected by a spell contained only within its own pages. There is a single witch capable of casting the spell to renew it. The incantation lasts exactly three moon cycles, and there is no other way to dispel it. To even *touch* the grimoire while the spell is active means instant death. The current owner has his witch recast the spell as soon as it wears off."

"She's dead."

A pause. Then, "The witch who casts the spell?"

"Died unexpectedly four months ago. Aneurism. The grimoire's owner is training her replacement, but until the training is complete, there is no spell guarding the tome. Other measures, yes, but not that one."

Silence. I strained to catch Karl's thoughts, but instead picked up snatches of others' thoughts. Ones that told me this conversation was about to go sideways. Fast.

I texted Karl. No message. Just a text to vibrate his phone. Then I did it again. That was our code: one buzz meant I was in trouble and a second meant he was.

"It's a very intriguing offer," Karl said. "I would consider it for two million."

"Two million?" Birkan laughed. "I am not *buying* it from you, Mr. Marsten."

"Yes, in essence you are, because your having gone to all this trouble to get me here tells me I'm your only option. And if I was really selling you the book, I'd charge ten times that. Two million presumes you—or Ms. Avery—have already done your research, and I will have access to it, in addition to any resources I need."

"So we have a deal?"

"At two million—plus clearing my name—you have my assurance that I will seriously consider the offer. I will do my own research, independent of yours, and you will have a firm answer within a week."

"I'm afraid that won't do, Mr. Marsten. I paid very well for this tip, and I've just given it to you for free. Which means you will do this job at the agreed price. And you will not be leaving the grounds until Ms. Avery escorts you to Belgium to fetch the grimoire. Which you will do while wearing a device that ensures your cooperation."

Karl laughed.

"You find this amusing, Mr. Marsten?"

"Oh, sorry, I thought you were quoting dialogue from a James Bond film. Equipping me with a device to guarantee my cooperation? That's very Hollywood of you. I expected better. One week. And you have my word that I will not attempt to steal the grimoire for myself."

"Your word?" Now Birkan was the one laughing.

"You don't like that? All right. Let's negotiate."

My first bullet shattered the huge sunroom window, scaring the crap out of everyone inside. The second hit the guard in his right shoulder, making him drop his gun. Karl pounced, and in a split second Birkan was facedown on the table, Karl's hand on his neck. Avery wheeled on me, hand going for her gun, only to see mine pointed at her.

"Uh-uh," I said. "Hands up. Also? Stop casting that spell."

She gave me a closer look, and then nodded and complied.

"Do you know how many guards are surrounding this place?" Birkan said.

"Yes, actually," I said as I carefully lifted my leg to step through the window. I retrieved the gun the guard had dropped, making a quick check to make sure the bullet had only passed through his shoulder, doing no serious damage.

"There are two left," I said. "One at the gate, and one on the opposite side of the property doing his rounds."

"You will now text both," Karl said. "Tell them that everything is fine, and that if they set foot in this house, I'll break your neck."

Karl watched as Birkan sent the text.

"Killing me won't get you the grimoire," Birkan said.

"If I wanted to kill you, you'd be dead. I don't kill potential clients unless they double-cross me. Your job now is to tell me why I shouldn't consider *this* a double cross. I came to your home in good faith. I listened to your offer in good faith. I promised to consider it, do the required research, and respond within a week. All sound business procedure. And yet, somehow, that was grounds to attempt to kidnap me and force me to do the job."

"It sounds like a double cross," I said.

"It does," Karl mused.

"*You* violated my trust first, by bringing uninvited company." Birkan jerked his chin my way.

"You didn't know that when you betrayed me. I was coming to the home of a stranger who had framed me for a crime I didn't commit. Of course I'd bring backup."

Birkan looked at me. "Backup? She is a very pretty girl, but I think a man of your reputation would hire a slightly more intimidating bodyguard."

"Considering your current situation . . ." Karl pressed his forearm against Birkan's neck. "I believe she's quite capable."

"Still, bringing her along on this trip tells me you're slipping, Mr. Marsten. Getting soft in your retirement. Hiring some tempting little tidbit to amuse you on the job? I really did expect better."

Avery cleared her throat. "That's his wife."

Birkan snickered. "Bringing your wife on business trips? That's even worse."

"Actually, she's a—" Avery began.

"As long as she's here," Birkan said, "we'll amend my offer. Put her to use. You may leave, Mr. Marsten. I'll keep your wife as a guarantee against you bringing me the grimoire."

"I believe you're misunderstanding the situation." Karl pressed down on Birkan's neck again. "We're both leaving. Leaving your home and your offer, and in light of what you've done, you'd better hope you can hire another capable thief quickly . . . one who will beat me to the grimoire."

"Do you really trust that your *wife* did a good enough job scouting my property? I have more guards, Marsten. Ones I can't call off with a text message. Either I walk out the front door in ten minutes or you and your wife are dead."

"He's bluffing," I said. "He's kicking himself for not hiring extra guards as Ms. Avery advised. And he's furious with you"—I nodded at the guard I shot—"for not only failing to stop me, but for standing there now, whimpering about your shoulder. He's decided you won't leave this house. He can't just fire you—not after you heard about the grimoire. So you're getting a permanent exit package."

Birkan stared at me, his mouth open.

"Hope Adams," I said. "Expisco half-demon."

"Which is what I was trying to tell you, *sir*," Avery muttered.

"Expisco? What the hell is that?" Birkan's accent had vanished, along with his vocabulary.

"A chaos demon," I said. "Fathered by Lucifer."

"Lu-Lucifer?" Birkan aimed his glare at Avery. "And you didn't see fit to tell me this? In advance?"

"It didn't seem pertinent at the time. But I was trying to warn you before you made any inadvisable threats against her."

Birkan snorted. "Demons don't care about their offspring. They're the ultimate deadbeat dads. Being half-demon, I know that better than anyone."

"Not entirely true, sir," Avery said. "Lord demons are known to occasionally take an interest in their children. And Lucifer, as I'm sure you know, isn't an ordinary demon."

"He's a fallen angel," I said. "But I'll be honest: if you put a gun to my head, he won't come running. He can't, because he's the only demon who cannot be summoned, and if he ran to my aid, all anyone would need to do is *put* a gun to my head to get his attention. But if you *harm* me—or his grandchildren—you will pay. And I don't think he accepts American Express."

"Sir?" Avery began. "I would suggest—"

"I can handle this," Birkan snapped. "All right, then, Mr. Marsten. Well played. You have the deal on your conditions. Two million and the clearing of your name, and you may have twelve hours to consider it."

"I don't need to consider it. You threatened my wife. Her father isn't the only one who takes that poorly. No deal." Karl backed off Birkan, letting the man rise. "Now you will walk ahead of us to the door as a good host should."

"Two and a half million."

Karl hesitated before saying, "No," and Birkan couldn't hide his smile.

"Three," Birkan said.

Karl looked at me. I nodded.

"Three million and twenty-four hours," Karl said.

Birkan snickered and said, "Of course, Mr. Marsten. So glad you found it in yourself to overlook my insult to your wife. Now let's discuss details."

NINE

*K*arl had no intention of doing that research. He planned to walk out of there and spend the night in Lausanne with me and then contact Birkan with a refusal. I talked him into it. This was indeed the chance of a lifetime. The perfect cap to an incredible career. No one would know the protective incantation had worn off, and thus it would seem he had done the impossible. The ultimate heist for a master thief. Plus three million for his retirement fund.

Or that was the argument I made. It was partly true. But I was also thinking of the promise to clear his name. And, let's be honest, if there was a job that might excite him enough to come out of retirement? This was it.

I contacted Clayton and explained the situation. Clay appreciated that I'd bypassed Elena, and I pretended that was why Karl didn't call himself: it would be wrong for a Pack wolf to circumvent the Alpha. Really, it was just a good excuse to avoid forcing the two into conversation. I think they both appreciated it.

As for the grimoire, Clay didn't give a damn about that. It wasn't historically significant. Well, not to him, anyway: the world's witches and sorcerers might beg to differ. The point was simply that he'd been consulted, and now, in stealing the grimoire, Karl wouldn't be breaking any promises to his Pack.

For a job like this, Karl would normally take weeks to prepare. We didn't have weeks. And I say "we" because there was no question of me going home. Well, yes, Karl had suggested it, but my look had answered for me. This wasn't an ordinary gig. The risk of moving fast was that he was relying on the intelligence gathered by others, and therefore he really needed his trouble detector at his side.

As Birkan said, the grimoire was in Belgium. By late afternoon, we were there, scoping out the estate, verifying the maps and blueprints Avery had provided.

"Ugh," I said, looking at the house.

"I thought you wanted to visit a castle."

"*That* is not a castle. It's a monstrosity." I caught his smile. "And, yes, I can recognize bad taste. At least when it comes to architecture."

I like castles almost as much as I like museums. Centuries of bloodshed and betrayal and heartache, all under one roof. You just don't get history like that back home. But there was no history in this particular "castle." It was a reconstruction. With as much fake-medieval crap as the owner could squeeze onto one building.

"Is that actually a moat?" I picked up the blueprint. "It is. What do you think is in it? Crocodiles? Piranha?"

"The climate is too cold for either."

"Sea monsters?"

He didn't respond. The man lacks imagination. Well, in some things.

Karl's phone buzzed. He frowned and jabbed in a quick text.

"The witch," he said, meaning Avery. Birkan had insisted on sending her, along with a small team, presumably to watch our backs, but neither of us was under any illusion that they'd do anything except run if we were caught. Avery was obviously our babysitter. The rest of the team was here to stop us if we tried to make off with the prize.

Once Karl was done with the text, he laid out the maps and said, "Tell me what's wrong."

I compared them with what I saw and pointed out all the missing structures or misleading landforms as well as all the potential safe places to hide . . . and the places that could be hiding danger. Not that Karl needed a second opinion. It was a teaching moment. Werewolves love them. It's the Pack instinct to pass on what they know. Which makes them great fathers. In our case, Karl included me in these particular lessons because, with the lives we lead, there's no telling when I'll need to know how to break into a place or—more likely—break out.

We spent a few hours scouting the square mile surrounding the estate. While it may have been an architectural nightmare, some-one had chosen the location as if it were a real castle, in need of defense. Which it was, in its way. The owner was Gustav Nast, former CEO of the German branch of the Nast Cabal. As CEO, he'd focused on amassing spells and grimoires for his Cabal. That was his hobby now that he was retired, and even his own Cabal would love to get their hands on his collection. Rare spells are a valuable commodity. Nast housed his treasures in a fortress worthy of the Ottoman Empire.

Avery had planned how we were going to breach Nast's fortress walls, and she'd apparently charged Birkan a half million for the plan alone, along with assembling a small team of experts who'd worked on independent sections with no knowledge of the whole. Karl still found flaws. And that was just the exterior.

For the interior, we had to rely on blueprints and aerial photog-raphy. Hours more work there, now back in our hotel room. Many more alterations to the Avery plan as I made some phone calls, checking out a few things.

"If you need more time . . ." I said as Karl rubbed his eyes.

"No," he said. "An extra day or two won't help. I'd prefer a week, but as it stands . . ." He pushed aside the plan and tugged me onto his lap. "It's good enough. Safe enough. If it wasn't, I'd never take you in. However, if you're concerned . . ."

"If the plan isn't foolproof, all the more reason to have me scout-ing for trouble."

"No plan is foolproof."

I put my arms around his neck. "But with you, it's as close as it can be."

"True."

I laughed and kissed him. "As your partner, then, I'd suggest taking a few minutes to clear your head before you look at those plans again."

He hoisted me up. "Perhaps more than a few," he said, and carried me into the bedroom.

Avery wasn't pleased with Karl's plan. Specifically the part that left her on the sidelines.

"Mr. Birkan hired me to oversee this," she said as we stood at the edge of a forest, a half mile from the estate.

"I understand," Karl said. "However, he hired me to get the grimoire, and I suspect he's more interested in having it than in having you at my shoulder. That is Hope's job. You may position his men anywhere beyond a five-hundred-foot radius of the building. They may be armed with anything you like, including binoculars. If they see me attempting to make off with the grimoire, they are free to take me down. Being guarded is not the issue. Being babysat is."

"I realize you're a lone wolf, Karl." She glanced at me. "Well, relatively speaking . . ."

"No," he said. "Not relatively speaking. There is only one exception. And she's standing beside me. Adding anyone else also factors in personal discomfort and decreases the likelihood Birkan gets his grimoire and the likelihood you get your final payment."

"I can help," she said. "Hope? You've worked for Rhys Smith, right? So have I. Call him. He'll vouch for me."

"He has," I said. "I already investigated you and spoke to him. It's not a question of trust. It really is about controlling the variables. Your presence is a variable."

"To the moat, then. Let me help you get that far. Then I'll stay outside and watch for trouble."

"Fine," Karl said, "you'll accompany us to the moat. I will find you a place to stand to wait. You will not leave it unless there is an immediate threat, and even then you will message Hope first."

"Understood."

It was a beautiful night. Karl and I had spent a week last year in the Scottish Isles on our annual Nita-free vacation, and tonight reminded me of that—the open and craggy landscape so familiar that if I closed my eyes, I could imagine the smell of heather and rain and wet wool rolling across the moors.

Under the circumstances, Karl wasn't nearly as enamored of the open ground. But as I said, Nast had chosen a defensible location for his faux castle. Which meant if the nearby forest had once extended this far, he'd chopped most of it down. There were still craggy hillocks, though, and stands of trees. Also, a quarter moon sliding between cloud cover. The old wives' tale says that thieves are more active under a full moon because they can see, but the truth is that they're a lot more worried about *being* seen. With Karl's werewolf night vision, the cloudy night was perfect.

We moved from cover to cover until Karl spotted our target: one of the three patrolling guards. He glanced past me to Avery, who had to stay at least twenty feet behind us. A grunt, and Karl took off, loping over the open ground.

Karl got within ten yards before the guard even cast a squint-eyed glance his way. It wasn't just the darkness—it was the fact that Karl was a black wolf, perfectly suited for blending into the night.

Karl looped past the man. I started padding toward them as Karl pulled the guard's attention his way. I kept my chaos sensors attuned for trouble, but the guard only squinted, perfectly still now, like a hiker who spots a wild animal and doesn't dare move for fear of scaring it off before he gets a good look.

I got right up behind him before he heard me. He tensed, ready to turn, and I jabbed a hypodermic into his arm. Karl was in flight. By the time he knocked the guard down, the guy was out cold. Karl grabbed his jacket between his teeth and dragged him to the nearest stand of trees. Then we set out after guard number two.

This one was a little more alert than his colleague. Or maybe less of a dog lover. The moment he spotted Karl, he went for his gun, and I was still too far away to jump him. Karl darted to the side, veered, and ran straight at the guy, who was still pulling his weapon when Karl pounced. A shot in the arm—plus my hand over his mouth before he realized he should shout for his coworkers— and it was over. Two down, one to go.

Number three was a fire half-demon. He managed to grab me as he was going down, but he was a minor subtype, and I barely even felt his heat through my jacket.

On to the castle. Avery's information told us where the outside security cameras were, and Karl had confirmed that with the aerial photos. He kept us in the blind spots while Avery provided further cover with a blur spell.

When we neared the moat, Karl made Avery and me take cover while he circled the building. As he came back around, I watched him, his blue eyes the only thing I could see in the darkness. Then I caught a flash of white teeth as he lifted his nose, sniffing loudly enough that I could hear it, his jaws opening slightly, trying to get as much scent as possible. I couldn't see his ears, but I knew they'd be swiveling, working as hard as his nose. He was trying to pick up a very specific smell or sound: those that indicated a canine in residence.

The contact who'd sold Avery the information was a former household employee—fired recently and happy to sell what she knew. She'd said there weren't any dogs—guard or pet—because Nast was allergic. But Karl still checked.

Karl circled twice. Then he came back and shook his head. No dogs. Which was good, because he'd rather face a gauntlet of booby traps. Karl's scent will drive even the friendliest pup into a frenzy.

"You can go Change back," I whispered. "I'll test the moat."

That was the plan, but apparently someone was as curious as I was to see if this moat contained anything but water. Karl stayed at my side as I took a bag from my backpack and moved to the edge. I peered into the murky depths. Then I shone a flashlight into those depths but saw nothing except brown water.

Glove on, I reached into the bag and pulled out a sedated mouse. We'd picked them up at a pet store earlier and drugged them. I told myself the little guy wouldn't feel a thing and, if all was well, the cold water would wake him and he could swim to shore and live free. But I still felt bad as I tossed him gently into the water.

Sparks flew up, making both Avery and me jump back. A zap and a sizzle and the poor little mouse . . . well, he was free now, in a way.

"Electrified water," Avery said. "Good thing you checked."

Karl's grunt said that only a fool *wouldn't* check. I hunkered down beside him.

"You can leap over it in wolf form," I said. "Change back on the other side. That means I stay here, though . . ."

He growled. By this point, it was safer for me at his side.

"Two alternatives, then," I said. "Find something to put across the moat." I looked around and realized the extreme unlikelihood of a large broken tree limb appearing. "Or stop the electricity at the source."

I turned to speak to Avery and saw her ten feet away, crouching by the water.

Karl growled. She lifted a hand, and I thought I heard her whispering. Then there was a zap, light flashing, and she rose, smiling.

"Problem solved," she said. "I hope."

She walked over and took a mouse from the bag. Then she tossed it in. I braced for an electrifying end to the tiny life. Instead, there was a squeak as the mouse woke and madly paddled for shore.

"The source is down there," she said, pointing to where she'd been crouched. "I used an energy bolt spell to fry it."

"Good call," I said. "Thank you."

Karl grunted. Then he growled, and Avery said, "Yes, I know that doesn't mean I get to come inside. I'll still point out that I think I've proven I'd be useful, but I'm not going to fight you on this. We don't have time for that. Go shift back, and let's get you two inside."

TEN

We had to bypass two security systems—one protecting the window and a separate one that sensed a breach into the room. For Karl, this was the easy part. The tricky thing was dealing with supernatural security. Karl had spent forty years in a world where other supernaturals were no more than rumors. Fortunately, I'd launched my own investigative career in a world where a break and enter means more than locks and an alarm system.

According to Avery's contact, Nast relied primarily on technological security. He did, however, have one rather unusual bit of supernatural protection: a werewolf night guard patrolling the castle. That may have been what helped us with the other guards— they thought the wolf was their colleague and were trying to figure out why the hell he was out for a run.

It makes sense to post a werewolf indoors. His ears can detect a break-in or unexpected footsteps. His nose can track an intruder. His strength can overcome that intruder. None of that helps when the intruder is another werewolf . . . who knows he's there. Karl followed the guy's scent until he was close enough for the guard to catch a whiff of him. The guy spun and two seconds later he was on the ground with Karl administering the sedative.

From there, it was on to the grimoire. That was in the center of Nast's collection, which meant bypassing more security, all technological. It would have been easy for Karl to stuff his pockets with other valuables as we passed them, but that would be greedy and unsportsmanlike. He had come for the grimoire.

We had to pass through three rooms before we reached the one we wanted. As Karl disarmed the door, I stood guard. The house was silent and still, not even a—

"There," a voice whispered. "It's disarmed."

It was a male voice . . . but not Karl's. I turned to see a blond man crouched in exactly the spot I'd last seen Karl, by a hidden wall panel that housed the security. Another man stood right next to me, doing my job, his fingers raised as if ready to cast a spell.

A vision. I was seeing—

"*Après vous*," the other man said, waving to his partner.

The blonde grinned and stepped into the room . . . and a fireball shot from the darkness. A massive fireball, knocking him back into his partner, and then *they* were the fireballs, their clothing igniting so fast it seemed doused in gasoline. They screamed, terrible agonized shrieks as they fell to the ground, human torches, their skin blackening, the fire consuming them impossibly fast, supernaturally fast.

"Wait here."

Karl's voice jolted me out of the vision, and I saw him stepping through that doorway.

"No!"

I grabbed him just as the fireball exploded in the darkness. He was already twisting, on guard for trouble and diving at me the moment he saw it. We hit the ground, and it shot over our heads. I braced for it to slam into the wall and engulf it in fire, but instead it struck and disappeared, extinguishing as it contacted something other than living flesh.

I squeezed my eyes shut. Then I felt Karl pulling me to him, both of us still on the ground. He kissed me. Kissed me hard, and I could taste the heart-pounding relief and the belated fear. I moved against him, losing myself in that wonderfully chaos-ripe kiss, until he pulled back and murmured, "Thank you."

"You were ready for it," I said.

"I'm ready for anything. But thank you."

I shook it off, getting my bearings, and he hugged me again. I rose carefully, still trembling as I told him what I'd seen.

"It's a good thing we brought lots of mice," he said.

We used the mice as, well, guinea pigs, to get us into and through that room. Most survived. The fireball was apparently triggered at the doorway, at about waist level. Crawling through was safe, and once inside, we didn't encounter any more booby traps.

We could see the grimoire a few feet from the door. I took out my flashlight and shone it on our prize. It looked . . . unimpressive. No glittering gilt pages or encrusted jewel cover. It wasn't bound in human skin or written in blood. Just a very old book, with a worn leather binding, patched and repaired, a few pages jutting out as if they were no longer affixed to the spine. I could make out writing on those loose pages. Very faint, handwritten words crossed off and added in margins. A working tome for a witch.

Karl reached into the bag for another mouse. He drew his hand back and—

"It's bullshit," a voice said, the accent American.

Karl disappeared, and the room filled with daylight. A young man led a young woman toward the grimoire. She was dressed in a maid's uniform, and he wore a suit, looking like a driver or a guard. The styles were maybe ten years out of date. I smelled mortar, and through the window I saw scaffolding. The "castle" was still under construction.

"Bull-sheet," the girl said, in a French accent.

He grinned. "Exactly."

"And if it is not?"

"It is," he said. "A grimoire protected by a spell in a lost language, contained only within its own pages?" He rolled his eyes. "The old man is senile if he expects anyone to believe that."

"Yet I see you do not go too close," the girl teased.

"Hell, just wait here and I'll bring it over. Maybe you can find a new spell, one that will polish the silver for you."

"No," she said. "One that will clean the windows. Have you seen how many there are? *Mon Dieu!*"

He laughed and strolled toward the grimoire. The girl sucked in a breath. He kept going. He reached for the book. And then he stopped, his fingers resting on it.

The girl's tinkling laugh rang out. "Changing your mind?"

The young man said nothing.

"Come on, then," she said. "I hear footsteps, and if Monsieur Nast catches us in here, there will be—how do you say?—hell to pay."

When he didn't move, she grabbed his arm. "Come. Quick—"

She let out a shriek and stumbled back, still holding his arm, and he started to fall. No, he started to topple, and she screamed, and her whole body flailed, as if she couldn't let go of his arm. As he toppled toward her, his leg struck the base of the grimoire stand and he . . .

He shattered. His body fractured into a thousand bloodred shards, tinkling to the floor, and the girl let out an impossibly high-pitched shriek, and I tore my gaze away from those shards and saw her backing away, her arm held out straight, rigid, her hand still clasping his elbow. That's all she held—his elbow. She swung around, and her arm struck another marble stand, knocking a book off it, and her arm . . .

Her arm shattered.

Her arm shattered from the shoulder down, and blood spurted from the stump, and she screamed, a horrible, terrifying scream, as footsteps pounded and blood sprayed the room. And then I was the one staggering back.

Karl caught me. He held me against him, and I buried my face against his chest, and when I could finally speak, I said, "They shatter. It's—it's like liquid nitrogen. It freezes them and they shatter."

"I know."

I pulled back and looked up at him. "You *know*."

"It's instantaneous death. That's what I told you. How it happens is hardly—"

"No," I said, gripping his jacket with both hands. "You're not touching that book."

I braced for him to argue. Instead, he said, softly, "All right."

"I mean it. We're—"

"I said all right, Hope. If you don't want me doing this, I won't do it. I don't need to." He put his hand under my chin and lifted my gaze to his. "You understand that, don't you? I don't need to do this job or any other one. I can quit. Right this second, I can turn and walk out that door."

I took a deep breath. "But you promised a client—"

"Doesn't matter. I'll deal with any repercussions, because I will not do a job that frightens you. They all frighten you. I know that. You worry from the moment I leave until the moment I return, and yes, I want to be able to look our children in the eye when I tell them what I do for a living, but more important than that, I don't want to be the selfish son of a bitch running around stealing jewels while his wife sits home, terrified this will be the time he doesn't return."

He was right. Every time he left for a heist, I sat by the phone until I got the call saying all was fine.

I hated what he did, because it put him in danger. But that danger is what kept him going, the same as chaos kept me going. The impossible quandary for both of us. I want him to be safe. He wants the same for me. Yet "safe" kills something inside us.

Did I want Karl to retire?

Hell, yes.

I would just never ask him to stop, never admit it's what I want, because it's not what he wants.

No, it's not what he *needs*.

I could say the word now and he would walk away. But beneath that panic swirling inside me, I knew that wasn't right. Even when I was sick with worry, I reminded myself that he was a professional and did not take risks. I'd seen him on the job, in the visions he shared with me. He worked as he had tonight, with consummate care. He'd double- and triple-checked all Avery's work. He'd insisted on testing the moat water. He'd seen the fireball coming. He would test the grimoire as many times as it took to reassure himself it was fine. He had this. He always did.

I took a deep, shuddering breath. "No, let's do this."

"I—"

"Thank you. For offering. But you are about to steal the most unstealable artifact in the supernatural world. You know what you're doing. And if you say it's safe, then it's safe."

He leaned down and kissed my forehead. "This is what I do, Hope. It's what I'm good at. Quite possibly the only thing I'm truly good at."

I looked up at him. "No, you're a good husband and a good father."

His lips curved. "I'm working at both, but I'm hardly a professional yet. What I mean is that I would not do this job if I believed it put either of us at risk." He stepped back and picked up the bag of mice. "I am going to thoroughly test to be sure the spell isn't active, and if you still feel you don't want me touching that book, I won't."

I nodded. He tested with all the mice we had left, dropping them right on the book, from every angle.

Nothing happened.

"May I?" he said, gesturing at the book.

I nodded.

He picked up the grimoire. Then, without even a moment's pause, he slid it into the bag, turned to me, and said, "Ready to go?"

I let out the breath I'd been holding and nodded.

ELEVEN

We met up with Avery on the other side of the moat. Under cover of her blur, the three of us hurried to a spot where she and I would wait by a small grove of trees while Karl Changed into wolf form so he could scout the way out.

He handed me the bag and slipped into the grove. We could still see his fair skin as he took off his shirt, hung it on a tree, and then moved behind a bush.

When the first grunts of his Change came, I turned away. That's when I felt the bag slide from my shoulder, and I spun to see Avery with her fingers extended, spell at the ready. Her other hand grasped the bag straps.

"I'll take this," she said.

I went for my gun. She sent me flying with a knockback spell.

"Hands where I can see them," she said. "I won't invoke Lucifer's wrath by killing you, Hope, but I noticed your husband isn't included under that protection. He's in a very vulnerable position right now . . ." She glanced over to where we could hear the soft grunts and snarls of Karl shifting forms. "I don't particularly want to kill him, either, though, so how about you just sit on that stump, hands on your head, and I'll bid you good night."

"Birkan double-crossed us," I said.

"Birkan?" She gave a low laugh, keeping her voice down so Karl wouldn't hear. "Fredrick Birkan is an idiot who fancies himself a dangerous man. No, this is all mine, sweetheart. Birkan was the bankroll, nothing more. Now, I will take this—"

Karl jumped her from behind.

"Or not," I said, when he had her on the ground, hands pinned. He put her hands behind her back and yanked her up.

"Oh my God," I said, staring at Karl. "You mean you just took off your shirt and *faked* Changing?" I took the bag and looked at Avery. "Did you really think he'd take the time to shift forms after he's stolen a priceless grimoire? I said I'd talked to Rhys about you. I also talked to Vanessa Callas, who's seeing one of Karl's Pack brothers. You remember Vanessa?"

"That—" Avery spat.

"She doesn't like you much, either. She said you two butted heads, lots of drama and competition . . . until she caught you moonlighting and stealing the agency's clients. She promised not to tell Rhys if you resigned quietly. But she told me enough to confirm you really *aren't* a team player. That had us on high alert. Then your chaos vibes confirmed it."

"What? No. There's a spell—"

"—that blocks chaotic thoughts and vibes from an Expisco? I've never heard of one, but apparently you have, and it works great. That's the problem. We're in the middle of a dangerous heist, and you weren't giving off so much as a twitch. Obviously you'd found a way to block me, and you wouldn't do that unless you planned to betray us."

"We can make a deal," she said. "I'll tell you how to evade Birkan's men—"

"No need. Oh, yes, we do plan to take the grimoire. There's nothing else we can do. You and Birkan set Karl up *twice*."

She opened her mouth, as if to say again that Birkan wasn't involved, but I hurried on.

"After that, Karl has to keep it. Otherwise, he'd look a fool. It's about reputation. And his rep says if you play fair with him, he plays fair back. Otherwise . . ." I lifted the bag and shook it. "Now, as for you, two choices. One, you can run and alert Birkan's men and try to stop us. Two, you can get the hell out of Belgium before Ivan Price arrives."

Her head jerked up at that name.

"You remember Mr. Price? I hope so, considering how Vanessa says you screwed him over. She always felt bad, letting you get away with that. So she's making it right. She's told him where he can find you. No rush to decide, though. You can sleep on it."

Karl injected her with our last dose of sedative, laid her in a comfortable position on the ground, and we took off.

Evading Birkan's men was simple enough. We'd worked it into the plan because Karl knew that Avery or Birkan planned to double-cross him. They'd gotten him here by underhanded means. They weren't going to suddenly play straight once the prize was in hand.

Two hours later, we were in a rental car crossing the border between Belgium and France, as Karl made a call using the speakerphone.

Once Birkan had stopped screaming obscenities in several languages, Karl said, "You double-crossed me, Mr. Birkan."

"I sure as hell did not—"

"You and Ms. Avery set me up. You had no intention of paying me for my work. That is unacceptable."

"I have no idea what you're talking about."

He kept babbling denials and accusations until Karl played him the recording. The one of Avery offering to get us past Birkan's men, in which I accused them both of setting us up . . . not giving her a chance to clarify that Birkan hadn't been in on it.

When the recording finished, Birkan denied playing any role in Avery's plot and swore vengeance on her, but there was no way he could keep claiming Karl hadn't been double-crossed. Which meant, as a matter of professional pride and reputation, Karl could not hand over the grimoire to Frederick Birkan. And no one would expect him to.

TWELVE

The next day, we were arriving in Philadelphia by private jet. One owned by the company of the man waiting for us.

"Hey, Troy," I said, giving him a hug. "Did the boss send you personally to escort the treasure home?"

"Nope." Troy waved at a man standing farther back from the aircraft. "The boss came himself for this one."

Benicio Cortez. CEO of the Cortez Cabal. And the man who had readily agreed to pay five million for the Eteocypriot grimoire, along with an assurance that he would personally handle any fallout from the Nast Cabal.

After a hug, Benicio took my arm and helped me to the waiting SUV as if I were nine months pregnant and ready to pop. Inside, he had cold water, hot tea, and an entire breakfast waiting.

"Your jet served breakfast," I said. "Twice as we crossed time zones."

"You're eating for two."

"That second one is currently the size of my fist."

"Perhaps not, but still, you *are* pregnant. And jetting across the world to break into fortified castles hardly seems . . ." A look Karl's way. "Appropriate."

"I'll be spending the next year tied down by my belly and then a tiny baby. I need to get my adventures while I can. And you got a very sweet prize."

I passed him the grimoire. He examined it, smiling like a kid with a new toy, as Karl fixed my tea.

"And the other prize?" Benicio said when he finally closed the grimoire, his hands still resting on it. "May I see that?"

"It doesn't work," I said. "Just an expensive bauble with an interesting history."

"Still, I would like to see it."

I took out the Eye of Pldans, which Karl had exchanged for a replica when Birkan had insisted on showing it off.

Benicio's eyes glittered as he took it.

"It doesn't work," I reminded him. "I tried it."

"Perhaps under the right conditions . . ."

I took it back. "Uh-uh."

"The original price was five hundred thousand. I'll double it."

Karl shook his head. "I have plans for it. If you want it, you know where to find it."

"*After* it leaves Pennsylvania," I added.

"All right. Now, I think there's a little girl who's waiting to see you. I thought I'd take you for lunch—Paige tells me there's a place Nita likes."

"Princess tea," I said, rolling my eyes.

Benicio chuckled. "Nothing wrong with that. Ask your mother to join us. I'm presuming that's who she's with."

"My mother does have a boyfriend," I said. "Two right now, actually."

Benicio smiled. "I would expect no less. Ask her along, and tell her I would love to see her again."

I sighed and took out my phone.

The next day, we were back at Lady Fitzwilliams's estate. She'd summoned Joel, and he'd brought us along. The police were also present, as was Bradley Fitzwilliams . . . who'd gotten a call last night with very specific instructions for saving his ass from jail.

"It was a stupid mistake," Bradley was saying, sweat beaded

across his forehead, chaos vibes throbbing. "I wanted to see the necklace, so I came over and Mom was busy, so I took a look myself. Then my girlfriend called—she was mad at me about something—and I got flustered and put the necklace back in the wrong safe."

"And didn't notice?" the detective said.

"I wasn't paying attention. Last night, I realized what I'd done and called Mom."

Lady Fitzwilliams confirmed that after she'd gotten the call, she'd opened the other safe and there it was, hidden among her other jewelry. A preposterous story. I'm sure the police and Joel didn't buy it. I'm sure Bradley's mother didn't, either. Clearly Bradley had stolen it and had a change of heart, but all parties decided not to pursue the matter further.

Joel took us to a celebratory lunch afterward. As we ate, Karl said, "If you still have a security position for me . . ."

Joel grinned. "I absolutely still have a position for you, since I apparently still have a security division, now that this whole mess can be laid at the client's feet. We're in the clear, and your job is waiting."

"Part-time," Karl said. "No more than two half days at the office or on location. The rest will be done from home. And I want to work alone, on projects separate from the team."

"Understood. You can start Monday."

And so Benicio got his grimoire. Lady Fitzwilliams got her necklace. Joel's company recovered its good name. And so did Karl, along with a story, spreading fast through the supernatural underground, of how Fredrick Birkan and Sharon Avery had tried to set him up, and he walked away with both the Eye of Pldans and the most unobtainable object in the supernatural world.

"Out in a blaze of glory," I said as we sat curled up by the fireplace.

Karl smiled and sipped his nonalcoholic champagne.

"Is that it, then?" I said. "You really *are* out?"

He tugged me further onto his lap. "Do you want me to be?"

I met his gaze. "I want you to be happy."

"And I want *you* to be—"

"Yes, I worry. But no more than you do if I'm off on a mission and you can't join me. You don't ask me to give those up because you know I need them, and you know how careful I am. I know you need this, and I know you're even more careful than me. Seeing you in action reminded me of that. I don't want you to retire. I just want you to be happy."

"Right now, I am. I could not imagine being happier." He shifted me into his arms. "I want to try it this way, Hope. Work security part-time for Joel. Stay home with our children because that's not a chance I'll ever get again. Take jobs from Elena and with you, and see if that scratches the itch and, yes, it probably won't, completely, but if it doesn't, I'll step back in the game now and then, for the right job at the right price. Minimal risk for maximum payback—in profit and adventure. So . . ." He shifted me again, until I was curled up on his lap. "Semi-retired. *Mostly* retired. Ready to start a new stage in my life and see how it goes. All right?"

I reached up and kissed him. "Absolutely all right."

FORBIDDEN

1. MORGAN

*M*organ Walsh struggled to get the map open over the steering wheel, preferably without detouring into the ditch. It really wasn't a maneuver to be attempted by someone who hadn't driven in almost two years. When a horn blasted, he glanced up to see headlights in his lane. He cursed and yanked the wheel as the pickup roared past, kids shouting out rolled-down windows.

"Yeah, yeah," he muttered.

He shoved the map onto the passenger seat and peered out the windshield. There had to be a town along here somewhere. It was ninety miles to Syracuse, and he was starving. He *shouldn't* be starving. He'd spent the last two years in Alaska, living as a wolf, only eating every few days. Now he couldn't seem to go a few hours without his stomach threatening to devour itself.

He glanced at the side of the road. He should just pull over and check the map, but the shoulder was slick with snow. Snow. In early November. Even Anchorage didn't see this much of the white stuff so soon.

As he thought that, more began to fall. He flicked on the wipers and heard his brother's voice, from their call, three days ago.

"Got a foot of snow last week. If you're coming home, you should do it soon. You know how it can get."

Oh, yeah. Morgan knew. Compared with winter where he grew up in Newfoundland, Alaska was positively balmy.

"You *are* coming home, right?" Blaine had asked.

"Maybe for Christmas."

They both knew it was a lie. It wasn't the shitty weather that kept him away. Even in the breathtaking wilds of Alaska, he'd dreamed of rocky coasts and pounding surf and winds that could knock the breath from your lungs and set your eyes blazing.

But he *hadn't* dreamed of the life he'd had there, up before dawn with his father and his brother, fishing for cod whose stocks had been depleted twenty years ago by factory fishing. And he hadn't dreamed of long nights in their cabin, far from any semblance of civilization, listening to his father rage against the Department of Fisheries and Oceans—and rage against Morgan, too, when he'd suggest it might be time to find a new livelihood. Walshes were fishermen and, by God, that's what they'd keep doing until it killed them.

Morgan had decided it was not really the way he cared to die. Or to live. So, at twenty-four, he'd packed a bag and set out to see what else the world had to offer. Four years later, he was still looking.

He hadn't told his brother where he was going. If he'd even said the words "New York State," Blaine would have flipped out. Might even have come after him. Which wasn't such a bad idea—it might be the only way to get Blaine off the Rock.

To the Walshes, as to most North American werewolves, New York meant one thing—the home of the American Pack. Growing up, Morgan had heard stories of the Pack the way other kids heard stories about strangers in white vans. The Pack. Madmen and murderers, every last one of them, endlessly scouring the country for innocent, peace-loving werewolves and slaughtering them for sport. *Stay in Newfoundland*, his dad had said, *or the Pack will find you.*

Nearly eighteen months ago, the Pack did find him. They'd been in Alaska hunting other werewolves. Not for sport, but because those others were exactly the kind of wolves his father claimed the Pack were. Madmen and murderers. Rapists and man-eaters.

The Pack had invited Morgan to visit when he was done his experiment—living as a wolf in Alaska. They wanted to recruit him. They hadn't said that exactly, but he'd gotten the hint—come and hang out with us, and if we still think you're a decent sort, we'd like to sign you up.

Was that what Morgan wanted? He had no idea. But it couldn't hurt to stop by. He'd say he was just passing through, remembered they were there, decided to call and say hi, maybe take them out to dinner.

Speaking of dinner . . . His stomach rumbled again. In the distance, he could see what looked like a town sign. He peered through the falling snow until it came into view. Then he blinked. And laughed.

It was indeed a town sign . . . with a snarling wolfman welcoming visitors to Westwood, home of the champion Westwood Werewolves. Across the bottom, the sign declared, "Westwood Loves Its Werewolves!"

Morgan chuckled again. "That's just too good to pass up."

He found a diner at the end of the main street. There were only two cars in the lot, both covered in snow, but the light seeping through the diner windows gave him hope.

It was open. Empty, though. Through the window he could see a server reading a paperback novel. As he walked in, he noticed the sign on the window: "10% off for all Werewolves and their families."

Wonder if they'll give me the discount.

He went in and sat down. The menu offered what he guessed you'd call home cooking, but it wasn't the kind of fare he ever got at home. His dad was a meat-and-potatoes man. Heavy on the potatoes, usually, unless he'd been lucky enough to hunt up moose or rabbit. Tonight's dinner was meat-and-potatoes—meat loaf with scalloped potatoes—but it was a damned sight better than anything his father ever cooked. And the apple pie was delicious. Morgan was finishing his second slice when the server stopped by to ask how he was enjoying his meal.

"Hungry, I see," she said.

He flashed her a big smile. "Always."

She returned the smile and gave him a good view of her cleavage as she cleared his dishes. She hadn't shown much interest in her novel since he'd arrived. He got the message: there was more than food on the menu tonight, at least for him.

She was cute, in a dyed-blond, being-homecoming-queen-was-the-best-day-of-my-life way. Comfort food, like his dinner. He was seriously tempted to partake. A hunger for food wasn't the only appetite that'd slammed back as he returned to human life. This one surprised him less—there hadn't been much opportunity for sex as a wolf. Sure, one of the females had thought he looked mighty fine, but *that* experience had definitely not been part of his experiment.

So he'd been making up for lost time, and he'd have been happy to let the cute server help, but he really did need to hit the road. Being in New York State meant he was technically trespassing on Pack territory. He couldn't afford to linger.

"Anything else I can get for you?" she asked, standing close enough for him to smell her rich, soapy scent.

"Just the check," he said with regret. "I need to hit the road before this snow—"

A wave of nausea rocked him. The room seemed to swirl, lights dimming. He gripped the edge of the table and blinked hard.

"You okay?" the server asked.

"Yeah." He took a deep breath and straightened.

"Maybe that second slice of pie wasn't such a good idea?"

As he nodded, his back started to itch. He looked down at his hands. The skin bubbled, like something was trapped under it. He yanked his hands out of sight under the table.

Damn it. He needed to be more careful. Take things slower. Like not embarking on a cross-country trip when he was so used to living in wolf form.

He reached for his wallet and slapped a twenty on the table. Then he rose, his hands shoved in his pockets.

"You sure you're okay?" the server asked. "You shouldn't be driving if you're not."

"I'm fine." That came out a little too close to a growl, and he coughed to cover it.

"We've got a couch in the back." She slid in front of him and smiled up. "Or my place is just down the road. I make a pretty good nurse."

He shook his head and started to walk away. She caught his sleeve. He wheeled, eyes blazing, fever coming fast.

"No," he said, in what was definitely a growl, deep and guttural, barely human.

She staggered back, and he hurried out the door.

Morgan wanted to move his car, considering that he'd just said he was leaving. But he was in no shape to drive. He needed to Change. Now. Luckily, the diner, being on the edge of town, backed on to forest. He headed straight there, cursing himself as he tramped through snow up to his knees.

He should have Changed last night. He should Change *every* night until his body got used to being human. Sure, willingly transforming nightly was akin to volunteering for anesthesia-free surgery. But he could not take chances. Seeing the look on that server's face, he knew he'd taken a chance. And on Pack territory, too.

Goddamn it!

The snowfall lightened as he trudged deeper into the forest, but he barely noticed, too caught up in his thoughts. What exactly had the server seen? Had his face started Changing? Or was she only startled because he'd growled at her? God, he hoped that was it.

A branch slapped his face, and he shoved it aside, growling, only to smack into a tree trunk. He blinked and rubbed his eyes. Everything looked slightly out of focus. He blinked harder.

He felt disoriented, like he had in the diner. That wasn't normally part of the Change. How long had he been driving? He calculated. Shit. Too long. No sleep. No exercise. Not nearly enough caffeine. That might explain this sudden need to Change.

He stumbled into the nearest clearing. Off came the clothing, shivers turning to near convulsions as he tried to hang it in branches, up off the snow.

Then he got down on all fours and started the transformation.

*T*he process went faster than usual. No less painful, but the compressed time frame made it seem better.

Lies we tell ourselves.

At least he was warmer, with the wolf coat. His fur was dark red, like his hair. Once, when he'd been spotted by hunters in Alaska, they'd mistaken him for an Irish setter, which was kind of insulting. Despite his coloring, he was clearly a wolf. But being mistaken for a setter was better than having the hunters return to town with stories of a massive, dark-red, green-eyed wolf.

He chuffed and looked around. Normally, it would be time to run. Work off the excess energy that came with being part canine. But he was still woozy, and dinner felt like a dead weight in his gut. A nice, leisurely evening stroll seemed more his speed—

"Are those footprints?" a distant voice said.

"Looks like it," a second man answered.

Shit. Rule One of Changing in a populated area? Get away from the damned population first.

Morgan had barely leapt from the clearing before he stumbled and plowed into a drift. He pushed up, shaking snow from his fur, and looked back at the branch that had tripped him.

Where'd that come from?

He blinked, and when he looked again, he saw two branches, blurred.

Where did they both *come from?*

Shit. He was really out of it. He should get farther into the forest and rest until it passed.

A branch cracked to his left. He peered through the trees. He could make out a bulky shadow about twenty feet away. Hunter? Bear? He wasn't in any condition to deal with either.

He ran. The snow had stopped falling, leaving the forest pitch-black, the dense treetops barely allowing any light from the quarter moon. His night vision had kicked in, but everything was blurred.

He stumbled over another branch and pitched headfirst into a gully, his skull cracking against a half-buried boulder as he fell. When he hit bottom, he managed to get to his feet. He teetered a few steps and then dropped as everything went dark.

Morgan surfaced to the sound of a woman's voice. He groaned and struggled to remember the night before. Something about a woman. A server in a diner?

"Come on. Wake up!"

Obviously, she was in a damned hurry to get him out the door. Was she married? Shit. He was usually careful about stuff like that.

It took some effort to pry open his eyes, and when he did, a blast of light almost made them close again. He squinted and saw a blurred figure bending over him. Then an icy wind blasted over his bare skin.

"Jesus," he muttered. "Someone close the damned—"

The figure above him came into focus. It was a pretty, dark-haired, dark-eyed woman, his age or a little older. Huh. He'd lucked out last night. Now if he could actually remember—

"Get up!" she said.

He blinked and rose on his elbows. Damn, it was cold. Why was it so—?

He got a good look at the woman. She wore a dark brown parka over a khaki shirt and trousers. It looked like some kind of uniform. And there was a gun in her hand. Pointed at him.

A ray of sunlight glinted off a police badge on her parka.

Morgan sat up fast, realizing as he did that he was lying in the snow. Naked. Surrounded by cops.

"Uh . . ." he began, as he looked around.

His gaze fell on the tracks in the snow. Wolf tracks.

Shit.

3. JESSICA

Westwood police chief Jessica Dales stood inside the station house door, struggling to close it against a gust of wind. She finally won the battle and paused to stamp the snow from her boots. A blast of furnace-hot air greeted her. She closed her eyes and let her cheeks thaw before she stepped into the office.

Wes Kent looked up from his paperwork at the front desk.

"Weatherman's right," Jessica said. "Another storm's blowing up. Crazy weather." She swiped snow from her hair, then hooked her thumb at the holding cell, just past an open doorway. "Speaking of crazy, is our streaker talking yet?"

"Nope," Kent said. "No ID, either. I ran the plates. Seems he bought the car in Vancouver for a grand last week. Guy let him 'borrow' the plates for a few hundred more."

"Nice of him."

Jessica walked to the open doorway and looked into the cell. Their new prisoner—their *only* prisoner—sat with his back to the bars. Before they'd located the car, they'd found his clothing in a nearby tree. It'd been soaking wet. They'd offered him a dry shirt and pants from some extras they kept in back, but he'd refused, putting on the wet ones instead.

"If he bought the car in Vancouver, he crossed the border," she said. "So he must have a passport."

"Should. By that accent, I'm guessing he's Scottish."

It was an odd accent, not one she remembered hearing before. She supposed it could be Scottish, but that seemed a strange fit for a guy who looked like he had a generous dose of Native American blood, despite the red hair and green eyes.

"I'll head back out and search his car," she said. "We know where he started his trip. If we can figure out where he was going, that will help. A place. A name. Anything."

"How about both?" Kent asked. "Plus a phone number."

He held out a map with a thick black circle around Syracuse, New York. Beside it, someone had written "Elena" and a phone number.

Jessica took out her cell.

4. ELENA

I stood just beyond the study doorway, out of sight. The low-burning fireplace tried to lure me in, with its inviting crackle and pop, rich smoky smell, and tendrils of heat. Clay's voice was an enticement, too. After three days of snowstorms, I just wanted to curl up on the sofa with him, drowse in the firelight, and—

"You already moved!"

"I didn't take my fingers off it!"

"Doesn't matter. That counts. Dad! Tell her it counts!"

Three days of snowstorms. One sprained ankle. Two serious cases of cabin fever.

"Let's go outside, guys," Clay said. "I'll pull Kate on the toboggan."

Make that three cases.

I steeled myself and walked through the doorway. Clay was on the couch, leaning over as the kids played chess on the floor. Logan and Kate had just turned five in September. With every birthday, there's a part of me that hopes this is the one where their energy levels will drop a little. I might as well hope that the moon will turn purple. They're the children of werewolves—those energy levels aren't dropping until they're a *hundred* and five.

"I don't wanna get pulled," Kate said. "I wanna walk!"

"You can't," Logan said. "You sprained your ankle, stupid."

Kate jumped on her brother. "I'm not stupid!"

Clay grabbed Kate's sweater and lifted her off her brother, snarling and spitting, more wildcat than wolf.

"Logan," I said as I walked in. "Did you forget the rule? Call her stupid and you earn an hour in your room."

He looked up at me. "That's not the rule. The rule is an hour if we call each other an *idiot*."

"Logan . . ."

He scowled. "It's her fault we can't go outside. She's the one who fell."

"Because you pushed me off the slide," Kate said.

Logan leapt up. "I did not! You fell, and I grabbed your coat. I was trying to *help* you." He spun on me. "I wouldn't push her. Tell her, Momma."

"I know. She does, too. She's just angry."

I scooped him up, ignoring his wriggling, and sat on Jeremy's recliner with him on my lap. I looked over at Clay, holding an equally squirming Kate.

"I'll grab the duct tape if you find the rope," I said.

He chuckled.

"I heard that," Logan grumbled.

I kissed his cheek and got a scowl in return. We sat there for a minute, just holding the kids. Cuddling and calming them. Or restraining them. It's a fine line some days.

I looked at Kate, her blond curls swinging as she struggled to get free. Clay bent down to her, whispering. There was no mistaking them for anything but father and daughter, with matching blue eyes and golden curls, Kate's down past her shoulders, Clay's cropped close. Similar in temperament as well as looks. Jeremy says that Clay was more like Logan as a child, quiet and serious, but Kate definitely takes after him now, squirming and shooting furious glances his way, refusing to be still until she damned well wants to be still.

Logan had already stopped squirming, saving his energy for the glares he kept firing at his sister. He has my dark-blue eyes and my straight hair, though his is a slightly deeper shade than my silver-blond. I'd like to think his off-the-charts IQ comes from his mom, but I have to cede that to his PhD father. As for his uncanny ability to maintain long, angry silences, I have no idea where that comes from. Really.

"Okay," I said. "We need a plan. How about some apart time? Dad will take Logan for a walk while—"

"That's not fair!" Kate said. "I want to go for a walk, too!"

"I was going to suggest you help me bake cookies."

"But I want to bake cookies!" Logan said. "And we haven't finished our chess game. You can't let her quit just because I was winning—"

"You weren't winning," Kate said. "I had a plan."

Her brother snorted.

"I did!" Kate said. "You'll see."

She jumped back onto the floor. Logan scrambled down beside her.

The phone rang. Clay and I collided pouncing on it. I won, grabbing the receiver and jogging away. Yes, it's a sad day when getting to answer the phone is a victory. Especially in a household where it normally rings through to voice mail, with three people sitting within reach of a receiver.

"Is this Elena?" said a woman's voice when I answered.

"Yes . . ."

"This is Jess Dales, chief of police for Westwood, New York. I have someone here . . ."

I listened as she explained. When I hung up, Clay said, "Trouble?"

"Maybe. I need to talk to Jeremy."

Clay shuttled the kids to the kitchen and left them there to make peanut butter and jam sandwiches while he followed me to Jeremy's studio.

"Do you think that's such a good idea?" I nodded toward the kitchen. "There are knives."

"I don't think the situation has reached that point." He glanced back. "The sharp ones are locked up, though, right?"

"They are. It'd be butter knife injuries. Or, more likely, a jam-flinging fight."

"After which we can make them take turns having baths and cleaning the kitchen, which means at least twenty minutes of apart time." Another glance over his shoulder. "Should I go back and get out the honey, too?"

"Tempting."

The door to Jeremy's studio was closed. Well, not exactly—he'd left it open a few inches, but for Jeremy that was a clear Do Not Disturb sign, and one even the kids would respect. I rapped first, and he called, "Come in."

Jeremy was standing at his easel, with his back to us. His shirt-sleeves were pushed up, feet bare, a pair of clean socks lying on a nearby chair. We'd gone for a walk outside earlier talking about Alpha business, and he'd gotten his feet wet. When we'd come in, I'd grabbed him a dry pair, but obviously he'd gotten too wrapped up in his painting to remember to put them on. Just like he'd gotten too wrapped up to realize he really shouldn't push back his hair when his hands were dappled with paint. There were blue streaks through it. Maybe I'd tell him about them; maybe I wouldn't.

I couldn't see what he was working on, and I didn't try to peek. He'd show it when it was ready. For now, he just lifted a finger and finished his brushstroke. Then he pulled out his earbuds. Jeremy never paints to music. Yet another sign that the chaos around here had become a little too much even for our unflappable Alpha.

"Remember Morgan Walsh?" I said as I perched on the window seat. "Newfoundland werewolf in Alaska?"

"The mutt who was living as a wolf?" Clay said. "Kinda hard to forget."

True. It wasn't something that happened very often. So rarely, in fact, that we'd added a page for Morgan to the Legacy—our book of Pack and werewolf history. There was a section for oddities. While his "experiment" was unusual, the guy himself had seemed normal enough. Until this call came.

"He was *what*?" Clay said when I finished explaining. "On Pack *territory*? Did I say the guy was a little crazy, darling?"

"He's not crazy. Just young. Trying to find himself. Some guys go backpacking in the Himalayas. He tried living as a wolf."

Clay's snort said "a little crazy" described it. This from a guy who was himself more wolf than human. As much as he loved being in wolf form, though, it wasn't anything he'd choose long-term. I wouldn't, either, but I could better understand Morgan's identity crisis. Clay has always known exactly what he was. It took me a lot longer to figure it out. Some days I'm still trying.

"We can overlook the trespassing," I said. "It seems he was heading to see us."

"And the rest of it?" Clay said. "Being found by the cops? Naked? In the snow? Surrounded by paw prints?"

"That might require intervention."

"You think?"

I shot him a glare and then looked back at Jeremy, who'd been quietly listening. "We could ignore this. Let Morgan dig himself out of the mess. But considering it's on Pack territory . . ."

"We should handle it," Jeremy said. "If he had your phone number, he was planning to announce his visit. That means his detour was a youthful indiscretion, not a deliberate one."

"The guy's older than Reese," Clay grumbled. "That's not *youthful* enough to excuse it."

"How old is he again?" Jeremy asked me. "Twenty-seven, twenty-eight?"

"About that."

Jeremy took off his music player and wrapped the earbud cord around it. "I seem to recall that isn't too old to do something rash

and impulsive. Something that might have far-reaching conse-
quences."

Clay flinched, despite Jeremy's casual tone. It was a subtle
reminder that Clay had been that age when he bit me.

"I'll drive up and take care of it," Jeremy said.

Clay and I both stared at him.

"Yes?" he said, pocketing his player.

"You're still Alpha," I said. "You make decisions and send out
your trusty minions to enforce them. That would be us."

Kate shrieked from the kitchen. "Give that back!"

"I believe I should handle this," Jeremy said. "You've been preparing to take over as Alpha. Likewise, I should prepare to resume
duties as a Pack member."

"Nice try," I said. "No adventures while you're Alpha. That's
the rule."

"I don't believe I ever said—"

Clay clapped him on the back as we headed out. "Don't worry.
We'll take care of this."

"It's not a matter that requires both—" Jeremy began.

Logan raced past the open doorway, a sandwich in each hand.
Kate stumped after him, limping on her bound foot.

"The Alpha-elect needs a bodyguard," Clay said. "That's another
rule. Sorry. Love to stay. Gotta go."

We snuck to the front door and grabbed our coats and boots.
Jeremy followed.

"Enjoy it while you can," he said to me. "Once you're Alpha, no
more adventures."

"Pfft. That's *your* rule," I said. "When I'm Alpha, I'm changing
it. That's the beauty of being the bitch in charge."

Clay grinned and handed me my gloves. At the sound of footsteps, Jeremy stepped into the foyer with us. We all stood silently
watching as Kate clomped past down the hall. She had both

sandwiches mashed in one hand and was taking a bite. When she didn't notice us, I exhaled in relief and grabbed the door handle.

"Mom!" Logan shouted.

"We'll be back before bedtime," I whispered to Jeremy.

"You'd better be," he said as we made our escape.

5.

*S*tonehaven is a rural estate outside the small town of Bear Valley, New York. The closest city is Syracuse. According to the GPS in Jeremy's SUV, Westwood was almost an hour west of that, off a regional highway. We'd been driving for about thirty minutes when the snow started falling again and the radio announcer declared another blizzard was set to hit before nightfall.

"I don't like the sounds of that," I said.

"It'll be fine." Clay turned up the windshield wipers. "I'm planning on getting this done before dinner. And since we said we'd be back by bedtime—and not sooner—that gives us a few extra hours."

"For a nice meal, without screaming kids and flying food?"

"I was thinking more like . . ." He pointed to a roadside motel as we passed. "Unless you'd rather go out to dinner."

I grinned. "Not unless we're done early enough to swing into Syracuse and get a hotel with room service."

He put his foot on the gas.

About an hour later, we finally reached Westwood . . . complete with a werewolf leaping off the town welcome sign.

"Walsh chose to Change *here*?" Clay said as we passed the sign.

"There must be a good explanation."

Clay jerked his chin toward an old feed mill on the edge of town. Through the snow, I could make out a wall mural of a snarling werewolf.

"Yeah, there's an explanation, all right," Clay said. "The guy's an idiot."

I refrained from comment. Whatever Morgan's explanation, it had better be good. By this stage, I was starting to think Clay had a point. Which meant Morgan Walsh's bad day was about to get a whole lot worse.

We parked on the main street, a few doors down from the police station. As we tramped along the snowy sidewalk, we passed a shop with a huge WARNING: WEREWOLF TERRITORY sign in the window.

"Did I mention the idiot part?" he said.

I sighed.

"I don't care how good his excuse is—" Clay began.

I spun to ward off . . . nothing.

I stood there, fists clenched. I hadn't heard anything. It was just . . . a feeling—the hair on the back of my neck rising, some deep-rooted instinct flicking on my fight-or-flight response.

"Elena?" Clay said.

Down the street, someone was coming out of a shop. On the road, a single car was trying to get traction, engine whining. That was it. Just one car and one person.

"Sorry," I said, shaking it off. "That's what happens when I don't leave the house in a week. I get outside, and I feel like someone's watching."

"Small towns. Someone's always watching."

"No kidding." I took a deep breath. "All right, then. Let's sort this mess out and go home."

The police station was actually just a storefront along the main street, wedged between the hardware and the bank. I was a little concerned about signs in the hardware advertising bolt cutters and shotguns. Maybe the Westwood cops were bored, hoping to convince some drunken local that breaking into the bank next door was easier than he thought.

The station's front door opened into a small foyer. A sign asked visitors to leave their boots on the mat. Clay ignored it. I was pulling mine off when I saw the puddles leading inside, suggesting no one else had obeyed, either. I tugged mine back on. I did feel guilty about it, though. I'd spent most of my life doing as I was told; it's a hard habit to break.

There were only two officers in the main room. One was a man in his early fifties, sitting behind the desk, talking to the other officer—a young woman sipping what I presumed was coffee until my nose told me it was cocoa.

When we entered, both officers looked up.

"Elena Michaels," I said, walking over, hand extended. "Chief Dales called me?"

"That's me," the young woman said, rising to shake my hand. That threw me for a moment. In such a small town, I was surprised that the police chief was a woman; I certainly didn't expect one who didn't look past her thirtieth birthday.

A noise came through an open doorway. I looked to see Morgan gripping the bars of a cell.

"Elena? Um, hey. What are you . . . ?" His gaze traveled over my shoulder, to where Clay stood. "Uh, Clayton . . ."

Clay walked toward the cell. The officers looked over but made no move to stop him.

Morgan took a slow step back.

"Er, I can explain," Morgan said.

"You'd better hope so," Clay said, too low for the non-werewolves to pick up.

I turned back to Chief Dales. "I'm really sorry about this. We were worried sick when he didn't show up last night. I guess he made a pit stop for a few beers." I mustered a glare in Morgan's direction. "Good thing those coyotes didn't decide to take a taste of him."

"The paw prints were too big for coyotes," Chief Dales said. "And we didn't find any human tracks. Just the paw prints. All around him."

I sighed and looked at Morgan, shaking my head. "You were out there long enough for the snow to cover your footprints? You're lucky you didn't get frostbite anyplace you really don't want frostbite. Or get bitten by that dog that came sniffing around."

When I looked at the police chief, she caught my gaze and held it. I gazed back, calm and cool.

"Is that what you think happened?" she asked.

"What else?"

"What else, indeed?"

More staring. Which I'm sure would have worked out a whole lot better for her if I was a small-town perp, not a werewolf who'd spent twenty years covering up mutt kills and, sometimes, dead mutts. I waited patiently until she spoke again.

"Do you want to hear my theory?" she asked.

"Sure."

She stepped back. She tried to make it casual, just moving, not retreating. But that's another thing about being a werewolf for so long—I've become almost as fluent in body language as I am in English, especially when it comes to expressions of dominance and submission.

"You've seen our town has an . . . affinity for werewolves," she said. "I think that has something to do with your boy's run through the forest."

I laughed and glanced at Morgan, who looked worried. "What? You got drunk and decided to go werewolf hunting?"

"Not hunting," Chief Dales said. "Staging. He's not the first person to try it. Frat boy passing through, decides to pull a prank on the local yokels."

"Frat boy?" Morgan said. "How old do you think I am?"

Clay moved in front of Morgan. I couldn't see the look he gave him, but it shut Morgan down fast.

"Too old for this crap," I called to him, then turned to Chief Dales. "I'm so sorry. He's a friend of the family. We haven't seen him in years. Obviously, he has a few issues"—a glare in Morgan's direction—"to work through. If there's anything we can do to fix this . . ."

She walked back behind the desk with the older officer, who'd been watching in silence. "It's his lucky day. Got another storm coming. Otherwise, I'd slap a public indecency charge on his ass. I expect him to present his ID so I can file a report, but otherwise, just get him out of my sight. And out of Westwood."

6. JESSICA

When the paperwork was done, Jess led her three guests out of the station. Then she stood at the door and watched them drive away. Once they were out of sight, she exhaled and leaned against the wall.

A close call. Damned close.

She should have made the connection. Guy turns up in their woods surrounded by paw prints, has a map marked with Syracuse and the name Elena. As in Elena Michaels, the only female werewolf.

Years ago, when Jess was at college in Buffalo, she'd made contact with a few local supernaturals. That always helped, for support and companionship. When she told them she'd gotten a job with the Westwood police, one guy had said, "Isn't that werewolf territory?" She'd thought he meant the local football team. He hadn't.

"The Pack lives up there," he said. "Somewhere near Syracuse."

Someone else said they'd heard the rumor, but it was just that—a rumor. The Pack lived on the west coast. Another said there *was* no Pack: werewolves weren't bright enough to organize like that. They were just dumb brutes running around slaughtering people. Like in the movies.

Jess had still done her research. But how exactly *did* you research that? Google "werewolves in New York State"? That was a ticket straight to Weirdsville. She'd searched police files instead, looking for signs of possible werewolf kills. Nothing.

So she'd chalked it up to rumor. Yet, having heard it, she couldn't help paying attention when other supernaturals talked about werewolves. She'd eventually learned there definitely was a Pack. One member was a woman named Elena Michaels. It was a common enough name and, really, not worth researching—she didn't have time for idle curiosity. She'd heard other names over the years, including Elena's mate, a guy named Clayton who was supposed to be a really nasty son of a bitch. But none of those stories ever mentioned Syracuse or upstate New York, so they didn't concern her.

Until now.

Even when the woman had introduced herself, the light bulb hadn't flashed. While Jess didn't consider herself one of those who believed werewolves were all Neanderthal brutes, apparently she did have some preconceptions. And they didn't extend to a friendly blonde who, with her ponytail and worn blue jeans, looked like a movie star going incognito. It definitely didn't cover the guy with her, a seriously hot thirty-something who wouldn't look out of place on a billboard—preferably wearing as little as possible.

When the guy called him Clayton, Jess had nearly choked on her cocoa. Even then, there was a moment when she told herself she had to be mistaken. Right up until she looked at Walsh shrinking back as "Clayton" bore down on him.

There were werewolves in Westwood. Three of them. *Real* werewolves. It would be damned funny if it didn't scare the shit out of her.

Jess took another deep breath.

No reason to overreact. It was a freak encounter. Walsh must have been driving past, seen the signs, and been unable to resist a detour. He'd stopped at the diner and had a few shots. More than a few, according to the server, Marnie. The booze had washed away his common sense, and he'd extended his visit to include a run in their forest.

Now the Pack had come and scooped him up. From the looks of things, he was in serious shit. They'd bustle Walsh out of town and steer clear for a very long time. Which suited her just fine.

Jess straightened and strode back into the station before Jaggerman wondered what happened to her.

*W*hen Jeremy first told me I was his choice for Alpha, I thought he'd lost it. Maybe it was stress. Maybe a fever. Clearly something, because the idea was ludicrous. Okay, I'll be honest for a moment and put aside the false humility. I didn't think, "I can't handle it." I could. Oh, I'd struggle. I'd screw up. I'd never really replace Jeremy. But I *could* be Alpha. That didn't mean it wasn't a crazy idea.

First, I'm not a hereditary werewolf, obviously. The gene passes through the male line. I didn't grow up in the Pack, either. Even after Clay bit me, I spent ten years boomeranging between the Pack and my old dream of a "normal" life. Eventually, I came to realize that Pack life *was* normal for me. Everything I'd wanted—stability, family, acceptance—I found there.

But I've only fully embraced werewolf life for the past decade. Plus there's the gender issue of being the only female werewolf. With the Pack, I think that actually worked in my favor—they didn't quite know what to expect, so they didn't really expect anything. I could be myself.

Beyond our territory, though, I can win a dozen challenge fights and I still won't be accepted as "one of the guys." I'm a chick in wolf's clothing. That makes me mate material. It also makes me a target for all the mutts who'd love to hurt Clay. But it does not make me a "real" werewolf, much less an Alpha.

I'd come to realize, though, that Jeremy didn't have a lot of candidates to choose from. Clay wouldn't take the job and, let's be honest, I don't think Jeremy would give it to him anyway. There was nobody more important to Jeremy than his foster son, but there was also nobody he understood better. If Clay became Alpha, all the reforms Jeremy had instituted would begin a slow backward slide. Clay would try to respect them, but he didn't always understand the rationale behind them.

No one else was suited to the post, either. Antonio was a year older than Jeremy. Nick wasn't Alpha material. Nor was Karl Marsten. Maybe someday Reese would be, but he wasn't even out of college. That left yours truly. Which meant that, when faced with a problem like Morgan Walsh, I could no longer just call up Jeremy and say, "Hey, what do you want me to do?" I was expected to make my own decisions. Which, sometimes, really sucked.

But this problem was mostly resolved. Morgan had "found" his ID and Chief Dales had processed his official release. We were leaving Westwood.

Snow was still falling, coming down heavier, which put some extra speed in our strides. It was mid-afternoon. There was definitely time for a stop in Syracuse. Which should not, admittedly, be my first priority. But I wasn't Alpha yet; I was allowed the occasional spurt of bad judgment. I needed to decide what to do with Morgan in the meantime, but that was best done after we'd hightailed it out of Westwood.

"Look, I know I screwed up," Morgan said as we left the station.

"You think?" Clay muttered.

"But I did *not* ask them to call Elena. I would never have gotten you guys involved."

"Which was the last in your long string of mistakes," I said. "If you get in trouble like that, you call us. Otherwise, if the problem gets out of hand, you don't get me coming to your rescue. You get him." I nodded toward Clay.

Morgan tried for a smile. "Complete with chainsaw?"

"Nah," Clay said. "You risk exposing us? On our territory? You don't get the chainsaw. I hang you from the nearest tree, rip you open, and let the vultures feast."

"Er, I can explain."

I stopped beside Jeremy's SUV and opened the back door. "We'll get to that part. First, we're going to take you to your car. Then I'll drive it, following you and Clay, to someplace where we can chat."

We all climbed in. I kept one eye on Morgan, in case he decided to bolt, but he just fastened his seat belt. Clay started the SUV and put it in drive. It lurched forward with an odd thump. He frowned and pressed the gas. Another lurch. Another bump.

"Shit," Clay muttered.

He threw it into park and got out. I did the same and looked down at the front passenger-side tire.

"Flat," I called over the hood. "Good thing we have a spare."

"Yeah, but we don't have two."

"Seriously?"

I walked to the front of the SUV. *Both* tires were flat. Not much chance that was accidental. I peered along the snowy street, but we were the only people in sight.

"Guess we're taking your car," I said to Morgan as he climbed out. "We'll call a truck for this. It's a long tow, but I don't want to stick around."

We trekked down the main street to the diner, where Morgan had left his car. As we walked, I decided we had time for him to explain the events of the night before. So he did.

"And that's how they found me." He took a deep breath. "I screwed up. No alcohol involved—I know better than that. And I wouldn't have Changed so close to town if I thought I was in any shape to drive away. But obviously I'm not accustomed to being in human form yet and I let myself get too tired. Add in a big meal, and something just . . . went wonky. In my defense, I can say that it's *never* happened before. I've been Changing every three days since I left Alaska, and that's worked out just fine. But, yes, I screwed up. I know that. I'll—" He stopped. "Son of a bitch!"

Morgan broke into a run. I squinted through the falling snow to see a single car in the diner parking lot. Morgan's, I presumed. Someone in a parka was crouched beside it, slashing the rear tire.

"What the hell?" Clay muttered.

He took off after Morgan. I followed.

"Hey!" Morgan shouted.

The vandal looked up. He was dressed in a dark parka, the hood tunneled, hiding his face. Seeing us, he took off running toward the forest.

I raced to the car and crouched beside it. The rear passenger tire was slashed. When I ducked to look underneath, I saw the same on the other side.

"Damn it!" I said. "Two tires here, too. We'll need to—"

I straightened and looked around the parking lot. I was talking to myself. The guys were gone.

*I*t was a scene straight from a horror movie. The heroic—
and slightly brain-dead—guys go racing into the forest
after the madman with the knife. The clueless blonde stumbles
after them, yelling, "Guys! Hey, guys! Wait up!"

If it were a horror movie, I'd be about two cinematic minutes
from meeting a grisly end as I realized—too late—that the deranged
killer had purposely led my menfolk into the woods to separate me
from them. Also, I'd be topless.

As it was, I was tramping through knee-deep snow in a very
unsexy pair of hiking boots and an old ski jacket. I was also wearing sock-monkey mittens—a gift from Kate last year. It's a new
kind of horror movie. Forget screaming, half-naked coeds. Time to
slaughter a few "did I even remember to brush my hair before I left
the house?" moms.

"Couldn't just let it go, could you, guys?" I muttered as snow
melted down the back of my neck. "Oh, no. Gotta catch the bastard. Can't let him get away with that." I snorted. "Men. You don't
see me tearing off into a strange forest in the middle of a snow—"
I looked around. "Never mind."

I squatted to peer at the snow-covered ground. I could smell the
guys' scents, but their footprints were already covered, the snow
coming down hard.

I stood. "Clay! Morgan!"

No answer. Damn them. I should just go back to the car and
wait. That would be the non-dumb-blonde thing to do. It would

also be the non-Alpha-elect thing to do. I sighed. At least I was pretty sure knife-wielding guy was a vandal, not a serial killer. Even if he was, this blonde came with super-strength and a kick-ass secret disguise.

I followed Clay's scent. Soon I could see only a few feet ahead of me.

Whiteout.

Damn it, guys. Five more minutes and I am turning back before I can't find my way out.

I walked, hands extended, making sure I didn't waltz into a knife. Or, more likely, a tree. I did narrowly avoid a silver birch that blended with the snow. As I touched it, my fingers ran across deep grooves in the bark. I moved closer for a better look.

There was a symbol carved in the trunk with a deep-red substance rubbed into the grooves. Not blood—I'd smell that. Meant to look like blood, though?

I turned around, the snow no longer driving into my face, giving me a clearer view of my surroundings. I was in a circle of silver birch, all with that red mark carved into them.

I got out my cell phone to take a photograph. That had nothing to do with being a werewolf and everything to do with being the wife of an anthropologist specializing in religion and ritual.

As I was pulling my mittens back on, something moved, off to the side. When I looked that way, the forest seemed empty. But I'd seen something. I knew I had.

"Clay?" I called. "Morgan?"

Brush crackled to my left. A shadow loomed over me. I spun, fists up.

Morgan looked down at my hands.

"Nice mittens," he said.

"They hit just fine," I said. "Which you will discover if you ever sneak up on me again." I lowered my fists. "A little warning next time, please."

"Sorry." He walked over and brushed snow off a partly covered symbol. "Huh. Weird."

"Not really. Many pagan practitioners conduct rituals in the forest. Perfectly harmless rituals. I've never seen these marks before, though. Clay might know what they are. I wouldn't suggest asking him, though, unless you're prepared for a twenty-minute lecture." I looked past him. "Speaking of which, where is he?"

He shook his head. "I lost track of him a while ago. I figured I should head back and find you."

At least the guy had good Pack instincts. Always a bonus in a potential recruit, even if his suitability had dipped since last night's episode.

"Let's head back to town." I stepped from the birch grove and stared out into the seemingly endless expanse of white forest. "If we can find it."

I took off my mittens again and pulled out my cell phone. I raised it to get a lock on the GPS.

"Gotta love modern technology," I said, and led Morgan out of the grove.

"You know," he said, "you could probably use that handy gadget to find Clayton, too. By calling him."

"That only works with people who also embrace modern technology. Clayton—"

I stopped as a smell drifted past on the breeze. I lifted my face to sniff better.

"You smell him?" Morgan said. "Damn. You *are* good. I can't pick up a damned thing out . . ."

I was already on the move, walking fast through the evergreens, pushing branches out of my way as Morgan jogged to keep up.

"It's not Clay," I said. "Thankfully."

I followed the scent to a massive evergreen.

"Oh, wait," Morgan said, inhaling. "Is that . . . ?"

I crouched and pushed aside the ground-level branches to see something sheltered and hidden at the very base of the tree. A corpse. A long-dead, frozen, decomposed corpse.

"Definitely not Clay," Morgan murmured.

I pushed back the branches to get a better look at the body. It hadn't been out here long enough to fully decompose, but it was well along that route. Judging by the clothing, it had been a man. Fully grown.

It didn't look as if he'd curled up under this tree and died. The pose was too awkward for that. Someone had shoved him in here postmortem.

Morgan crouched beside me. "I didn't do it."

"I didn't think you did."

"Thank you."

"The body's partly decomposed. You only got to town yesterday."

"I'm not a man-killer." Morgan sounded annoyed.

"Yeah?" Clay said as he walked over. "Well, I've never met a mutt who claimed otherwise."

"No offense," I murmured to Morgan. "We've learned to be skeptical."

"So, what've we got here?" Clay knelt and pushed back the branches. "Huh."

I hunkered beside him as he examined the body. No expression crossed his face. No revulsion. No pity, either. There was a time when that bothered me, when it seemed a sign that there was something missing in Clay, something vital, something that made us human. There was. He *isn't* human.

Clay could barely remember a life when he wasn't a werewolf. He lacked the ability to look at a stranger and see anything more than a potential source of aid or threat. That's how the wolf sees anyone who isn't in his Pack—either they can help you or they can kill you, and it's probably the latter.

"Something's taken a few bites," he said, leaning close enough to the corpse that my own gorge rose. "Can't tell if it's a scavenger or a predator. Seems to be missing a hand, too."

"We can't poke around too much if we're going to report it," I said. "Which is the big question."

Clay nodded and moved back, letting the branches cover the body.

"Why report it?" Morgan said. "He's been there awhile. No one's going to know we found him." He paused. "I mean, yes, reporting it would be the right thing to do. He has a family out there somewhere, wondering what happened to him, and maybe a killer who's gone free—"

"Not our concern," Clay said, standing.

"Unfortunately," I added. I thought that every time I had to hide a body. Somewhere out there, a family would never be able to bury their dead, would never be able to mourn properly. But werewolves had to put their Pack first.

"It would be better if we could bury it," I said. "But the ground's frozen solid."

"Why can't we just leave it?" Morgan asked.

"Because we've been here," Clay said. "We've left a shitload of tracks to a dead body and we can't just trust they'll all be covered by snow. We were chasing someone who might be watching us right now, as we stand over a corpse. And we left our names—our real names—at that police station."

"We didn't have anything to do with this," I said. "So it's safest to play it on the level. As if we were just regular citizens. I'll—"

A noise to my left made me pause. I couldn't see anything, but once again I had the distinct feeling I was being watched. I took a few steps into the woods, lifting a finger for Clay and Morgan to wait.

I walked about twenty paces in the direction of the noise. While it was just past four o'clock, the sun was already dipping fast, shrouding the forest in long shadows.

When I saw what looked like snow-dimpled footprints, I bent, brushed off the layer of snow, and inhaled.

As I did, I sensed someone walking up behind me. Even with the wind going the other way, I knew who it was.

"Do you know what this means?" I asked, waggling my index finger.

"Wait one minute," Clay said. "I waited two."

He came closer. "Are those tracks?"

"Yes." I pushed to my feet. "Ours."

I walked to Clay. Morgan hovered a few steps back.

"I felt like we were being watched again," I said. "I heard something, too. But there's no sign of a trail. No scents on the breeze." I shook my head. "I think I've been housebound too long. I'm turning into a paranoid hermit."

We walked back to where we'd left the body.

"Better get this over with," I said. "Can one of you stay with it? So we don't lose the spot?"

"I'll stay." Morgan gave Clay a look. "And I promise not to snack."

9. MORGAN

*M*organ huddled in the lee of the evergreen, rubbing his hands together. Elena and Clay had left without even commenting on his crack, as if he'd been seriously reassuring them. He shook his head. To them, labeling all "mutts" potential man-eaters seemed to be nothing more than a cautionary reflex. Like not leaving cash lying around the house when you had service people over. But it wasn't like that at all. It was like presuming all men lusted after thirteen-year-old girls until they proved they didn't. Insulting on a moral and personal level.

Morgan shivered, hunched against the cold, and shoved his bare hands under his armpits. Maybe he'd made a mistake, coming to see the Pack. Morgan, his father, and his brother had grown up isolated from the very culture of being werewolf. His father and brother viewed it as an affliction. A genetic condition that you learned to live with. Morgan didn't agree, which was why he'd lived among wolves: to get in touch with that side of his nature. But to the Pack, being a werewolf wasn't just about being partly wolf. It really was an all-encompassing way of life.

He'd found something in that Alaskan wolf pack that he'd never experienced before: a sense of community. He wasn't ever going to get that back home, where it was just the three of them, mingling with the outside world as little as possible.

Of course, the problem with the wolf pack was, well, they were wolves. Intellectually, it was a little stifling. So, from that perspective, the werewolf Pack intrigued him. Community and brotherhood complete with intelligent conversation, poker games, and movie nights. Like a frat. Only without the stupid pranks and rituals and codes of behavior.

Except that the Pack had its own way of looking at the outside world, which included calling non-Pack werewolves "mutts" and suspecting them all of being too stupid or too weak to avoid the temptation to hunt humans. In that way, they were a little too elitist.

A twig cracked somewhere in the forest. He peered out, but saw only snow and trees.

Oh, sure, Elena, I'll stay out here, alone, after you thought you sensed someone watching us.

It was probably just the moron who'd slashed their tires. Or it could be a deer. Most likely a deer. In Alaska, he'd noticed that the Pack werewolves were a little paranoid. Of course, that suspicious nature had saved their lives. Maybe his, too.

He walked around the evergreen, watching, listening, and sniffing the air. When a faint scent wafted past, he stiffened. Yep, there was definitely someone out there. It wasn't strong enough for him to tell whether it was the vandal they'd chased, but it was clearly human.

Damn.

Morgan wasn't confrontational by nature. That's how he'd been raised. Avoid contact and avoid trouble. It had served him well in Alaska, where he'd managed to duck the notice of a group of werewolf-like evolutionary throwbacks called Shifters. More important, he'd avoided a group of werewolves whose claim to be fully evolved had been debatable, given their behavior. The bunch were exactly the kind of murdering, raping thugs people expected werewolves to be.

He'd known what kind of men they were, and he'd done nothing about it. He still felt the guilt—and the shame—of that. Sure, he'd had plenty of excuses. There were a half dozen of them, all career criminals, who never went anywhere alone. If they'd found him, they would have killed him. When Elena and Clay showed up, he'd helped them find and stop them. But he should have done more and done it sooner.

So maybe lying low wasn't always such a good plan. Excellent for self-preservation. Not so good for the conscience.

He squinted into the growing shadows and sniffed again. Yep, there was definitely someone out there. And if he still entertained thoughts of joining the Pack, he couldn't let Clayton Danvers come back and discover that Morgan had hidden and waited for a potential threat to go away. He'd be branded a coward, and if that got out to the werewolf community at large, he might as well hightail it back to Alaska.

The scent had vanished, but Morgan knew where it had come from. He headed in that direction, his head high, gaze fixed forward, ready to—

Something pressed against the back of his neck. Cold metal. Then he heard the distinct click of a rifle.

10. ELENA

I reported the dead body. I explained that our tires had been slashed and we'd pursued the vandal into the forest. Then I fudged the truth and said we got engulfed in a whiteout and ended up farther in than we expected. As we were searching for the way out, we thought we spotted someone crouched under an evergreen. We investigated and found a corpse.

Chief Dales rounded up the older officer we'd seen earlier—a guy named Jaggerman—and a younger one named Kent. Then she had to call one of the night shift in early to cover the station while they were gone. Apparently, a dead body warranted full departmental support. I asked her when was the last time they'd had one—just making conversation on the walk. She didn't answer. She'd told us to get out of town and wasn't happy we hadn't listened, even if we had a good excuse.

Contrary to what I'd told her, Clay and I both have a very good sense of direction . . . aided by a very good sense of smell. So we were able to escort the police right to where we'd left Morgan and the body.

The clearing was empty.

"Morgan?" I called.

Clay shouted louder, voice edged with annoyance. "Morgan!"

No answer. I looked around. I could faintly make out his footsteps, though they'd nearly been filled with falling show.

Beside me, Clay muttered, "Better not have bolted." He said it too low for the cops to hear. I nodded and motioned for him to subtly start searching. When Morgan had offered to stay behind, I should have considered the possibility he'd decided to take off. But he'd had a chance to do that while we were all tromping separately through the woods. Maybe being alone just gave him time to think. Or maybe he'd decided that reporting a dead body was more than he'd bargained for.

I bent to pull back the branches. "I don't know where he went, but the body is—"

I swore under my breath. The body was gone, too.

"Looks like you've got the wrong spot," Chief Dales said. "Time to tell your friend to invest in a cell phone."

"No, I can definitely smell decomp. This is the place."

"How do you know what decomp smells like?" Jaggerman asked, eyes narrowing.

"We live in the country. We come across enough dead things to recognize the smell."

The officers nodded. Living out here, so close to nature, they knew it was true.

Chief Dales gazed out into the empty forest. "Then I guess we need to go back and organize a search party. For a living guy and a dead one. Though how the hell they went missing together is a mystery I'm not sure I want to solve."

I started to move off, my gaze fixed on Clay, a hundred feet away, waiting for me to come find Morgan. If he'd taken off, he wasn't getting far without a working car. I doubted Westwood even had a cab company.

"We'll look for our friend," I said.

"No, you reported a dead body. You're coming back to the station. You can join the hunt for your friend after you give a statement."

As we walked, we kept our eyes and noses open for any sign of Morgan. I thought I caught a faint whiff of him once, but the scent vanished before I could snag it. I glanced over at Clay and considered asking if I could handle the statement while Clay went hunting, but Chief Dales didn't exactly seem open to reasonable suggestions. We made the trek in silence. The younger officer—Kent—tried to start conversation a few times, but glowers from his chief were seconded by Jaggerman.

As we walked into the station, I caught the stench of perspiration strong enough to wipe out everything else. I glanced at the thirty-something officer behind the desk, but the smell seemed to come from the guy standing in front of him, a heavyset middle-aged guy in a camouflage jacket, his bald head shining with sweat. A rifle rested across the counter.

"Uh, Chief," the officer said. "Mac here—"

"Got something for you, Jess."

Mac beamed over at Chief Dales, then motioned with a flourish at his trophy. It was Morgan, hands bound behind his back.

"Found this vagrant walking away from a murder scene," Mac said.

Morgan's brows shot up. "Vagrant?"

"Oh, sorry," Mac said sarcastically. "Homeless person. Or do we have to say domicile-challenged these days? This ain't Syracuse, boy. You're a vagrant or a drifter. And you should count yourself lucky, because you're about to get three squares a day and a warm cell to sleep in."

As Morgan sputtered, Mac turned back to Chief Dales. "Like I said, found him leaving the scene of a crime. A murder, no less. So I brought him in for you." An almost sheepish look now, like a boy presenting a cute girl with a bouquet of wildflowers. "Even brought you the body."

He waved toward the side door. I stepped forward and looked through a small window into what seemed to be the chief's office. There was the decomposing frozen corpse, in several pieces, atop a garbage bag on her desk.

To Chief Dales's credit, she remained calm. She thanked him and nicely explained that, should he find more corpses in the forest, it was really best to just make note of them for the police. Then she grabbed Kent, with a camera and crime-scene kit, and headed back out, pausing only long enough to make sure Jaggerman knew to call the coroner.

We were forgotten. Which would have been a pleasant surprise, except that we had no place to go. After we untied Morgan, we asked the night-duty officer about a garage that would repair our tires, and he said the only mechanic—with the only tow truck—was currently out on calls. He'd have the guy phone us when he could, but given the weather, it would likely be "a while." As we left, I called Jeremy to update him and say we might be stuck here overnight.

"Did I hear you right?" Morgan said as I hung up. "You're going to stick around?"

"Doesn't mean *you* need to," Clay said. "Better for us if we don't have to worry about rescuing you a third time."

Morgan's face darkened. Before he could respond, I cut in. "Obviously you can't leave until your tire is fixed, which isn't happening anytime soon. If you want to hole up and wait it out, that's fine. If you'd rather pitch in, we can always use the extra help."

"Or a decoy," Clay muttered.

Morgan ignored him. "Help with what?"

"We have a dead body with chew marks. As long as we're stuck here, we should investigate." I waved at a wall mural of a wolfman howling at the moon. "Just in case you're not the only werewolf who thought it'd be funny to hang out in Westwood."

11.

$\mathscr{I}$f I'd found this case on the Internet, would I have investigated? Not if it wasn't so close to home. Even then, I wouldn't rush. A corpse with evidence of predation was hardly a sign of werewolves. While we were extra-paranoid about potential killings on our own territory, this would have gotten little more than a cursory closer look. But as I'd said to Morgan, we were stuck here anyway.

The first thing I wanted to do was get a really good look at that body. If we were considering a werewolf diner, we needed more than Clay's casual observation. I'd tried to get a better look at the body in the police station, but Chief Dales had closed and locked her office as soon as she realized she had a corpse on display.

Before we'd left, I'd listened in on Officer Jaggerman's phone call to the coroner. The doctor wouldn't be able to get to it right away—he was the town physician, too, and had evening appointments today. He also didn't particularly want a decomposed body in his office, which doubled as his home. They'd decided to take it to the high school. Whether he planned to work on it there or just keep it there temporarily, I had no idea. Apparently, in Westwood, storing a decomposing body in the school science lab was a perfectly fine solution.

So we needed to pay a visit to the school. Preferably after all the kids were gone. It was nearly five, meaning I figured we had another hour to wait, to be sure.

We checked in at the local motel. Morgan followed us down the sidewalk. His room was the one past ours, so I thought he would just keep going. He didn't.

When I opened our door and he was still standing there, Clay turned to give him a look.

"You said we were doing this case together," Morgan said.

"Yeah," Clay said. "The case. Not—"

I cut him off. "We're waiting for the school to empty out."

"So we have got time to kill."

"Yes," I said, stepping into our room. "Yes. We do."

"You want to grab something at the diner? Food's good."

"Why don't you do that. We're going to take a nap."

"He's not five, darling." Clay turned to Morgan. "You need to get lost so we can have sex."

Morgan backed away fast.

"Subtle," I said to Clay as Morgan hurried off, and he closed our door.

"Subtle wasn't working."

Clay paused. Then he opened the door, hailed Morgan, and called, "Looks like we're the only guests checked in. How about you go on over to the diner. Get an early meal."

Morgan seemed ready to protest. Then he caught Clay's look, nodded, and headed off, looking confused.

"See?" Clay said. "Subtle doesn't work."

"He did as you asked."

"Yeah, because he's scared of me. Not because he has the faintest clue why we might not want him in the next room while we're having sex."

"Not because he's slow—because he's young. He's not yet reached that wonderful stage in life where there's no greater gift your roommate can give than offering to take your kids out for an hour."

"I seem to recall we were pretty damned happy when Jeremy left *before* the kids came."

I laughed. "True."

That was the problem with having a permanent housemate. It's not that we'd shock him. Werewolves aren't high on privacy. We run and hunt together whenever we can, and I'd long passed the stage of scrambling for my clothing as soon as I Changed back. And Jeremy has long since stopped opening a closed door—any closed door—without knocking first. The problem is that even with the door shut, he's still going to *hear* what's going on. It's that pesky enhanced hearing. Clay and I aren't particularly loud in bed, but there is still . . . noise. So we need to be careful not to do or say anything that might be a little awkward to recall when sitting across from Jeremy at dinner. Or I'm careful. Clay doesn't care.

But we had the room—and the motel—to ourselves, with no need to worry how thin the walls were.

As the door closed, Clay tried to grab me around the waist. I danced out of his reach.

"You know what?" I said. "We have an hour, and we're used to making do with a lot less. I should probably do some research first."

I waited for Clay's inevitable growl and pounce.

"You're right." He waved at the bed. "You do that. I'll take a nap."

When I hesitated, he looked over at me.

"What? You did want to work, right?"

"Umm . . ."

"You weren't just saying that to tease me, were you? Expecting me to jump you because I'm a guy, so naturally I want sex a lot more than you do?"

Damn.

"Well?" he said. "Do you want to work? Or were you engaging in some highly sexist teasing?"

Damn.

"I . . . should do some research," I said. "That'd be the responsible, Alpha-elect way to spend a free hour."

"Absolutely."

He strolled to the bed, plunked down, and stretched out on his back, eyes closing. "Wake me up if you change your mind."

Damn.

As I started for my laptop, Clay sat up and stripped off his T-shirt.

"Hey," I said.

"What? It's warm in here." He slanted a look my way. "It doesn't bother you, does it?"

I've been seeing him naked for twenty years. Watching him take off his shirt should hardly put my hormones in a tizzy. I'd deny it . . . if I wouldn't be so blatantly lying that I fear my nose might grow.

When I didn't answer, Clay chuckled. He undid his belt and slid it out of the loops, then popped the button on his jeans.

"Hey!" I said. "It's not that hot in here."

"Not yet." He glanced over. "Unless you're interested in changing that."

"I'm fine," I growled.

"Well, if that changes at any point, you know where to find me."

He stretched out on the bed again. I admired. I knew I shouldn't, but it was such a nice view, that muscled chest, that faint line of golden hair leading down to—

I turned away. Clay laughed. I continued heading for my laptop. As I walked, I undid my own jeans. I slid them down and kicked them aside. Then I bent down to pick up my laptop, taking my time, giving him a view of his own.

"When did you have time to change into *that*?" he said.

I was wearing my thong. I own only one—bought when I found panty lines showing on a new dress. Of course, I don't wear dresses very often. I didn't wear the thong that often, either. If you've been together long enough, you learn that, despite the temptation to wear something your partner likes every day, it'd quickly lose its allure that way.

"We were getting low on clean laundry," I said.

"Not that low," he said. "You didn't have time to change before we left, so you must have put it on this morning. What were you planning to do? Strip down tonight and tease me, knowing no way in hell we'd get Jeremy to take the kids out in a snowstorm?"

"No, I thought *we* could go out in a snowstorm."

He rose on his elbows.

"I was planning to ask if you wanted to go for a run after the kids were in bed. Or, if this"—I plucked the thong—"made you decide you weren't so keen on the running part, I'd stashed a sleeping bag and some blankets out there. Cold snow. Warm blankets. Hot sex. I seem to recall you like that."

A growl answered. I turned and bent again. As I did, I unbuttoned my shirt and shrugged it off. Then I picked up the laptop, straightened, and turned.

His gaze dropped to my bare breasts. "I see we're *really* low on clean clothes."

"We are."

I could feel him watching as I lay down on the bed and propped myself up on the pillows.

"You go ahead and sleep," I said. "It looks like you could use the rest. In the meantime, since you're obviously not that into it, I'll see if I can find something to amuse me on the Internet. Maybe hot werewolf sex. I hear they have that."

"I've got that right here."

I looked over. "Do you?"

"Yep. Just gotta ask." He stretched out, jeans riding down his hips, zipper parting to show what was on offer. "Or take."

Damn.

I glanced at the clock. I could hold out, but time was ticking. One thing you learn in marriage is the art of give-and-take.

This time, I took.

he storm was blasting now, wind and snow whipping around us as we stood outside the high school, hidden behind a massive sign that read "Football Semifinals Saturday! Go Werewolves!" It looked like a typical country school—a one-floor cinder block with no redeeming architectural features. The simple layout would make infiltration easy. There were only two cars left in the parking lot, both almost buried under snow, making me wonder if the owners had just left them there.

I glanced at Morgan. "I'm going to ask you to stand guard. Come near the side door with us, watch the lot, and whistle if you see anything. Don't engage: just whistle."

Morgan nodded and followed us around the side of the building. When we reached the doors, they were flush with the wall, leaving him no recess to hide in.

"Better take cover," I whispered.

"Yeah," Clay said. "We don't want to spring you from the cop shop again."

Morgan scowled and stalked off to hide behind a cluster of evergreens. When he was gone, Clay examined the door, then looked around.

"Too exposed," he said.

I nodded and waved to the back. Not only was the door there recessed, but it backed onto the football field, which was surrounded by forest.

As Clay checked the lock, I said, "The Pack needs wolves, and he seems like a good kid."

"Yeah, but if he can't take direction and criticism? Pack's the wrong place for him."

"He's taking direction just fine. It's the criticism that's causing problems."

Clay heaved on the door until the lock snapped. Then he opened it an inch, inhaling and listening. He seemed to be ignoring me, but I knew he was processing what I'd said.

He was capable of being nicer. Hell, our kids have never heard a critical word from him. Disapproval is a gentle growl and nudge in the right direction, rather than a snarl and snap. He'd do the same with any Pack child. That's the wolf in him.

But a grown wolf like Morgan got the snarl and snap, reminding him of his place and booting him into it. Once Clay was sure Morgan understood that, he'd treat him like Noah and Reese, more gently shaping their behavior as he taught them everything they needed to know to survive and flourish as a werewolf.

"He's twelve years older than Noah," I said. "Six years older than Reese. He isn't a kid, and he doesn't appreciate being treated like one."

Clay closed the door and looked at me. "You want him in the Pack?"

"I want to have the chance to evaluate that."

Clay's chin dipped. "Fair enough. I'll take it down a notch."

"Thank you."

"But if he screws up—"

I lifted a hand. That's all I needed to do. We'd already taken a chance, coming here to help Morgan. If he messed up another time, he'd be escorted to the state border and told—in detail—what would happen to him if he ever trespassed on Pack territory again.

We entered the school. It had a very simple layout. Two

corridors ran lengthwise to side doors and a short one connected them to front and back doors. The first hallway was empty.

Clay headed along the connecting corridor. I followed. When we reached the corner, I peered down the long front hall to discover a woman in a nurse's uniform sitting at a table doing a crossword. Standing guard over the body? Looked like it. Smelled like it, too, from the faint scent of decomp wafting past on the furnace heat.

I backed us up to the rear corridor, the empty one. We went down it. The third door led into a classroom decorated with fading DNA and cell posters. A door at the back was conveniently labeled Lab. It was locked, but Clay's sharp twist on the handle fixed that.

Clay peeked through the door. I glimpsed a sliver of the lab. When I stepped to the side, I could see the main door to the hall. It was half open, showing the corner of the nurse's table.

Clay opened the door a little more, craned his head in, then withdrew and shut it.

"Body's right there," he whispered. "If she gets up and looks in, she'll see us."

I took a deep breath. "Can you manage a quick examination?"

He nodded. Clay's a cultural anthropologist, not a forensic one, but he's done a fair bit of cross-reading and studying.

Clay quietly opened the door again and went in. He crept soundlessly to the left, where I could see the edge of the examining table. Then he bent over the body, pencil in hand, to poke and prod at the corpse.

I listened for any noise from the nurse's post. She didn't move. Then Clay stopped, his head tilting. I caught the sound a split second after he did. Morgan's whistle.

Clay hurried back into the classroom with me. A moment later, we heard the faint whoosh of the front doors opening. Then the louder sound of footsteps. Boots. Heavy. A grown man, I was guessing. Alone. His footsteps approached the nurse's station.

"Hey, Miz Morrison. Doc got you standing guard?"

The voice sounded vaguely familiar. I motioned for Clay to crack the door a little. He did, and we caught the scent of Officer Kent.

"He does," the nurse replied. "At least until he figures out how to handle this. Do the autopsy here or bring that thing back to the office without making his family sick from the smell."

"Well, you can take a break from the smell yourself. Why don't you head over to Polly's and grab a coffee? I'll be here awhile. Chief wants pictures."

"Didn't she get enough earlier?"

"Apparently not. You know how she is."

"Thorough," the nurse said. "Which is more than anyone could say for her predecessor."

Kent murmured something under his breath that could be taken as agreement, but I got the feeling he'd rather his boss was a little less dedicated to her job.

There was scuffling as the nurse gathered her things, clearly eager to be gone. As Kent walked her to the door, he asked if the janitor was around.

"Snowed in, last I heard," the nurse said. "I'm hoping he'll show up soon. Doc said I can leave if he does. Otherwise, I'm stuck here until he's done his evening appointments."

As they talked, Clay leaned over and whispered, "I got enough."

I looked back at the classroom door. "I think we'd make more noise leaving than staying. We'll go as soon as Kent settles in."

Clay nodded. Footsteps sounded in the hall again. I watched through the crack as Kent entered the science lab, big camera in hand. He walked to the table. Then he stopped and seemed to be listening, as if waiting to see if the nurse would come back. After a moment, he laid the big camera on the edge of the table. Then he started taking photos . . . with his cell phone.

For at least ten minutes, Kent took shots, from every possible angle. Then he grabbed the big camera and snapped a few pictures, with nowhere near as much care as he'd taken in getting the ones for his private collection.

When he finished, he stood over the body, staring at it. Then he reached out and—

The front doors creaked open. Kent shoved his cell phone into his pocket, picked up the camera, and strode from the lab.

"That was fast," he called.

"Polly closed the coffee shop early," the nurse answered. "Too much snow and not enough business, I guess, but . . ."

We slipped away as they talked.

We were waiting for Officer Kent when he left the school. He headed for his personal pickup, apparently, which wasn't surprising, given that I was pretty sure he was here on his own time, pursuing his own interests. What interests could involve taking photographs of a decaying corpse? None that he'd add to an online dating profile.

He could sell them online. There are people who'll buy that sort of thing. Selling them didn't seem as bad as the possibility he wanted them to satisfy his own perverse interest in dead bodies. But the most heinous explanation was the one I liked best, because it would mean our killer wasn't a werewolf—he was a small-town police officer who couldn't resist more photographic trophies of his handiwork.

We waited behind the sign as Kent crossed the parking lot. While he was distracted clearing snow from his vehicle, I motioned for Morgan to loop around behind him. Kent didn't notice Clay and me until I called, "Officer?"

He jumped and swung the brush up like a weapon. Then, as snow crunched behind him, he turned to see Morgan approaching from the other direction.

I smiled. "Seems like a never-ending task today, doesn't it?"

"Wh-what?"

I motioned at the snow brush.

"Oh, right."

I came closer and stopped in front of him. Clay halted behind me.

"I heard the body was here." I waved at the school, then at the camera around his neck. "Were you taking pictures for Chief Dales?"

"Uh, yes."

"I'll let her know you're hard at work," I said, and then set off, Clay beside me.

"What?" He scrambled toward us so fast he slid in the snow.

"We're just heading to the station to see how things are going."

"No, umm . . ." He looked from me to Clay, then cleared his throat. "Chief Dales isn't at the station. She's off trying to ID the victim."

"Oh? Well, that shouldn't take long. You can't have many missing people in this town."

He hesitated. He knew he shouldn't tell me anything, but he didn't want me going to the station, either.

He moved closer, lowering his voice conspiratorially. "Between you and me? Guy's obviously a drifter. We get them through here all the time. He wouldn't be the first to disappear."

"No?"

He shrugged. "It happens everywhere."

Actually, it doesn't. Not in a place the size of Westwood.

$\mathcal{W}$as Kent serious about drifters going missing in Westwood? Or just saying that so we'd back off? There was an easy way to find out. Research.

First, we needed to let Jeremy know this was definitely an overnight trip. The local mechanic had finally phoned to say he was stuck handling a pileup on the highway and was heading home—ten miles away—when he was done.

Normally, we'd Skype to break the news to the kids, too. Ever since they discovered they could see us, too, they weren't going back to regular calls. But the Internet here was too slow. So Clay used my cell phone to talk to them while I started digging for information, which was slow going enough. Morgan headed to the diner to grab takeout for all of us.

A half hour later, Clay was still on the phone, when Morgan passed the window. A rap sounded at our door.

"Come in!" I called.

"Yep, that's Mommy," Clay said. "She's doing some work while we're stuck here. I'm going to pass over the phone to her. Dinner's arrived, so I want you to keep her busy until I eat it all, okay?"

I heard Kate giggling as he handed me the phone.

"Hey, guys," I said. "What's up?"

They were on the speakerphone. That's something else we learned from Skype—calls home work a lot better when the kids aren't battling for the receiver. They both chattered away, telling me about the Clue tournament they'd played with Jeremy and the phone call from Uncle Nick, who'd promised to bring Reese and Noah up for a weekend of snowshoeing and cross-country skiing.

They didn't complain once. I should have been happy about that. But there was this little part of me that worried they were being on their best behavior because they suspected we'd fled to escape them.

I promised we'd be home tomorrow. Even if we still had work to do, Westwood was close enough to home for us to spend the night at Stonehaven. Jeremy had said that if his SUV wasn't fixed by then, he'd rent another in Syracuse and pick us up.

I was wrapping up when Morgan asked Clay if I'd found any more possible murder victims. Clay motioned him to silence and jabbed a finger at the phone. To his credit, he didn't back that up with a scowl. Just a stern look. Which was as close to "being nice" as I could hope for.

"Sorry," Morgan murmured. "Forgot your kids have super-hearing. That must be fun."

I signed off and started fixing a plate from the food containers covering the bed.

"Kent was right," I said. "This place is a regular Bermuda Triangle for drifters. In the last five years, three have been reported missing in the region. I can imagine how many more *weren't* reported."

"Preying on those who won't be noticed or missed. That's a serial killer MO, isn't it?"

"Man-eaters, too."

Morgan shrugged. "Same thing."

I shook my head. "Obviously a repeat man-eater is a serial killer, using the strictest definition of the term. And certainly some man-eaters are classic serial killers—they kill because they enjoy it. But others just screw up."

"Repeatedly," Clay muttered.

"Because they don't have a family or a Pack or anyone to teach them not to Change around humans until they can control the urge to see them as prey."

"But it *could* be a human serial killer," Morgan said.

"Yes," I said. "All three missing persons are young men—late teens into twenties. Young guys on the road, looking for work and a place to call home. Not the most common serial killer prey, but not unheard-of."

"So what did you learn from the body?"

"He matches the pattern of the missing drifters," Clay said. "Male. Young, but past adulthood. Definite predation. *Major* predation—not something taking a nibble. But a large predator would usually scatter body parts, taking pieces home for later. Everything seemed intact except for that missing hand."

"Then it could be a werewolf."

"Living this close to us for years? Possible, but I doubt it."

"Which won't stop us from investigating," I said. "Man-eater or not, we've got people disappearing a little too close to home. Especially if we have partly eaten bodies." I glanced out the window at the darkness. "Time to see if we can sniff out any more corpses."

The snow had stopped falling a while before we headed out, leaving pristine streets without so much as a set of tire imprints; everyone had retreated home after dinner and stayed there. Forest bordered the whole north edge of town, so we didn't need to walk far to reach it.

It was easier to see than it had been this afternoon in the snowstorm. The quarter moon shone from a nearly cloudless sky, lighting the world for our enhanced night vision even inside the tree line.

The forest was silent and still. No sign of footprints or snowmobile tracks. No scent of people or gasoline fumes.

"Is it hunting season?" Morgan asked.

"Deer," Clay said. "Maybe wild turkey. Can't remember exactly when that ends. Depends on the location."

"Do they hunt either at night?"

"Sunrise to sunset legally," I said.

"I'm actually asking because of those guys I heard in the forest last night. It was too late for hunters, and I didn't smell snowmobiles. I wonder what they were doing out there."

"Lots of reasons people go into the woods at night," Clay said. Then he paused, softened his snap by adding, "But if you hear the same voices again in town, let us know. Might be worth figuring out what they were up to."

"Looks like a clearing over there," I said, waving. "Good place to Change."

"I'll stand guard. Morgan—"

"Find my own spot. Got it." He stepped into the clearing ahead of me. "How about just over there—"

He stopped. I followed his finger to see a small animal pelt hanging from a tree. I took another step and saw more tiny pelts hanging from trees marked with a familiar symbol.

"We saw these earlier," I said to Clay. "The symbol, not the skins. They were on the trees near where I found the body. I was going to show you the photos to see what you made of the symbol. Apparently it's more than a one-off. It could have something to do with the men Morgan heard in the forest."

"Maybe. The pelts are tiny. Moles, voles, mice . . . No ritual significance I can think of there."

He flipped over a pelt and shone a penlight on it. On the back, someone had burned a crook and flail into the skin.

"Osiris," he said, then added for Morgan's benefit, "Egyptian god of death and rebirth. Cults of Osiris and Anubis used to hang pelts from sticks."

He examined the symbol on the next tree.

"Definitely not Egyptian. Possibly Mesopotamian. Someone's mixing their mythos."

Morgan leaned toward me. "So he really is an anthropologist? I thought that was a joke."

"Everyone does," I whispered back.

"I heard that," Clay said. He was making a circuit of the clearing, checking every tiny pelt. "Same symbols at the other spot?"

I held out the cell phone photo in answer.

"Yeah, it's the same. But no pelts?"

"Not that we noticed. The snow was coming down hard, though."

He peered up into the trees, then down at the ground. "Could be something under the snow. Ritual circle, maybe. But if we clear the snow, we'll only disturb what was there." He took another slow look around. "Snap some more photos. That's all we can do for now. It's time to Change. Morgan?"

"I'm on it."

I went first. That was part of the move to our new positions. When I became Alpha, Clay would be my bodyguard. It wasn't the most comfortable transition, for either of us. We'd always been partners, and I'd taken pride in that—my mate was the most powerful werewolf in the country, yet he didn't feel the need to shove me behind him, where it was safe. He knew that I was safe at his side, able to protect myself and him, if necessary. But that didn't work for the Alpha and her beta. When it came to plotting and planning, I had to step forward and he had to step back. In matters of safety, the situation reversed. So when we Changed, he wanted me to go first. That way, if danger struck while he was mid-Change, I'd already be in wolf form, better able to protect myself.

I entered the thicket and Changed. It hurt like hell, as it always does and always will, sadly.

When I finished, I took a moment to orient myself. Most werewolves do—the shift to another reality is always jarring. Clay is, of course, the exception. There seems to be no discordance for him. The moment he's a wolf, he's ready to get out and run.

While he began his Change, I ran about a dozen strides away, flying through the snow, feeling the exhilarating cold of it chase away the last aches of the Change. I stopped short and then tore around in circles, ripping up the snow, rolling in it. Making a mess, basically. Then I hunkered down, muzzle aimed at the tree line just beyond the clearing, where we'd trampled the snow coming in. I checked my trajectory, crouched, and sprang, flying clear over the unbroken snow and past the tree line.

I looked back at my handiwork. A straight path from the thicket where we Changed, ending in that ripped-up patch. It could look like a fight, but there were no other scents. I wouldn't worry him like that. He'd see it and sniff it and think I'd just been goofing around. And then? Well, then I vanished. Just vanished. No sign of where I'd gone. A straight trail to an empty trodden patch, surrounded by unbroken snow.

I chuffed, pleased with myself. Then I crept to the other side of the thicket, downwind of him, where he couldn't smell me. I settled in, head on my paws, tail curled around me. Inside the thicket, I could hear Clay finishing up. I could see him, too, his yellow fur bright through the brush.

He started out the way he'd come in. Then he stopped. I could imagine him there, looking at the track-story I'd left, puzzling it out. I wriggled lower. With my pale fur, I'd blend with the snow. If he couldn't see me or smell me or hear me . . . I resisted the urge to give a chuckling growl.

Clay stepped from the thicket, vanishing from view. I waited. As much as I strained, I couldn't hear him in the soft snow. Was he just standing there, still puzzling? Had I given him enough time to recover from the Change? Was he fair game now? I lifted my hindquarters, preparing to race up behind him and pounce.

I was just about to launch when a yellow blur tore around the thicket. Coming straight at me.

I tried to leap out of the way, but it was too late, and he barreled into me, sending me flying. Before I could scramble up, he was the one pouncing. He pinned me, teeth gripping the loose ruff around my neck as he held me down, growling and shaking me.

I sighed and let my paws slide out from under me, admitting defeat. He released me and backed off. I played submissive—head down, ears flat, tail lowered—while I bunched my legs, ready to—

He pounced again, knocking me on my side this time. I got hold of his ruff, though, biting and growling as we tumbled through the woods, mowing down innocent saplings.

I let go, sprang up, and started to run. Just then, Morgan emerged from his Changing place across the clearing. I made the mistake of pausing to glance over and got plowed down by Clay. He hit me in the side and knocked me flying into the snow. Then he turned to Morgan.

Clay lowered his head. Classic standoff stance, but he wasn't growling and his ears weren't back, meaning he was just goofing around. Given Morgan's experience with real wolves, he should recognize that, but his body language said he wasn't so sure . . .

Finally, Morgan's nerve broke and he took a slow step back. Clay charged. He hit him square in the chest, nearly flipping him backward. Morgan went down. Clay zoomed back to me, paws spitting up snow in his wake. I chuffed and shook my head.

I glanced over at Morgan. He was on his feet, shaking off the snow. His gaze was fixed on Clay. Evaluating his intent. I resisted the urge to intercede. It's damned near impossible to communicate "he's kidding" in wolf form. Morgan would figure it out eventually, and he seemed to do just that when Clay let him approach without knocking him flying again.

Clay nudged my flank.

I gave him a look to say, "If I get up, are you going to let me *stay* up?"

He exhaled, his breath steaming, and backed up. I slowly rose, flicking my tail and my ears. Then I charged. He feinted out of the way. I nearly plowed into a tree. When I turned around, I swore he was laughing. Morgan, too.

I swished my tail and snorted, then pulled myself up and growled to say playtime was over. Clay rolled his eyes to say I was a sore loser. Then he took off, racing through the snow. I loped up beside him, Morgan falling in behind.

We ran only long enough to take off the edge that play-fighting hadn't dulled. Then we slowed, fanning out, sniffing the air and pausing for a closer sniff at large evergreens. We'd been out there for maybe an hour when I caught a scent. I motioned to Clay and he lifted his muzzle and then shook his head. It was too faint for him.

I followed the smell to a spruce. Branches fanned the ground. Carefully, I pawed one aside. The smell was almost hidden by the astringent odor of the needles. I pushed my head into the dark cavity under the branches. It took a moment for my eyes to adjust. When they did, I saw white bone. A skeletal arm encased in a ragged sleeve.

The skeleton's hand was missing. As I pushed farther under the tree, I could see other parts were missing, too, including the skull. Did scavengers often make off with skulls? I couldn't recall encountering that—like the hands, there wasn't much "meat" there.

I eased back for a more critical look at the body. It'd been reduced to clothing-covered bones. The clothes were ripped too badly for a struggle, suggesting predation. It looked like male clothing. The body seemed small, too. Not child-small, but not adult-sized, either. On both counts, though, I was just guessing. So I backed up and let Clay in for a look.

He spent a few minutes examining the remains. When he was done, he couldn't tell me what he thought, obviously, just gestured that we could move on.

We made a mental note of our surroundings, then headed out in search of other bodies. Yet if there were more, it quickly became apparent that they were either a lot farther into the woods or too old for me to smell.

I stopped to tell the guys we should head back. When I looked around, though, I saw only Clay's golden fur. I threw back my head and howled. After a moment, a distant yip from Morgan replied.

Clay chuffed and shook his head. I howled again. Morgan yipped back. Damn it, when I called, he was supposed to come.

I didn't glance over to see Clay's expression. I didn't dare. Just gave one last howl, edged with anger, and then set off after Morgan.

14.

We found Morgan at the foot of a steep hillside. He was standing by a clump of bushes, staring up at a pie pan hanging from a branch. The pan twisted in the breeze, glinting in the moonlight. Great. How the hell was I supposed to convince Clay that Morgan could be Pack material if he was distracted by every shiny object he saw?

He didn't even seem to notice us until I let out a chuff, and he glanced over, casually, as if he'd heard us all along but had really been more interested in the pie plate. I sighed.

He nosed around the bushes for a moment, then looked at us, head tilted as if to say, "Well, are you coming?"

To do what? Join his rapt contemplation of baking tins? I grunted. He yipped, then dove through the bushes . . . and disappeared into the hillside.

Oh.

Clay bounded over, stuck his head through the bushes, then pushed in until the tip of his tail vanished. I followed.

The bushes disguised the entrance to a cave. The pie plate must have been someone's way of marking it. When I got inside, I smacked muzzle-first into Clay's rear end. He chuffed an apology, his nails clicking on stone as he moved farther into the inky blackness.

Only slivers of moonlight managed to get past the entrance. I backed out and held down one of the biggest bushes under my paw. Moonlight flooded into the cave. Inside, Morgan dipped his muzzle as if in thanks. When he started nosing the floor, exploring, Clay let out a low growl.

Morgan looked up, confused. Clay head-butted him toward me. More confusion. I released the bushes a little and then stepped on them again and jerked my head toward him. It took a moment, but he figured out what I meant. He sighed, came to the mouth, and took over the job of holding down the branches while I went into the cave for a look.

I suppose it's a testament to how long I've been a werewolf that I didn't feel guilty. It was simple hierarchy. He'd get his look around . . . after we got ours.

The mouth of the cave was narrow, which is why we'd smacked into each other. Now Clay squeezed to the side to let me through first. Again, hierarchy, not chivalry. That feels a little strange sometimes— taking precedence over my mate, my partner. We'll be fine as long as the imbalance in power doesn't extend beyond this, and I can be damned sure Clay is never going to allow that.

I trotted into a second, bigger chamber. It stank of woodsmoke, as if someone had used it for a bonfire. Everything was dark for a moment, as Clay came through the mouth and blocked the moon-light. Then he stepped aside and I looked around.

There was a moment where I thought I'd found some ancient cave painted by Neolithic man. In my defense, it was only a brief moment. I may not have Clay's background, but I know we're a long way from anyplace with Neolithic cave paintings. When my eyes adjusted, I could see these weren't even mock paintings. They were symbols, sketched with what looked like chalk and soot.

They weren't the same symbols I'd seen on the trees, but some were similar. As I stepped forward for a better look, Clay nudged my flank and whined. Telling me to stop. I looked over at him. He bent his muzzle to the cave floor and nosed what looked like a white, tubular rock. Then he jerked his head toward the rest of the floor.

We were on the edge of a ritual circle, adorned with more symbols. In the center, ashes and burned wood explained the smell. There were dark splotches just to my left. I carefully picked my way over to them. Dark red. I lowered my nose and inhaled. It was hard to get past the smell of smoke that permeated the cave, but I detected blood. Animal or human, I couldn't tell—it was too old— but it was definitely blood.

Clay nosed the white rock again, then gestured to a pile of them in the middle of the circle. I walked in, being careful not to step on the markings or the dried blood. When I reached the pile, I realized they were finger bones.

Was this where those missing hands ended up? If so, they hadn't been scavenged. These bones were bright white and smelled faintly of sodium hypochlorite. Boiled clean and bleached.

I needed a better look. Which required fingers, a camera, and a penlight. Time to Change back. I communicated that to Clay, then had him hold down the bushes while I let Morgan take a look around before we started the long run back to our clothing.

I snapped pictures while Clay examined the symbols. Morgan hung back and watched.

Clay said, "They look like a mix of elements. That could suggest a supernatural ritual, not a human one."

I nodded. "The bones and blood point to necromancy. The symbols look more witch or sorcerer. I'll send the photos to Jaime and Paige."

I was taking another picture when my cell phone beeped, reminding me I had a message. It must have come in while I was in wolf form. A text from Chief Dales asking us to stop by the station. She'd sent it at nine, and it was just past ten now.

I told Clay and Morgan, then said, "We can drop by, but I'm guessing she'll be gone for the night."

"Are we reporting this?" Morgan waved at the cave.

I shook my head. "Not this and not the other body. Finding two corpses in one day is a little much. We'll have to hope they conduct a thorough search of their own." I looked at the cave. "And hope they don't find *this* until we figure out what the hell it means."

So what *did* that cave mean? I could be optimistic and say it had nothing to do with the dead bodies. Sure, it was a little coincidental finding corpses missing hands, then hands missing a corpse. Maybe someone had found the hands carried off by animals and decided to boil them for ritualistic parts rather than turn them over to the police. You know, you're out, walking your dog through the woods, he brings you back human hands, and you think, *Huh, I could use those.* Perfectly plausible.

Actually, if the dog walker was a necromancer, it *was* possible. They needed human remains for rituals, and they didn't require fresh ones, so they got creative. Jeremy's longtime girlfriend, Jaime Vegas, was a necromancer, and she did use "bits and bobs" from dead bodies, most of them ancient. Still, she'd never claim random body parts found lying about. And she didn't use blood. Dried flesh and old bones signify death, which is the domain of the necromancer. Blood signifies life.

It seemed more likely to be spell-casters. Witch, sorcerer, or maybe one of the rarer and weaker races. While 99 percent of magic has nothing to do with ritual sacrifice, there is that 1 percent. The highest level of magic, requiring the highest level of sacrifice: a human life. But I wasn't sure the blood was human. It could be animal sacrifice . . . paired with human remains from someone conveniently killed under completely separate circumstances.

Any explanation other than a ritual murder was a stretch. A big one. No matter how rare it was in the supernatural world, I had to entertain the very strong possibility that's exactly what this was.

✥

I expected to find the police station shuttered. Or, at the very least, nearly dark, with only the night officer on duty. Instead, all the windows were ablaze and I could hear voices from a hundred feet away. It seemed every set of footprints on the street led straight to the station doors. The only three cars in sight were parked out front.

"Party at the cop shop?" Morgan said.

"Something's going on. I just hope Chief Dales's message didn't mean 'get your asses over here fast because we have a situation.'"

"No reason it would involve us," Clay said.

"I hope not."

I sent Morgan back to the motel. I wasn't sure how far news of his escapade had traveled, but my experience with small towns said the answer was "far." Best to leave him out of this.

Clay and I stepped inside to find three people hanging out in the small foyer. They moved aside for us but didn't say a word. I kicked the snow off my boots and opened the interior door.

Officer Jaggerman manned the front desk. Three more people stood in front of it, all leaning in, holding Jaggerman's attention. A couple in their late thirties cast anxious glances at us. Another in their forties sat off to the side. I could hear Chief Dales's voice coming through her closed office door. Talking to Kent, it sounded like. Or hiding in there with him. If so, I wasn't sure I blamed her.

Two of the people in front of Jaggerman seemed to be a couple. Maybe my age. Latino, like the younger couple to the side. With them was a man of about thirty-five, balding and beefy, a worn Westwood Werewolves team jacket straining over his broad chest.

"I demand to see that body," the woman was saying, loud enough to make my ears ring.

"It won't help, Mrs. Rivera," Jaggerman said. "You wouldn't be able to tell if it's—"

"Are you telling me I wouldn't recognize my own son?"

"The body is in"—Jaggerman swallowed—"poor condition."

The guy in the football jacket laid his hand on Mrs. Rivera's arm. "If it is Ricky, you'll know as soon as they do, Maria. Some of the other team parents"—he gestured at the sitting couple—"have volunteered to take turns staying here all night until Jess has an answer."

As if on cue, Chief Dales's door opened. She walked out, papers in hand.

"No one needs to stay," she said. "I just got Doc's preliminary report. As we thought, the body is that of a man in his early twenties, too old to be Ricky. Even more conclusively, there were several tattoos. That means it definitely isn't your son."

Chief Dales offered a few quieter words of sympathy. I could tell she was struggling. I recognized that look—*I can feel deeply for people, but I have trouble expressing it, especially to those I don't know well.* Yet her sentiment did seem genuine.

Mrs. Rivera muttered something under her breath and then stalked out, leaving her husband and the guy in the team jacket to hurry after her. None of them paid any attention to us. Nor did Chief Dales as she walked to the front desk, still holding the pages.

"Doc confirmed it looks like homicide," she said to Jaggerman. "I've compiled a list of persons of interest. All our local recluses."

"You want me to take a run at them tonight?"

"Your shift ended two hours ago, Phil. I told you to go home then, and after that visit, I bet you're wishing you listened."

He chuckled. "No kidding." He glanced at us. "Uh, Jess, we have—"

"I'll leave these addresses here," she said. "Take Wes in the morning and see who you can round up for questioning."

I approached the desk as she set the pages on it. "You texted me?"

She glanced over sharply, as if startled. A little *too* startled. As if she'd only been pretending she hadn't noticed us.

"Oh," she said. "You didn't need to stop in."

"The message said—"

"I just wanted to know if you're spending the night in Westwood."

"We are. No luck getting our tires fixed with all the storm calls."

"Staying at the Red Cedar, I'm guessing?" She struggled for a tired smile. "Only place in town."

"It is."

"Good. I may have more questions in the morning. If I don't stop by before you leave, give me a ring."

"All right."

I started to turn away.

"Grab yourselves a coffee before you head out," she called. "It's a cold night." Then, to Jaggerman, "Phil? Got a few things for you to sign."

They disappeared into her office as I was pouring a coffee. She shut the door behind them and I sidled back to the front desk and glanced down at the pages she'd left there. Clay came up beside me.

"A list of the local loners?" I said. "Otherwise known as a list of potential mutts or supernaturals involved in nefarious business."

"Handy."

"No kidding."

I took out my phone. He stood guard as I snapped photos of the pages.

15

I got outside the police station before I took a sip of the coffee. It tasted like roasted tree bark. I prepared to dump it into the snow.

"Uh-uh," Clay said. "We've got a long night. You're going to need that."

He was right. The best time to investigate this list was while it was dark enough to skulk around and before the local cops tackled the job themselves.

So I choked down half the coffee as fast as I could manage. We were heading toward the motel when a woman's voice called, "You there!"

We turned to see Mrs. Rivera bearing down on us while her husband scrambled from their parked car.

"Maria!" he called.

We waited until she planted herself in front of us. "I saw you at the police station. Then I remembered someone said strangers found the body. A blond couple."

"Yes, it was us," I said. "We were hiking—"

"Maria." It was the other man from the station, the one in the football jacket. He came up beside her and lowered his voice. "They only found the body. They didn't have anything to do with it."

"Of course they didn't," she snapped. "They arrived today. I just wanted to ask if it could be him."

She held out a photo of a teenage boy. He was heavyset and soft.

I would have guessed he was about thirteen, but he wore a football uniform, so he had to be in high school.

I stared at the photo. He was grinning at the camera. So proud of that uniform. So young. When had he disappeared? *How* had he disappeared?

"You recognize him," she whispered.

I shook my head. "I'm sorry. It's just . . ." I looked up at her. "He looks very happy. I'm so sorry."

The man took the photo. "And I'm sorry to bother you," he said to me. "We're all very upset, as you can imagine. This . . . discovery has only brought it all back." He held out his free hand, first to Clay, who had to be nudged to shake it, and then to me. "Tom Hanlon. I'm a teacher up at the high school. I coach the football team."

I introduced us.

"We'll let you get on with your night," he said, putting an arm around Mrs. Rivera's shoulders as he handed back the photo.

She knocked his arm away and turned to us. "Are you sure it couldn't have been—?"

"Jess said the body has tattoos," Coach Hanlon said. "Ricky didn't."

"I don't care what she said. I don't know *how* she got that job. Or who she slept with."

"Maria!" The coach's eyes widened. "Jessica Dales is the chief of police because she was better qualified—"

"This is my boy, Ricky," she said, shoving the photo at me again. "He went missing just after last Thanksgiving."

I shook my head. "The man we found was older and died much more recently. It wasn't your son. I'm sorry."

It took a few minutes—and her husband's help—to get Mrs. Rivera back to the car. I didn't leave until she was gone. We just stood there, waiting. As the car drove away, we set off slowly, not wanting to seem like we had better things to do.

"The guy we found this afternoon definitely wasn't him," Clay murmured as the rear lights of their car faded in the distance. "But the second body? The smaller one? Hard to judge exactly, but I'd say it's been there about a year."

"I know."

Two hours later, we were hiding in the forest watching an old woman with a rifle stalk around her dilapidated cabin, her gaze on the ground as she searched for footprints. She didn't find any—I'd been careful to approach only as close as I could get without leaving the forest. She stomped back to her porch and stood there, faded nightgown whipping around her spindly legs.

"You better run!" she shouted. "This is private property, you hear? Don't want no damn hunters. Or kids. Or sledders. Or . . ." The list went on, covering everyone who might break the sacred seal of privacy she'd created out here.

"Aliens?" Morgan whispered.

"Bet she's been beamed up a time or two," Clay muttered.

"It's like something out of an old hillbilly cartoon," I marveled as I watched. "I thought the last cabin was bad."

"They're all bad," Clay said. "The only difference is whether they're half crazy or all the way there."

He was right. We'd checked out four cabins so far. With two, I'd barely gotten close enough for a good sniff before someone came thundering out, as if they could sense trespassers. In the other two, I'd peeked in the windows to see them sleeping . . . beside empty bottles.

"Is every paranoid survivalist in America living in these woods?" I said.

"Only half," Morgan said. "The rest are in Alaska."

We waited until the old woman went inside, then we set out again. Finding the people on Chief Dales's list was getting tougher with every name we crossed off. The first three had been locals who lived in town. That was easy enough. But these past four were forest cabins, and only the first was even on a proper road. To find the rest, Dales had listed coordinates. We'd taken the portable GPS unit from Jeremy's SUV. It still wasn't easy.

We continued walking for about ten minutes before I could make out a distant, unlit cabin. We veered to the side, approaching from the forest.

"Do you want to handle this one?" I asked Morgan.

He didn't answer. Just spun and wrenched Clay's arm, yanking him hard. Clay caught Morgan's wrist and threw him down on his back and then loomed over him.

"Don't ever—"

Morgan cut him off by pointing. We both looked to see metal almost buried in the snow. Watching Clay, Morgan rose, then reached for a nearby stick, waved us back, and poked at the metal. A bear trap sprang, jaws snapping the stick in two.

"That's another thing I saw a lot of in Alaska," he said.

I peered around and pointed to a second one, almost hidden under a fallen branch. "And there are a lot here, too, apparently. I don't think these are meant for bears, though."

We continued, armed with sticks as we poked our way forward. When we drew closer to the cabin, Morgan stopped us again. Penlight in hand, he waved it along a metal wire running at knee level. We approached with care and bent for a better look.

"Razor wire," I murmured. "Someone really doesn't want visitors."

With this many booby traps outside, I couldn't send Morgan up there alone. As we drew close, I listened, but heard nothing from the dark building. There was a generator to the side, but it wasn't running.

"Looks like no one's home," Morgan whispered.

I was nodding when I caught a scent. Not human, but almost as familiar.

Morgan went still and I knew he'd picked it up, too.

I glanced at Clay.

"Yeah, I smell it," he murmured at my shoulder. "Let me have a look."

He took one step around the side of the cabin, then stopped. I hurried over to find him standing in front of a darkened window, staring up. A gleaming wolf skull stared back.

The cabin seemed unoccupied. Clay snapped the door lock. It was a simple one—apparently, with all the traps, the owner didn't expect anyone to get close enough to try the door. Clay went in first, looking and listening and sniffing. I waited until he'd checked the small cabin and came out to say he was absolutely sure it was empty. Then I stationed Morgan on the porch and slipped inside.

Clay had lit a lantern. I didn't make it past the hall before I stopped. I stood there, gaping into the main room. If the old woman with the nightgown and rifle looked like something from a cartoon, this looked like a set from a horror movie.

Our blond heroine, having miraculously survived being chased by a knife-wielding vandal into the forest, soon finds herself lost. She stumbles through the snow until, in the distance, she sees lights. It's a cabin. An unoccupied cabin, to be sure, but she's freezing—being half naked in a snowstorm can do that to you. So she rushes toward the cottage, finds it unlocked, and stumbles in gratefully, then looks up to see . . .

Dead animals. A whole lotta dead animals, all staring back at me. Some were stuffed and mounted, while others were just pelts, heads still attached, glass eyes inserted. That was creepy enough. But in any good horror movie, you need more. You need weapons. Here, they lined every wall—ancient guns, machetes, knives . . .

Clay stood by the wolf skull. There were actually three of them— one facing out the window, two facing in. All sat atop a wolf pelt.

"That explains the smell," I said, waving at the pelt. "Not a werewolf. Just someone who really likes wolves." I looked around, seeing a few more skulls and pelts. "Dead ones, at least."

While the wolf skulls on the table suggested they deserved a place of honor, the cabin owner was an equal opportunity predator fan. Every skull and stuffed beast and pelt came from one. I must have subconsciously realized that when I walked in, which is what stopped me in my tracks. It's also what made the room look more like a scene from a horror movie than a simple hunter's retreat. Not a single buck's head or stuffed duck. Instead, I saw coyotes and foxes and bobcats and weasels. There was even a wolverine pelt, right above a polished bear skull. I could smell them all, too, and it was putting my nerves on edge.

I looked over at Clay, who was absorbed examining something on a shelf. I could make out a white sliver of skull. I walked over and, for the second time, stopped short. There were, again, three skulls on display. All from the same predator.

"Those are . . ." I began. "I mean, they are, right? They aren't apes . . ."

"Human," he said.

The outer two were yellowed with age. The middle one was slightly smaller and polished white, like the finger bones in the cave. I moved closer and lowered my head for a sniff.

"Bleach," I murmured.

Clay nodded. "The others are old. This one isn't." He bent for a closer look. "Can't tell much from a skull, but it looks young and male."

Morgan appeared in the doorway. I waved him in.

"So that skull belongs to the missing kid we found?" he said. "Ricky Rivera?"

"No," Clay said. "We're guessing that it *could* belong to the dead body we found, which *could* be Ricky Rivera."

Morgan looked annoyed, as if Clay was making a petty distinction. He wasn't. If you start making leaps like that, you end up in all sorts of trouble. Years of investigating have taught us to keep everything theoretical until we have proof.

I started for the door, planning to take over guard duty on the porch. I'd seen everything I needed to—time to let Morgan satisfy his curiosity while Clay searched for more. As I was leaving, I noticed a low shelf covered in bones.

I bent to examine them. Morgan reached over my shoulder for one. I stopped him.

"Paw bones," I said. "They look animal."

"These ones aren't," Clay said.

I turned to see Clay crouched by a set of bookshelves. It was stuffed with books, but one lower shelf had a gap between the tomes, scattered with small bones.

I walked over to see that they weren't "scattered" at all. They were finger bones, like the ones we'd seen in the cave, arranged in a pattern.

"They're a little bigger than the ones in the cave," Clay said. "Bleached, too, though more recently."

I could smell that. The bleach on the others had been faint, like the skull. This was strong enough to smell from several feet away.

Clay stood, head tilting to read the titles on the books.

"Someone likes anthropology," he said. "Lots of folklore and ritual. Can you snap shots of these, darling? I don't recognize some of the titles."

I took cell phone photos while Morgan watched.

"This guy seems to be our killer," he said. "And we don't smell a werewolf here. Meaning the murderer isn't a man-eater. So this isn't the Pack's responsibility, right?"

"Just because this guy has the bones doesn't mean he killed anyone," Clay said.

Again, Morgan looked annoyed. "And the blood in the cave?"

"Could be animal."

"Clay's right," I said. "We have lots of pieces here, and it's natural to want to fit them together. But we need more. Are these definitely from those bodies? Is this the murderer or a scavenger? And what about the eating? Animal scavenger? Man-eating werewolf? Cannibal human? Dark magic? Once we eliminate the supernatural possibilities, we're free to go. Until then, we'd better get comfy in Westwood."

$\mathcal{W}$e made it back to town, coming out on a residential road just north of the main street. As we walked, I kept thinking about what we'd found. Sure, that was pretty much all I'd *been* thinking of, but in an abstract way. How did those victims die? Who did it? Why?

Seeing the houses was like a cold slap, waking me up and reminding me that we hadn't just found bodies—we'd found people. Two young men who'd been murdered, their bodies mutilated.

There was a time when I'd blame Clay for my lack of empathy. Clearly I'd been around him too long and started seeing things the way he did. But that gives him too much credit. Or perhaps it gives me too little—that I'd be so easily influenced. I can't blame him. I can't blame being a werewolf. I can't even blame the fact that I've seen so many bodies that I've built up an immunity. I have changed. It takes me longer these days to recall that I'm dealing with lost lives. But the truth is that I've never been someone who could see a dead body and instantly mourn a life lost. I know people who do, and I feel like I should. But I don't. I do mourn; it just takes longer.

"You okay?" Clay whispered.

"Mmm-hmm. Just thinking."

Morgan cleared his throat. "I don't know about you guys, but I'm freezing. I'm going to kick it up a notch and get back to the motel."

Clay nodded and Morgan took off, jogging down the snowy sidewalk. I watched him go. When he reached the corner, I took a deep breath, sucking in cold air to wake myself up.

"Okay, we need a plan," I said. "We've got our booby-trapping, predator-fixated hermit's name on that list, so I can research that. You can look up those books from his cabin. I'll touch base with Paige and Jaime on the symbols." I sighed. "Lots of little pieces, none of them seeming to add up to—"

I stopped, my attention caught by a sign in a yard. We stood in front of a small two-story house with a car in the drive. Just your typical family home. On the lawn were two signs, one a weathered, "Our Son is a Werewolf!", the other newer and larger, dominated by a huge picture of Ricky Rivera, and "Please Help Bring Our Ricky Home!"

I stared at that sign. Then I wrenched my gaze away and looked at the house. It was dark except for a single second-story light. Was that Ricky's room? The light left on, as if he'd be back any minute?

Clay's arm went around me, his warm breath on my cold cheek as he bent to whisper, "That body might not have been him."

"I know we're trying to keep an open mind. But we know that was him, and I just keep thinking what if it was . . ."

"I know."

"I don't think I could handle . . ."

"I know."

As we stood there, I thought of the playground back home, in Bear Valley. Of what had happened just last week. The weather had been nice—cold but sunny—and I'd jumped at the chance to take the kids to the playground for some much-needed socializing. Yes, my children's idea of socializing is to be in the same place as other kids, interacting only when physical contact occurs and avoiding that as much as possible. But it's better than total social isolation, which is our natural bent.

At the playground, I'm one of *those* parents. Like hawks watching their fledglings' first flight from the nest, endlessly circling, endlessly hovering. I'm not standing on the sidelines yelling, "Don't go up there! Hold on tight! Watch your step!" But that doesn't mean I'm not thinking it, cringing with every reckless move my little daredevils make.

That day, though, I'd resolved not to hover. On the drive, I'd been encouraging them to join in with other children's games, and then I settled in and saw the other mothers huddled on the benches, sipping coffee and chatting, with me off to the side, oblivious and alone. I'd realized I really wasn't setting a good example for the twins. So I took out my thermos, went over, and sat with the other parents. I talked, too, letting the conversation engage more and more of my attention, until . . .

Until Kate's scream of pain.

She'd fallen when I wasn't paying attention. I heard her scream and I leapt up and I saw her there, huddled beneath the big slide, Logan shoving past other kids as he backed down the ladder.

They'd been arguing, they later admitted. She wanted to slide down together and he didn't. They tussled. She fell over the side. And I hadn't seen it. I hadn't heard them fighting. I hadn't seen her fall. I hadn't been there to catch her. I'd been preoccupied and she'd been hurt and it could have been so, so much worse.

I shoved my hands in my pockets. "Are we being careful enough? Should I *become* Alpha? What if a supernatural did this and tries to retaliate when we catch him? What if some mutt, at any point, tries to retaliate for whatever—"

Clay cut me off, both arms going around me. "No one protects their kids like we do. They have the whole Pack watching out for them. If you stopped chasing guys like this or didn't become Alpha, that wouldn't make anyone less likely to come after our kids. You need to do exactly what you are doing—carrying on as if no one would dare touch our children while making sure they're so well guarded that no one could."

He was right, of course. Holing up in my cave with my pups was a sign of fear. Fear was a sign of weakness. Killers—werewolves or not—prey on that.

Clay continued, "I'm sure this boy's parents watched out for him, but they aren't werewolves."

I nodded. I knew he was telling himself that made a difference. Because he needed to believe it. He's Clayton Danvers and we're the Pack and our children are safe. But the truth was that all it took was one distracted moment in a playground, and they could be gone. Forever.

I looked back at that lit window and let Clay prod me back into motion along the sidewalk.

At the motel, Morgan's light was out.

Clay sighed when he saw where I was looking. "He's probably just gone to bed, but yeah, I'll check on him."

"Sorry," I said. "It's just . . ."

"I know."

Clay walked past as I opened the door. Then he wheeled and pushed past me into our room. As I regained my balance, he lifted a hand, telling me to stay back. He looked around, eyes narrowing.

"The room is empty," I said. "The door was locked. No one is under the bed . . ."

"Someone's been in here."

"Yes, restocking the minibar, which I'm about to appreciate. Just as soon as *I* go check on Morgan."

Clay was there in a shot, gripping my elbow.

"Hold on," he said.

Before I could say a word, I caught the intruder's scent. Half the drawers were cracked open. A water bottle I'd left on top had been knocked over, water pooled on the floor.

I inhaled deeper. "It's the same guy who slashed our tires. The room's been searched. Better see what's missing."

A few minutes later, a knock came at the door. Clay opened it to find Morgan standing there.

"I stopped at the gas station—it's the only place open to grab a pop," he said. "Someone has been in my room. Nothing's missing, but I doubt this place has turndown service. And I don't want to be paranoid, but it smelled like—"

"The vandal we chased earlier today," I said. "Whatever he was looking for, I don't think he found it. My laptop was still hidden."

"I'll check your room," Clay said. "Elena?"

"Lock and bolt the door behind you," I said. "Yes, sir."

17. MORGAN

*M*organ glanced over his shoulder as Clay followed him back to his room. He'd like to take this sudden show of interest as a positive sign—the guy was concerned about him. But he knew better. The guy just didn't trust him to conduct a thorough sniff-search on his own.

Clay walked in, looked around, and grunted. It could be approval for Morgan's housekeeping—the room was spotless except for the duffel in the corner. Or he might just have gas.

Clay walked to the duffel bag, bent, and opened it.

Sure, go ahead. Look through that. I don't mind.

Morgan pretended to sniff-search the rest of the room. He'd already done it, but he didn't dare just stand by.

"Our intruder rifled through your bag," Clay said. "Was there anything to find?"

"I know better than that."

Clay rose. "You gonna be okay here tonight?"

Morgan glowered at him. "I am capable of looking after myself. I know I've screwed up, but—"

"It was a question, not an insult."

Clay turned to leave.

"Wait," Morgan said.

Clay stopped at the door, one hand on the knob. He turned.

"Look," Morgan said. "I know I stayed out of the fight in Alaska. I know that didn't impress you."

"You're not Pack. I didn't expect you to fight for the Pack."

Clay started out the door. Then he stopped, as if considering. He backed inside, closed the door again, and turned to Morgan.

"Elena seems to think you might be interested in joining the Pack."

"I . . . haven't really decided . . ."

"But you might be. That's why you were coming to Stonehaven, wasn't it? To check things out."

When Morgan didn't answer, annoyance flickered across Clay's face. Morgan didn't blame him really. Obviously that's why he'd been on their territory, heading to their home. So why couldn't he admit it?

"The Pack needs wolves," Clay said. "Finding them is Elena's job. Pretty soon the whole Pack will be her job."

Morgan blinked, taking a moment to process that. "She's going to be Alpha?"

"Is that a problem?" Clay's voice had dropped to a growl.

"Um, no. I just . . ." He straightened. "It's not a problem. Just a surprise. But I guess it shouldn't be. I saw how she handled things in Alaska. And here. She'll make a good leader."

A little too kiss-ass? Clay didn't exactly light up with pride. Yeah, too kiss-ass. Morgan swallowed. Damn it, why was this so complicated? It was like walking a tightrope, never sure exactly where to find the sweet spot between submission and assertion. That must come naturally to guys who'd grown up in the Pack. Not for him.

Clay took another step into the room, making Morgan inch back in spite of himself.

"In five years, she's found two suitable wolves," Clay said. "Reese and Noah. You met them in Alaska. One's in college and one's not even out of high school. They're great kids, but they won't be full Pack members for years. She's frustrated and discouraged." He took another step. "You want in? Step up. Don't toy with her. Understood?"

Morgan nodded. "Understood."

18. ELENA

I was in bed on my laptop looking up our predator-obsessed cabin dweller when Clay came back. He didn't say anything, just went into the bathroom, then came out, undressed, and crawled into bed, being careful not to disturb me.

An hour later, when I stopped to stretch, I was sure he'd fallen asleep. But he opened one eye and said, "Find anything?"

I shook my head. "No. I think that's why we call them hermits. He's not a mutt. I can't find out if he's in the council records until morning, and even then, I doubt this"—I pointed at the list—"is his real name if he's a supernatural. Hell, it probably isn't his real name if he's a human, so how am I going to . . ." I shook my head. "I'm too tired."

Clay pulled me against him. "We're gonna find whoever did this. Supernatural or not. Then we'll make sure the kid's parents know. Give them some closure."

I reached up to kiss his cheek. "Thank you."

He tugged me on top of him, one arm around my waist, the other hand on the back of my head. "Now, let's see about helping you get a good night's sleep."

The problem with most motels? Lack of room service. It's not usually a huge issue. I normally roll out of bed and hunt down breakfast myself. But this particular small town wasn't exactly bulging with dining options. The motel didn't even have vending machines, as Morgan had discovered last night. So Clay and I were dressed within minutes of waking and heading out the door.

We'd been up so late, we'd slept in and it was past ten. That meant our ride—scheduled to get its tires fixed at eight—should be done. Except, as we jogged along the main street, we could see the SUV ahead, buried in snow.

"That doesn't look ready to drive," I said.

"No," Clay growled. "It does not."

I kept going, just in case the mechanic had miraculously managed to change the tires while not disturbing the SUV's snow blanket. He hadn't, of course. There weren't even boot prints in the surrounding snow to suggest someone had taken a look.

I called the garage. It took a while for someone to answer. When a woman did, I explained the problem.

"We really do need to get home," I said. "We have young children and this wasn't supposed to be an overnight trip. What time is the mechanic coming?"

"You need to make an appointment." The receptionist sounded bored, TV blasting in the background.

"I did, as I just explained. For eight this morning. He said we didn't need to be here—he'd change the tires and bill us. Is he running behind?"

"If he is, he hasn't told me. But *that's* not your problem. Your problem is that you canceled the appointment."

"What?"

She spoke slower, as if to someone of limited intelligence. "You called this morning and said you didn't need service."

"If I did, I would remember it, wouldn't I?" I bit my tongue and softened my tone. "Okay, clearly there's been a mix-up, so—"

"No mix-up. You called. Elena Michaels, just like on the work order. You said you didn't need service."

"And I spoke to you? Did it sound like me?"

A pause. I knew it hadn't—my Canadian accent doesn't stand

out around here nearly as much as Clay's Southern drawl, but it was distinctive enough.

"I didn't pay no mind," the woman said finally. "Woman calls, says she's Elena Michaels, getting her tires fixed this morning, that's good enough for me."

"All right, then. When can I reschedule for?"

A deep sigh, then a creak, as if I'd made her get out of her chair. A moment later, paper shuffled. "Same time tomorrow."

"What? No. Look, I understand there was a mistake, and it's not your fault, but I have children at home and I need to get back today."

"Then you shouldn't have canceled the appointment."

Clay, who'd been listening in, held out his hand. I hesitated. Then I decided she deserved it—and I really did want to get home— so I handed over the phone.

Clay went easy on her. But even his "easy" is more effective than my worst. He managed to get her to agree to have someone out before nightfall. That was the best we could do. Then we continued toward the diner on foot.

"I'll call Jeremy," I said. "He might be able to get someone sooner. If not, at least he can be ready to pick us up for the night himself. It's not like we're stuck in the middle of nowhere." I looked around at the empty, snow-filled streets. "It just feels like it."

"I know. We'll get home tonight. Even if we don't, the kids will survive."

I nodded. Just yesterday, I couldn't get out of the house fast enough. That seemed to be the way it went. We'd go stir-crazy if we were home too long, but it didn't take much time away before we wanted to go back.

"The dispatcher didn't seem too bright," I said. "Do you think she just screwed up? Or did someone really call and cancel our appointment?"

"Hard to say. But if a woman called, there's only one woman who knew we were getting our car serviced this morning."

"Chief Dales."

"Yep."

I glanced over my shoulder at the police station.

"Food first," Clay said. "I'm too hungry to stand back and watch you be diplomatic."

"And I'm too hungry to be diplomatic. Food it is, then."

19. MORGAN

*M*organ rolled over and looked at the clock. It was after ten. No wonder he was so hungry. He stretched and yawned. As he did, he noticed a white piece of paper under the door. The bill?

He padded over and picked it up. It was a handwritten note.

Checking car, then going to diner for breakfast. Join us when you're up.

Ten minutes later, Morgan was still in his shorts, sitting on the edge of the bed, staring at the note. Elena wanted him in the Pack. No, that was overstating it—she wanted him to put his name forward so he could be evaluated for Pack membership. The "evaluated" part didn't bother him. It was like any other club—if it'll take just anyone, there's a catch. Of course, one always hoped that, having made your acquaintance, they'd be happy to have you, no admission tests required. But if Elena offered him membership based on their short acquaintance, he'd be suspicious. He should be flattered they were even considering him.

He *was* flattered. Maybe even a little surprised. That's where the problem lay. The Pack offered brotherhood and protection, which he wanted. But it was a reciprocal relationship. You got the brotherhood and the protection because everyone joined in to provide it. You couldn't take without giving back.

So what did he have to give? Most werewolves couldn't have joined a real wolf pack and lived with them for almost two years as he had. The social isolation would drive them mad. Morgan had missed the human world, but not enough to quit his experiment. That was a good clue that he wasn't the most sociable guy. If he did join the Pack, how often would he have to attend the meetings and other gatherings? He did want that brotherhood, but there would be times when he just wasn't in the mood to offer it back.

The bigger problem was the second part of the equation. Protection. The Pack needed fighters, and Morgan was not a fighter by any stretch of the imagination. He'd gone to a rough-and-tumble rural school but managed to avoid most brawls, namely because he was so damned average. Even being part Native Canadian hadn't mattered, given that half the school was the same. He wasn't smart enough or different enough to be bullied. He wasn't big enough or athletic enough to be challenged. He'd been raised to stay under the radar. Be invisible. Avoid confrontation. He couldn't afford to risk revealing his enhanced strength. He could count on one hand the number of altercations he'd gotten into, and he'd lost every one because he hadn't stuck around to finish the fight.

Elena would anticipate he'd need training. So would Clay—Morgan doubted any recruit would meet *his* standards. But when Clay found out they'd have to begin at square one, with "how to throw a punch without breaking your fingers"? Morgan would sink so low in his regard that he'd never climb back out again.

Clay was right. If Morgan wasn't sure he wanted to join the Pack, then he was messing with Elena. She didn't need that. And Morgan didn't need to piss off Clayton Danvers. They'd already been pulled into this mess because of him. He should back out while he could.

He got up and dressed, then wrote a note of his own and put it under Elena's door.

So now what? Morgan thought as he headed along the sidewalk, hunched against the cold. Walk to the highway and hitch a ride to . . . ? To where? Back to Alaska? To Newfoundland? No, there was nothing for him there.

He stopped and looked around. What the hell was he doing? He'd driven nearly a week to get to the Pack and now he was having second thoughts? No, not having second thoughts. Chickening out. Running away.

Maybe he didn't think he was Pack material, but wasn't that up to the Pack to decide? There wasn't a penalty for trying. Elena had told him that in Alaska. He could go to Stonehaven, hang out with them for a weekend, and if he wasn't interested, that was fine. If he did apply and was rejected, he'd be no worse off than he was now. They weren't going to chase him to the state border and vow to kill him if they ever saw him again. It would be an amicable parting. Elena would see to that.

He'd be upfront with Clay about the fighting issue. Or maybe he'd tell Elena instead. That felt a little cowardly, but it also seemed safest. He could explain the situation to her, and she could warn Clayton. They might count it as a strike against his membership, but at least Morgan would have been honest about it.

Before he even realized he was walking again, he found himself back in the motel parking lot.

I made a bad impression, he thought, *but I can fix it. I will fix it. Just—*

He stopped as a scent wafted past. Turning, he saw a teenage boy sliding a key card into Morgan's motel room door. He was wearing a parka, with the hood down. While Morgan didn't recognize his face, he did know the parka—and the scent. It was the vandal who'd slashed his tires.

The kid turned, as if sensing Morgan there. Morgan leapt forward. The kid bolted. Morgan tossed his duffel into the bushes and tore after him.

*P*ancakes were on the menu, so that's what I ordered. We got biscuits, too, just to have something to keep our stomachs from growling while we waited for the meal. I'd already had two—and a cup of coffee—and was trying not to eye the kitchen impatiently.

"You know," I said, "I'm getting that feeling of being watched again."

"Huh." Clay ripped apart his fourth biscuit. "Don't know why."

The diner was nearly full, and I swore every one of those patrons—plus the server and even the cook—had found an excuse to walk past our table. At least half of them were gaping at us.

"This is why I hate small towns," Clay muttered.

"You also hate small cities. And big ones. The common factor? They all contain people." I glanced around. "We should take advantage of our popularity. Ask about our hermit guy. But we need to be discreet. Subtly follow someone out—"

Clay turned his chair so fast it squeaked, startling the guy behind us, who'd been leaning in to eavesdrop.

"Hey," Clay said. "We were hiking yesterday and nearly lost a leg in a bear trap near a cabin. You know anything about that?"

The guy yanked his chair back fast. "Nope."

Clay turned to the woman on his other side, who'd been doing her share of gaping—though only at him. "How about you?"

"N-no." She dropped her gaze, blushing furiously. "Sorry."

Our breakfast arrived as I was glaring at Clay.

"Hey," he said to the server. "Got a question—"

I kicked him under the table. He shot me a look and then turned back to her as she set out the food.

"Were you the one who served our friend the other night?" Clay said. "The guy whose car is stuck in your parking lot?"

"Uh-huh," she said, laying out the plates.

Now the man behind Clay perked up again. "Oh, is that the one who was running around naked in the woods?" He laughed. "You better tell your friend he needs to learn to hold his liquor better." He poked the server. "And you need to learn when to stop serving drunk guys, Marnie. Even if they are handsome young men."

I looked up at the server. "He was drinking?"

She swallowed and then said, casually, "Uh-huh. He seemed fine, so I kept serving. It was only a few whiskeys, but I guess he can't hold his liquor very well."

She was lying. Even if I hadn't been able to tell that from her gaze, I would have smelled liquor on Morgan yesterday morning. He'd said he hadn't had a drink and nothing about his scent had claimed otherwise.

I glanced at Clay. He was already attacking breakfast. The server backed away and scampered off.

"She's lying," I said.

"Yep."

"Why?"

"No idea." He waved at my plate. "Eat up. We need to leave so someone can follow us out."

"What?"

"Just eat."

After we left the diner, I started to walk back to our motel, but Clay waved me over to Morgan's disabled car, a snowdrift in the lot.

"What are we—?" I began.

"Stalling."

"Because . . ."

"Someone will talk to us. Just not in there."

I should have known that. I'd learned long ago that some people, particularly in small communities, are happy to gossip with strangers . . . just not in front of their neighbors. That's what Clay had been doing when he'd asked about the traps—seeding the clouds. I've pulled similar ploys, though a little more discreetly. The fact that I didn't realize what he was doing proved just how little sleep I'd gotten, my dreams haunted by missing children.

Sure enough, as we were clearing off Morgan's car with our hands, a family came out and headed our way. The couple was around our age. Regular-looking folks, a dark-haired man and his red-headed wife. They had two kids with them. The woman leaned over and whispered something and the kids took off for the family's car.

"You're going to need a snow brush for that," the man called as they came closer.

"Or a shovel," I said with a smile.

"I can help with the brush," he said. "Let me go grab mine."

While he headed off to retrieve it, his wife introduced herself.

"Michelle Woodvine," she said. "I heard about the traps. I'm so sorry. I've said before that there should be warning signs. Everyone in town knows they're there, but visitors don't."

"We saw them, luckily," I said. "Do you guys actually get bears around here?"

She sighed. "No. It's just . . . It's Charlie. He's . . . having some problems. Psychological problems. Everyone remembers how he used to be, though, so no one wants to make a big deal. Like he'll just wake up one morning and snap out of it."

"Charlie?"

"Lacoste," Michelle said, though I already knew the name from Chief Dales's list. "He grew up here in Westwood. Headed off to college in New York, then went backpacking and didn't come home for nearly twenty years."

Her husband came back and Clay took the brush, cleaning while we chatted.

"Charlie got wrapped up in all kinds of crazy stuff out there," the husband said. "Witchcraft in Africa. Voodoo in the Caribbean. Mysticism in the East. Then he came back. Married a local woman with a little boy. Taught history at the high school. Just a regular guy again."

"Until his wife died," Michelle said. "He got in a big fight with his son. And he started . . . losing it. Living in the woods, setting traps, scaring off anyone who came by."

"Sounds dangerous."

The three of us stood there, the silence broken only by the *swish-swish* of the snow brush as Clay cleared. They knew I was thinking of the body we'd found. I could tell by their expressions—almost guilty, as if they'd played some role by not pushing harder to get help for Charlie Lacoste.

Finally, Michelle said, "If he killed that young drifter, it wasn't intentional. We were thinking about that earlier. Maybe the young man wandered onto his property, got hurt, then wandered off again. Bled to death or died of exposure."

Which still made Charlie Lacoste guilty. But I didn't say that.

"I'm sure Jess would have already brought Charlie in for questioning if she could," the husband said. "But he went missing a couple months back. No one's seen him. Not even his son."

"His son lives in Westwood?" I said.

They nodded in unison. Then Michelle said, "His name's Hanlon.

Tom Hanlon. He kept his dad's name when his mother married Charlie."

"Tom Hanlon. The football coach?"

Another simultaneous nod. With that, we had our morning planned out. A visit to Chief Dales, followed by one to Coach Hanlon to talk about his stepdad.

21. MORGAN

The kid who'd slashed Morgan's tires apparently wasn't keen on getting caught. It wasn't exactly a fast chase, though—the sidewalks were covered in fresh snow. In fact, as Morgan slid and stumbled after him, it probably looked pretty damned ridiculous. Like a chase scene shot in slow motion. The kid fell once, which might have helped, if Morgan hadn't fallen twice.

The kid kept glancing back, his expression growing darker each time, as if to say, "Are you still there? Give up already, dude." But Morgan was nothing if not tenacious.

Finally he chased the kid into the commercial heart of Westwood. The sidewalks were shoveled here and people were out and about, shopping and socializing. The kid wisely decided running down a busy street might not be his best option. He ducked between two shops. Morgan chased him along the narrow alley. The kid veered behind the shop . . . and went flying as his boots slid in snow-dusted mud.

Morgan tackled the boy, grabbed him by the front of his parka, and put him up against the wall. The kid struggled. He struggled quite well, actually, suggesting there was an athletic build under that bulky parka. Not that it did any good. Morgan might not be a fighter, but he was a werewolf, with a werewolf's strength. As the boy struggled, Morgan took a better look at him. Acne-pocked cheeks. Short dark hair. Sullen expression. Maybe sixteen, even seventeen.

"Who told you to slash my tires?" Morgan said.

"No one. I don't like strangers."

"So you just slashed my tires and my friends' for kicks? And broke into our motel rooms for fun?"

The kid hadn't denied that he was the vandal. He didn't deny this, either—didn't even seem to pause to wonder how Morgan knew. Clearly not someone with a lot of criminal experience. Or a lot of brains.

"I was looking for money," the boy said. "You city folks always have money."

"You left fifty bucks in my bag. My minibar wasn't even opened. You were hunting for something specific. And someone gave you key cards to find it."

Now the kid started thinking. And looking worried. "I-I don't know what you're talking about."

"My door wasn't broken. My friends' door wasn't broken. Those motel doors close and lock automatically, meaning whoever came in used a key card, which he could only get from someone who worked there. Someone who does gave you those cards, probably the same someone who told you to break in, and told you what to look for."

"N-no. I found your card. It was . . ." He looked around. "In the snow. You must have dropped it."

"And my friends dropped theirs, but both magically reappeared in our pockets later." Morgan shook his head. "How about you tell that story to my friends. See what they think of it." Morgan flipped the kid around and grabbed the back of his jacket. "Walk."

The kid took two stumbling steps, as if trying to figure out his next move. Morgan was giving him a helpful shove when a figure walked out from the alley.

"Thought I heard voices," the man said. "What's going on here?"

Another man joined him. Both were about Morgan's age, big and burly. One wore an old Werewolves football jacket. They bore down on Morgan, coming close enough for him to smell last night's beer on their breath.

"You like little boys?" asked the guy in the team jacket.

"Only ones who slash my tires and break into my motel room."

The guy leaned right into Morgan's face and he continued to hold on to the kid. "You made a mistake."

"Um, no, I—"

"Yeah, you did. Now let him go."

Morgan paused. "All right. I will. At the police station. They can settle this. If he didn't do it, I'll even apologize."

A third guy had appeared. Middle-aged. Hanging back, watching, uncertain. When Morgan tried to nudge the kid forward, the guy in the team jacket grabbed the boy and thrust him toward the older man.

"Bill? Take Jason home. Blake and I will handle this."

"Handle what?" Morgan said, voice rising as Bill led the boy around the corner. "I didn't hurt the kid. I chased him and cornered him, and now I want to take him to the police station to straighten this out. You can escort us there if you'd like."

The guy in the team jacket took a swing. Morgan saw it coming and ducked. He backed up.

"Look, maybe you don't like outsiders accusing town kids of committing crimes, but this isn't the way to handle—"

The other guy—Blake—swung. Morgan managed to dodge again, only to come up straight into Team Jacket's fist. Apparently they weren't interested in handling this properly. Not when the alternative gave these two thugs a chance to beat the crap out of a stranger.

Morgan fought back. He wasn't completely inept. And he had the advantage of strength, so it wasn't nearly as humiliating as it would be against a couple of werewolves. He managed to land a hard right to the side of Blake's head. The guy dropped. Team Jacket charged. Morgan grabbed him by the coat, threw him aside, and raced for the alley.

He rounded the corner to find himself facing a small mob headed by a middle-aged Latino woman.

"What did you do to my boy?" she demanded.

"Boy?" He looked toward the street. The guy with the kid was gone. "If that was your son, I apologize for chasing him, but he broke into—"

"That wasn't her son," one of the men snapped. "She's Ricky's mom."

Ricky? Shit. The missing kid. Ricky Rivera.

Morgan backed up, hands lifted. "I didn't do anything to anyone. I just got here the night before last. I—"

Team Jacket charged Morgan. He stepped aside and the guy went flying. As Morgan turned, someone in the mob took a swing. An awkward swing, from someone even less accustomed to fighting than him. He managed to catch the guy's arm and throw him down. Then he wheeled to find Mrs. Rivera in his path again.

"Are you going to attack me, too?" she asked.

"I haven't attacked anyone," he said, struggling to keep the snarl from his voice. "I've defended myself against a bunch of—" He swallowed the last words. Insulting the locals really wouldn't help. "Just take me to the police station and I'll explain—"

Two men jumped Morgan from behind. He went down, face-first in the muddy snow, his attackers piling onto his back.

"You'll explain now," Mrs. Rivera said. "I don't trust that lady cop—"

"This isn't the way you folks want to handle this," said a distant voice, growing closer. "Whatever you think of Jess Dales, Maria, she's the chief of police here. I'm going to take this man to the station and let them handle it."

The mob parted. A hand reached down to help Morgan up. He took it.

22. ELENA

*A*s we were walking away from the diner, a police cruiser pulled into the lot. We waited as Officer Kent got out.

"Fueling up before tackling that list the chief gave you?" I said as he approached.

"What list?"

"Of the guys living off the grid around here. I heard her mention it last night when we stopped by the station. She said you and Officer Jaggerman were checking on all the names this morning."

We stepped aside for an elderly couple exiting the diner.

"Right," Kent said. "No. She changed her mind. Has me running errands today."

We said goodbye and headed for the road.

"So," I said, "Chief Dales just happened to leave that list where we'd see it and then decided not to follow up on it? And a woman just happened to cancel the car service that could have let us leave Westwood this morning?"

"She's getting free help," Clay said.

I glanced over.

"I bet she's found out you're a journalist," he said. "Looked you up online and saw you've covered missing persons cases in Canada. Hoped maybe you'd decide to do some investigative reporting as long as you're stuck here. Doesn't seem like the local cops are exactly homicide experts."

"But she runs the risk that I *will* write an article, and that it won't exactly be complimentary to the Westwood PD."

He shrugged. "Maybe she's hoping negative publicity would boost the budget. Get her some decent cops. Or maybe she's just making a very stupid mistake. She's young."

"Either way, we should have that chat with her. Coach Hanlon can wait."

We arrived at the station to find Officer Jaggerman behind the counter.

"Chief's out on the case," he said.

"Do you know when she'll—?" I began.

An officer I hadn't met walked in from the back room, cordless phone in hand. He went over to Jaggerman.

"Just got a call," he said. "There's a disturbance over behind the old feed store."

"Disturbance?" Jaggerman said.

"Couple guys going at it."

Jaggerman snorted and waved him off. "Cabin fever. Let 'em duke it out." He turned back to me. "No, I don't know when she'll be back. I tried her cell a few minutes ago and she wasn't answering. When she calls, I'll let her know you're looking for her."

Clay and I returned to the motel. I'd left a note for Morgan to join us for breakfast, and hoped he hadn't headed there while we were in the station. It looked like he might have—he didn't answer when I rapped on his door.

"Could be sleeping," Clay said. "You know what Noah and Reese are like. If they don't have school, they sleep until noon, and it takes a bullhorn to wake them up."

Morgan was likely past that stage, but I didn't say so. Clay would just snort that he still acted that age. He didn't. But, sadly, you reach that point in life where anyone under the age of thirty seems like a kid.

We went to the motel office. The elderly clerk sat behind the desk reading the newspaper. I approached as Clay hung back.

"Our friend in room six isn't answering his door. Could you ring his room for me?"

The clerk didn't look up from his paper. "He checked out."

I frowned. "Are you sure? He's—"

"Young guy? Long hair? Indian?"

Close enough, I supposed, given that the old guy's glasses were on his desktop instead of his nose. I thanked him and we headed for our room. When Clay opened the door, I saw the note shoved under it.

I'd better be moving on. Sorry for any trouble I caused. Thanks for helping me out. I owe you.

Clay read the note over my shoulder, then he walked down the sidewalk to Morgan's room. He snapped the lock and opened the door.

I walked into the empty room, looking and sniffing.

"No scent except his," I murmured. "Same for the note. It smells like him. No one else." I paused. "He's gone, then."

"I'm sorry, darling."

I nodded, wadded the note, and pitched it into the trash.

All day, we'd had no luck tracking down Chief Dales. Or Coach Hanlon. It'd be dark soon, so we decided to hike back to the cabin to take another look around. We were close enough to see it when we noticed footprints coming from the forest, deep ones, quickly filling with new snow.

"Someone else headed this way not too long ago," I said as I crouched beside a print. "Small prints made with heavy boots. A kid?"

"Any scent?" Clay asked.

I shook my head. "Too much snow."

"Follow the trail, then."

A few feet farther, we found a sprung bear trap, tracks leading up to it then moving past. Looking closer, I saw holes in the snow by each footstep. Someone poking a walking stick into the snow. Someone who knew about the traps.

We'd almost reached the cabin when Clay stopped, head tilted. "Hear that?"

It took a second, then I caught a voice on the breeze.

"Someone talking?" I said.

"Sounds more like chanting."

The sound came from the other side of the cabin. We crept to the building, then paused. Definitely chanting. Not in English, either.

I snuck along the side of the cabin, then peered around it to see a circle cleared in the snow. Candles burned at each of the compass points. A woman knelt in the ritual circle, her back to us. Her hood was down, dark hair spilling out over her navy parka.

"Looks like we found Chief Dales," Clay whispered.

"And we found our witch."

23.

*I*f there were commandments for Alphas, the first would be "Thou shalt be decisive." When I'd first been bitten—and for years afterward—I'd mistaken Jeremy's decisiveness for narrow-mindedness. He never seemed to weigh options. He never even seemed to *see* options. When presented with a problem, he'd tell us how to handle it and that was that, as if there was only one possible solution. Of course, that wasn't true at all. If Jeremy and I have anything in common, it is that we see too many solutions—every way that a situation could be handled—and we agonize over the choice, knowing none are perfect.

The trick, as Alpha, is to *act* otherwise. To follow the Alpha's commands wholeheartedly, Pack wolves must believe those commands. Kind of like a cult, if you think about it, but when I jokingly mentioned that to Clay once, I got an hour-long lecture on cult dynamics versus Pack mentality. He was right. Werewolves don't obey because we're brainwashed into thinking our leader is all-powerful—we obey because the wolf in us is most comfortable following a strong leader.

So I needed to decide what to do about our spell-casting chief of police. Clay would march out there and confront her. Which is why, as he'd be the first to admit, he'd make a lousy Alpha. The problem is that, sometimes, I wish I had a little more of that decisiveness. Instead, I stood behind the cabin, shivering in the cold, as I replayed everything we'd discovered, all our interactions with Chief Dales and what they could mean, in light of our new discovery.

Then I texted Paige. I sent her the chief's name and a photo, and asked if she had any record of her. The Coven records aren't nearly as good as the Pack's dossiers. I could take some pride in that—I've been in charge of the dossiers for almost twenty years. But I need to track only a few dozen werewolves, not hundreds of witches. And, let's be honest, on a per capita basis, my guys are a whole lot more likely to get into the kind of trouble where I *need* to track them down, fast.

It took Paige only a few minutes to report that there was no Jessica Dales in her database, which only meant Dales hadn't been caught causing trouble before. There were a couple of witch families in the area, but most non-Coven ones had forgone their matrilineal system, meaning surnames were often useless. There had not, however, been any reported cases of witches practicing rituals requiring human sacrifice in upstate New York. Which, again, might only mean they hadn't been caught.

As I weighed all this, Dales started packing up and made my mind up for me. I walked around to the back of the cabin.

"Hey, Jess," I said. "Can I call you that? Jess? Or do you prefer Jessica?"

She jumped. "Oh, Ms. Michaels. I didn't hear—"

"You don't need to do that out here," I said, pointing at the almost-obliterated circle. "You can, if it helps for mental preparation, but that whole at-one-with-nature thing is just window dressing. You can perform rituals anywhere. I have a friend who can help you with that. Paige Winterbourne? Maybe you've heard of her. Her mother led the American Coven. Do you know them?"

As I chattered, I watched her expression. One, for signs she had no idea what I was talking about. Two, for signs she was shocked that *I* was talking about it. When I saw neither, it answered a whole lot of questions.

"I know you're a witch," I said. "What concerns me more is that I just started talking about covens and councils, and you aren't wondering how the hell I know all that."

"Which means you know what *we* are," Clay said.

He'd stepped out behind her. When he spoke, she wheeled and stepped back. She stopped herself, but that reaction erased any doubts.

"You've known since you called me, haven't you?" I said. "You figured out what Morgan was, and when you found my name on his map, you called me to come and take care of it. Get him off your turf. Fast."

"I-I don't—" She cleared her throat and came back stronger. "I don't know what you're talking about. Covens? Councils? Witches? I was waiting for the punch line."

"So you don't know what we are?"

"Besides crazy?"

I took a step toward her. She struggled not to shrink back.

"If you *did* know and you admitted it, we could work something out. I'm all for coexisting. But when people know what we are and pretend they don't, that's a problem. And we're very good at taking care of our problems. Which you'd know, if you knew what we are."

A pause, one so long I swore an inch of snow fell before she answered. "Let's talk."

"Good. We'll go inside."

She shook her head. "It's not my place. I just come here now that Charlie's gone. With all the traps, I know no one will bother me."

"We can open the door. As you said, he's not here."

She hesitated.

"Which would be illegal," I said. "Trespassing. Break and enter. That's not what you're thinking, though. You're a little more concerned about what we'll see inside. All those predators. Especially the wolves. Someone really likes wolves."

"That's Charlie, and it's completely unconnected to . . ." She glanced at us, then nodded. "Let's go inside." She paused. "And it's Jess. You can call me Jess."

"Yes, I know what you are," Jess said after we were inside the cabin. "And who you are. I didn't make the connection when I called you because everyone says the stories about your . . . group living near here are just rumors. Obviously not. I figured it out when you guys showed up, which also explained the issue with your friend. After that, I just wanted you to get the hell out of town. No offense."

"None taken." I took a seat in Charlie's living room. "I can understand why you'd want us gone, preferably before we found a dead body. Sadly, that didn't quite work out."

She stared at me. "What? You think—? Shit! Of course you do." She paced to the window, struggling to control her breathing, then turned. "I have nothing to do with that body. Witches don't sacrifice people. I thought you'd know that."

"They do for protection rituals," I said. "High-level magic like that requires a life given for a life protected."

"I protect myself with this." She opened her parka to show her gun. "And I protect my town with this." She gestured at her badge. "That body you found was partially eaten. And not by scavengers. Doc said he found human teeth marks on the bones. That made me think it might be one of yours. We've also had drifters go missing, which could mean we have one of you guys living out here. I know your . . . group is supposed to handle problems like that, which is why I called you to the station last night and left you that list."

"And stopped us from leaving today?"

"What?"

"A woman called and canceled our car repair this morning."

"That wasn't me," she said.

"You're the only one who knew."

"No, lots of people know. They saw the car. They asked us if you guys were okay. We said Jim was swinging by this morning to fix it."

"So someone slashed our tires to strand us here and then canceled our repair to keep us here?"

She finally took a seat across from me. "I presumed the tire slashing was just kids. We have a few idiots. Well, more than a few. It's a small town. They get bored. They know better than to lash out at locals, but strangers are fair game. I don't understand the mechanic call, though." She looked around. "And where's your friend?"

"He left."

She frowned. "How? I saw his car at the diner this morning. It wasn't going anywhere."

"Hitchhiked to the highway, I guess. Morgan's not one of ours. He was just coming out to visit us and, apparently, after everything that happened, decided to push on instead. But speaking of the diner, did the server tell you Morgan was drunk the other night?"

"Sure. Marnie said he had three, four whiskeys with dinner."

"Did you test him?"

She shook her head. "I couldn't charge the guy with public drunkenness after all that time."

"He wasn't drunk. He said he didn't have a single drink, and we'd have smelled it on him even the next morning. Your server lied."

"Why?"

"Answering that is your job, isn't it?" Clay drawled.

She looked at him, seemed to consider responding, then decided I was the safer conversationalist and turned her attention back to me.

"Also, if your coroner found human teeth marks on that body, it wasn't one of us. You'd have found teeth marks like those." I gestured at a wolf skull on the shelf. "Which means you have the kind of problem we can't help you with. And . . ." I rose and walked to the shelf with the three human skulls on it. "This middle one? It's new. It's been boiled, so I don't think you'll get DNA off it, but it's a pretty sure bet it belongs to Ricky Rivera."

"What?" She scrambled up and stared at the skull. She looked ill and I cursed myself for being so flippant. She'd known Ricky. She'd doubtless come to know him even better in the months she'd been searching for him.

"I'm sorry," I said.

She tore her attention from the middle skull and her gaze tripped over the whole trio. "No. That's not . . . Charlie wouldn't have . . . There's no way you can tell that from a skull."

"We found the rest of the body. Minus a skull. Also minus a hand, like our dead drifter. There are some finger bones there." I pointed at the bookcase. "We found more in a cave. We'll show you that, too. Before we do, though, tell us about Charlie."

24.

*J*ess started the same way as the couple from the diner. Charlie was a town legend, dating back before her time— the young man who'd gone off to see the world, come back, taken a wife, and settled down. The couple had said he'd been just a normal guy until his wife's death, but Jess told a different version.

"I think people forget," she said. "Or they rework the past to make a better story. I arrived shortly before his wife died, and he was already a little off. According to everyone I talked to, he'd always been that way."

"Off?"

"Eccentric, I should say. Not dangerous. Not ever . . ." She looked back at the skull, then away. "Some of this was here even before Susan died. Certainly the books. That's what he did abroad. He taught history to make a living, but his real passion was for traveling and gathering stories. Folklore. Myth. Whatever you call it."

"Ritualistic magic," Clay said.

Again, she looked over, as if surprised to hear him speak, and she nodded, before turning back to me.

"Yes, ritualistic magic. From all over the world. That's what drew me to him when I moved here. I heard a few things, and I wondered if he was a supernatural. So I asked about his interests. We became friends, of a sort. No one else was interested in his hobby, not even his wife and stepson. No one around here seemed to understand. It was just . . ."

"Weird," I said.

She nodded. "But it was purely an academic interest. He collected some of this, but he didn't do anything with it. He didn't try the rituals. He just learned about them. Until Susan passed away."

"His wife," I said. "How did she die?"

"Cancer. No foul play there. It was quick. Three months after the diagnosis she was gone. But during those three months . . ." She waved around. "That's when it went from books and memorabilia to all this. The skulls, the skins. He became obsessed with animals."

"Predators."

She blinked, as if she hadn't seen the connection. After a look around the room, she nodded. "Yes, predators, I guess."

"And the traps?"

"That came later. After the fight with his stepson."

"Coach Hanlon."

"Right. Don't ask me what it was about. No one knew. Just a big blowout that pushed Charlie completely off the rails. That's when he started living out here permanently, set up the traps, and told the rest of the world to go to hell. Even me."

Charlie Lacoste was still out here. He was probably even coming home every now and then, to add to his collection. He might be living in the cave, the smoke covering his scent. If my theory was right, he'd *become* his obsession—become a predator. A wild beast living in the forest, feeding on whatever he could catch. Including Ricky Rivera.

The sun was setting, and we were on the cabin steps when Jess got a call. She looked at her cell phone and winced.

"Mrs. Rivera," she said. "Always fun." With a deep breath, she answered.

I don't know if she realized we had super-hearing—her knowledge of werewolves seemed to be a little scattered—but she retreated into the cabin to talk. I managed to catch a few words. Something about a man who'd been arrested, and there might be a connection to her son's disappearance. Mrs. Rivera was calling to demand more information. Jess seemed to have no idea what she was talking about. A moment later, she came out.

"Well, it seems your friend Morgan didn't take off after all," she said. "According to Mrs. Rivera, he was caught going after one of our teens."

"What?" I said. "No. He wouldn't . . ." I glanced at Clay. "Our tire-slasher. I bet he spotted the kid." I turned back to Jess. "Clay and Morgan chased our vandal yesterday and lost him in the woods. Morgan must have seen him again and gone after him."

"I figured it was something like that. I tried to tell her yesterday that he couldn't have taken Ricky. It seems she's convinced that he took him and has come back for more. Because, if you're going to grab teenage boys, this is the only town that has them." She rolled her eyes.

"So what happened?" I asked.

"A flash mob," she said. "And not the sort that breaks out in song. I don't think they'd have done anything, but luckily, it never came to that. The voice of reason appeared, in the form of our football coach, who has more than his share of experience mediating when testosterone takes over. Mrs. Rivera said he took Morgan to the station. We'll get this straightened out. But you really need to keep your friend on a tighter leash." She glanced sharply at Clay. "No pun intended."

He only grunted.

She phoned the station to see what was going on.

"Yep, he's here," Jaggerman's voice came through the cell. "Coach thought this was the safest place for him. I figured we'd hold him until everyone settles down. I'll turn him loose."

"No," Jess said. "Tempers are probably still a little raw. I'll bring his friends down to make sure he gets out safely."

"I don't think that's nec—"

"Better safe than sorry. Just hold him until we get there."

A pause. "Not sure I'm comfortable with that, Chief. Doesn't it violate his civil liberties or something?"

"No, we can hold him for up to twenty-four hours. I'll be there as soon as I can."

"Where are you? I thought I saw your Jeep over by the woods."

"You did. I got a report of a second body. It might be . . ." She trailed off. "I don't want to say too much. Just hold tight and let Wes know what's going on. I'll call if I find anything."

We took Jess to see the grove with the pelts and tree markings first. She said she'd seen other trees with the markings elsewhere, and presumed they were Charlie's. The pelts, though, were new, and she had no idea what they meant.

We had a good idea where to find the body—I'd made note of the coordinates. As we approached, I noticed Clay slowing. Hesitating.

"Wrong turn?" I whispered as Jess trailed behind us.

"Thought I heard something. Wind's blowing the wrong way, though." He took another step, then lifted his hand, telling me to hold on while he investigated.

After a moment, he waved me forward. When Jess tried to follow, he put up his hand to stop her.

"Like hell," she said. "I'm the one wearing a badge here and—"

I gave her a look. Should I admit I was shocked when it actually worked? Maybe I was getting better at this Alpha thing. Or maybe that look just reminded her that I could rip that badge from her chest . . . and take her heart with it.

I crept over to Clay. He motioned for me to peer through the branches. When I did, I saw a figure in a parka heading for the body. A police parka.

"Kent," I whispered.

Jess had told Jaggerman to notify him. I should have said something then, warned her that we'd seen Kent taking way too much personal interest in the first corpse. Now it was obvious he wasn't just a creep with a camera. He was heading straight to the hidden body. Moving fast. Getting rid of the evidence.

I looked at Jess. She'd walked a few steps closer. I glanced toward Kent, then motioned for her to approach quietly. By the time she made it, Kent was crouching by the evergreen that sheltered the body. No time to explain. Well, yes, there was time, but I wasn't taking the chance that she'd blurt something and startle him. Instead, as she waited for an explanation, I motioned Clay around the other way. He took off.

I whispered, "Someone's there," and pointed to the spot where she could look through the branches. As she bent, I left her there and headed for Kent.

"I think you should let the chief handle that," I said as I walked up behind the crouched figure.

He jumped and turned and I saw his face. Not Kent. Jaggerman. He looked at me, then to the left, where Clay blocked his escape.

"What the hell is going on here?" Jess said as she strode over. "Phil."

"I, uh, had a report. Must have been the same one you got."

"She got that from us," I said. "We were leading her here."

"Then someone else must have found the body, too. I got a tip."

"Right after I said I was heading out here?" Jess said.

As Jaggerman continued backpedaling, it became very apparent why this career cop had been passed over for the chief's job. He was an idiot.

I let Jess handle it while Clay and I blocked Jaggerman's retreat. When he didn't even try to make a break for it, I started doing some logistical figuring.

"You weren't at the police station when Chief Dales called, were you?" I said. "You were already out here. Which means you have the station phone forwarded to your cell."

"I . . . No, I got the call, then I—"

"Put on your jet pack to beat us here?" I took a step toward him. "Where's Morgan?"

He paused, then managed a weak, "Who?"

Clay was on Jaggerman so fast he didn't have time to squeak before he was up against a tree, suspended by his shirtfront.

"Hey!" Jess said. "That's my—"

"Where's Morgan?" Clay said.

"I don't know who—"

"The guy you supposedly took into custody."

"Oh, right. He's, um . . . I let him go." He looked at Jess. "I know you said not to, but I really felt I should. He was threatening lawsuits and—"

"You weren't at the station when she called," I said. "We've already established that. The only reason you were so damned determined to release Morgan was because you never had him in the first place, did you? Which means . . ." I looked at Jess. "Mrs. Rivera said Coach Hanlon took Morgan."

Coach Hanlon. Charlie's stepson.

I closed in on Jaggerman, pinned against the tree by Clay. "Where is Morgan?"

When he started to protest, Clay leaned in and whispered in his ear. I was standing too far back to hear more than a few words, but when Jaggerman's gaze shot to the tree sheltering the corpse, the message was clear. *Tell us or you'll end up like that.*

"Jess?" Jaggerman said in a strangled voice. "You know me. I've worked with you for years. I'm a good cop. I—"

"Tell him where his friend is," Jess said. "Or I need to start a search party for the man, which means I'll have to ask *him* to escort you to the police station."

Jaggerman's jaw worked. Then he swallowed and said, "He's at the cave."

25.

 $\mathcal{W}$ e didn't get within a hundred feet of the cave before we found at least a half dozen sets of footprints, tramping through the new snow to the cave. The sun had set, so it was dark enough for us to creep around unseen, but the wind had died and the forest had gone so still that even our feet crunching in the snow echoed. We started walking in the other prints, which helped a little.

As we drew close, though, it became increasingly apparent there was no need for stealth. The cave was dark and silent. We crept near the bushes blocking the entrance. I could detect scents, but they were coming from the ground, nothing in the air.

Clay pushed through and disappeared into the cave.

"Empty," Clay called back, his voice echoing.

I went in. There were fresh marks on the floor and walls. Fresh blood. Not enough to be worrying, but I definitely smelled Morgan. Coach Hanlon, too, along with a few scents I didn't recognize. All male.

The strongest odor wasn't from a living thing. The cave stunk of a mishmash of scents that reminded me of Paige's teas. She made some for healing, some for protection, and some just for sleeping. I thought I detected a note from the sleeping brews. There was more, though. A lot more.

"Psilocybin mushrooms," Clay said as he lifted a couple of pieces from the floor. "Hallucinogens."

I didn't joke about how he knew what they were. The only way we can get Clay to take pain meds before being stitched up is if

Jeremy threatens to leave him unstitched. He doesn't like anything messing with his brain. He'd know what the mushrooms were because they were used in Central American religious rituals.

"I smell something like sleeping brew, too," I said. "That implies sedatives. But sedatives plus hallucinogens?"

"Drowsiness could accelerate hallucinations. Doesn't matter. Point is, Morgan was here and now he's not. We have a trail to follow."

Following that trail was easy. In fact, if I hadn't been so intent on *listening* for someone in the cave, I'd have noticed the footprints leading away from it sooner.

I did look for signs that someone—like Morgan—had been carried or dragged away. I didn't see any.

Admittedly, I'm about as straight edge as Clay when it comes to drugs. As screwed up as my teen years were, I'd never resorted to pharmacological or alcoholic escape routes. I'd grown up thinking my brain was my only ticket out of that crappy life and, like Clay, I did nothing to mess with that. But surely a guy on hallucinogens wouldn't just trudge along with the group.

We followed the trail into the forest. Deep into it, to the point where even the moon wasn't much help, barely piercing the thick tree cover. That's when my cell phone rang. It was Jess, who'd stayed behind to deal with Jaggerman. The reception was crappy and her voice kept cutting out. I caught a few words, like "football" and "ritual."

"You mean the football coach?" I said. "He's conducting a ritual?" I'd already figured that part out.

"Drugged . . ." she said. "Night . . ."

Yep, figured that out, too.

"What are they doing?" I said. "Who are we up against and what do they have planned?"

Static.

"Can you text me the details?" I said.

Silence. I checked my phone. The signal had disappeared. It came back at one bar for a second, only to vanish again. I typed a text message repeating my request and sent it.

We'd been walking as I'd talked, and I'd kept my voice as low as I could. When I stopped speaking, though, we picked up voices. Faint ones, distant enough that we didn't need to worry about how much noise we made. We picked up our pace and strained to listen as we jogged toward them.

Then the voices went quiet. We slowed. A gun fired, and we dropped to a crouch. Shouts followed. We froze, listening and straining to see.

Clay pointed and I picked up the faintest glimmer of a flashlight. Another shot sounded.

"There it is!" a man's voice bellowed. "A wolf or a bear. Did you see it, boys?"

Something crashed through the woods. More voices. Excited now. Cries of "I saw it!" and "There it is!" They were at least a couple of hundred feet away, so it couldn't be *us* they'd seen.

I looked at Clay.

"No idea, darling," he whispered.

I carefully stepped from behind the tree and peered around. I could see flashlights waving about and hear more crashing through the undergrowth. Then Morgan's scent slipped past on a breeze.

That snapped me back. It didn't matter *what* they were doing, only that they had Morgan. I held on to his scent as I started forward. We moved from tree to tree, all the while listening to the shouts and cries. There were other noises, too, as we got closer. Snarls and grunts. Human, though; I could tell by the tenor.

I lost Morgan's scent once, but found it again and we began circling wide, staying away from the noise. Gradually, as we got closer, the two separated, the cacophony to my left, Morgan's scent to my right. We crept in Morgan's direction.

Finally, I could tell where he was. In a cluster of trees. Staying in place, if his scent was right. I started motioning for Clay to go around and then stopped and told him to stay where he was. I'd circle. The noise was far enough to our left that he didn't argue.

I rounded the cluster of trees. I got just north of it when I heard the soft thump of feet running through the snow. I turned to see Morgan racing toward me. He was holding his hands in front of him and there was a gray strip over his mouth. Before I could say a word, he lunged and slammed into me. We both went down.

By the time Clay came running, I was sitting on the ground, pulling at the cord binding Morgan's hands. It wasn't easy. He kept struggling, his voice muffled against the gag. Clay grabbed him by the collar and I got his hands free. Morgan ripped off the duct tape over his mouth, hissing at the pain, then whispering, "Down!" to Clay, then to me, "Get down!"

As I motioned for us to move to the cluster of trees, dry branches crackled and snow crunched. A figure lurched into view. It was a teenage boy, staggering and stumbling. I shot to my feet.

"No!" Morgan said, but I was already running.

The boy stopped and stared at me with unfocused eyes.

"It's okay," I whispered as I got close. "We're—"

With a snarl, he swung something. I saw it coming and ducked just in time. It hit my shoulder, the blow barely penetrating my jacket. The boy pounced. He hit me full on. I staggered back, and I would have been fine if I hadn't slipped on something—a rock or a log—and lost my balance. I went down with him on top of me.

The boy tried to pin me by the shoulders. I saw a flash of teeth as his open mouth shot for my neck.

He's trying to bite me.

I grabbed the boy and held him off. Then Clay was behind him, hands on his jacket, whipping him up in the air. As the boy hung there, he gnashed his teeth and spat and snarled like a wild beast.

He swung something again. A club, I realized as I snatched it from him. A police baton.

Morgan slapped his duct tape over the kid's mouth. The boy continued to struggle and growl.

"I think we know where those hallucinogens went," Clay muttered.

"They're drugged," Morgan said. "They gave me something, too. A sedative, I think. Same as I was dosed with the first night I got here."

"Are you okay?"

"Woozy. They underestimated the dose." It takes a lot to knock out a werewolf. "And I know what it is this time, so I can fight it."

Still holding the struggling boy, Clay looked toward the noises on our left. "How many are there?"

"Minus this one? The coach and four players."

"Players?" I said. "Football?"

"It's some kind of—"

At a noise to our left, Morgan stopped and we all looked over. Everything had gone quiet. I tried to pick up a scent, but the wind was blowing the wrong way. A twig cracked. Then snow squeaked underfoot. I pointed in the direction of the sounds.

"Circling us," Clay said.

I took hold of the boy and sent Clay to investigate. Morgan followed. I glanced at the kid. Just a regular teenage boy. My height. Muscular. Wearing a team jacket.

A football player, Morgan had said. Why would the coach be drugging—?

A shot fired. Clay grabbed Morgan and knocked him down. I did the same with the boy. When he kept struggling, I dragged him over and tied his hands with the cord they'd used on Morgan. I peered over at Morgan and Clay. They were still on the ground, crawling backward toward us.

"One shooter," Clay murmured when he was close enough. "Over there." He pointed to where he'd been heading.

"It's the coach," Morgan whispered. "The kids have clubs. The coach has a rifle. He was shooting at me to get me to run."

"Hunting you?" I said.

He nodded. I'd experienced something like that before, years ago, a guy who'd captured and hunted supernaturals.

"Does he know what you are?" I whispered.

Morgan shook his head. "I don't think so. He kept talking about wolves and bears and predators, but he didn't seem to get the connection."

"Any sign of magic?"

"It's definitely some sort of ritual. That's what they were doing in the cave. The coach brought the kids there. He took me outside before they arrived, so they couldn't see me, but I could hear enough to figure out what was going on. He gave them something to drink. It sounded like they'd done it before—no one asked what was going on. Then he started leading them in some kind of vision quest. All this mumbo jumbo about how they were mighty hunters and—"

My phone vibrated. It didn't ring, but the vibration sounded so loud that I hit Ignore.

"The police chief?" Morgan said, leaning over.

I nodded. "I'm going to text her the coordinates and—"

A shot whizzed past.

"Boys!" a voice yelled. "Over here. I've got it cornered."

It. Why did they keep saying . . . ? Didn't matter, as Clay would say. He prairie-dog-popped up from the bushes, for a quick peek, then pointed and mouthed, "Hundred feet."

Damn. Unlike the kids, Hanlon was obviously good at sneaking through the forest. Our whispers must have been carrying more than we thought. Judging by that shot, he knew exactly where we were.

I signaled a plan. Then I went north, and Clay headed south. Hanlon kept shouting for the boys, which made him very easy to track. He wasn't moving anyway. Just standing there, yelling. We crept in until we could see each other on either side of Hanlon. Then Clay charged.

As Clay took Hanlon down, I heard Morgan shout. Then I caught the snarl and snap and pound of a running pack. Clay pinned Hanlon as Morgan raced over.

"They're—" he started.

The boys appeared. Four of them, running together, howling and waving their batons.

"Get it, boys!" Hanlon shouted. "It's the bear. Get it!"

The first one charged Morgan. I caught a whiff of the boy's scent and recognized him as the vandal who'd slashed our tires and broken into our rooms. Morgan tried to swing around to face him, but he stumbled. I swooped in, grabbed the kid by the arm, and threw him back with the others.

"It's a pack," Hanlon yelled. "You stumbled into a pack of bears. Kill them! Before they attack!"

The boys rushed us. I kicked one away. Morgan body-slammed another.

"We're not bears," I said. "We're people. *Look* harder. *Listen*."

The sound of my voice made them hesitate. That's why Hanlon had gagged Morgan—so nothing would disrupt the illusion. They hung there, clutching their cudgels, eyes struggling to focus.

"You've been drugged," I said. "You're confused. But we're talking. That means we're people. Just like you."

"No!" Hanlon yelled. "They're monsters. That's what we've been hunting. I thought it was bears, but it's monsters. Look over there." He pointed at the fifth boy, the one we'd bound and gagged, stumbling toward them. "It's Bryan. They caught him and they were going to kill him, just like they killed Ricky. You remember what happened to Ricky? The bear got him. We were hunting and it—"

Clay slammed Hanlon's face into the snow.

"Thank you," I said. "Now, boys, you're confused. You know you are. But we're here to help. You're from Westwood, New York. You're on the football—"

A hiss of pain behind me. I turned to see Hanlon with a knife. Clay let go just long enough for Hanlon to rise. Clay grabbed the back of his jacket, but Hanlon was wrenching down the zipper as I raced over.

Hanlon got free of his jacket and started to run. We went after him. The boys went after him, too. They barreled past me, shoving me aside. I thought they were running with him. Then I saw their faces and heard their snarls and realized what they saw— running prey.

They pounced on their coach, beating and biting as he fought and screamed.

26.

*S*o it wasn't an actual ritual," Morgan said as we sat at the police station. "Just a mishmash?"

"It's not an uncommon belief," Clay said as I bandaged his arm. "Imbibing the strength of your enemy."

"By literally imbibing *them*?" Morgan shook his head. "I hope those kids never find out what they did."

"They won't if their parents can help it," I said.

"What a mess," Morgan said, shaking his head. "A crazy, fucked-up mess."

It was indeed a mess, one that Jessica Dales and the town of Westwood would be digging out from under for a very long time.

Jess had kept us informed as she questioned Hanlon and Jagger-man, and we'd pieced together what we could. It had started with Charlie Lacoste. Like most academics, he'd focused his attention on one specific area of interest. For him, it was rituals of consumption and transfer, whether it was drinking bear blood or eating your ene-mies in an attempt to appropriate their strength. It was, as Jess had said, strictly academic. That's where the fight with his stepson began. Charlie's wife got sick and Tom Hanlon somehow got it into his head that one of his stepfather's rituals might help—if not to save his mother, then at least to give her the strength to undergo treatment.

When Charlie refused to help, Hanlon had done his own research, and after his mother's death he became obsessed with what he'd learned. He came up with a new application for his obsession—using these rituals to help his football team win.

Yes, football. It didn't seem any less crazy than it had when we first discovered the connection. Even after Jess talked to Hanlon, it didn't make more sense. Somehow, it had to Jaggerman, the volunteer assistant coach who'd been his wingman in all this. And to Hanlon's girlfriend, Marnie, the server, who'd canceled our repair service. She was the one who'd drugged Morgan the other night at the diner and called Hanlon to say she'd found a victim.

That's who they targeted: drifters. Young men, strong and healthy. They set them loose in the forests with the key members of the football team, who'd been drugged and brainwashed into thinking they were still in the cave, imagining a vision where they were seeing animals, which they'd hunt and then, yes, partially eat, to imbibe their strength.

It had even seemed to work, taking a losing team to the state finals for the past three years running. I'd say it was the power of suggestion. When these boys came out of their drug-induced state, they knew only that they'd undergone a powerful magical ritual that made them better players. They believed it and so it worked. In those three years, four graduating players got a full college ride, several more got partial scholarships. I think it was hard for me to really comprehend the importance of that for a town like Westwood. For many of these kids, college had never been an option. Now it was.

There was the matter of town pride, too. I think I couldn't quite understand the importance of that, either. But I could see it, in the signs and the murals. They had a winning team; their children were winners; their town was a winner. That's what drew Jaggerman and Hanlon's girlfriend into the mad scheme.

It *was* mad, of course. Tom Hanlon was not a sane man. No one could be, to hatch such a plot. He'd almost certainly murdered his stepfather. From what we could tell, Charlie finally had figured out what his stepson was doing. That's when he vanished.

And Ricky Rivera? That might be the biggest tragedy of all. Hanlon implied he'd been killed by one of their victims. Maybe he had, but Hanlon said a few things later that made Jessica suspect Ricky's own teammates had done it. Ricky had been weak, Hanlon had ranted. They'd tried to include him, but the others "smelled weakness." I don't know if that's true. I only know that if it is, I hope to God those boys never remember it. And I hope to God the Riveras never learn the whole truth.

We were in Jess's office, Clay and I, Morgan outside with Kent, so shell-shocked he really wasn't much help. There was no sign he'd played any role in what happened. If he had, I'm sure Jaggerman would have dragged him down with him. But why had he been taking photos? I wasn't asking, but I'd tell Jessica. She had to know he could be a problem.

"Are you going to be okay?" I asked.

She didn't answer, just sat there, drinking hot chocolate, staring into space. I asked again.

"I don't know," she said at last. "This is beyond . . . I've seen things. I've heard things. You know what it's like in our world. But this . . . I don't understand. I really do not understand."

"I don't think it helps to try," I said. "The state police or the FBI or someone will come in and take over and you just have to step back and let them. Protect your town. Protect the kids. They didn't do anything wrong."

"I know." She exhaled. "I have to question Jason, though—the boy who vandalized your vehicles. He searched your rooms, too, looking for information about you—he works at the motel sometimes. He was one of them."

"I know. I saw him."

She swallowed. "I'm hoping Hanlon just made up a story to get Jason to slash your tires and search your rooms, but . . . I don't know. Wouldn't the boy have thought it was odd if Morgan went missing after all that?"

"Maybe, maybe not. Hanlon seemed to have a real hold over them. He probably just fed him a really good story. Told him we were . . . I don't know, spies from a rival team? Faked Morgan's disappearance to upset the town and throw the team's game?"

"Football." She shook her head. "All this for football."

It was more than football, but as I'd said, it didn't help to figure out all of the motivations. Ultimately, what Hanlon, Jaggerman and Marnie did would always be incomprehensible.

"Question Jason," I said. "Question Hanlon *about* Jason. If the kid seems clean, keep a really close eye on him for a while. Just in case."

She nodded. "I will."

We left Jess to her work, with an invitation to call me if she needed to talk about anything on the case. Or if she had concerns about having the Pack living so close to her town. I gave her Paige's contact information, too, in case she wanted support from that angle.

Both cars had been repaired. We drove Morgan to his.

"Can I follow you guys to Stonehaven?" he said. "Or would you rather take a breather at home and I'll come by in a day or two?"

I twisted to look at him. "I thought you were leaving."

"I intended to. Then I changed my mind and came back, which is how I saw that kid and nearly got myself killed." He paused. "On second thought, maybe that's a sign."

"Only that you should have come to breakfast with us instead of taking off. Come for the weekend. The Sorrentinos are driving up tonight with the boys. It's not an official Meet, but a good way to observe the Pack in its natural habitat. As long as you don't mind the noise. Seven werewolves and two five-year-olds means a very chaotic household."

"As long as no one tries to kidnap or hunt me, I'm fine."

"Actually . . ." I glanced at Clay. "We can't guarantee that. But we will ask them to go easy on you."

We called Jeremy to tell him we were bringing Morgan. When we arrived, Morgan asked to head out back first, get a look at the property. Giving us time to say hi to the kids. I appreciated that, especially considering that our children seemed to have inherited some of Clay's "no strangers in my den" attitude.

Clay and I walked into the house and braced for shouts and pounding feet.

"We're home!" I called.

Silence.

"Hey!" Clay bellowed. "Anyone here?"

When no one answered, my heart started tripping. Ridiculous, I know. It's a big house. They could be in the back room, watching videos, or upstairs, Kate plugged into her iPod, Logan engrossed in a book.

I yelled again. Still nothing. I checked the garage. My car was there. So was Clay's.

I took a deep breath and went for the back door, moving fast. Clay didn't tell me I was being foolish—that Jeremy was with them, that this was our house, that nothing could possibly have happened. He knew it didn't matter. All I could think about was what had happened in Westwood. About those young men who'd passed through, lost young men, their families still waiting, hoping for a call, dreading a call.

Most of all, though, I thought of Ricky Rivera, the smiling boy in the photo, the horror of his death. I thought of his mother's rage, his father's quiet grief. I thought of that sign on their lawn. And I thought of that light. That single light, burning for the child who would never come home.

The back door was locked. As I fumbled with it, Clay reached over and pulled it open, then stuck his head out, shouting so loud it made my ears ring. I stepped outside. Morgan was in the yard. He turned to us, looking confused.

"Do you see—?" I began.

"Mommy!" a voice shouted behind me.

I turned as Kate thumped down the hall, dragging her foot. She launched herself and sent me smacking into the wall as I caught her.

"We were hiding," Logan said as he walked toward us. "You were supposed to come find us."

Of course. An old trick, one I should have guessed. In trying to take charge of the investigation, I hadn't shared much with Jeremy, certainly not enough for him to have any clue that I'd panic when the kids didn't come running.

When I didn't reply, Kate pulled back. "What's wrong, Mommy?"

I hugged her, as tight as I could. "Nothing," I whispered. "Nothing at all."

We couldn't be with our children all the time. But we could train them to look out for themselves. We'd already taken the first step last year, letting them know what we were. The door was open now, not to frighten them but to warn them, to make them aware of what it meant to be the children of the Pack.

I boosted Kate up onto my hip. "So I hear we're having company this weekend."

"Uncle Nick and Uncle Antonio and Reese and Noah."

"Maybe even Karl and Hope," Logan said. "Hope was talking to Jeremy and she said they have news. Special news. They might come up and tell all of us."

I glanced at Jeremy, beside Clay. He nodded. "Special news."

"Well, that does sound intriguing. We have another guest here, too. Someone I'd like you to meet. Come say hi."

With Kate still on my hip, I took Logan's hand, smiled at Clay and Jeremy, and led the kids to meet Morgan.

Angelic

ONE

*E*veryone needs a vacation now and then, and angels are no exception. It was a concept that seemed to elude the Fates. My annual stint as a celestial bounty hunter had been supposed to end last week, but complications had arisen, as they so often did. Retrieving hell-doomed souls and hunting down unruly demi-demons isn't a nine-to-five job.

But now I was finally finished. Kristof didn't know I was back yet, so I thought I'd get ready for our holiday trip and surprise him. I was looking in the mirror, making a few last-minute adjustments to my costume, when my house vanished and I found myself staring at a mosaic of a wedding, with lots of garlands, flowers, and flowing robes. The bride began to turn, so slowly it seemed a trick of the light. Over her head, a dove's wings moved, just a fraction. The mosaic of life—always changing, always the same. Deep.

I turned away from the wall and glowered into the white marble cavern that was the Fates' throne room.

"Hey!" I shouted. "I'm on vacation here!"

The floor began to move, as slowly as that damned mosaic. Atop the dais, a middle-aged woman with long, graying blond hair pumped a spinning wheel, gathering the thread as she wove. I clamped my mouth shut, not wanting to cut anyone's life unnecessarily short. She paid me no heed until she'd finished. Then she looked up and gaped at my low-cut, laced white bodice, skintight calfskin breeches, and knee-high boots.

"It's my vacation outfit," I said. "We're going to La Ceiba, so I have to look the part."

"La Ceiba?"

"The pirate town. Kris likes playing pirate." I paused. "Kris *really* likes—"

"Enough." The old Fate appeared, taking her sister's place. She had wiry gray hair, a bent back, and a shriveled face made even uglier by her perpetual scowl. "Wherever you're going, Eve, I hope *that's* not part of your costume."

She pointed a wizened finger at the four-foot angel sword slung across my back.

"Er, no. Of course not. That would be inappropriate."

Damn. Once I disenchanted the sword, I couldn't get it back until my next tour of duty. I pulled it off, the etched metal glowing, murmured a few words, and it vanished, replaced by a boring—if more thematically correct—scimitar.

"There," I said. "As I'm sure you already know, Trsiel and I finished the demi-demon contract. I've submitted my report. If there are any questions, he'd be happy to answer them. I'll see you ladies in six months—"

"We have another job for you."

I stared at her. She stared back.

"You forgot to flip the calendar again, didn't you?" I said. "I'm off duty. Technically, I was off duty last week, too. Not that I'm complaining . . ."

"You already did. Repeatedly."

The middle-aged Fate took over. "You'll get your break. As soon as you do this one last thing for us. A group of djinn have been tormenting people who summon them."

"Um, yeah, because that's what djinn do. According to the ancient treaty of something-or-other, they're allowed to toy with anyone who breaks the summoning contract. Screw them over, and they'll screw you back. Fair is fair."

The youngest Fate appeared—a pretty little girl with bright blond hair, so tiny she had to stand on tiptoes to see me over the spinning wheel. "Have some experience with that, Eve?"

"With the summoning contract, sure. That's what puts the *dark* in dark witch—we use whatever's available, including djinn. I was never stupid enough to break a contract."

"Neither were these people. They're supernaturals, too. Dark magic practitioners, like you, who know how to do such things safely."

I leaned on my scimitar. "Or so they think. That's the problem, as I always told my students. A djinn *wants* you to break the contract; otherwise, where's the fun in it? They're tricky bastards, so you have to be careful."

"These djinn recently entered into a contract with a young witch. When it came time for her to fulfill her end, they bound her and left her, without food and water, for two days, until the contract expired, when they were allowed to begin tormenting her for real."

"That's not fair."

"We thought you might agree."

Damn. They knew I hated hearing about witches getting screwed by demons—well, metaphorically. If they want the literal sort, that's their choice, one my own mother had made, and I appreciated the extra powers that came with being half-demon.

Still, a vacation was a vacation.

"Trsiel can handle it. Pair him with Marius or Katsuo—they're always up for a little extra adventure."

The middle-aged Fate returned. "They're all busy. Now, we believe the problem with the djinn is lack of leadership. With their demon master unavailable, they're testing the boundaries."

"Who's master of the—?" I stopped. My grasp of demon politics wasn't what it should be, but this one I knew. "Dantalian? Um, he's been unavailable for five hundred years, and the djinn just realized he was gone?"

The old one now, fixing me with a glower. "Naturally, he has under-demons handling his affairs during his exile. We believe one of them has finally decided to stage a coup."

"Dantalian's not going to like that . . . Ah, now I see. That's why you want me—I know the old guy. So I just pop over to Glamis castle, tell Dantalian about the evil scheme afoot, and he'll get his other flunkies to stomp it out. All right, then. Since it'll be quick, I'll do it. Consider it a favor." I lifted my hands for a teleport spell.

"You are not going to Glamis, Eve. You are not consorting with demons. You have not seen Dantalian since that unfortunate business with the Nix five years ago. Correct?"

I didn't even bother to answer. They knew full well that I'd been cultivating the exiled demon as a source. But God forbid they should admit it, because then they'd need to admit they thought it was a good idea.

In the beginning, I'd played along with them, happy to lie by omission as long as the Fates didn't interfere with my methods. I love an underhanded, authority-subverting scheme as much as the next person. But when I was continually expected to provide results and lie about how I got them, the bullshit started to stink.

"We all want this resolved quickly," I said. "So you give me the job, and I'll run off and fix the problem—"

"You are not going to Glamis, Eve. That is a direct order." The old Fate's gaze bored into mine.

"Fine. If you don't want Dantalian to fix this, you don't need me to handle it, do you? Get one of the others."

"They aren't available."

"Well, neither am I."

"You are now."

She waved her fingers and the throne room vanished.

TWO

The Fates teleported me to the ascended angel staff lounge. It's not called that, naturally. We aren't staff. This is a calling. An honor. A noble mission.

Bullshit.

It is a job—the first I've ever held. I'd spent my life avoiding exactly this, responsible only to myself and, later, my daughter. I'd left the Coven at seventeen, then spent years traversing the country, learning the kind of magic that gave the Coven Elders vapors. By twenty-five, I'd become a renowned teacher of the dark arts. Then I met Kristof Nast, got pregnant, left Kristof, had Savannah, and continued on, building my reputation, teaching my craft, staying one step ahead of the interracial council and my growing number of enemies, until one day I hadn't been fast enough to avoid the fate some would say I'd been running from all my life.

I'd been thirty-eight when I died. Ask me, though, and I'll say I was forty, just to avoid that "wink-wink nudge-nudge, *sure* you were thirty-eight" shit. I have my faults. Vanity isn't among them.

One fault I *will* admit to is an overdeveloped sense of loyalty. I do stupid things for people I care about, and that's what got me into the angel business. I'd made a deal with the Fates to protect my daughter. Now I spend six months a year with Kristof as a ghost, and six months as an ascended angel. Like Persephone banished to heaven instead of hell. Someone *else's* idea of heaven, I should say, because it sure wasn't mine.

I made the deal, and I don't regret it. Sure, I bend the rules, but that's why the Fates chose me. I was their fixer, the one they sent on jobs that required a less than angelic touch. In the relatively short time I'd been at it, my success rate matched that of ascended angels who'd been on the job for centuries.

Yet somehow I was still the bad girl, no matter how hard I worked, how much good I did. It was just like when I'd been alive—all anyone saw was what I did wrong. Back then, I hadn't minded, because my badass reputation kept Savannah safe. Here, it was starting to piss me off.

"You do realize that's not how real pirates dressed," said a deep voice behind me. Marius—another ascended—walked around me, slouched onto the sofa, and gave me a slow once-over. "Which is really a shame."

"Hey, angels can't ogle," I said.

"Can't or shouldn't?"

I shook my head and cast a spell to change into my usual attire—a blouse, jeans, and boots. Marius, dressed in a toga and sandals, looked like he was getting ready for a costume party himself. But he had an excuse. Most ascended angels were warriors in life. Marius had been a gladiator. He didn't need to keep wearing the same clothing, but he viewed pants much the same way I saw skirts—a fashion torture to be avoided at all costs.

Marius had been about my age when he finally lost a bout. He looked at least a decade older, with graying hair and a leathery, square face. The scars didn't help, but as with most warriors, he regarded them as marks of pride, and not something he'd consider having magically removed.

"I hear you got the djinn contract," he said. "I thought you were on vacation."

"So did I."

"Shit. Damn Fates."

I'm sure he didn't say "shit," "damn," or any such Anglo-Saxon curse. That's what I heard, though. With angelhood we get a few powers, and one is a built-in universal translator. Marius spoke first-century Latin and I heard twenty-first-century English, which could be a little odd, like watching a badly dubbed movie, the lips rarely matching the words coming from them.

"If you need help, I've had plenty of experience with djinn," he offered.

"You aren't on assignment?"

"Nah. I finished the last one early and the Fates don't have anything for me yet, so I'm just kicking back . . ." Seeing my expression, he stopped. "The Fates told you no one else was free, didn't they?"

"Uh-huh."

"What is their problem with you?" He shook his head. "Well, if you need help, I'm around. Seriously. Just ask." He grinned. "For me, demon butt-kicking *is* a vacation."

So the Fates picked me for this assignment knowing not only that Marius was cooling his heels but that he also had more experience with djinn? Enough of this bullshit. I wanted out. Time to stop bitching about it and do something.

THREE

*B*efore you take action, you need a plan. That's the part I'm not so good at, and there's no reason to do it alone when my partner-in-crime is a consummate schemer. It also gave me an excuse to go see him. Technically, I was still on angel duty—no conjugal visits allowed—but after the first year, I'd found a back door into our dimension of the ghost world. I didn't use it often and only for short visits, so the Fates wouldn't figure it out and plug the hole.

When I slipped through, Kristof wasn't at his houseboat or the courthouse. Yes, we have courts in the afterlife. Ghosts have disputes like anyone else. Kris is a defense lawyer.

The third place I checked was the hockey arena. I popped in behind the bleachers. A middle-aged guy sitting at the back turned and smiled at me.

"Hey, Eve. Welcome back. Looking for Kris?"

I nodded. "If you're here watching the game, then Brianna's playing, meaning Kris is playing, too." I scanned the ice. "But where . . . ?"

"Do you really need to ask?" He pointed.

I thanked him and headed for the penalty box, waving to Brianna as I circled the rink. In the afterlife, all teams are coed. I'd played a few times myself, but I'm not good at games with rules. And I'm not the only one.

It had been two months since I'd seen Kristof. He hadn't changed, of course. Ghosts don't. He would never pass his death age of forty-seven. His blond hair wouldn't continue thinning . . . nor would he regain what he'd lost. And no amount of hockey would tighten the slight paunch around his middle.

He still cut an imposing figure—broad-shouldered, six foot three, with a handsome face and piercing, icy-blue eyes. He also cut an intimidating figure, having inherited his full genetic allotment of Nast arrogance, with a glare that could freeze a witness mid-sentence.

He wasn't glaring at anyone now, though, despite his exile to the penalty box. In life, no one would have dared impose such a petty punishment on Kristof—he was too rich, too privileged, too powerful. In death, it was a welcome change of pace.

"Hey, you," I said as I came down the arena stairs and climbed into the row of seats behind him.

He turned, smiled, grabbed me around the waist, and swung me over the boards. No mean feat, I might add—I'm six feet tall. Nor was plunking me on his lap any easier—I'm not the lap-sitting type. When I resisted, though, he only held me tighter, his mouth coming to mine in a kiss that made me stop struggling.

If there was one mistake I made in life, it was running away from Kristof. Too bad it had taken death to make me realize that.

He slipped his hands under my blouse, grinning when his cold fingers made me jump. "So, are you ready to start that vacation?"

"It's been postponed."

His fingers stopped. "Let me guess. The Fates."

"Yes, they screwed me over," I said, and told him about my reassignment. "But this is the last time."

"I doubt that, whatever they might say."

The referee whistled, telling Kristof his penalty was over, but Kris waved him off.

"I have a few ideas on how to handle them," he said.

"Oh, I already know how to handle it. I'm going to get myself fired."

Kris frowned, as if he hadn't heard right. "Fired?"

"Let go? Pink-slipped? Sacked?"

He studied my face.

"I've had enough, Kris."

"I know. Let's— This isn't a good place. Hold on."

He gestured to his captain, telling her he was quitting early. Then he led me out of the arena to a playground behind it. There are few ghost children to play on that equipment—kids here continue aging until they reach adulthood—but most afterlife cities are exact replicas of human ones.

"You have every right to want to quit right now," he said, leading us both to a bench.

"Hell, yes. I had every right years ago. I'm pissed off." *And not just at the Fates.* I'd expected Kristof to jump in with schemes to free me from my obligation. One look at his face, though, and I knew what was coming—some variation on *slow down and think about this.*

We might share the same get-the-job-done-at-any-cost mentality, but Kristof had been the second-in-command and heir apparent to his family's multinational corporation. That meant we had very different approaches. He'd plot and plan, and proceed with care. I dove in where, well, where *most* angels feared to tread.

Sure enough, he told me to do this one job, then we'd discuss the situation when I returned.

"So you're not going to help me?" I said.

"Of course I'll help you. Just do this one job first and then we'll have six months to plan—"

I teleported out before he could finish the sentence.

FOUR

Without Kristof's help, I could forget any sophisticated exit strategy. That was fine. I like plain and simple, and there was a plain and simple way to get myself fired. Fast, too, which was a bonus.

I recovered my sword and transported to a field in living-world Scotland. The spires of Glamis castle shimmered in the early morning sun. I really needed to find a teleport code to get me *into* the castle, but using this one was safer, though it did mean tramping through a field of cow shit. Even Trsiel—who'd given me this code—didn't dare pop straight into the castle, for fear of alerting the Fates. As for why my full-angel partner had this code at all, let's just say there was a reason the Fates had paired us up.

I looked at the castle.

"'Glamis thou art, and Cawdor; and shalt be what thou art promised: yet do I fear thy nature.'"

A grazing Highland cow rolled her eyes.

"Hey, it's the only Shakespeare I remember. I'm damned well going to use it every chance I get."

I started tramping. The cows lumbered aside. Like most animals, they could sense ghosts—they just didn't realize that getting out of my way wasn't really necessary.

So I trekked over the field, across the castle grounds, through the big doors, up the winding staircase . . .

Finally, I heard a tour guide ahead.

"And another Glamis ghost is believed to peer out that very window," she was saying. "The White Lady, Janet Douglas, widow of the sixth Lord Glamis. A witch, they say. She was burned at the stake for conspiring to poison King James the Fifth. Historians have never found any evidence she was part of the conspiracy, though, and her death is believed to have been simple political revenge. Her ghost is said to haunt this staircase, constantly watching for the men who came to kill her." She led her group around the corner, her voice fading. "And so, with all the stories I've told so far, you can see why this is considered the most haunted castle in Scotland."

Actually, it was the *least* haunted. Having a high-ranking demon walled up here tended to scare off the regular spooks. I could see the White Lady, though, standing just where legend placed her, endlessly watching. She wasn't a ghost, but a residual—an imprinted image.

I cut through the polyester-clad tourist brigade and stepped through the wall, coming eye to eye-socket with a silently screaming skeleton. It never failed. There were only a half dozen of them along the wall, but I always smacked into one.

In the corner were more bones, piled up and covered in gnaw marks. Old bones, from a Scottish clan who'd been walled up in here for pissing off their lord. Knowing their souls were long gone didn't keep a chill from going through me each time I saw them. I tried not to picture the story the skeletons told.

The chill didn't last—the room was like a sauna. Clearly, Dantalian was at home. Not that he had much choice. He'd been walled up here himself, for pissing off *his* lord. The story went that the Lord Glamis responsible for these skeletons had been, like me, the half-demon offspring of a lord demon, in his case Baal. He'd offered the sacrifice of these men in return for a boon. Baal accepted. But the boon required Dantalian's powers of transmigration. Dantalian refused to cooperate, for reasons known only to him and his lord, and ended up walled in with the clansmen, sentenced to remain here for 555 years.

"Yo, Dantalian!" I called. "We need to chat."

A sigh whispered through the room, carried on a current of hot air that tickled the back of my neck. I didn't bother looking over my shoulder. I wouldn't see anything. In the living plane, even the lord of transmigration can't manifest without a body to possess.

"A little respect, perhaps, my lovely demon-angel?" he said, his voice deep and resonant.

"Sorry. Yo, *Uncle* Dantalian. We need to chat."

He sighed louder. It was his own fault. During one of my regular visits, he'd tried to curry favor by pointing out that my father, Lord Demon Balam, was his older brother, meaning we shared a blood tie. It hadn't gotten him what he'd wanted. Nice try, though.

"There's a problem with your djinn," I said.

"It's nice to see you, too. You look well. Still carrying that unfortunate sword, though, I see."

"Yep, want a closer look?"

I swung the angel sword off my back and sliced it through the air. He only chuckled . . . from the other side of the room, out of its reach.

"I'm interrupting my regularly scheduled visit to bring you an important message," I said. "I have a problem and, as it turns out, my problem is also your problem."

I explained the situation.

"I suppose it was only a matter of time before one of my underlings sought to take my place," Dantalian said. "The biggest surprise is that they haven't tried before now. This is easily handled, though. You'll simply need to take a message to one of my demons."

"And hope he's not the one staging the coup?"

"He isn't. He's an excellent soldier with no aspirations to be a general. He knows I'll reward him for his loyalty when I'm free, and he prefers his recompense to come without any pesky political responsibilities."

"Where do I find him?"

That, apparently, was going to be a bit of a problem.

FIVE

The best part about this scheme for getting myself fired? Not only wasn't I shirking my responsibility to stop the djinn, but I was also earning a shitload of gratitude from a very powerful demon. I'd still be drawing on this bank after Dantalian was free. The trouble was, in order to find Armaros—Dantalian's trusted soldier—I had to go someplace I'd really rather avoid.

I teleported into a desert, hot wind buffeting me, my long hair whipping my face, sand blasting my eyes. When I squinted, I could make out the hulking figure of an enormous slavering dog blocking my path. Cerberus. Contrary to myth, the guardian beast didn't have three heads. Like a lot of legends, it's a fanciful version of the truth. There are three dogs—the Cerberi—each facing a different direction, blocking all points of entry to hell. Well, actually, they're guarding a library, but close enough.

I pulled out my sword. Cerberus One sat and then stretched out, head on her paws, whimpering softly. Two and Three did the same, maintaining position, guarding the west and east.

"Good girls," I said, and paused to scratch behind One's massive ears. She made a deep noise in her throat that Trsiel insisted was a growl but I knew was more of a purr, her big head tilting, giving me better scratch-access. The other two looked over hopefully. I patted them, too. I'm not really a dog person, but it's wise to befriend the gatekeepers, especially when they have fangs the size of my forearms.

"You gals still going to let me past when I don't have this?"

I waved my sword. Cerberus One chuffed and grumbled and prodded my hand for more ear-scratching. I took this as a positive sign.

Returning my sword to my back, I headed up the vast marble steps of the Great Library of Alexandria. Yes, *that* Great Library, the one Caesar accidentally torched while burning the Egyptian fleets. Whoops.

In the ghost world, areas are sometimes frozen in time, usually at their zenith. So we still have the Great Library, though, as the monster guard dogs might suggest, it's not open to the public.

I have an uneasy relationship with the Great Library. It really can be my version of hell—endless aisles of moldy books that the Fates banish me to every time I get a new assignment. As a kid, I hated it when teachers told me to go look something up, and I appreciate it even less now. But books have their place, namely as repositories of arcane spells, and for that, nothing beats the Great Library. I can find more here in an afternoon than I could in years hunting through black-market grimoire shops. The Fates themselves didn't know all the books these vast halls contained, meaning I often found some real dark magic gems in here.

I could also find books on demonology that would lead me to Armaros. But that would take hours, days even. Instead, I walked through the special reference collection, past all the marble-topped tables and gray-haired scholars, and slipped into a secret passage to the very special collection, one that contained a single, priceless resource.

The hall was a typical corridor, lined with unnamed, locked doors, guaranteed to convince any wanderers that they'd taken a wrong turn. A little farther along, though, and the faint perfume of tropical flowers wafted past on a mist-laden breeze. Then the burble of running water grew louder until a waterfall blocked the passage. I kept going. I got soaked—the water was real—but a quick spell dried me off, and I found myself in a grotto filled with flowers and birds and butterflies. Don't ask me to name any of them—I know only that they were spectacular enough for me to slow down and admire.

In the center of the grotto, a dark-haired man sat under a tree, poring over a stained book. He didn't glance up as I approached, simply lifted a hand, waving as if in greeting, and I smacked into the invisible magical barrier he'd erected. He finished his page and then glanced up.

"Ah, Eve. Come in." Another wave and the barrier vanished. "Here to see Delphia?"

"I am." I reached into my pocket and took out an amulet.

His gray eyes widened. "Is that—?"

"Uh-huh."

A grin creased his face and he took the amulet from me gingerly, as if it might shatter on contact. Suck up to the gatekeepers. Works every time.

I passed him and navigated another waterfall into yet another grotto, this one extending as far as the eye could see, and far too large to actually be contained within a building, even the Great Library. It was an illusion, of course. I couldn't even imagine the amount of magic that had gone into this. The ultimate gilded cage . . . for the ultimate songbird.

Nymphs frolicked through the glade, splashing in the pools, chasing each other through the flowers, and doing what I suppose comes naturally when they caught one another. I stepped over one entwined couple. They didn't notice. I didn't blame them.

Nymphs look human. They *are* human, as much as any other supernaturals are, except nymphs are drop-dead gorgeous, every one of them. That's the only power they have—the ability to stop traffic with a single smile.

I passed a trio engaged in a more cerebral pastime—some ancient board game. They glanced up and smiled, giving no sign they'd seen me here before. If they had, they wouldn't remember it. Nymph ghosts clamor for stints in this paradise, but it comes with a price. While here, they lose their long-term memories and most of their short-term ones. By the time their game ended, they wouldn't remember who'd won the last round. They lived in the moment and for the moment. To me, that'd be hell, but for some, it's a chance at ultimate happiness, with the added bonus of serving Delphia . . . better known as the Delphic Oracle.

I found her sitting in a swing, watching a trio of Adonis look-alikes weave her a garland of flowers. The flowers were all she wore, and she was as beautiful as any nymph in her garden. When she saw me, she leapt from the swing, startling her suitors as she clapped in delight.

"You've come again. How lovely."

"You know her?" one of the young men asked, frowning at me.

"Of course. We met in Sparta, before the Peloponnesian War. Or was it Britannia?" She studied my face. "Perhaps we haven't met yet? Yes, that's it. We don't meet until after the third Great War. If there is one, that is. If there isn't, we may not meet at all. That would be a shame."

Memory. It is both a blessing and a curse. For Delphia, it's definitely the latter. In her head, she holds the memories of all times that have passed and all times to come. Except that, because the future isn't written, she sees the times that *could* come. All of them. Everything that was, and everything that could be. That's why the nymphs here must live in the moment—so she can, too, giving her the closest thing to peace she can find.

"Was it Britannia?" she asked. "Or America? No, neither. It was—"

Delphia stopped as I held up a pearl-like stone. She stared at it and then threw her arms around me.

"Eve! How delightful. It's been too long."

"Five months."

"And eight days, ten hours."

She was right. In myth, the Delphic Oracle speaks in riddles. In reality, she just gets very, very mixed up, with all those memories stuffing her head. To fix that, you need a focus stone. It's temporary, unfortunately. It also needs to be used sparingly, which is why the Fates make angels spend days digging through the reference stacks instead of just queuing up outside Delphia's grotto.

To get access to Delphia, angels had to plead their cases to the Fates, then be given temporary custody of a focus stone and an escort to get past her guard. As for how I got my own permanent focus stone, let's just say it wasn't easy. But it had saved me countless days of research.

Did I really think the Fates hadn't realized I had a stone and access to Delphia? Of course they knew. They just looked the other way . . . until I got caught by some higher deity, and then they'd claim to have known nothing about it. Yet another game I was sick of playing.

Delphia and I talked for a while. Just social chitchat. Not my thing, but she liked it, and I wouldn't begrudge her those few minutes of lucid conversation. Then I told her I needed to find the demon Armaros, and she looked deep into her crystal-ball brain, and dredged up his current location for me.

"When you find him— Oh!" She stopped short, blue eyes going wide and blank, her mental gaze turning inward. "Armaros. The djinn. You're going to . . ." She blinked, her eyes filling with alarm. "Oh no, Eve. You mustn't—"

She blinked again. Then those big blue eyes unfocused, her mind slipping away again. She smiled and touched my hand. "We've met before, haven't we?"

"We have." I squeezed her hand. "Take care, Delphia."

She smiled and fluttered her fingers in a wave. Then she leapt to her feet. "Wait! I was going to tell you . . ." She frowned. "I *was* going to tell you something, wasn't I?"

I was sure I knew what she'd foreseen—my plan to quit the angel corps, meaning I might never see her again. I managed a smile.

"It was nothing important," I said, and left.

SIX

*A*rmaros was hanging out in the human world, as demons are wont to do. According to Delphia, he was running some scheme in Tangiers, which is one of those places I'd heard about but wouldn't have a clue where to find on a map. For that, I *did* crack open a book. It was the fastest way to get the teleport code.

It turned out Tangiers was in Morocco, another place I was a little fuzzy on. Northern Africa, apparently, with Tangiers smack dab at the entrance to the Strait of Gibraltar.

I was going to miss this part of being an angel. I loved the PI work, tracking down ghosts and demons and humans to the far corners of all the dimensions. Even more than the hunt, I loved the chase. And even more than the chase, I loved the big fight at the finish. But I wasn't going to think about that. I wanted out. No time for second thoughts.

I got to Tangiers. Cool city. I'd have to save the code and bring Kristof here, though I suppose it wouldn't be as much fun without my built-in universal translator, letting me slink down exotic back alleys and eavesdrop on clandestine conversations. I found Armaros in a sidewalk café drinking a tiny glass of potent coffee with some very shady fellows. Armaros fit right in. He'd possessed the body of a guy who looked like a modern-day *Indiana Jones* villain— shaggy blond hair, old army jacket, aviator sunglasses, a few days of scruff. Carefree adventurer turned dangerous gunrunner.

And gunrunning did seem to be the order of the day. Supplying arms to some rebel faction. Typical. In the movies, demons are always trying to overthrow the world. In truth, they're not much different from the thug on the street corner who gives kids free drugs in hopes of turning them into regular customers.

People try to say there's no God, because if there was, He wouldn't let bad shit happen. He'd stop the demons, and then humans, free of temptation, would live happily ever after. Bullshit. Armaros wasn't forcing his guns on anyone—he was just facilitating a process humans had already started and reaping his chaos rewards.

When he glanced my way, frowning, I pulled out my sword. He flinched, lips forming an oath. Then his eyes narrowed and he settled back into his seat, scowling at me. Everyone else kept haggling over prices, even when I plunked myself down on the table's edge and started polishing my sword on my shirttail.

"What do you want?" Armaros growled under his breath.

"A fair deal," one of the men said. "That is all I ever want, Charles. A fair deal."

"World peace, too," I added. "He says he wants guns, but what he really wants is world peace. Kill everyone and things will be very, very peaceful."

Armaros glanced from them to me, then muttered, "I need to take a piss. Work it out while I'm gone."

I followed him to an alley. "I'm—"

"I know who you are. Balam's traitor whore daughter."

"Well, I can see why Dantalian said you make a better soldier than a politician."

His head jerked up. "Dantalian?"

"I'm playing courier angel today. I'd deliver his message as a singing telegram, but I can't pronounce the lyrics."

I handed him the note Dantalian had me write out. It had taken forever because the words were actually symbols—a demonic language.

"Huh," Armaros said after he'd read it. Then he fixed me with a quizzical look. Wondering why I was helping Dantalian, I was sure, but I wasn't explaining myself. Dantalian said Armaros would know the message came from him and wouldn't challenge it, and he didn't.

"Everything clear, then?" I said.

"Yeah. Can you take a message back to him for me?"

Another example of the language for my research? Couldn't argue with that. I conjured up a pen and paper, but Armaros waved it aside.

"Just relay a verbal message."

I motioned for him to go on. He said something in a language my translator didn't cover—the same one as the note, I presumed.

"Got that?"

I handed him the paper and pen. Again, he waved it off.

"Just pass on the message. Get it close enough and he'll understand. You need me to repeat it?"

"Uh, yes."

He said it again, then made me say it back to him. When I got it wrong, he tried again. I repeated it back and—

The alley disappeared.

I expected to arrive in the Fates' throne room. Instead, I teleported into what seemed to be a vacant house prepped for sale. I'd moved often enough in my life to recognize the look— the faint coating of dust on the windowsill, the walls gleaming off-white, new paint quickly slapped on. I walked to the window, but the sun shone too brightly for me to make out anything beyond it.

As I headed for the hall, I cursed Dantalian for a fool, but not before leveling the same curses at myself.

"Couldn't Armaros be the one betraying you, Dantalian? No? Okay, sure, I'll go chat with him, and when he asks me to repeat a line in demon tongue, I'll do that, too. Why not? It isn't like he's going to zap me to another part of the country, rally his djinn troops, and warn them that Dantalian knows all about his evil scheme."

I tramped down the hall, threw open the front door—and stared out into the blinding white light of nothingness. I cursed some more, then slammed the door.

"Better yet, zap me to another dimension. That'll slow me down."

I cast a teleport spell. Nothing happened. Tried another, and another, feeling my power level drain as my panic mounted.

"Cool it," I told myself. "You've been dimension-zapped before."

And that was exactly why I was panicking. Spells didn't work well in empty dimensions like this. It could take days for me to escape or be found. On my first case, the Nix I'd been chasing had teleported an ascended angel to another dimension, where she'd stayed for what had been—to her—centuries. She now lived in a padded room, raving mad.

"And that's exactly the sort of thinking that'll help you get out of here."

My voice echoed through the empty house. I turned into a room and sat cross-legged on the floor. When my powers had recovered, I'd try a few other things—

"Mom?"

I jumped up so fast my legs tangled and I fell backward, nearly impaling myself on my sword.

"Mom? Is that you?"

Savannah's voice drifted from somewhere above me.

"Savannah?"

Her laugh tinkled down. "That is you. Where are we? One second I'm typing a stack of invoices for Paige, and the next . . ."

Her voice drifted off.

"Hold on," I said. "I'll come find you."

Damn Dantalian. Damn him to a thousand hells. I strode into the hall, searching for the stairs. But the hall just kept going, an endless corridor of doors.

"Mom?"

"I'm coming, hon. Just sit tight."

As I went past a doorway, another voice stopped me.

"Yes, if you can find her again, I'd appreciate that. No, don't do anything. Just let me know where she is. Let me know she's all right."

"Kris?" I said.

I turned to look into a home office. Kris sat behind the desk, slumped forward, forehead resting on his hand.

"Daddy?" Across the room, a door opened and a blond boy of about five poked his head in.

When Kris lifted his head, I saw the face of the man I'd left twenty years earlier. The boy was Bryce, Kris's younger son, as he looked back then.

Kris managed a tired smile for his boy.

"Hey, bud. I was just coming to—"

"Was that your witch girlfriend?"

The venom in Bryce's voice made Kris flinch. "Girlfriend? No, I don't have—"

"Not anymore. Uncle Josef said she dumped you."

Kristof blinked back his surprise. We'd worked hard to keep our relationship a secret. "Okay, bud. How about we grab some ice cream and talk—"

"That's why Mom left, isn't it? Because of your witch girlfriend."

Kristof's surprise turned to shock. "No, that's not—"

Bryce ran off. Kristof hurried after him.

So Bryce had known about us? Blamed me for his mom leaving? It wasn't true—she'd abandoned them before I met Kristof.

That's why Bryce hates Savannah, a voice whispered behind me. *He hates that Sean treats her like a sister. He hates that his father died trying to save her. He's never gotten over it, and it's all your fault.*

I wheeled. No one was there.

Djinn.

As Dantalian's soldier, Armaros would command the djinn. And what was their specialty? Driving people insane.

"Mom?"

"Savannah?" I called cautiously now, realizing she was probably an illusion. I couldn't be sure, though. I continued down the hall.

"—bunch of stupid bitches—"

"Savannah, please," a familiar husky voice answered. "I know you're upset, but talking like that—"

"I'll talk any way I damn well want. You aren't my mother, Paige."

I followed the voices to Paige's old living room in East Falls. Savannah was there, thirteen again, pacing the floor. Paige sat across the room. She leaned back, long curls spilling over the chair back as she stared at the ceiling as if praying for guidance.

God, Paige looked young. I'd forgotten how young she'd been.

Twenty-two when you got yourself killed and dumped your daughter in her lap.

"You think my language is bad?" Savannah said. "You should have heard what they called my mom. Stupid little Coven bitches. Mom was smart. She left."

"You need to ignore what they say about her, Savannah. Don't pay any attention—"

"Just *let* them say those things? You're as bad as they are, Paige. As stupid, too. I hate them and I hate you!"

Savannah stormed off, smacking the wall as she went. A piece of molding popped free. Paige slowly got up and tried pushing the molding back into place, hands shaking, blinking back tears, muttering under her breath.

Cursing you, Eve. You know she was. Tell her not to bother fixing that—her house is going to burn down in a few months. That's what she got for taking in your kid. It destroyed her house, destroyed her reputation, destroyed her life.

"I screwed up, okay?" I yelled. "You think I don't know that?"

I tramped down the hall.

"You killed her!" Savannah's shriek echoed through the house. "You promised Paige would be safe, and you killed her!"

I broke into a run. I stopped only when I heard her scream again. I wheeled and saw a furnace. Savannah knelt on the other side of it, facing the wall, sobbing.

I looked at that room and my gut went cold.

"No," I whispered. "Not this. Come on. Don't—"

"I'm right here, Savannah," Paige's voice drifted from behind the furnace. "Nobody killed me."

"Oh, thank God." Another voice I knew so well. Kristof's. "See, sweetheart? Paige is fine."

"You killed her!" Savannah screamed. "You killed her! You promised! You promised, and you lied!"

Savannah's head dropped forward, tears streaming as she sobbed. Kristof stepped forward, arms opening to embrace her. Paige yelled for him to stop. He didn't.

Savannah turned fast, hands shooting up in a spell. Kristof sailed off his feet. His head hit the concrete wall with a horrible crack. His eyes went wide. Then they closed and he slumped to the floor. Paige ran over to check for a pulse.

There wouldn't be one.

She was calling for you, the voice whispered. *Before Kristof came. Screaming for you. But you didn't come. And he did. Do you really think she doesn't know what happened? Doesn't realize she killed her father? She knows, Eve. She knows.*

If only you'd told Savannah about Kristof . . . If you'd let her know he was a good man, let her know you loved him, none of this—

"Do you think I don't know that?" I snarled. "I know every fucking mistake I made in my life, and I don't need to be reminded."

How many people did you kill, Eve? Not just tangentially, like Kristof. But sent to the afterlife yourself?

"Oh, no." I gave a harsh laugh. "Now you're getting desperate. *That* I don't regret. I never killed anyone that wasn't just as big a threat to me as I was to them. I don't feel any guilt over them."

"No?" said a young voice behind me. "What about me? Do you feel guilty about me?"

I turned to see a boy of about ten. "I don't know you."

"I'm Terri Blake's son. My mom double-crossed you. You killed her. Do you know what happened to me?" He met my gaze. "Do you care?"

"Look, I—"

"What about me?" A woman stepped from another doorway. "John Salton's wife. Widow, I should say, though I never realized that. I thought he'd left me and the kids. Did a good job of hiding his body, didn't you?"

"He'd have done—"

"—the same to you," the boy and the woman chanted in unison, their voices joined by others, more people stepping from doorways, the endless hallway filling. "Had to kill them. Didn't have a choice. Kill or be killed. The law of the jungle."

John Salton's widow leapt at me, teeth bared. "Welcome to the jungle, Eve."

EIGHT

I don't know how long I spent in that hell, tormented by the ghosts of those I'd wronged. I didn't curl up and take it. I defended myself—verbally, physically, whatever it took. When that didn't stop it, I walked away, only to step into another scene from *This Is Your Life*.

I fought. I resisted. I raged. But eventually the djinn won. I don't remember anything after that.

NINE

I heard a voice whispering, "Shhh, shhh, it's okay," as a hand stroked my head. I opened my eyes. I was in one of those empty rooms, curled up on the floor, my head cradled on a lap.

I twisted to see Kristof.

"Hello, gorgeous," he said.

I stared at him. Then I blinked and pulled away. "It's not really you."

"No?"

"Prove it."

He paused, considering, then said, "How would I do that?"

I sat up. "What do you mean?"

"Well, the usual way would be for me to tell you something only I know, which would work if you suspected I'm an impostor. But if, as it seems, you've been hallucinating, then I could be a product of your imagination, meaning I'll say whatever you want me to say, which doesn't prove anything at all. On the other hand—"

I threw my arms around his neck and hugged him.

"Proof enough?" he said.

"It is." I pulled back. "How did you get here? Wherever here is . . ." I looked around.

"Tangiers, it seems."

"No. I was in Tangiers, and then . . . You said I was hallucinating. I'm still in Tangiers, aren't I?"

"Apparently. You're trapped in some sort of mental construct. A typical djinn trick."

"Which I'd know if I'd done my research. But how'd you find me?"

"You called, I came. As for how I got here, as you know, I'm a master of teleportation."

I laughed and settled in, hugging my knees to my chest. "Like the time you tried taking me to the beach and we ended up in the Sahara?"

"It had sand. I only *appear* to have trouble teleporting because I need to conserve my powers to properly fulfill my role as the hero's wise and nurturing girlfriend."

I sputtered a laugh.

He continued. "Every hero needs a sidekick. I'm the wise and nurturing girlfriend, who sits on the sidelines, counseling him to make better choices, and picking him up when he invariably ignores her advice and falls."

"Ah, but if you were a real hero's girlfriend, you'd be the one needing rescue."

"True." He sighed and stretched his legs. "It's the one part of the role I'm finding difficult to fulfill. But I'm working on it."

"Are you working on the *girl* part, too?"

He arched his brows. "Do you want me to?"

"Never."

We sat in silence for a moment. My hands started shaking again, and I shoved them into my pockets.

"I screwed up, Kris. Big surprise, huh? You tried to slow me down, and I ignored you. But you won't even say *I told you so*."

"You beat yourself up enough, Eve. You don't need anyone else doing it for you." He pulled me onto his lap. "We can fix this. Just tell me what happened."

"I—" I glanced around and shivered. "I will. Just— I want to get out of here and clear my head first."

"A distraction? Now that is definitely one of my sidekick specialties."

He murmured a teleport spell. The house evaporated and I dropped a foot onto a soft mattress. I looked around to see Kris's houseboat.

"Nice aim," I said.

"Did I mention those expert teleportation skills?"

"How about those expert distraction skills?"

"Coming right up," he said, his mouth lowering to mine.

A half hour later, I was in bed, covers twined around me, telling Kris everything that had happened as I watched him fix me a snack. Ghosts don't need food any more than they need sleep or sex, but an afterlife without passionate nights, lazy mornings, and breakfasts in bed isn't the kind of eternity I want.

Ghosts do the things they enjoyed in life, necessary or not, and for Kris, one of those things was cooking. His ex-wife took off when their boys were little more than toddlers, and he'd been determined that they'd never suffer the lack of anything for it. Including homemade meals.

Today he was keeping things simple. When he brought over my tray, it held a glass of milk and a peanut butter and jam sandwich. My ultimate comfort food.

"You really do this nurturing thing well, you know," I said.

"It's a front. Underneath, I'm a cold, ruthless bastard." He sat on the end of the bed and pulled my legs over his lap. "So you think Armaros is behind the coup?"

"Of course. What else—?" I caught his expression. "I'm missing another possibility, aren't I?"

"You could be. Dantalian perhaps?"

"Overthrowing himself? That makes no sense. Why would he stage—? Wait. Key word there? *Stage*. You think it's a setup. If the djinn cause enough trouble, the easiest way to subdue them would be to grant Dantalian early parole. And the last thing he'd want is me poking around. So he sent that coded message telling Armaros to distract me. That double-crossing son of a bitch. I'm going to—"

Kristof didn't cut me off. He didn't need to. I may not be PhD material, but I am occasionally capable of learning.

"That's exactly the attitude that got me into this mess in the first place, isn't it?" I said. "Dantalian will only deny it, so I'm wasting my time, which is better spent stopping Armaros and his djinn before they do more damage. Then I can deal with Dantalian." I glanced at him. "Right?"

He smiled. "Right."

I'd already spent too much time in the ghost world, so twenty minutes later I was back where I'd started, in the ascended angel staff lounge, where a stocky, dark-haired guy cursed as he tried to get the coffeemaker working.

I conjured a fresh cup for him.

"Show-off," he said.

Katsuo was a former samurai who looked more like a college student, right down to the jeans, fitted tee, and sneakers.

"Can't stay away from us, can you?" he said.

"Actually, I'm still on the clock."

"Yeah, I heard that. Something to do with the djinn, right? Marius has been moping around, waiting for you to call him in."

"That's why I'm here. I need to pick his brain."

"Research?" Katsuo made a face. "I don't think that's quite what he had in mind."

I wasn't the only ascended who preferred swinging swords to reading books. I may not have been the usual recruit, but in some ways I fit right in, and I'd made friends here. Good friends, like Katsuo. Would I ever see them again after I quit?

"I'd better go find him."

"He's in his quarters." Katsuo snagged my elbow before I could walk away. "Eve?"

"Hmm?"

He lowered his voice. "He'd never say this himself—he's too proud—but he really wants to help out. He— He's had a few assignments lately that didn't go too smoothly."

"Got it."

"Great. And if you need *more* help—of the ass-kicking sort, that is . . ."

"I'll give you a shout."

"How to summon a djinn?" Marius said, frowning.

We were in his private quarters, which looked like the quarters of any career soldier—a small room, simply appointed.

"Multiple djinn, if possible. I knew how to do it when I was alive, but . . ."

"That doesn't work after you're dead." He sat on the edge of his bed. "Usually I just hunt them like any other demi-demon. I suppose you could try to find a living supernatural who's already attempting to summon one."

"That could take days. Same as hunting one down."

"Hmm. How about you leave it with me? You're supposed to be on vacation, so go see Kristof." He smiled. "I'm sure you know how to sneak into the ghost world."

"No, I should stay on this. But when I'm ready, I'll call you and Katsuo in to help with the collar."

ELEVEN

y first stop was a theater, where, according to my "Jaime beacon," I could hope to find my living world liaison. Jaime Vegas is a necromancer, meaning she can see and hear ghosts. We have an agreement—I scare off unwanted ghosts for her and in return, she does the stuff I can't, like getting information and contacting people in the living world.

Backstage, I saw a familiar figure in the wings. He was a couple of inches taller than me, slender, with an angular face and black hair laced with silver. He watched the show through the curtains, hands in his pockets, gaze fixed on Jaime out on the stage.

When I approached, he stiffened and glanced over his shoulder.

"Hey, Jeremy. Good to see you."

He didn't answer. Not being a necromancer, he couldn't see or hear me. He sensed me, though. That could be the wolf in him . . . or the fox. Jeremy is another dual-parentage supernatural: were-wolf on his father's side, kogitsune on his mother's. Until Jaime told me a few months ago, I'd never heard of kogitsune, a very rare, almost extinct type, the offspring of humans and kitsune—Japanese fox maiden demi-demons. Seeing Jeremy now, I also saw a shortcut to the djinn. Unfortunately, it wouldn't be just the Fates who'd balk at this idea.

Applause still thundered as Jaime left the stage. Her assistant, Tara, swooped down with ice water and a clipboard full of messages. A small group of super-fans broke through a gap in the curtains, calling after Jaime and snapping pictures. Two security guards rushed to pull the gap closed. Jaime got about ten steps—out of groping range—and turned, smiling and waving. She motioned for the guards to let one besotted middle-aged admirer stumble through the line and give her a bouquet of slightly wilted lilies.

With tousled red hair, a toothpaste-ad smile, and legs that go farther than my best teleport spell, Jaime looks like a lounge singer. Her true claim to fame?

"Jaime!" a woman shrieked from the crowd. "Did you see my father tonight?"

Jaime waved for the woman to come forward. The guards bristled and glowered, moving closer to their charge.

Jaime clasped the woman's hands. "No, I didn't, hon. I'm sorry. It can be difficult for spirits to cross, but I can sense him here, with you. I know if he could get a message through, he'd tell you—"

I repeated the words with her. "—he misses you, but he's happy and he's in a good place."

Jaime's head whipped around, her eyes meeting mine.

"Jaime?" someone called from the crowd. "What is it? Do you see something?"

"I'm not sure." She shivered. "I sense . . . trouble."

"Ha-ha," I said. "I'm behaving myself, aren't I? Just standing back, another of your adoring fans."

She rolled her eyes, gave a few more smiles, signed a couple of autographs, then discreetly signaled Tara, who stepped forward to stage-whisper to Jaime that she had an appointment. Jaime apologized to the group and the guards closed the gap as she walked toward the wings. Tara trotted at her side, giving her a rundown of real appointments, attendance figures, technical glitches, all that boring postshow stuff. Jaime answered, but her gaze flitted across each passing face, searching for one special one. When she found it, she lit up like a kid spotting a Free Ice Cream sign.

She waved Jeremy over, and he fell in step beside her, murmuring, "Good show." Tara said something about checking the schedule and hurried off.

"Eve's here," Jaime whispered, jerking her chin at me.

"Ah." Jeremy glanced over as I fell in on her other side. "Hello, Eve."

"Tell him I said hi."

She did, and we continued in silence to the dressing room. As much as I longed to start explaining—it's not as if the security guards would hear me—I'd learned not to talk to Jaime when she was around humans. She can't help listening to me and responding, even if it's just a nod.

In the dressing room, I dropped into the nearest chair and rested my boots on a magazine-covered table. Jeremy glanced at Jaime.

"She's there," she said, pointing.

Jeremy took another chair.

"Welcome back," Jaime said as she plucked pins from her hair. "You're just in time. I have a favor to ask."

"Actually, I'm not quite back from angel duty yet. I will be soon, though. What's up?"

"Nothing that can't wait."

She forced a smile and grabbed the cold cream. In other words, some bastard was haunting her. There was no sense pushing her to admit it. She'd never let her own problems distract me from my higher calling, no matter how hard I argued.

"So what do you need?" she asked.

I told her. Her smile froze, then dropped from sight.

"You want Jeremy to do *what*?"

He looked up from the newspaper he'd been reading, his brows arching in question, too polite to interrupt.

"The answer is no," she said. "Absolutely not."

A moment's silence, then Jeremy cleared his throat. "As that refusal concerns me, may I ask what it's regarding?"

"No." She flushed and murmured an apology to him before turning on me and snapping "No" again.

Jeremy folded his paper. "I'd like to know."

The murderous glare she shot my way would have worked much better on someone who could be murdered.

"Yes, I'm putting you in a bad position," I said. "Now you have to tell him, and he'll consider doing it. But I wouldn't ask if it wasn't important, and you know he's not in any danger as long as I have this—" I pulled out my sword.

"So it's . . . that kind of a job."

"If it wasn't, do you really think I'd ask? I need to get answers fast, and this is the best way to do it. I'd planned to get you to ask Paige or Savannah, but that means another stop and another delay."

Again, Jeremy cleared his throat. Jaime tried to ignore him, but his patient, direct gaze wore her down.

"She wants you to summon a djinn," she said. "But I think Savannah is much better suited for it."

"Because you need a spell-caster in order to summon one?" he asked.

"A human can if they know the ritual, but they'll come faster for someone with magical abilities."

"Like me. All things considered, I'm probably a safer choice than Savannah."

He had a point. Savannah might not be in any danger from a djinn, but . . . let's just say *Savannah's* safety wasn't always the main concern. My daughter will be twenty in a few months, but in some ways she's still very young.

Jeremy glanced in my direction. "Ask Eve to tell me what I need to do."

TWELVE

*W*e didn't have all the ingredients necessary for a proper ritual. It didn't matter. When Jeremy summoned, the djinn came like starving curs smelling raw steak. I was sure they'd never been summoned by a werewolf, let alone the Alpha of the American Pack *and* a member of a nearly extinct race. They were dying to see what he wanted.

I'd barely had time to send up a mental smoke signal for Marius and Katsuo before the djinn started appearing. By the time Marius arrived, I already had three djinn skewered on my sword.

"I need a bigger sword," I said.

Marius grinned. "We'll have to requisition one for you."

I glanced behind him. "Is Katsuo with you?"

"Haven't seen him, but I'm sure we can handle these three."

The djinn looked human—or close to it. Unlike most demons and demi-demons, they can manifest in the living world. And like most who *can* manifest, they bore some resemblance to their mythical counterparts, in their case the genies of Arabian lore.

The djinn were bald and muscular, and wore only billowing pants. Their yellow eyes and copper skin glowed. They were barely five feet tall, but I'm sure to humans who summoned them they looked *much* bigger.

Skewering them on my sword didn't kill them. But whatever makes an angel sword glow is like celestial Krazy Glue for demons. Once they touch it, they aren't going anywhere, no matter how much they curse and struggle, and these djinn did plenty of both.

"Want me to take these guys into custody while you wait to see if any more show up?" Marius asked.

"First I need to interrogate them and find out exactly what Dantalian is up to."

Marius shrugged. "I say don't bother. You've done enough. Let someone else handle interrogation."

Very tempting. But any thought of getting myself fired had faded under the need to finish this job. So I asked him if he would stay and watch for more djinn. Then I thanked Jaime and Jeremy, and hauled my captives off to a dimensional holding cell.

The djinn didn't want to talk, naturally, but I can be very persuasive, especially when I've called in Kris to help me play bad cop/psychotic cop. This was another reason I'd left Marius guarding the arrivals gate—I don't mind breaking the rules, but I won't let an angelic colleague be party to it.

Kris had been right: it was all Dantalian's idea. The djinn were only foot soldiers, so they knew little about the overall plan, only their small part in it, which was to work overtime responding to all summonings and give the summoner an automatic pass to crazy land.

When the divine powers realized the djinn were breaking their compact, they'd send in the angels, who'd find the problem spreading like eldritch fire. The lord demons would see the angel troops being marched out and they'd get involved—not to muster their own troops, but to stamp out the fire fast.

The battle between good and evil is really a cold war. Each side makes small forays against the other, struggling to keep the power balance tipped slightly in their favor, each knowing they don't have the martial supremacy to risk a full-blown attack.

So the lord demons would want a quick resolution to the situation. That's where, presumably, Armaros would suggest a surefire way to end the conflict. Release Dantalian. After all, he'd served most of his sentence. He'd learned his lesson. Grant him early parole and he'd be eager to prove himself by stopping his djinn. Then, the moment he gave the word, the djinn would fall in line. Problem solved.

I was still finishing the interrogation when Marius popped in. No more djinn had appeared, and he was eager to hand these three to the Fates. I let him take them. I had a more pressing appointment to keep.

"Yo, Dantalian!"

I strode through the wall, narrowly avoiding a skeleton. Kristof wasn't so lucky and cursed beside me.

"Jaime and I talked about having her do a 'special broadcast' here," I said as he disentangled himself. "Great publicity for her, but we didn't want to take the chance of freeing Dantalian."

"Oh, I'm sure that wouldn't happen," Dantalian's voice slithered past.

I snorted and walked over to the couch, where I sat.

"I see you brought your boyfriend," the demon said, a petulant note creeping into his voice.

"No, I brought my lawyer."

"You had a binding agreement with Eve, Dantalian," Kristof said. "You're in violation of section three, clause two, which means—"

"I like the lawyer even less than the boyfriend. I'm quite sure you and I can work this out, Eve."

"Kris? Continue, please."

"You're in violation of section three, clause two of Eve's agreement to visit you biannually in return for services already rendered. Therefore, she is now free of her obligation and you may consider this your last visit from her."

"Perhaps we can renegotiate."

"You're not even going to deny what you did, are you?" I said.

"I respect you too much to engage in such petty machinations—"

My burst of laughter cut him short.

He tried again. "It was business, not personal, and I'm sure, of all people, Eve, you understand that. I'm really very fond of you."

"Fond? Your djinn tried to drive me crazy."

"Only temporarily, and I assure you that when I was freed, I had every intention of compensating you for that inconvenience." His voice slid around me on a warm breeze.

"You'd find me much more useful as a free demon."

"Nice try. But you're staying here. I captured three of your djinn. They told me everything."

"Ah."

"They're on their way to the Fates now, and when *the Fates* hear the story and relay it up the food chain, then over to Lord Baal . . ."

"Ah." He sighed. "I suppose I'll be serving my full sentence, then. Pity."

My eyes narrowed. "You don't seem very upset about it."

"No sense raging against fate. Or the Fates, in this case. As you so quaintly put it, it was a nice try. Now about our contract. I believe renegotiations are in order."

"You really aren't the least bit worried about what Baal—" I stopped short. "Shit!" I spun on Kris. "Can you get yourself back home?"

He nodded.

"Go."

THIRTEEN

I popped into the Fates' outer chambers first, in case I was wrong. But as I feared, there was no sign of Marius. I returned to the theater, just in case. Jaime and Jeremy were long gone and, again, there was still no sign of Marius. I searched the building anyway, and finally found him backstage, sitting on the floor, shell-shocked.

When I shook him, he didn't respond, just kept staring, unblinking. I shook him harder, calling his name, and was about to resort to a magical wake-up call when he jumped, right hand sailing to his sword hilt . . . only there was no sword there.

"Marius?"

He looked up at me, blinking. "Eve?"

"Where are the djinn?"

"Djinn?" His lips formed the word as if he didn't quite recognize it. Then he leapt up, looking about. "No. No, no, no!"

"What happened?"

"I—" He blinked hard. Then he looked up at me. "I don't know. I had them on my . . ."

He glanced down at his empty hands, then into his empty scabbard, and he swore, the end of the curse rising in panic. Outstretched fingers trembling, he stammered through the incantation. When the sword appeared in his hands, he tottered with relief. I didn't blame him. For an angel to lose his sword to a demon? Let's just say it is one of those things I'd heard about, but I'd never met anyone it had happened to, and suspected there was a good reason for that.

"You must have unconjured your sword somehow, and they escaped," I said. "Do you remember anything?"

He gave a slow shake of his head. Then his eyes snapped wide. "I remember . . ." He glanced down at the sword still lying across his palms. His voice dropped to a whisper. "I saw an angel sword. Then everything went dark."

An angel sword meant an angel. In other words, his attacker was one of us. A traitor. I wasn't shocked. I'd already considered the possibility when Dantalian hadn't seemed too worried about his djinn being hauled before the Fates. He knew they'd never arrive. Which meant he needed an angel in his pocket.

What surprised me was my gut reaction: grief and outrage. A little voice reminded me that I often broke the rules, and had even planned to quit. But a betrayal on this scale would never occur to me.

"Katsuo." Marius swallowed. "He didn't come when you called for help, but he must have heard the summons and knew you had the djinn. He knew where we were." A sharp shake of his head. "No, I'm sure I'm wrong. Katsuo would never . . ." He trailed off uncertainly.

"Either way, we need to get those djinn back."

"If . . . if it was Katsuo, I know where he might have taken them."

"Lead on."

Waves battered the rocks, drenching me with each crash. I squinted, but even my Aspicio powers didn't help me see through my hair, whipping in front of my eyes. I licked my lips, tasting salt. The ocean. A ghost world version, if I could feel and taste the water.

I tied my long hair in a plait, hands moving automatically, gaze traveling around me, Aspicio powers kicking in, letting me see through the mist. I stood ankle deep in water on a rock that jutted from the stormy sea. It was a small outcropping, barely big enough to pitch a tent on. Beyond that, there was no land as far as my bionic eyesight could see.

"—down—cave—"

Behind me, Marius shouted to be heard over the crashing waves and howling wind. I turned to see him hunched against the water's blast, one hand shielding his eyes from the wind, the other pointing to a narrow hole in the rock, descending into darkness.

"Katsuo—we found—assignment last year—said—perfect place—"

I didn't catch the rest but could fill it in. That cave on this forsaken outcropping was the perfect place to stash a prisoner—or three.

"I'll go down," he yelled. Then he grimaced in what would probably have been a wry smile if not for the icy rain pelting his broad face. "—your job—you want to do—I'll stand watch."

"No," I shouted back, moving closer so he could hear me. "You go on down and get them. I'll stand guard out here."

He sluiced water off his face as he shook his head. "No, you should get credit—"

He jerked back, my sword point at his throat.

"Eve?" His eyes widened. "You're the traitor?"

"No, not me and not Katsuo, but you know that. I'd ask you why, but the truth is, Marius, that I don't give a shit why you did it. There is no excuse."

"You think *I'm* the one who—?"

"Am I wrong? Great. Go on down there and prove it."

He didn't move.

"So where does that lead?" I asked, nodding at the hole. "A cave? A portal? A hole to the center of the—"

He kicked my shins. I staggered back, but recovered in time to leap out of the way. He lunged for me. I danced around him, blade flashing. He ducked and charged. I sidestepped. My foot slipped on the rock. He dove at me, knocking me toward the hole. I couldn't get any traction. My sneakers hit open air. I dropped my sword, rushing through the incantation to unconjure it as I grabbed the hem of Marius's toga. I fell into the hole . . . and he came with me.

We seemed to fall forever, grunting and kicking and punching, into a darkness even my Aspicio vision couldn't pierce.

I landed flat on my back with a bone-jarring crack that left me dazed.

I listened, but of course heard nothing. Ghosts—even angels—don't breathe. Marius could be right beside me and I wouldn't know it. Beneath me, the ground was slick and cold. Rock? Marble? Glass? I had no idea.

I could conjure a light ball, but that would only show him where I was, so instead I struggled to see. My powers, though, like any night vision, need a light source, however faint, and here there was none. When I did make out a faint glimmer, I leapt to my feet, spinning as Marius's glowing sword sliced toward me.

I dove into the darkness. My sneakers squeaked. Hearing that, Marius flew at me. I raced out of the way, then hopped, yanking off my shoes as I went. When I pitched one, he tore off that way; I ran the other direction and then hunkered down.

He picked up my shoe, cursed, and whipped it into the shadows.

"You're too good for this job, Eve," he said. "We both are."

I bit my tongue against answering.

"They don't treat you right and you know it. It's your demon blood. They can't get past their prejudice. You could be the best angel they've ever had, and they'd still treat you like shit."

I could faintly see him by the glow of his sword. He walked carefully, his chin up, listening for any sound that would give me away.

"Can you imagine how the demons would treat you? Daughter of a lord demon? Master of the dark arts? Former ascended angel? I'll be well paid for my part, but I'd be lucky if they'd even let me be your bodyguard."

My socks whispered as I moved. He stopped, his head jerking to follow the sound. I crouched and threw my other shoe, letting it skip lightly across the hard ground. When he turned that way, I scampered in, coming up behind him—

He wheeled. I fell back.

He chuckled. "Nice one. Not quite quick enough, though. Do you forget my claim to fame, Eve? I'm a gladiator. I've fought giants and dwarves. I've fought wild animals and savages. I've fought one, two, a dozen at a time, but what finally killed me? My partner. Stabbed me in the back. I learned my lesson. Do unto others before—"

I rushed at him straight on, catching him off guard. He stumbled back, his sword flashing. I grabbed the blade. Felt the pain, searing, unbelievable pain, but I held on. I wrenched the sword from his hands, spun, and threw it as far as I could.

And darkness fell again.

We fought. It wasn't easy—he was as good as he thought he was. But he was fighting blind, and the distant glow of his sword was enough for my enhanced night vision. I could make out his figure, duck his blows, and deliver my own. Soon I had him pinned.

"Need some help?" asked a voice behind me.

"Took you long enough."

Katsuo laughed and took out his own sword, waving it so he could see by its glow. "You're lucky I could follow your beacon down here. And you're lucky I brought a little magic dust to take us away. Ready?"

I was.

FOURTEEN

*W*hen Katsuo and I brought Marius back, the Fates were shocked and overcome with gratitude. They saw the error of their ways, and promised me a permanent extra month of ghost-time each year.

Right.

We handed Marius over to the guards outside the Fates' throne room. One took a message in and returned to say they'd be with us shortly. After waiting for an hour, I told Katsuo to cover the meeting—I was starting my vacation.

I found Kris back where I'd left him, with Dantalian. I told him what had happened. I didn't say a word to the demon, but he could hear, of course, and knew his plan had failed. He cursed—some serious cursing, too. None of it, though, was directed at me. As he'd said, betraying me had been purely business. I *did* understand that.

Before I left, he was already making offers to renegotiate our contract. I ignored him. I *would* listen, but only after he'd had a few months to stew and panic and get very, very lonely. Then, if I decided to come back to see him, I'd make damned sure he compensated me well.

I teleported us back to Kris's houseboat. When we were safely settled on his couch, Kris asked how I'd figured it all out.

"I knew something was up when Katsuo didn't answer my page. And there's no one less likely to betray us—samurai loyalty and all that. The guy loves his job. Marius . . ." I shrugged and tried to ignore the stab of pain. "I knew it was a possibility."

"He blocked your signal to Katsuo?"

"Apparently. Luckily, my follow-up call worked or I might still be in that hole." I slumped into a deck chair and sighed. "You know what I can't believe? That when Dantalian's goons went looking for an ascended to turn, they didn't even try me. Some rebel angel. I'm a fraud, and everyone knows it."

He slanted me a look. "I hope you don't expect me to respond to that."

He was right, of course. I wasn't a fraud. I'd always prided myself on keeping my word. Granted, I didn't give it very often, but if I did, I kept it. That was the key to success in the dark underbelly of the supernatural world. You can be as bad as you want to be, but if you expect to survive and thrive, people have to know that if you agree to teach them a deadly spell, you won't turn it on them and empty their bank account.

"So . . . I guess I don't want to quit my job," I said. "But you knew that all along, didn't you?"

He didn't answer that, either.

"As much as I love it, though, I can't take the bullshit. I just can't."

"I know."

I looked over at him. "I need your advice."

He smiled. "I thought you'd never ask."

The Fates summoned me within the hour. When I arrived, Katsuo was gone. The youngest Fate was at the loom, weaving. She didn't even glance at me.

"You guys knew there was a traitor in the ranks, didn't you?"

She looked up, her bright eyes dancing. "We know everything."

"Then you didn't need me to find him."

"*Almost* everything."

"Why did you pick me? Because you thought one troublemaker would recognize another?"

The middle-aged Fate took over. "No, dear, because we knew if there was a traitor, you wouldn't quit until you found him."

"And I did, so now I can start my vacation, right? And on that subject—"

"You want an extension," she said with a put-upon sigh.

"No."

"No?" The old Fate appeared. "You'd better not want anything else, Eve Levine. We don't grant favors to angels for doing their job. We'll give you exactly the number of hours you lost, because that's fair, but don't you dare push—"

"I wasn't going to. I'll take compensation for the hours I lost. I know I don't deserve special treatment."

Her eyes narrowed.

"I figured a few things out while I was gone. At first, I was mad as hell, ranting about how unfair it was. Then I realized you guys aren't being unfair at all. I'm a celestial pain in the ass, always sneaking around, getting into trouble, breaking the rules. If I want to be treated better, I need to act better. I need to be a proper angel."

She eyed me, waiting for the punch line.

"When I come back, I'm going to follow the rules. All of them."

"No one asked you to—"

"I get that. You've been very patient with me, but it's been five years and it's time for me to shape up and toe the line."

The three Fates morphed in and out, as if each was clamoring to speak. Then the old one asserted herself and, for a minute, there was silence. I met her gaze, mine as open and guileless as I could make it.

"Fine," she harrumphed. "Take an extra month, but don't—"

"No, I'm serious. You want the Good Witch? I can be the Good Witch."

"Six weeks." She scowled. "And that's my final offer."

"Wow. Well, okay, I guess. But you do want me to behave myself, right? That's what you're always getting on my case about: my misbehavior. Ergo, you must want—"

"We want you to do your job."

"And I want to do it." I locked gazes with her. "I want to do it right. My kind of right. If you want the same thing, then you need to back off and let me work."

We stood there a moment, staring each other down. She dropped her eyes first, grumbling under her breath before saying, "Go. We'll talk when you get back."

I turned away, smiled, and teleported off to meet Kris in La Ceiba. Time to play pirate.

THE UNGRATEFUL DEAD

I see dead people. Unfortunately, they also see me.

One of the first lessons a necromancer learns is the art of playing dumb. When strolling down Fifth Avenue, searching for that perfect pair of shoes, pay no attention to the guy in the Civil War uniform. If he notices the glow that marks you as a necro, he will attempt to make conversation. Pretend you don't see him. With practice, you'll learn to finesse the act—pursing your lips, tilting your head, murmuring, "Oh my God, would you look at those darling Jimmy Choos!"

Eventually, the ghost will decide you're untrained—or just plain stupid—and wander off before getting to the part that begins with, "Say, could you do me a favor . . . ?" Of course, one problem with playing dumb is that it seeps into your everyday life. But that has its advantages, too. No one ever asks me to help them with their taxes.

Now, as I stood behind the stage curtain, I searched for signs of any otherworldly presences. Nothing screws up a séance like the appearance of a real ghost.

I heard my intro begin. "This is their world. A world of peace and beauty and joy. A world we all wish to enter."

I tensed, flexing my calf muscles.

"Jaime . . ." Brett warned as he fixed my hair. "Stand still or this piece is going to wave like a bug antenna."

Achieving an artlessly windswept updo is, truly, an art form. But it was part of the "sexy librarian" look I adopted for my shows.

The pinned-up red hair, the modestly cut but curve-hugging dress, and, of course, the wire-rimmed glasses. Admittedly, at forty-six, I was pushing the limit of how much longer there would be any "sexy" in my librarian. Keep the house lights low, though, and I looked damned hot.

My cue came. I walked to the curtain, cheeks twitching as I struggled to keep my smile on, reminding myself I'd need it for the next two hours.

As I stepped onto the dimly lit catwalk, I could hear the breathing of the sold-out crowd. Their excitement ignited mine and my grin broke through. I bit my cheek.

"Come with me now," my recorded whisper snaked through the hushed theater. "Let me take you into their world. The world of the spirits."

I stopped. The speakers hissed as the recording switched to a man's voice.

"The Globe Theater proudly presents . . . internationally renowned spiritualist . . ." Another hiss as the volume swelled, the house lights rising with it. "Jaime Vegas!"

"I'm getting a male relative," I said to Patty, a round-faced woman with big tortoiseshell glasses straight out of the eighties. "His name starts with *N* . . . no, wait . . . *M*. Yes, *M*."

Statistically speaking, *M* is one of the most common first letters for male given names. Somewhere in Patty's mental file, she'd find a deceased Mike, a Matthew, or . . .

"Mort!" she shrieked, like she'd correctly answered the Double Jeopardy question. "My uncle Mort."

"Yes, that's right. Your moth . . ." I drew out the word, watching for her reaction. At her frantic nod, I said decisively, "Your mother's brother."

Interpreting cues is the key to cold reading. Sometimes it is only a slight widening of the eyes or a faint involuntary nod. But there were people like Patty, so eager to praise and encourage me that I felt like a puppy who'd finally piddled outside.

I spent the next few minutes postponing the inevitable message, with "Wait, he's fading . . . No, here he comes . . . I think he's trying to say something . . ." It's a two-hour show.

I was in the midst of "reeling" Mort back when a voice said, "You called?"

I glanced behind me. There stood a sixtyish bald man with a round face, bearing a striking resemblance to Patty. Uncle Mort. It doesn't matter that I rarely summon ghosts on stage. Sometimes they just show up.

"Mortimer!" I beamed a smile as his gaze nestled in my cleavage. "How wonderful. I thought I'd lost you."

"Uncle Mort?" Patty bounced, clearing her seat by a good three inches. "It's me, Patty."

Mort squinted. "Patty? Shit. I thought you said *Pammy*, her sister." His eyes rolled back as he smiled. "Mmm. Pammy. She was always the cute one, but after she turned sixteen? Boom." He gestured to show what part of Pammy's anatomy had exploded.

"Uncle Mort would like to tell your sister, Pammy, that he's thinking of her."

"Ask her if Pammy's still hot," Mort said. "Last time I saw her was at my funeral. She wore this lacy little black number. And no panties." He chortled. "That's one good thing about being a ghost—"

"Uncle Mort remembers that black silk dress Pammy wore to his funeral."

If Patty bounced any higher, she was going to take flight. "What about me? Does he remember me?"

"Yeah," Mort said. "The fat one. Even as a baby she was a little tub of lard—"

"Uncle Mort says he remembers what a beautiful baby you were, so cute and chubby with red cheeks like apples."

Patty spent the next few minutes telling Uncle Mort about Cousin Ken's cataracts and Aunt Amy's arthritis and little Lulu's lazy eye. Uncle Mort ignored her, instead peppering me with questions about Pammy.

"Are you even listening to me?" Mort said finally.

"Uncle Mort appreciates the update," I said. "And he'd like you to pass on a message in return. Tell everyone he misses them dearly—"

"Miss them? One more Christmas with those people and if the cancer didn't get me—"

"—but he's gone to a good place, and he's happy."

"Would I be *here* if I was happy? I'm bored out of my frigging skull."

I crouched beside Patty, clasped her hands, and wished her all the best. Then I returned to the catwalk. "Uncle Mort has left us now."

Mort jumped in front of me, waving his arms. I walked through him.

"She's ignoring you," another voice said.

"I'm waiting for a new spirit to make contact," I continued. "I can sense them just beyond the veil." I pretended to scan the room, to get a look at the new arrival without letting on I'd heard him. More secrets of the successful spiritualist.

A young man had climbed onto the catwalk. Dressed in a striped Henley shirt and cargo shorts, he was about twenty, stocky, with manicured beard stubble. A frat boy, I guessed. A ghost, I knew. The fact no one noticed him sauntering down the catwalk gave it away.

I continued to survey the room. "A spirit is trying to break through the veil . . ."

"Don't bother, buddy," Mort said to the other ghost. "She may be a necromancer, but she needs some serious remedial training."

"Actually, I hear she's very good. Comes from a long line of powerful necros."

"Yeah? Well, it skipped a generation."

"I have a name," I intoned, eyes half closed. "Is there a Belinda in the audience?" In seat L15, if my sources were correct.

"See?" Mort said. "She doesn't even know we're here."

"Oh, she knows." The frat boy's voice carried a burr of condescension. "Don't you, Red?"

"Do I have a Belinda in the audience? Hoping to contact her father?"

A bingo hall shriek as an elderly woman—in L15—leapt up. I made my way over to her. Mort stomped back to his afterlife. The frat boy stayed.

After the show, I strode down the backstage hall, an icy water bottle pressed to my cheek.

My assistant, Tara, scampered along beside me. "We have a ten a.m. tomorrow with the *Post-Intelligencer*, then a two o'clock pre-tape with KCPQ. Friday's show is totally sold out, but you can plug the October one in Portland."

"Will do. Now, can you find Kat? Let's see if we can't get that sound system fixed before Friday."

I slipped into my dressing room, closed the door, and leaned against it. A slow clapping started across the room.

The frat boy slid off my dressing table. "Okay, show's over. You done good, Red. Now it's time to get to work. Be a real necromancer."

I uncapped my water and chugged.

"Cut the crap," he said. "I know you can—"

"—hear you. Yes, I can." I mopped my sweaty face with a towel. "But a dressing-room ambush really isn't a good way to get my attention."

His full lips twisted. "Oh, please. You think I'm going to peep at you undressing? You're, like, forty."

"I meant it's rude." I tossed the towel aside and grabbed my hairbrush. "If you'd like to talk, meet me at the rear doors in twenty minutes."

"Um, no. I'm going to talk to you now and I'm not leaving until I do."

Rule one of "how to win favors and influence necros"? Never threaten. I'd say if you're lucky enough to get one to listen, you should fall on your knees with gratitude. But that might be pushing it. A simple "okay, thanks" will do.

I'm not heartless. In fact, in the past few years I've made a real effort to listen to ghosts, and I'd had every intention of hearing this one out. But he was fast blowing his chance.

I turned to the mirror and brushed out my hair, pins clinking to the floor.

"Don't turn your back on me," the ghost said.

"I'm not. As I said, I'll be ready in twenty minutes."

He walked through the dressing table, planting himself between the mirror and me. "Fine. How about this?"

He shimmered, then shot back, clothing drenched with blood, stomach ripped open, safety glass shards studding his intestines. A brain-splattered metal rod protruded from his ear. One eye bounced on his cheek.

"Oh my God! No, please," I mock-pleaded. "Not the death body. I'll do whatever you want!" I reached through his intestines for my cold cream. "Do you really think you're the first spook who's tried that? I've seen decapitations, burnings, drownings, bear maulings, electrocution . . ." I leaned to see my reflection past the rod sticking from his head. "A couple of years ago, there was this one ghost who'd been cut almost in half. Industrial accident, I guess. That one *did* give me a start. But car accidents? Pfft."

I met his eyes—or the one still in its socket. "Did you see that segment on E! last month? About celebrities addicted to plastic surgery? They talk and it's like watching a ventriloquist's dummy. Only their mouths move. *That* scares me."

I went into the bathroom to wash my face. The ghost followed. He'd changed back to his regular body, and stood behind me, arms crossed. Now, I've played this game before, and I could usually hold out longer than any ghost. But then my cell phone rang.

Even without the special ring tone, I knew it was my boyfriend, Jeremy. He always called me after a show to see how it went and he always timed it perfectly, giving me a chance to wind down but catching me before I headed out for a postshow talk with my staff.

The call also reminded me that he was coming to Seattle after my Friday show. Our schedules allow only weekend visits every couple of months, and there was no way in hell I was spending this one with a ghost in residence.

So I told Jeremy I'd call him back, then said to the ghost, "What do you want?"

"My cousin died in the same accident as me. I want you to open his coffin."

"I'm not a grave digger."

"He isn't in the ground. Our family has a mausoleum."

"And why would I want to open his coffin?"

He looked down his nose at me, not easy when he was no more than my five foot six.

"Because you're a necromancer. You serve the dead. I'm dead. So serve."

Of course, I said no, in increasingly descriptive ways. Of course, he didn't let it go at that.

The problem with refusing a ghost's request is that you can't say no and walk away. Wherever you can go, they can go. At my staff meeting, Frat Boy stood between me and them and shouted the Pledge of Allegiance. When I called Jeremy back, Frat Boy mocked and mimicked my conversation. In the rented limo, he sat on my lap and switched in and out of his death body.

Being unable to touch anything in the living world squashes a ghost's threat potential. But they can be damned annoying. And this guy was a pro, making me wonder how many other necros he'd hit up before finding me.

When it came time for my shower, I declared war. I've had enough ghostly Peeping Toms to get over any modesty. But Frat Boy would do more insulting than ogling, and as healthy as my ego was, I didn't need a twenty-year-old studying me for signs of sagging and cellulite.

So I filled a censer with vervain, set it alight, and banished him. A temporary measure that worked until 4:10 a.m., when the herbs burned up and I woke to him screaming the Pledge in my ear. I added more vervain, and went back to sleep.

When I woke, there was no sign of Chuck. I had no idea what the ghost's name was, but he looked like a Charles Willingham III or something equally pretentious—he reeked of money and privilege, too much of both, the smell as strong as BO and just as offensive. If he was a Charles, I'm sure he'd be Chas. I'd call him Chuck.

I hoped he was gone for good and naming him was premature. The last bit of vervain still smoldered, though. When it disappeared, he'd be back.

I added another pinch, and noticed I was getting low. That happens when I'm on tour. There's a limit to how much dried plant material you can take on a plane. Even if I explain I'm a spiritualist and produce documentation, a satchel of dehydrated herbs begs for a trip to the little white room and a cavity search.

Half of my remaining supply of vervain gave me time to dress and escape. But as I walked into the TV station that afternoon, Chuck found me. I spent the next half hour with a ghost prancing naked between the interviewer and me. Though I kept my cool, I knew my distraction would show—eyes a little too round, gaze darting a little too often, laugh a little too shrill. That wouldn't do. Part of my appeal is that, yes, I can be spacey, but in a ditzy, C-list-celebrity way, not one that screams, "I just got my day pass."

Afterward, sitting in the cab, listening to Chuck do a stand-up routine of sexist jokes, I envisioned him harassing me through my Friday show and into my weekend.

I can take abuse. But there are two things no one interferes with: work and Jeremy. The warning shots hadn't scared this guy away. Time to haul out the howitzer.

Normally, my "big gun" comes in the form of a sword-wielding, ass-kicking spirit bodyguard. Eve is a half-demon and a part-time angel, proving even the afterlife has moved to nondiscriminatory hiring practices. But Eve was on a celestial stint, and incommunicado.

So I had to do this myself. That meant the heavy-duty banishing ritual, one that required a lot of time, effort, and ingredients. The last was the sticking point. Vervain wasn't the only herb I was low on. So I placed a call to my west-coast supplier.

Paige Winterbourne is a witch who lives in Portland and has everything a spell-caster or necromancer could need. She doesn't sell the stuff. She's just better organized than me . . . or anyone else I know.

It was still late afternoon, and Paige never went home early, so I called the office.

"Cortez-Winterbourne Demon Hunters," a voice sang. "Get 'em slayed before you get flayed."

"That's new."

"Yeah, needs work, though. The rhythm's off." A pause and a double thump, and I imagined Savannah leaning her chair back, feet banging onto the desk. "So how's the celeb necro biz?"

Savannah was Eve's nineteen-year-old daughter and Paige's ward. From the way she answered the phone when she recognized my number, I knew Paige wasn't there.

"Lucas is off in Chicago defending a client," Savannah said. "Paige and Adam are in San Fran with Cass, checking out a vamp problem. Guess who's stuck behind answering the phone? I told Paige that's why God invented voice mail. But now I have a feeling my week is looking up. So what kind of trouble are you in? Kidnapped again?"

"Ha-ha. No trouble. I just need ritual supplies from Paige. Do you have access to her stash? Or does she still keep it under lock, key, and security spell so you don't blow anything else up?"

"Ha-ha. The shed was an accident. So what's the ritual for? Summoning or banishing?"

"Banishing." I listed what I needed.

"Ooh, big-ass banishment. What did your spook do to deserve that?"

"The usual. Tormenting me. Insulting me. Blasting me with the Pledge of Allegiance."

"Allegiance assault? The bastard."

"It's probably the only thing he'd ever memorized. Anyway, if you could courier the stuff to Seattle—"

"Seattle? You're just around the corner."

"A hundred and fifty miles around the corner."

"I'll be there by seven."

"No! I appreciate that, but really—"

"Staying at the Olympic, as usual?"

"Er, yes, but—"

"Seven it is. Don't eat without me."

Savannah arrived at 7:20, bearing pizza and beer. I wasn't asking how she got the beer. With Savannah, I'm better off not knowing.

She kicked off her knee-high boots, peeled a slice from the box, and folded her long limbs into a chair, pulling her feet up under her. "So, what does he want?"

"Who?"

"Your spook. Does he have a name?"

"I call him Chuck."

"So Chuck presumably asked you for a favor. You couldn't do it. He's making your life hell. You need to banish him. Which is why you shouldn't let them ask in the first place."

"It was more of a demand, really. But I have been trying to listen more often, help with little things like passing on messages."

"Uh-huh. How's that working out for you? Though I guess that"—she jabbed her pizza slice at the burning vervain—"answers my question. About Chuck, though. What does he want?"

I took a beer and sat on the sofa. "He and his cousin died in a car accident. They were interred in the family mausoleum. He wants me to open his cousin's casket."

"And . . ."

"There is no 'and.' Apparently, as a servant to the afterlife, it's not my place to question the will of the dead."

"Asshole." She chugged half her beer. "If he's got a mausoleum, that means he's got money—or his family does. I bet there's something valuable in that casket, and jerk-wad is just too stupid to realize it won't do him any good, being dead. So, if we did find something, we'd keep it."

"No, I'd give it back to his family."

"Shit. Jeremy's rubbing off on you, huh?"

"I'm sure there's no treasure in that casket."

"Then why does he want you to open it? Aren't you curious?"

I wasn't. Another necromancer lesson: never stop to question. There are too many opportunities. Like the residual in Savannah's house—a woman forever watching out the window. I should wonder what she's looking for, why it is so emotionally powerful that the image of it is seared forever within those walls. But necromancers can't afford idle curiosity. They'll go mad chasing questions whose answers don't really matter. That doesn't keep me from feeling like I *should* be curious, though.

"It is odd . . ." I said finally.

"Good." Savannah smacked her bottle down. "Let's go take a

look and get rid of this spook, so you can skip the nasty banishment ritual. You don't want to be wiped out when Jeremy's here, right?"

I hadn't thought of that. One problem, though . . . "If I do it, he wins. I'll have ghosts lining up to scream the Pledge of Allegiance at me."

"I'll handle that." She tamped out the burning vervain with her fingertips. "Yo, Chuck!"

After a moment, he appeared. "Who the hell is Chu—?" He saw the pizza and beer. "A party for me?" His gaze moved to Savannah. "Whoa. You even brought party favors. Sweet."

Savannah's gaze followed mine and fixed on a spot near the ghost. "Sit down, Chuck. Grab a beer." She sucked back the rest of the bottle, eyes rolling in rapture. The pizza came next, dangled over her mouth, twisting the cheese strands around her tongue. "*So* good. Want some?"

His eyes slitted. "Teasing little—"

"He appreciates the offer," I said. "But respectfully declines."

She set down the pizza. "Come here, Chuck. I have a proposition I think you'd like."

Hope glimmered in his eyes, then guttered out as he remembered his noncorporeal state.

"We're going to open your cousin's casket. No, you didn't wear Jaime down. I'm curious, so I talked her into it. Give her any grief, though, and she has the shit now to do a full banishment. And if you ever come around again? Or tell anyone we did this for you?" She recited a spell. A fireball appeared at her fingertips. "I'll replace your balls with these."

"Bitch."

"He agrees to your terms," I said. "And thanks you for your help."

She pulled on her boots. "Off to the graveyard we go, then. My first mausoleum break-in." She paused at the door. "Actually, my second, but if Paige asks . . ."

"It was your first."

⚜

It wasn't the first mausoleum break-in for me. Or the second. A practicing necromancer needs "artifacts of the grave" and the easiest way to get them is from bodies in crypts.

Between grave robbery and graveside summonings, I'd been in enough cemeteries to write a guidebook. I could also write a security manual for cemetery owners. I rarely encountered more than floodlights and an hourly rent-a-cop drive-by.

This cemetery had taken the extra step of locking the gates after dark . . . a gate attached to a fence with gaps you could ride a horse through. They'd splurged on lights, too; from a distance, the place looked like a runway. But all the lighting in the world doesn't help when you're outside the city limits, a mile from the nearest house.

As we drove up in Savannah's car, I suspected Chuck had played us—this cemetery looked too small and new for family mausoleums. Apparently, though, it'd been designed by someone with a background in real estate, creating "mixed-dwelling" communities. Here, you had your apartments (columbaria), single-family dwellings (graves), and McMansions (mausoleums). The latter targeted families with too much money, too high an opinion of themselves, and too little time to actually check out the product before plunking down the cash. The buildings were little more than faux Graeco-Roman sheds.

Savannah picked the lock and we stepped inside to what looked like a summer-camp bunkhouse, stinking of damp wood, the walls lined with berths and a few coffins.

"So which—?" I began.

Chuck motioned for silence and made me relay it to Savannah.

"Um, okay," she said. "But someone should tell him 'waking the dead' is only an expression."

And, it seemed, we were the only ones supposed to stay silent. Chuck kept up a running commentary as we cast our flashlight beams around. When Savannah approached his cousin's casket, he got louder.

"Do you hear that?" Savannah asked.

"I can't hear anything with Chuck yapping." Which I began to suspect was the point.

"Something's in here." She bent to open the coffin. "Are mice scavengers? If so, I think we have a nest of them chowing down at the body buffet."

My "Wait!" came out like the squeak of a mouse, which must be what she mistook it for, because she threw open the lid. The corpse leapt up like a jack-in-the-box, shrieking and gobbling, fingers worn through from battering the casket, bone tips clawing the air, flesh tatters waving.

I'd seen this coming, but I still fell back. Even Savannah did, uttering a "Holy fucking shit!"

At the sound of her voice, the zombie went still. His head swiveled toward her. Then, with the grace of a landlocked hippo, he lurched over the side of the casket. Savannah stepped back and the zombie, his internal bits and bones out of whack, hit the floor, limbs sprawled.

"Dude, chill." Savannah brushed a stray bit of flesh from her jeans. "Do we look like grave robbers? Your cousin brought this nice necromancer here, and I'm guessing he wanted her to help you out of your predicament."

The zombie looked around but, of course, couldn't see Chuck, who'd taken a seat in an empty berth and watched, arms crossed, waiting for me to get on with my job.

After a moment, the zombie got up. It wasn't easy. His left leg had evidently been broken in the accident and coroners don't reset bones on dead people.

He propped himself against the wall and looked at us, his gaze keen and very human. A real zombie isn't the shambling brain-chomper of movie myth. It's a ghost returned to its corpse. Simple . . . and simply horrifying.

"So how did this happen?" I asked.

"What the fuck does it matter how it happened?" he shouted, wheezing through a hole in his throat. "Get me out of this rotting corpse!"

"You know, it shouldn't be rotting," Savannah said. "Someone went cheap with the embalming, dude."

"Stop calling me 'dude.'"

"Would you prefer 'decomposing hunk of stinking meat'? Speaking of which, he is damned ripe, Jaime. Can we crack open the door before I hurl?"

I motioned for Savannah to tone it down and made a mental note to give her zombie-sensitivity training later.

"Again," I said. "How did you—?"

"What the fuck does it matter, you dumb twat?"

He did not say "twat." The word he used made Savannah grab him by the suit collar and shake him.

"Show some respect, dick-wad. She's trying to help you." A sharper shake. "That right hand looks a little loose. If I smack it off, it ain't growing back."

I motioned for Savannah to release him. Zombies are notoriously unhygienic.

"The reason I'm asking," I said calmly, "isn't to satisfy my curiosity. I don't really care how you got in there. But until I know, I can't get you out." I swept off a dusty niche and perched on the edge. "Why don't I take a guess? You and Chuck—"

"It's Byron," said the ghost.

"You and your cousin. You die in a car accident. You come back as ghosts. You find a necromancer. You demand something and you won't let up, so he teaches you a lesson by shoving you back into your body. Am I close?"

The zombie tried unsuccessfully to cross his arms. "I only wanted him to bring us back to life."

"And he did," Savannah said.

"I didn't mean like *this*."

"That's the only way it can be done," I said. "I'm sure he tried to tell you that. You didn't believe him. So he showed you. Now he's let you stew for a few days before setting you free." I took my flashlight from the berth. "I'll go talk to him and get this sorted. Where is he?"

Chuck said, "Not good enough to do it yourself, Red?"

"No, I'm not 'good enough' to free another necro's zombie. It can't be done."

The zombie turned on me. "What? No way."

"It doesn't matter. I'm sure I can persuade this guy—"

"He's gone," Chuck said.

"Gone where?"

"If I knew, do you think I'd bother with you?"

The cousins each gave their own rambling account, drowning out and often contradicting each other. After wading through the bullshit that blamed everyone but themselves, I figured out two things. One, some people never learn. Two, I wasn't getting Chuck's cousin un-zombified anytime soon.

After their pestering led the necromancer to return the cousin's soul to his body, Chuck had decided the best way to fix it was to pester the guy some more. The necro had opted for an impromptu vacation to parts unknown.

"Okay," I said. "I have a lot of contacts, so tell me everything you know about him and, hopefully, in a few days—"

"A few days!" the cousins said in unison, then launched into rants that could be summed up as: "You're useless and stupid and if you don't get him out of that body, you'll regret it." After a few minutes of this, I began to think that, while I never thought I'd condone zombification, I could see the other necromancer's point.

If I could have stuffed Cousin Zombie back into his casket, I would have, but getting him there meant risking a noxious scratch or bite. So I agreed to attempt a soul-freeing ritual. And I kept attempting it for an hour before I gave up. That's when Savannah mentioned she knew a spell that might work.

"Why the hell didn't you say so?" the zombie said.

"A spell for freeing souls?" I said. "I've never heard of that."

"Because it's not meant for zombies. I'm thinking outside the box."

"Thinking?" the zombie said. "Must be a new experience for you."

"Do you want back *inside* the box? Nailed shut?"

"So, this spell," I said. "The real application is . . ."

"Knocking the soul out of a living person."

"Temporarily, I hope."

"Supposedly . . . but that's why I haven't tested it. Lack of volunteers."

The zombie cleared his throat, air whistling through the hole. "This is all fascinating, ladies. But in case you haven't noticed, this body isn't getting any fresher."

Savannah looked at him. "I want to be clear this is an untested, very difficult, very dangerous dark magic spell, intended for use—"

"Oh, for God's sake. Do you want me to sign a fucking liability waiver?"

"No, but I happen to be a mixed-blood witch," Savannah said, switching to a tone that sounded eerily like Lucas's legalese-speak. "That means when I cast a spell, the results can be more vigorous than intended. I'm trying to become a more responsible spell-caster by considering the ramifications—"

"Rotting here . . ."

She glanced at me.

I nodded. "If anything goes wrong, I'll tell Paige you gave him the disclaimer."

Savannah cast the spell, and cast, and cast again. The first two times, nothing happened, and the cousins started their heckling. By the third cast, her eyes were blazing as she spit the words. I probably should have stopped her, but when I saw the zombie's skin balloon and bubble, like it was in a pressure cooker, I thought his soul was about to pop free. Something did pop. His left eyeball, shooting out, bouncing across the floor, then coming to rest, optic nerve quivering like a sperm tail.

Cousin Zombie screamed, breaking it off in a string of profanity long enough to hang someone with. From the looks he shot Savannah, there was no doubt whom he'd hang.

"Hey, I warned you." She prodded the eyeball with her boot. "You know what they say. It's all fun and games until someone loses—"

He lunged at her. She hit him with a knockback spell, smacking him against the wall, the flimsy mausoleum trembling. He bounced back, fists swinging.

"Watch out," Savannah said. "That hand is really wobbling."

He ran at her. She caught him in a binding spell.

"Damn, this isn't easy," she said through clenched teeth. "It doesn't work as well on zombies."

"Nothing does."

"We've got about ten seconds before he breaks it. And he's really pissed."

"No kidding!" yelled Chuck, who hadn't been silent, just ignored. "You popped out his eye, you incompetent—"

I returned him to ignore mode.

"Should I try the spell again?" Savannah asked, face straining with the effort of keeping the zombie bound. "I think I was close."

I looked from Cousin Zombie, frozen in a savage snarl, to Chuck, spitting dire vows of vengeance, and I decided, at this stage, "close" wasn't really an issue.

"Go for it," I said.

This time, the spell worked in the sense that it didn't fizzle. It didn't release his soul, either. Just that loose hand, which sailed off and flopped like a trout at my feet.

"Did anyone *not* see that coming?" Savannah asked.

The zombie broke the binding spell then and Savannah showed off her single year of ballet lessons by pirouetting out of his way as he lumbered after her.

"Forget her!" Chuck shouted. "Get the necromancer. She's old and slow."

Great advice, if only zombies could hear ghosts. His cousin kept dancing with Savannah, who, after a few rounds, zapped him with another binding spell. Caught off balance, he tottered and fell sideways.

She whisked off her belt. "Are you over this 'I should be more helpful' shit yet?"

"In general, no," I said. "In this case, as you may recall, I was done with Chuck before you got here. Then you convinced me to open Pandora's casket." I walked closer, skirting the zombie in case the spell broke. "We aren't getting this guy back in that box without a fight. Even if we manage it, someone could find him, and I'll be the only council delegate who's ever had to haul her own ass before a disciplinary committee."

"Molly Crane."

I stared at Savannah.

"You remember Molly." She looped the belt around the zombie's ankles.

"Dark witch? Your mother's contact? You sent me to her for information, she knocked me out, dragged me into the woods, tried to torture me and dump my remains in a swamp? I vaguely recall her, yes."

"So what do you think?"

"About what?"

She untwisted her scarf. "Molly would *love* to babysit this guy for you. Not only does she get a slave, but the bits that fall off are gold on the black market. Then, when you've found that necro, he can de-zombify this guy, preferably after Mom's back to deal with him."

Again, I could only stare.

"What?" she said as she gagged the zombie with her scarf.

"Last time you saw Molly Crane, you left *her* gagged and bound."

"I didn't gag her. And she'll be over it." She knotted the scarf. "If not, then this is the perfect olive branch. She'll be happy for the excuse. I'm Eve Levine's daughter. Having me in her contact book is almost as valuable as those zombie bits. Of course, there is an alternative. We can put him in my trunk, take him to your hotel . . ."

"Do you still have her number?"

"Right here." She took out her iPhone.

Chuck leapt from his perch. "Am I hearing this right? You're going to sell my cousin into slavery?" He strode over to me, switching to his death body for effect. "You do this and you will regret it. You think I was bad before? That was nothing compared to what's coming. I'll haunt you every minute of every day, and there's nothing you can do about it."

"Nothing?" I said softly.

He crossed his arms. "Nothing."

I took a slow step back toward the middle of the mausoleum.

A smirk rippled his defiant scowl. "So, Red, I'd suggest you start speed-dialing those contacts of yours."

"Uh-huh." I scanned the crypt, then walked the perimeter.

"That's right. Find a place to get comfy. It's going to be a long night."

I stopped at a casket and my gaze settled on the plaque. Byron Carruthers. "Your name's Byron, right?"

"That's what I said. And you'd better start using it. No more of this Chuck shit. Got it?"

I unlatched the casket.

"What the hell are you doing?"

"Just getting a look." I heaved it open. "Seems you've rotted even worse than your cousin. That's not good."

"Yeah? So what?"

I retrieved my Gucci makeup bag of necromancy supplies. "Savannah?"

She pulled the phone from her ear. "Hmm?"

"Tell Molly we have a special today. Two zombies for the price of one."

I knelt beside the casket and started the ritual.

ZEN AND THE ART OF VAMPIRISM

*I*n Miller's Bar, the only thing that smelled worse than the bathroom was the clientele. Of the three humans there that night, two were already so pissed I could have walked over, sunk my teeth into their necks, and they'd never have flinched. Tempting, but Rudy the bartender likes me sticking to beer.

Cultural assimilation is a lofty goal. Yet every minority needs a place to kick back with her own kind, a place to trade news and gossip that wouldn't interest outsiders. For supernaturals in Toronto, that place is Miller's.

The clientele isn't exclusively supernatural. That kind of thing is hard to enforce without calling attention to yourself, which none of us wants to do. But the ambiance alone is usually enough to discourage outsiders.

Tonight the only sober human was a guy in a suit sitting at the bar, drinking in his surroundings and telling himself that, despite his house in the suburbs and corporate parking spot, he was still a badass. And as long as he was misbehaving, the Japanese girl in the short skirt and knee-high boots looked just right to cap off his evening. I'd already rejected the two drinks he'd sent my way, but he wasn't getting the message, not even when I blatantly eyed the blond half-demon girl at the other end of the bar.

While I'd have settled for an introduction to the half-demon, what I really wanted was a job. My rent was due, my bar tab was overdue, and if I didn't get a gig in the next week I'd be digging through my stash of goodies looking for something to fence. I supposed I *could* return my new red leather jacket and matching boots, but I hoped to resolve the situation long before it became that desperate.

A job might be forthcoming. According to Rudy, a guy had come by last night, asking about hiring me. I don't usually take jobs without referrals, but desperate times . . .

I swore I heard the bells of St. James toll midnight when the guy I was waiting for walked in. He slunk through the door, looking around furtively, hands stuffed in his overcoat pockets like a perv getting ready to flash. The overcoat didn't help. Nor did the rest of the outfit—skintight pleather pants, an open-necked shirt and chains. Someone had watched *Underworld* one too many times.

Rudy said the guy had introduced himself as José. If there was an ounce of Hispanic blood in him, I'd drink cow's blood for a week.

He'd made it halfway to the bar before Rudy pointed me out to him. The guy stopped. He looked at me. He looked some more.

Obviously, I wasn't what he expected. Unfortunately, he was exactly what I expected—scruffy, stringy hair, wild eyes. Toronto doesn't get a lot of new supernaturals and those who do land here are usually on the run from trouble south of the border. I only hoped José didn't want me to permanently fix that trouble for him. I'm a thief, not an assassin, but I've had more than one client imply that it shouldn't make a difference. Vampires kill; therefore, they should have no compunction about doing it for money.

José walked to my table. "Zoe Takano?"

I motioned to the chair across from me.

"It's, uh, about a job," he said.

I motioned at the chair again.

His gaze skittered about the bar. "Shouldn't we, uh, take this outside?"

"Does anyone in here look like an undercover cop?"

He gave a nervous chuckle. "I guess not."

Actually, the hulking half-demon in the corner *was* one, but we had an understanding.

"Tell me what you have in mind," I said. "Just leave out the identifying details until I've agreed."

It was a theft, something about a ring. I didn't pay much attention, because after two lines of his story I knew there was no job. That's when he'd turned to call a drink order to Rudy, and his hair swung off his neck, revealing the ghosts of a half-dozen puncture wounds.

Vamp freak.

Just as there are humans who get off on bloodletting, there are supernaturals who do, too. The difference is that supernaturals don't need to find someone to play vampire for them. They can get a real one.

Toronto didn't have any resident vamp freaks. There was no point, since I was the only vampire here.

I let José natter on, then set my beer aside. "You're right. Let's take this outside."

He jumped up so fast he set the table wobbling. Rudy scowled from behind the bar, José's drink in hand.

"Pay the man," I said.

José opened his wallet and stared in confusion at the multi-colored bills.

"This one's pretty," I said, plucking out a red fifty. I handed it to Rudy, mouthing for him to apply the extra to my tab. Then I waved José out of the bar.

I led José to an alley two blocks away. He trailed at my heels even when I said he could walk beside me. Someone had him trained well. I shivered and briefly wondered who.

I got far enough down the alley to be hidden from the street and then turned sharply.

290 · KELLEY ARMSTRONG

"No," I said.

"No?"

"I'm not interested."

"In the job? I thought . . ."

He stopped as I moved in, so close our clothing brushed. Then I lifted onto my tiptoes. I didn't say a word. Just gave him the look. His pupils dilated. His heart raced, the sound of it echoing through the alley, the sight of it pulsing in his neck making my fangs lengthen. He let out a groan and shifted forward, his erection rubbing my leg.

I stepped back. "*That's* what I meant. And the answer is no."

"Please? Just a bite. Just a taste."

I swallowed my revulsion. My fangs retracted. As I took another step back, a crackle sounded behind me. A foot treading on trash.

He kept babbling. "I'm a clean-living Druid. *Totally* clean. No booze. No dope. No cigarettes. I haven't even taken aspirin in months."

"And do you know what all that healthy living is going to get you? A comfy berth in the morgue."

He shook his head. "No, I'm always careful. I know what it feels like when you need to stop. I have a safe word—"

"Which works just fine until it's time for your master's annual kill. That's how it ends, José. That's how it always ends. So take my advice and find a human playmate who'll bite your neck for you and—"

I spun, my kick connecting with the kneecap of a hulking figure. Another spin, another kick—this one to the back of her knee—and she went down.

The woman lying on the ground was at least six foot two and well muscled. A flaxen-haired Amazon. Admittedly, I have a weakness for strong blondes, but I knew drag queens who could pass for female more easily than this woman.

"Brigid Drescher, I presume," I said. "Pleased to meet you."

She snarled, spittle speckling my boots. I bent to wipe it off, then spun fast, fists and foot flying up. The dark-ponytailed vampire sneaking up behind me raised his hands.

"Hey, Hans," I said. "It's been a while."

Forty years, give or take a decade. Last time I saw Hans, he was still going by his real name: John. I kicked myself for not figuring out who "owned" José. If his rechristening hadn't given it away, his costume should have. Last I heard, Hans was on an Anne Rice kick, but judging by his outfit he'd progressed to *Underworld*. Either that or he spent his off-hours in a bordello.

As Brigid got to her feet, he turned to her. "I told you there wasn't any use trying to trick Zoe."

Brigid brushed off her leather corset. "I thought you said she didn't fight."

"Only in self-defense. Isn't that right, Zoe?"

I ignored his mocking lilt and managed a perky smile. "You got it. So what brings you two to Toronto?" I had an idea, and hoped I was wrong.

"José," Brigid said before Hans could answer. She snapped her fingers, and motioned the vamp freak to her side. He pretended not to notice and kept slinking closer to me. I sidestepped. He slunk. Sidestepped. Slunk.

Hans laughed. "I think your boy found something he likes better, Brig. Sorry, José, but you're not Zoe's type. Or gender."

José frowned, taking a moment to get it. Then he smiled and sidled closer.

"Go," I said, flicking my fingers at him. "Shoo."

"José!" Brigid barked.

He slid a look her way, shuddered, and wriggled closer to me. Brigid strode over and grabbed him, yelping, by the collar.

"When I tell you to come, you come."

His gaze shunted my way, and Brigid's head shot down to his neck, fangs sinking in. I started to say this wasn't the time for a snack. Then Brigid's head ripped back, a chunk of José's neck in her teeth, arterial blood spurting against the wall. She dropped him and spat out the flesh. José convulsed on the ground, gasping and jerking, hands pressed to his neck, eyes rolling as he tried to stop the flow.

I looked down at him, knowing there was nothing I could do, feeling the old serpent of rage uncoil in my gut. My gaze shot to Brigid, but at the last second I wrenched it away and turned aside.

"What's the matter, Takano?" Brigid said. "Don't like the sight of blood?"

I counted to five, until the serpent relaxed and slid back into hiding. Then I turned and smiled.

"I have a weak stomach, what can I say?"

José lay on his back now, sightless eyes staring up.

"Well, that was a waste," Hans said, stepping away as the blood seeped toward his boots. "You really need to control your temper, Brig."

"Can we get this conversation over with?" I said. "I'd really rather not be found standing over a dead body." I kept my gaze on Hans, my tone light. "And I do hope you plan to clean this mess up. It's terribly bad form to leave bodies in another vamp's town."

"That's what we're here to talk about," he said. "Your town."

"It's not yours anymore," Brigid said.

That's what I was afraid of. Hans and his little gang had lived in New Orleans. From what I'd heard, they'd been thrilled when Hurricane Katrina hit—a chaos-gripped city makes for easy pickings. But after a year, they'd realized trailer-park life really wasn't their style. Since then, they'd been hunting for a new place to settle.

"Toronto?" I laughed. "Seriously? Sure, it's a world-class city, multicultural, blah, blah. But it's *Toronto*. There's a reason a third-rate vamp like me lives here. No one else wants it. Long, cold winters. Hot, humid summers. Smog so thick you can taste it. Taxes are outrageous, and for what? Free health care? Like vampires need that."

"You aren't going to give us any trouble, are you, Zoe?"

Hans's voice was smooth and soft, but there was an arrogant tilt to his chin and a condescending twist to his words.

For a moment, I reveled in a vision of what I would have done if he'd said those words a hundred years ago. A vampire's invulnerability makes it difficult to inflict any sensation like pain. But there are ways. And I know them all.

"You're welcome to fight for your territory," Brigid said. "But I hear you're a bit of a coward."

"Coward is a strong word."

She came so close I could see a shred of José's skin caught between her teeth. Then she took another step and towered over me.

"Is it?" she said.

I sidestepped to face Hans. "I'll be gone by Friday."

I was born Kioko Takano in 1863. My name meant "happy child," and I fulfilled its promise. My life was unremarkable. I was a cheerful girl with loving parents, who grew into a cheerful young woman with a loving fiancé.

A month before my wedding, a group of missionaries came to our village. One of them was Jane Bowman, a blond English girl not much older than myself. When I met her, I realized why, as dearly as I cared for my fiancé, I could feel no more passion for him than for a brother.

I fell in love with Jane. Madly, desperately in love. She was vibrant and brilliant and worldly, all the things I was not. I soon learned why she had so much experience, despite her youth—she was a hundred-year-old vampire. I didn't care. It only made her more exotic and wonderful. I loved her. She loved me. Nothing else mattered.

I ran away with Jane. The next few years were glorious. Then came my twentieth birthday, and to celebrate it she offered me the gift of eternal life. Become a vampire. Be young forever. Be with her forever.

I refused. She wheedled, pleaded, begged. I refused. She called me a coward. I laughed and refused. And then, I discovered, she really wasn't *asking*.

Being a gracious hostess, I offered to show Hans and Brigid around Toronto the next day. I'd introduce them to the supernatural community and make the transition easy. For a fee, of course.

We had to wait until after dark. Apparently, Hans was sensitive to daylight. He seemed to think this made him a more authentic vampire. I thought it made him an idiot.

And I wasn't the only one. Rudy got one look at the pair, dressed like they were heading to a BDSM convention, and marched into the back room. He emerged only when I hopped over the bar and helped myself to a beer.

"Not until you pay your tab, Zoe." He plucked the bottle from my hand. "And if you think you're cutting town and not paying? I will hunt you down and rip that pretty little—"

"I'll pay. Just give me a couple weeks to settle into my new place."

Rudy put the beer back and turned to Hans. "You're the new vamps Zoe told me about?"

Hans glanced about us, but it was early and the only patron was passed out, probably from the night before.

"Yes," Hans said. "We'll be taking over—"

Rudy slapped a paper onto the bar. "Pay her tab."

Brigid snorted. "We aren't going to—"

"You ever want to set foot in this place again?" Rudy asked.

Hans looked around. "Not particularly."

"You want to take Zoe's place in this city? Be part of the community?"

"We aren't really joiners."

Rudy stuffed the tab into his pocket. "Fine. Just remember, we've got over a hundred sorcerers, witches, half-demons, necromancers, and shamans in this city, and the only vampire they've ever known is Zoe. Now, if a *real* vampire comes to town, it's going to make folks nervous—"

"How much?" Hans said.

"Seven-hundred and eighty-two dollars."

Hans pivoted to me. "How much do you drink?"

"Only one beer a night. It's the paying part that gives me trouble."

"Make it an even grand and you'll get my personal seal of approval," Rudy said.

Hans sighed, pulled a wad of cash from his pocket, and peeled off the bills.

As Rudy counted them, he said, "My first piece of advice? Make sure this one"—he pointed at me—"shows you the ropes."

"That's what I'm doing."

He met my gaze. "*All* of them."

"What do you mean?" Brigid asked.

Rudy looked at her. "Toronto has its peculiarities."

"Like the transit system," I said quickly. "Buses, subways, street-cars, high-speed trains to the suburbs." I rolled my eyes. "It's so confusing. Let's go check out the subways now."

I hustled them off, leaving Rudy glaring after me.

Back when I'd refused to become a vampire, Jane had invited me to a weekend with her undead friends. To persuade me, she teased. Only there was to be no persuasion. It was a conversion.

Like Jane, most vampires inherit the genes and are reborn on death. There is a second way to become one, but the process is hor-rific. They say you can't force it on another person. They're wrong.

By the time Jane and her friends were finished with me, months later, I was half mad. But I was a vampire. She expected me to be grateful. Hadn't she proven how much she loved me, to what lengths she'd go to keep me?

I killed her. As slow and horrible a death as my own conversion. When she was finally gone, I hunted down her friends. Then I slaughtered their human servants and thralls. Every last one of them.

Next stop on our Toronto tour: Trinity Church.

As I walked to the front doors, Hans and Brigid stopped short, earning choice words from the stream of shoppers exiting the mall next door.

"What is that?" Brigid said.

"The Church of the Holy Trinity. Pretty, isn't it?"

They stared at me. I reached an arm through the open doors and wiggled my fingers.

"See any smoke yet? I hope not. I really like this jacket."

When they didn't answer, I walked in and waved my arms. A homeless guy circled warily around me.

"We are not going in there," Brigid said.

"Suit yourself."

In the side courtyard, I found a dark-skinned, fortyish guy in a gym shirt and sweatpants tending to one of the regulars who refused to set foot inside a building. I led Hans and Brigid to him.

"You need to have that tooth pulled, Frank," Randy was telling the old man, who was dressed in ten layers of clothes despite the warm night. "A dentist *should* do it, but I will if you want."

"What's he doing?" Hans whispered.

"Running a medical clinic for the homeless," I said.

"Why?"

I lifted myself up to his ear. "For the money."

Hans shot me a look.

"Seriously," I said. "Why do you think they wear all those clothes? They're stuffed with cash."

Hans snorted, but Brigid started eyeing the old man.

"I'm kidding," I said, before I was responsible for a wave of homeless deaths.

As the old man tottered away, Randy packed his medical bag.

"Hey, Doc," I said.

"Don't 'hey' me." Randy straightened. "Are these the vamps who are taking over?"

"Yep. Randall Tolliver, meet—"

"Are they taking over your work for me, too?"

"Um, no, I don't think—"

"What work?" Brigid asked.

"Medical supplies," Randy said. "The clinic can't run without them and we're too underfunded to buy all we need. Zoe obtains them."

"Steals them," I said.

"How much does that pay?" Brigid asked.

"If I could afford to pay for the theft, I could afford to pay for supplies."

"So it doesn't pay?"

"Sure it does," I chirped. "Huge dividends in self-satisfaction. You'd love it."

They looked at me as if they'd rather swallow a crucifix.

"Well, that's just great," Randy said. "You piss off and leave me in the lurch with, what, two days' notice? Thank you, Zoe."

He turned to leave, then slowly pivoted back. "She has warned you about Tee, hasn't she?"

"Tee?" Hans said.

"Tea," I said, taking Hans's arm and leading him away. "Being part of the British Commonwealth, Canadians like their tea. Hot tea, not iced. It takes some getting used to."

"If you don't warn them, Zoe—" Randy called after us.

I coughed to cut him off. "Now, ahead is the Eaton Centre, one of Toronto's largest shopping malls."

Hans waited until we were at the mouth of a deserted walkway, then stopped me.

"You really think I'm stupid, don't you?" he said.

I decided it was best not to answer that.

He went on anyway. "I see what you're doing, Zoe, and it's not going to work."

"Doing?"

"First the bartender warns us of some unknown danger in Toronto, and then your doctor friend mentions a monster named Tee."

"Monster?" I gave a nervous laugh. "There's no monster."

"Of course there isn't. Really, Zoe, I gave you credit for being a lot more clever than this. Do you think Brigid and I are going to be scared off by wild stories? I've been around for two hundred years—too long to be frightened by demons."

"Who said anything about—?" I blurted, then stopped. I stepped back into the shadows and shoved my hands into my pockets. After a moment, I sighed. "I'm sorry. The guys were having some fun with you—playing a prank on the new vamps. I was running interference because I was afraid you'd take it the wrong way." I adjusted my collar. "I really don't want to cause any trouble."

"Of course you don't," he said smoothly as Brigid rolled her eyes. "That's why we want to make this transition as painless as possible."

"So do I."

"Good. Let's get on with it, then."

For my first ten years as a vampire, I never fed and left a victim alive. I didn't need to—I found enemies everywhere. If someone so much as shoved me at the market, it would awaken that serpent of rage. I killed and I killed and I killed, and the rage was never sated.

Eventually, I stopped.

There was no dramatic epiphany. No wise vampire showed me a

better path. One day I was sitting by a river, caught a glimpse of myself in the water, and wished the old lore was true—that vampires cast no reflection. I realized then that the lifetime of a vampire was too long to spend being someone you couldn't bear to see in the mirror.

I moved to the New World and rechristened myself Zoe—a lighthearted, cheerful name. I'd been lighthearted and cheerful once and I vowed I would be again.

And so I reinvented myself. Zoe Takano, cat burglar extraordinaire. The always calm, always cool Zen master of vampirism. Fun, good-natured, and easygoing. If you need someone to liven up a party, I'm your girl. To help you in a fight? Not so much.

That's the problem with swearing off the dark stuff. Like an alcoholic, I'm only one good fight away from losing control. It's happened before and it was a long, ugly road to recovery. I can't travel that route again. I might not find my way back.

The next evening, I played Realtor, showing Hans and Brigid my apartment.

"It's one of the few units in the building that's still rent-controlled," I said as I led them down the hall. "Being downtown, you get mainly young, single tenants. They come and go so often that I've been here thirty-seven years and no one has noticed I haven't aged a day."

I put my key in the lock.

"And how much would this illegal transfer of tenancy cost us?" Hans asked.

"Three grand, which is an absolute steal. Around here, that wouldn't buy first and last month's rent for a place like this."

"And that's on top of the thousand I already paid you for playing tour guide?"

"Er, yes, but it's negotiable."

"Seeing as how we've been such good customers," he said dryly.

I faced him. "Whether I leave tomorrow has nothing to do with whether you pay my bar tab or hire my guide services or take over my apartment. I could say you owe me relocation expenses, but we both know I'm not going to challenge you on that. If you don't want to see the apartment, fine. I just thought—"

"Show it to us," he said.

I didn't move.

"Show us the damned apartment," Brigid growled.

When they walked in, I could tell they were impressed. I'd spent twenty years in Toronto searching for exactly the right place to live, and this apartment was it, with its huge bank of windows taking in a postcard view of the skyline.

They admired the night sky and the panorama of colored lights below, and then Hans checked out the apartment itself. Again, it was perfect. Minimalist, but warm and inviting. Every piece had been selected with care, from the leather chairs to the ebony dining set to the priceless artifacts I'd "picked up" over decades of museum heists.

"How much for the whole thing?" Hans asked. "Fully furnished."

Brigid's gaze swept over the apartment, her lip curling. "It's not really my style—"

"It's mine." He met my gaze. "How much?"

"A lot. I don't think you want—"

"I do."

His tone said either I named a price or he'd take it for nothing. The serpent uncoiled. I clenched my stomach muscles, sending it back to sleep.

"We'll discuss it," I murmured. "For now, if the location is to your—"

A shuffling rasp came from the bedroom. I went still. But they didn't hear it, only frowned, wondering why I'd stopped.

I put my hands on Hans's back, propelling him toward the door. "Actually, let's discuss this over drinks. My treat. I know this amazing place on Queen West. Much more your style than Miller's."

He let me push him two feet before locking his knees. "I want this apartment, Zoe."

"Actually, you know, transferring the tenancy might not be that easy . . ."

The shuffling sound reached the bedroom hall. Brigid heard it now, pivoting that way.

"You want more money?" Hans said. "Is that what this is about? It better not be, because I've dealt fairly with you, and if you screw me over—"

"*Mein Gott*," Brigid whispered. "What is that?"

Lurching from the bedroom hall was a woman. I already knew her gender—otherwise, it would be impossible to tell. Gauzy rags encased her skeletal limbs. A tangled mass of matted white hair hid her face. She shuffled forward, her bony fingers waving in front of her as if she were conducting an orchestra no one else could see. Her head bobbed, sunken eyes glittering with madness, fleshless lips moving soundlessly.

Seeing me, the woman stopped. She squinted, head weaving like a hawk trying to get a better look at its prey.

"Tee," I said. "Hi. I, uh, was just—"

"Going somewhere, Zoe?"

I bit off a nervous laugh. "Uh, no. Of course not."

"That's not what Tee heard. She heard you're leaving us. Running off because big bad vampires have come to town again." She looked at Brigid and Hans, and sniffed. "Are these them? Nasty creatures."

"Hey!" Brigid stepped toward Tee, then thought better of it and stopped, crossing her arms over her chest. "Whatever that monster is—"

"Monster?" Tee unfurled her limbs, pulling herself up until she was almost as tall as Brigid. She shuffled toward her, rags whispering against the hardwood floor. Brigid tried holding her ground, but when she caught a whiff of Tee, she drew back.

"A monster kills and does not feed," Tee said. "A monster leaves pretty boys to die in ugly alleys."

"José?" Hans said. "That was—"

"There was another, last night. The one this naughty vampire didn't tell you about." She drew herself up again to look Brigid in the eye. "The pretty boy with the pretty red hair and the pretty red shirt and all that pretty red blood."

"How did you—?" Brigid began.

"Tee knows everything. Her friends tell her."

Tee swept a hand around the room. Brigid and Hans followed it, but saw nothing.

I stepped forward. "And that is the great thing about you, isn't it, Tee? You have a regular army of spirit informants."

Tee rocked back on her heels, lips smacking in self-satisfaction. "Tee and her friends help little Zoe."

"Exactly, and now you can help Hans and Brigid."

Her lips pursed, and she eyed them. "One vampire is enough for any city." She sidled toward Hans and whispered, "Give Tee the naughty one, and she won't ask for morsels for a very long time."

"Morsels?" Hans's gaze shot to me.

"Er, yes," I said. "See . . ."

I motioned him to one side. When Tee tried to follow, I waved her away. She grumbled, then stumped over to a chair.

"Tee's a demon," I said, voice lowered. "She got trapped in a human body over a century ago. Being a demon, she can't die, which is why she . . . looks like that. But over the years, she's misplaced a few of her marbles."

"A few?"

"Most of the bag. Anyway, she's convinced that she's alive because she's found the key to immortality: consuming the flesh of the living."

"What?"

I motioned for him to keep his voice down. "Usually she just takes a few nibbles off dead bodies. Sometimes she does hunt—"

"Tee eats what she hunts," she called. "Not like some people." She glowered at Brigid.

I lowered my voice another notch. "We discourage the hunting. It's messy. Instead, Tee and I have an arrangement. Her spirit friends help me, and in return I feed her."

"Feed her what?"

"If you're looking for immortality, what's even better than the flesh of the living?"

Hans stared at me. He blinked. Then he eased back with a harsh laugh. "If you really expect me to believe that you feed her—"

I took a penknife from my pocket, sliced a strip of flesh from the underside of my forearm, then walked over and gave it to Tee. She gobbled it down like a strip of bacon.

Behind me, the room went silent. I flexed my arm. The flesh was already filling in the furrow. In an hour, it would be back to normal.

"That's all there is to it." I smiled brightly. "Now, let's get that drink and we can talk terms. There are a few pieces here I couldn't bear to part with, but the rest is negotiable."

I walked to the door. Hans and Brigid didn't move.

"We don't like them," Tee muttered. "We don't like them at all. Nasty things. We like Zoe."

I sighed. "Yes, it'll be an adjustment, Tee, but you'll get used to them." Another bright smile. "I'm sure we all taste the same."

"Okay," Brigid said, hands flying up. "That's it. Zoe might put up with your shit, demon, but I won't. If you ever try to take a bite of me—"

Brigid sailed off her feet, smacked into the wall, and collapsed at the bottom.

"She's a demon, remember?" I whispered. "You don't say no to a demon."

"The hell I don't," Brigid snarled.

She leapt up . . . and got hit in the gut with an energy bolt. The smell of burning flesh filled the room. Tee hadn't budged, just sat placidly stroking the leather chair.

"We don't like her." Tee looked at Hans. "We don't like you, either, but we like her less. Give her to Tee. Tee has a good hiding place, dark and cold. She'll save all the naughty vampire's bits and eat them slowly."

Brigid let out a growl, pawing the ground like a bull.

I went over to Tee and squeezed her shoulder. "Ah, Tee, you're such a joker. You'd never do that, would you? Not to a big, strong vampire like Brigid."

"Even vampires sleep," Tee murmured. "Yes, they do." Her gaze darted around as she listened to her spirit counsel. "That's how we'll do it. We'll get her when—"

"Tee," I said sharply.

She pouted and grumbled under her breath.

"I'm not staying in the same city as that thing," Brigid said. "Either she goes or I do."

Tee launched herself at Brigid. The vampire stumbled back, arms sailing up to ward her off. Then she stiffened and fell over.

"Shit!" I said. "Her binding powers. Hans, grab her before—"

Too late. Tee was on Brigid, biting chunks of flesh from her shoulder. Hans and I managed to get her off. I restrained her, thrashing and howling, as the binding spell broke and Brigid scrambled to her feet. As they ran for the door, I dropped Tee and tore after them.

"Wait! We had a deal! I'll give you a discount on the apartment—"

I caught up with them in the stairwell. We had a brief discussion, the upshot being that I could keep my damned city and they were never setting foot in this godforsaken town again. I begged. I pleaded. I cajoled. All to no avail.

I walked back into my apartment. Rudy and Randy were helping themselves to my bar.

I said, "Well, that's that. Thanks for the spells, guys."

Rudy and Randy were half brothers. With different mothers and twenty years between them, they didn't look much alike. The only thing they shared was their father's sorcerer blood.

Tee was back in her chair, stroking a Maori mask she'd plucked from the shelf. She whispered under her breath. Talking to her spirits. Tee isn't a demon—just a very old, very powerful, very crazy necromancer who is terrified of death, certain it will condemn her to an eternity of serving ghosts.

I cut another strip from my arm and handed it to her. She gobbled it down. Randy turned away; Rudy glowered at me.

"It grows back," I said. "And it's better than having her hunt humans."

"Just don't do it while I'm here, okay?" Rudy helped himself to my daiginjō-shu.

"That'll be twenty bucks," I said. "You can add it to my credit."

"Credit?"

"You got a grand for a fifty-dollar tab, most of which José already paid off. I expect at least five hundred in credit."

"Sure, we could do that." He headed for the couch, circling wide around Tee. "Or I could introduce you to that blond half-demon. She asked about you last night. Of course, not having any experience with vampires, she's a little nervous . . ."

"Keep the money."

He sat. "I'm sure you had fun with this scheme, but you could have saved yourself a lot of trouble and just killed them."

"Me?"

He gave me a look that said I didn't fool him. I never had.

Randy handed Tee a glass of my cheaper sake. She whispered under her breath and petted his hand.

"Normally, I'd be all for the humane solution," Randy said, grabbing a spot on the sofa. "But in this case, killing them might have *been* the humane solution."

True. I did the world no favors by sparing Brigid's life. I could argue that in killing her, I would have risked unleashing a worse predator inside me, but that's bullshit rationalization. I let her live because I wouldn't chance the personal hell that could come with killing her.

I have a good life here. A damned near perfect one. Would I kill to keep it? I'd rather not find out. Someday, I'll be tested. Just not today.

I pulled out the watch I'd swiped from Hans when we were struggling with Tee.

"Anyone want a Rolex?"

COUNTERFEIT
MAGIC

1. HOME SWEET HOME

*C*ortez-Winterbourne Investigations. How may I help you?"
I smiled as Savannah's voice echoed down the hall.
Even the fake-cheerful lilt was a welcome sound.

Cortez-Winterbourne Investigations. Not the Lucas Cortez
Agency. Not even Cortez and Associates. After three days of being
treated like my husband's assistant, it was good to come home and
hear my own name.

When his father had phoned, Lucas had been away on a case.
Benicio told me he was calling an emergency meeting at Cabal
headquarters in Miami. Could Lucas attend? No? How about me,
then? I'd gone with some trepidation, but Benicio had treated me
as his son's partner, soliciting my opinions and listening to them.
Unfortunately, he was the only one who had, and as a result I was
extra glad to be home.

"Paige!" Adam swung out from his office and slung his arm over
my shoulders. "Damn, I'm glad to see you."

"Laptop on the fritz again?"

"You got it. I put it in your office. When can I expect it back?"

I launched a knockback spell, but he ducked it, grinning, then
followed me into the meeting room.

"How was Miami?" he asked.

"They asked me to serve coffee again."

Savannah came in. "I hope you dumped it over their heads this
time."

"No, I simply suggested that it was a task better suited to the administrative staff. And on that note, a tea would be wonderful."

She snorted and plunked into a chair. That was the problem with having an admin assistant who'd been your ward—a definite lack of decorum and respect. Adam was a little more cognizant of office etiquette, maybe because I've been bossing him around since we were kids. When I hinted that I'd like a tea right now, he poured me a cup of steaming water, passed it over, and flipped me a tea bag.

I smiled. "It's good to be in charge again."

"Yeah?" Savannah said. "Well, don't get too comfy, boss. You have a new client arriving in five minutes. Plus, I put a pile of paperwork on your desk."

"As long as you don't ask me to check with Lucas before I do any of it. For three days, I couldn't go five minutes without hearing, 'Shouldn't you run that past your husband?' and, 'What's his opinion?' and, 'Are you sure you're authorized to speak for him?'"

"Condescending bastards," Savannah said. "I'd have smoked 'em with an energy bolt."

"Didn't Benicio stand up for you?" Adam said.

"He did." Which only made things worse. I didn't want my father-in-law defending me. I wanted the Cabal board of directors to hear my opinions and say, "Hmm, she has a point." It had been three years since a family crisis had forced Lucas to start playing a role in the Cabal. Three years of trying to prove myself. Yet nothing changed.

I kicked off my shoes and took a sip of tea. "So, there's a client coming?"

"Er, right." Savannah got to her feet. "Actually, I don't know what I was thinking, telling her to come by as soon as your plane landed. You're tired. Let me reschedule—"

"No. I've had my pity party. Getting back to work is the best thing for me."

"Hello?" a woman's voice called.

"She's here?" I said.

"Apparently," Savannah muttered. "She's a Tripudio"—a low-level teleporting half-demon—"so I had to break the wards before she came by earlier."

"And you forgot to reactivate them?" Adam said. "Nice one."

She glared. "Hey, even *I* wouldn't be rude enough to teleport through someone's front door."

"Hello?" the voice called again.

Savannah strode into the hall. "Oh, hello, Ms. Cookson. I'm sorry, I didn't hear you ring the buzzer. I'd really suggest you do that next time. We have some seriously nasty security on this place, and I'd *hate* to see you—"

"Is he here?"

"Mr. Cortez isn't available, but—"

"I thought you said he'd be here."

"No, I said you could come by for a case intake session. Ms. Winterbourne will be handling that."

"Who?"

I stepped into the hall. The woman was younger than I'd have guessed by the sound of her voice. No more than a year or two older than Savannah. Tall, blond, slender, and fashionably dressed. And, judging by the way she was squinting at me, in serious need of glasses. The scowl on her face didn't do her any favors, either. Without it, though, I'm sure she was very attractive.

"Paige Winterbourne," I said, extending my hand.

She looked at it, then back at me. "Oh. The wife."

"No, the *partner*," Adam said, coming out of the meeting room.

"The *boss*," Savannah said. "The woman who will decide whether we take your case or not."

I stopped them both with a look, then said, "Lucas is away until later this afternoon, so—"

"I'll wait." She sailed past Adam and sat in a meeting room chair. "I take my coffee black."

"And bitter, I'm sure," Savannah muttered under her breath. She raised her voice so Ms. Cookson could hear. "There's a coffeemaker right behind you. It does a cup at a time. Very easy to use. You may want an espresso, though, to keep you awake. It'll be a while before Lucas gets here and even longer before he's ready to talk to you. He's been away from his wife for a week, so he'll want to . . . visit first."

I shot Savannah another look. I got a look, too—from Ms. Cookson. A slow once-over that said, really, she couldn't imagine why Lucas would bother. Now she was truly being a bitch. While I wasn't tall or blond or slender, I didn't need a paper bag over my head.

I walked to the coffeemaker. "Mild, medium, or dark roast? We have flavored, too. French vanilla and hazelnut cream."

"His favorite," Savannah said, shooting a thumb at Adam.

I waved them both out. Savannah went. Adam lingered, giving me a look that said I should be kicking this client out, not making her coffee. That was his way and Savannah's. Yet when people insult and underestimate me, it only makes me all the more determined to prove myself.

It's not as if being overshadowed by my husband is anything new. Even back when I was Coven leader and Lucas was an unemployed lawyer, he was still the one whose name made people sit up and take notice.

My father-in-law is the CEO of the most powerful Cabal in the country. Lucas is his illegitimate youngest son. He is also the one Benicio has named as heir, despite the fact that Lucas has devoted his adult life to fighting Cabal injustices. Pretty hard to compete with that reputation. So I don't try. I believe in his cause—helping supernaturals—and I join him in it, knowing that to most people I'll always be "that witch who married Lucas Cortez."

"I want to speak to Lucas," Ms. Cookson said as I handed her a coffee.

"You will. When he gets here. But we'll be working your case together—"

"I want Lucas."

"You'll have him." I forced a smile. "But it's a package—"

"*Only* Lucas."

I sat down, opened her file, and started to read it.

"Ava," I said. "May I call you Ava?" I continued before she could protest. "Although Lucas and I are partners, there are tasks that only one of us handles. Legal work, for example. He's a lawyer; I'm not. Technical work is my forte. I'm a computer programmer; he's not. Beyond those obvious differences, there are tasks one of us does to reduce conflict and confusion. Such as case intake. While clients may—and often do—present a potential case to Lucas personally, I'm the one who decides which ones we take."

"I bet you like that, don't you?"

"The power of choosing the cases? Hardly. We usually evaluate them together and—"

"I mean the power to get rid of clients you don't like. Ones who might pose a threat to your . . . position."

It took me a moment to get her meaning. When I did, I laughed. I didn't mean to; I just couldn't help it. Her eyes slitted, her lips thinning to a scarlet line.

"Um, no," I said. "Sorry, but no. I'm perfectly willing to consider your case, Ava. I need to know what that case is, though, so I can present it to Lucas when he returns and give him my recommendation."

She continued to eye me, like a cat that suspects it's being teased. She shifted in her chair. Then, slowly, she began to talk.

2. HEDGING A BET

*A*va Cookson was twenty-two. Unmarried. High school education. Lived in Los Angeles. Worked in a clothing store. Had a brother. She didn't tell me any of this—it came from the intake form, including a little notation Savannah had made by the name of the store Ava worked at—"overpriced crap made in sweathouses and marketed as designer." All that was incidental . . . except the last fact. *Had a brother.*

One brother. Two years her junior. Attended San Francisco State. Or he did, until his body washed up on the shore near Santa Cruz.

"He was murdered," Ava said. "And it's my fault."

Ava was a half-demon, meaning her brother didn't share her demonic father or powers. He wouldn't have known what she was. That's the theory, anyway.

"He caught me teleporting once," she said. "You can't explain away something like that."

Which is why you have to be very, very careful.

"You think that's what got him killed," I said.

Her eyes flashed. "Of course not. Don't accuse me—"

"I'm not accusing you of anything. We investigate cases involving the supernatural world, so if you're here, I presume his entry into that world—through you—somehow resulted in his death."

"Maybe. But Brody was in other trouble, too. He made the wrong kind of friends in college. At first, it was just innocent stuff, like poker. But then it was serious gambling. He owed money."

That would seem a more obvious cause of death, but I only nodded, encouraging her to continue.

"I told him I might know a way for him to make money fast. I'd heard of this fight club outside Santa Cruz. For supernaturals. They're always looking for women, especially hot girls, so I figured I could fight and win some money to help Brody pay his debt. They don't even ask what your power is. That's part of the challenge. I can teleport— not far, but far enough to avoid getting hit. It seemed so easy."

It always does.

"It would have been, too," she continued. "Only they cheated. They set me up against this chick who actually knew how to fight."

Imagine that.

"I did fine for the first few rounds, but then I started getting tired, and I couldn't teleport as fast. So she won."

I could never have seen that one coming.

"So I'm talking to Brody afterward, and my mouth is bleeding and swelling up, and I'm telling him how sorry I am, and he's saying it's okay. Then this guy walks over, thumps him on the back, and congratulates him. Says winning his first bet is always a good sign."

Ava looked up, eyes blazing. "He bet *against* me. My *brother* bet against me. I stormed out. He came running after me . . . to hand me the car keys. Tells me he's going to watch a few more rounds, and asks if I can drive the rental car back. So I did. All the way back to LA. When I return the car, his credit card is refused. I call to give him hell, and I can't get hold of him. I figure he's just avoiding me, so I pay for the rental. A week later, someone found his body."

I took her back to the beginning. When had she told him she was a half-demon? Could he have told anyone else? Had she introduced him to anyone?

We were going through this when I heard footsteps in the hall. Light ones, barely noticeable, but part of me had been listening for them since I sat down.

The steps stopped outside the meeting room door. I turned my chair, as if getting comfortable, and carefully slid my gaze to the partly open door. Lucas peeked around it, finger to his lips, then motioned me out before withdrawing silently.

I waited for a suitable break in Ava's narrative, then excused myself to "ask Savannah to compile information on fight clubs."

Lucas was in the hall, waiting. Silently, he backed into the stockroom. I was barely through the door before he caught me up in a breath-stopping kiss.

I threw my arms around his neck, reveling in the familiar tug of his hands entwined in my hair, the taste of breath mints hastily chewed on his way up the stairs, the faint citrus scent of his shaving lotion. Whatever problems I had with my husband, they weren't problems *with* my husband. They were the issues that came with his world and the life he'd been thrust into. I was as crazy in love with the guy himself as I'd been when I married him.

When he began unbuttoning my blouse, though, I pulled back. "Client."

"Call Savannah." Lucas flicked open the top button. "She'll cover for you."

"Normally, yes, but this client is a teleporting half-demon. A very impatient one who's liable to jump in here any second now."

"We'll move to our office, then." He popped the front clasp on my bra. "It's warded."

"And involves sneaking past the meeting room's open door."

He cupped my breasts. "You're arguing, but you're not stopping me."

"I'm enjoying it while I can. But maybe there's enough time to make *you* a little more presentable." I pressed my hand to his crotch, then lowered myself to my knees. "You know I have a thing for storage rooms."

He chuckled. I unzipped his pants.

"Where'd she go?" Ava's voice rang down the hall. "Is that Lucas's suitcase? Is he here?"

I sighed and zipped his pants as I stood.

"If he's here, I want to talk to him," Ava demanded.

I opened the door and stepped out. Lucas followed. Savannah walked up behind Ava, who stared at us, nose crinkling.

"What were you doing in there?" Ava said.

"Duh," Savannah muttered. She passed me a file. "The information on fight clubs you asked for, boss." The meeting room was wired to her office, and she eavesdropped at will. "Did you find a box of toner in there or are we out?"

"Out."

"Told ya."

While we'd been talking, Ava had managed to zip between Lucas and me, so fast she must have teleported.

"Ava Cookson, sir. Pleased to meet you. *So* pleased to meet you."

She stared up at him with the kind of adoration usually reserved for rock stars. Behind me, Savannah snickered, and I had to admit, it looked very odd. I love my husband dearly, but the word most often used to describe him is *geek*. I happen to think it's completely unfair, but Lucas is comfortable with the term. He even propagates the image, refusing to wear contacts or more flattering suits, keeping his hair in a short, nondescript style any barber can manage. He likes to be unassuming, invisible even.

When Ava gazed up at him in adoration, he inched backward, gaze sliding to Savannah and me, as if begging for rescue.

"I was just taking Ava's case history," I said. "If you'd care to join us . . ."

"Oh, we don't need you." Ava waved me off, eyes never leaving Lucas. "He can take it from here."

Lucas protested. When she insisted, he became visibly annoyed, which for Lucas meant she was seriously pissing him off.

Finally, I said, "Actually, that's probably best. You go on. I'll start a file."

Lucas asked Ava to excuse us. Savannah practically had to drag her away, but finally she got her back in the meeting room.

"She's a twit," I said. "And she's got a serious crusader crush on you. But I think you can handle it."

Spots of color warmed his cheeks. "Of course I can. It's not that. It's—"

"—that you don't like her insulting me. I get that. But you arguing that I'm important doesn't make me important." I lifted onto my tiptoes and kissed his chin. "All things considered, I'm just as happy not dealing with her. I'll listen in on Savannah's line and, when she's gone, we can go look for more toner. I'm sure there's a box in there somewhere."

He smiled, but it was a wistful smile. He kissed me, though, a long, delicious kiss that promised a very good night to come, and when we parted and I thought I caught a touch of sadness in his eyes, I told myself I was imagining it. I had to be. Everything was fine. Well, *we* were fine, and that was all that mattered.

3. CRUSADER CRUSH

I found both Adam and Savannah eavesdropping on Lucas and Ava from Savannah's desk. They didn't try to hide it. Lucas and I didn't care. If we did, we'd say so, and they'd stop. With such a small office, confidentiality only means we don't discuss cases with anyone outside it. Listening to intake sessions just saves us explaining the whole thing later.

We moved into the office I share with Lucas, where the meeting could be broadcast on my speakerphone. I sat at my desk and reviewed Ava's file as I listened. Adam stretched out on the divan, jotting notes and exchanging quips and observations with Savannah as she paced.

Ava insisted on retelling the whole story to Lucas. This recital was a lot more emotional. When she spoke of her brother, I could imagine her dabbing moist eyes. When she spoke of his disappearance, she choked up. Yet even in her grief, she managed to flirt outrageously.

She gushed about Lucas's reputation. Simpered about how honored she'd be if he took her case. Added a few extra heartfelt sobs in hopes he'd come over and comfort her. He didn't, of course. His comfort was offered with words, polite and sympathetic, but distant. Which only made her try all the harder.

"Sounds like someone is hoping to pay her bill with an exchange of services," Adam said.

Savannah snorted. "Her ego will take a beating if she tries."

They laughed. I didn't. It was insulting, having a woman throw herself at my husband when she knew I was in the next room.

"So it seems we have two avenues of investigation," Adam said. "The gambling debt and the fight club. I'll take the fight club and—"

"Excuse me?" Savannah strode over. "No offense, fire-boy, but you're a one-trick pony. I'm a dual-purpose, ultra-charged spell-caster."

"And an attractive young woman, which they like," Adam said. "That's why I was about to suggest you come with me."

"Whoops."

"Uh-huh."

"Sorry." She lifted his legs from the divan, sat down, and let them fall across her lap.

As they bantered, I kept my gaze on my notes. Savannah has had a crush on Adam from the day they met, which wouldn't be so bad if she hadn't been twelve at the time and he'd been twenty-three. If Adam noticed, he never gave any sign of it and had treated her like a little sister. I'd figured she'd grow out of it, and if she was going to have a teenage crush, Adam was as safe a bet as I could want—someone who'd treat her well, and leave her with a good impression of guys in general.

Except, well, maybe for Savannah the impression Adam left was *too* good; no boy her own age could live up to it. At twenty-one, her infatuation has mellowed into a solid friendship, but I know she hopes more will come of it. As for Adam, if you'd asked me what his feelings were a year ago, I'd have said friendship. Strictly friendship. Lately, though, I've caught hints that something's changed, something he isn't quite aware of himself.

I don't have a problem with the age difference—let's face it, maturity-wise, Adam has always been on a slow curve. There's a part of me that wants to give things a push. But I know better. They'll have to figure this out for themselves.

⚜

Once Lucas had everything he needed, he extricated himself from the meeting. It wasn't easy, and Savannah was chomping at the bit to rescue him. I wouldn't let her; if Ava thought Lucas hadn't ended their meeting of his own free will, it would make things worse.

It didn't help that he hadn't jumped to take her case. Eventually, he got her out of the building and joined us in our office, where I met him with a double shot of espresso.

"Thank you," he said.

"I think we still need toner," Savannah said. "Unless that meeting wore you out."

A faint smile. "No, but I think Ava Cookson was enough work for everyone today. I declare the workday officially over."

"Is that a hint?" Savannah said.

"It is."

"Grab your coat, Adam." She stopped beside me. "We're going for drinks, then a movie. I'll be home late, so don't wait up."

"You buying?" Adam said.

"We'll expense it. Coworker bonding time."

They left. Lucas sipped his espresso until the stairwell door alarm clicked on. Then he downed the rest and crossed to my chair.

4. DIVVYING UP DUTIES

By the time we left the office, it was past six. We grabbed takeout and headed back to the house. Normally, I prefer to cook, but after three days away I couldn't trust there'd be anything left in the fridge.

We hadn't discussed Ava's case yet, but it didn't take long before conversation turned to another aspect of work. My Cabal visit. I gave him a rundown, focusing on the reason for the abrupt summons to Miami: a diplomatic situation.

When I met Lucas, the thought that he—let alone *I*—would ever hurry off to Miami to help the Cortez Cabal would have been absurd. Lucas *fought* the Cabal; he didn't *help* it. Then came the night when everything changed. Lucas's two oldest brothers had been murdered, leaving only Carlos, whose greed and amorality might make him a good Cabal leader if he weren't so damned incompetent.

Benicio needed help. Benicio needed Lucas.

In those early days together, I don't think Lucas would have responded. He'd have let the Cortez Cabal crumble. Now he was older, no less idealistic but more realistic, and he'd come to realize that as corrupt as the Cabal was, it was the best of the North American Cabals. If it failed, the supernatural world would suffer.

Lucas still refused to claim the role of heir, but he did play a role in the family business. And so, when they needed help, he came. And if he could not, I did, in his place.

In this instance, the problem was a French Cabal accusing the Cortezes of poaching a shaman employee. They hadn't—they'd hired a Romanian national who'd failed to disclose the fact he was employed by the Moreau Cabal. The shaman claimed the Moreaus had blackmailed him into working for them, and he had proof.

In the past, Benicio would have returned the shaman to the Moreaus to avoid straining international relationships. These days he has to show Lucas that the Cortez Cabal can become the kind of organization he'd be comfortable leading, which doesn't include handing over innocent supernaturals, knowing they'll be imprisoned and possibly killed.

"My advice was to negotiate with the Moreaus," I said. "Give them an option. Take the shaman back on a one-year contract, promising no mistreatment. Or give him to the Cortezes and accept a finder's fee for training him."

"Good idea," Lucas said after finishing a bite of his spring roll. "Excellent, actually. I'd have been inclined to confront them with proof of blackmail and force them to drop the matter. Your solution is far more elegant."

"Thank you."

"My father agreed, I presume."

"He did, and that's the solution he chose."

"As he should." He speared a piece of lemon chicken, eyes on his plate. "And he had the backing of the board?"

When I didn't answer, Lucas's shoulders drooped. A faint reaction, but noticeable, like the lines beside his mouth that seemed to deepen.

"Who argued against it?"

"Carlos. Or, I should say, several of the VPs disagreed and subtly conveyed their opinion to Carlos, who voiced it."

Lucas made a noise that sounded shockingly close to a growl.

"Hanging out with the werewolves too long," I said. "Clay's rubbing off on you."

"No, it's just Carlos. I suppose I should be glad he's showing up for meetings."

"And showing up sober."

Lucas tried for a smile. The fact was, he'd be a whole lot happier if Carlos showed up drunk or high. At least then he wouldn't be a threat. But on his brothers' deaths, Carlos had seen an opportunity to seize his birthright, which to him meant seizing all the power—and money—he could. Unfortunately, he was finding supporters in everyone who opposed Lucas and was pleased to have a straw man they could put forward in his place.

We ate in silence for a few minutes, then Lucas said, "I know those meetings couldn't have been easy."

"I survived."

"Naturally, but I really think we should talk—"

"Tell me about your trip."

He hesitated.

"Please," I said.

He nodded, and I thought I saw that sadness flash in his eyes again. Frustration, I decided. He didn't like the situation, and having me dwell on it wasn't going to help. Push it aside and move on. Better for both of us.

"The trial went well," he said. "Nothing unexpected, although there was a minor glitch when the client's nerve wore thin and he began thinking perhaps he should admit to having set the fire, albeit accidentally . . ."

We had a good night. Didn't get much sleep, but it wouldn't have been nearly so good a night if we had.

We arrived at work at nine, late for us. Lucas caught a ride in with me, which is rare—he usually rides his motorcycle, knowing one or both of us will be zipping off at some point during the day and two vehicles will likely be needed. We used to do most of the legwork together, but lately, well, lately it just seems more efficient to divide our resources.

Savannah drove in separately—on *her* bike. She has no excuse, spending most of her time in the office, but she likes her independence. In some things, at least.

I'd texted Adam to say there would be a meeting at nine, and we met up with him and Savannah in the stairwell.

"So we're taking the Cookson case?" Adam said. "Time to divvy up duties?"

"It is," I said as we moved into the meeting room. "We have two avenues to investigate—"

"I called dibs on the fight club." He glanced at Savannah. "Sorry, *we* did."

Lucas took a seat. "Actually, Paige and I are going to take that angle."

Savannah sputtered a laugh. "Yeah, I know you can fight, Lucas. But seriously? Those guys will make you the minute you show up."

Adam nodded. "According to the files, this club is notoriously anti-Cabal."

"I planned to effect a disguise, naturally."

"It won't be enough," Adam said. "They're so worried about Cabal interference, they probably have your family's photos tacked up in the office. And don't tell me you're going to stay in the background and let Paige fight, because . . ." He looked at me, and the corners of his mouth twitched. "Um, no. Just no."

He was right. I could defend myself, but I was no fighter.

"Perhaps you have a point," Lucas said. "But if you've read those files, then you know there are certain types of supernaturals they really don't like in a ring. It's a short list, but it includes Exustio half-demons. An energy bolt spell is one thing, but your powers inflict third-degree burns. As soon as they realize what you are, they'll throw you out and make a note of your face, so you never get near the doors again."

"Leaving one option for your fighter," Savannah said.

I glanced at Lucas, who nodded, reluctantly.

"Yes, it'll have to be you, Savannah," I said. "And if Ava's right and they like young women, having you show up with Adam is going to limit your sex-object potential. So I'll play manager."

"I'll accompany you and stay in the background," Lucas said.

"Leaving Adam to check out the gambling lead and no one in the office?"

"I'll take the gambling lead and Lucas can play secretary." Adam caught our looks and sighed. "Or Lucas follows that lead, too, while I sit on my ass and look pretty."

"Because you're so good at it," Savannah said.

Adam sighed again.

Lucas didn't seem thrilled by the division of duties. Not unhappy, just not thrilled. To be honest, I was surprised he'd suggested taking the fight club lead himself—he knew he couldn't slip around the supernatural world as easily as he had five years ago. And accompanying Savannah and me? That made no sense at all.

Maybe he'd foreseen the next turn of events. Ava insisted on going with Lucas to check out the gambling angle. When she'd been in San Francisco with her brother, she'd met his debtors. She couldn't remember where they'd been, but she could find the way, and she couldn't describe the men, but she'd know them if she saw them.

So he was stuck with her.

5. THE FIRST RULE OF FIGHT CLUB

*W*e flew to San Francisco, rented a car, and drove to Santa Cruz. On the way, I read over everything Savannah had compiled on fight clubs.

Unlike the movie, the first rule of supernatural fight clubs was not "don't talk about it." Most people plugged into the seamier side of our world knew about them. The difficult part was supposed to be finding them, and even that wasn't all that tough if you knew whom to ask. Our records named organizers in over a dozen cities. Find them and, theoretically, you'd find a fight club. In the case of the Santa Cruz club, the owners had been running it in the same location for years.

While Adam was right that fight clubs were anti-Cabal, again, the truth wasn't so simple. While outwardly they professed complete independence of Cabals, our records showed that about half were underwritten by a Cabal. That didn't include the Santa Cruz one, which *was* known to shun all Cabal overtures.

A supernatural fight club is exactly what it sounds like. Supernaturals—usually young, usually male—work off pent-up frustration and energy by fighting. People bet on the outcome.

If there *are* rules to our fight clubs, the first would be "don't permanently maim or mutilate or murder your opponent." Our files hinted at underground clubs where anything went, but the average one was very strict about the rule. They had to be. No kid would get into the ring knowing he could be up against a werewolf capable of snapping his neck with a single twist.

Kill your opponent—even accidentally—and you'd be banned from every fight club for life. Inflict serious damage and the fight would be called at your forfeit. Too many deaths could shut down a club, so the owners didn't take any chances.

The address in our files led us to a house in the country. An abandoned house that was past ready to be condemned, every window and door gone, the roof collapsing, the house listing to one side. The outbuildings weren't much better. The surrounding field was so overgrown I wasn't even sure we could *get* to the house.

Savannah idled the car on the road as we looked around. "Looks about right."

"Have some experience with these places?"

"No, but if I was running an illegal supernatural fight club, this is where I'd put it."

"I don't even see a place to park. It doesn't look like there's a neighbor in sight, but wouldn't someone notice if there were cars lined up and down this road?"

She swung the rental car toward the ditch. The tires found a pair of ruts that led past the wire fence and behind a thick patch of trees. There the lane opened into a parking lot surrounded by grass higher than my head. A vintage Mercedes and a gleaming new pickup were parked at the far side.

"Great, we found the right place," I said. "Now let's get out of here before—"

"No one's around," she said as she finished casting a sensing spell. She got out of the car, walked over to the vehicles, and peered inside.

I rolled down the window and looked around. We might have found the club, but Savannah couldn't just walk in and say, "I want to fight." It was invitation only. Ava had provided us with the name of the half-demon friend who'd gotten her invitation, and she said he'd be happy to give one to us, too, but we had to be a little more discreet than that.

"We'll come back tonight and scout around," I said. "In the meantime, we'll run those license plates and—"

Savannah strode toward a path leading from the lot.

"Hey!" I whispered, as loudly as I dared. "Don't—"

She disappeared into the long grass.

By the time I caught up with her, she was heading through a small door into the barn. From inside came the *thwackity-thwack-thwack* of someone hitting a boxer's speed bag.

I picked up my pace and joined Savannah inside. The door led into a small room with a coatrack and a sign warning that the management wasn't responsible for stolen articles. Underneath, someone had written "I'm not either" and signed it "Rico." The bouncer, I guessed. Fortunately, he wasn't around now.

From there, we walked through a second door and straight into the fight club. It wasn't a state-of-the-art gym cleverly disguised as a crumbling barn. If it was, I'd have known the Cabals were involved. Still, the place was a lot nicer than you'd expect from the outside.

A professional boxing ring dominated the large open area. Bleachers stretched along two sides. The third was an empty space for bystanders, with a betting window to the rear. The fourth side was the staging area, where a guy in his early thirties was pummeling a speed bag, dancing in place, sweat dripping down his bare back, wavy dark hair plastered to his forehead and neck.

Savannah paused to admire the view while my gaze moved on to a second man, tapping away on a laptop just inside a tiny office at the back. He was also dark-haired, bearing a strong resemblance to the fighter, but his hair was short, his physique hidden under a golf shirt and pressed trousers.

The fighter ducked to avoid a hard swing-back and caught sight of us. He said something to the other man, who rose, frowned, and stepped out of his office.

"May I help you?" he asked.

"I hope so," Savannah said, mimicking my Boston accent. "I want to fight at your club. Only thing I'm missing is the invitation."

The man's frown deepened. He was handsome but somber, late thirties, a man who'd look more at home in a corporate office than at a fight club. I was going to hazard a guess at his name. Ethan Gallante, club owner along with his brother, Shane—the speed-bag boxer.

"This isn't how it's done," Ethan said.

I stepped forward. "I know, but Georgia here is new to the circuit. We knew where you were, but don't have any contacts we could get her an invitation from. Our only other option was to hang around the parking lot tonight, find a gullible-looking guy, and convince him to invite us."

"Which could be fun," Savannah said. "But I thought you'd rather we didn't stalk your patrons." She flashed a smile. "And I was really hoping to start fighting tonight."

Ethan walked over and circled her. It was a cool appraisal. Not rude, just uninterested in anything but her potential as a fighter. Shane was the one giving her the more personal once-over, grinning as if he liked what he saw. Most men do. Savannah looks like she belongs on a runway. Six feet tall and lithe, with straight dark hair that stretches to the middle of her back and huge eyes so blue she's often accused of wearing color contacts. Her features are strong—severe even—but it only makes her more arresting, paired with those innocent, wide blue eyes.

Savannah looks strong and forceful, direct and confident, and men like that . . . until they realize that the packaging promotes the product accurately. I'd never tell her to tone it down, though. She doesn't need to change. She just needs a man who's confident enough in himself to accept and appreciate her. Like Adam.

I could tell Ethan approved of her height, but the rest of the package was a little too fashionable.

"How much experience do you have?" he asked. "Real fighting, without your powers."

"I don't go looking for bar brawls, but I can hold my own."

His expression said he doubted it. "Well, Georgia, I'd love to give you a chance to test that, but I don't see a gym bag, and that outfit definitely isn't—"

Savannah unbuttoned her blouse and tossed it aside, revealing a sports tank in place of a bra. Then she kicked her boots aside and peeled off her jeans. Underneath, she wore spandex exercise shorts. She was in excellent shape. She worked out with Adam, and I swore they were into every outdoor sport imaginable.

"All right, then." Ethan pointed to the ring. "Shane will give you a few rounds. You can save the supernatural stuff for an audience. This is strictly hand-to-hand combat."

Shane grinned. "Which keeps the playing field level for me."

I knew from my files that the Gallantes were a family of necromancers. Unlike witches and sorcerers, a necromancer's powers hit only a few members every generation. Ethan had them; Shane didn't.

Shane and Savannah climbed into the ring. It was more a test than a fight. Shane was clearly a pro and he didn't want to show her up, just put her through her paces, see whether she could throw a punch and block one.

When they finished, Shane congratulated her. Ethan only eyed her for another minute, then said, "Do I know you from somewhere, Georgia?"

"Not unless you hang out at Harvard," she said.

Shane laughed. "Definitely not."

"You look familiar," Ethan said. "Maybe I've met a relative?" Without waiting for an answer, he walked over to his laptop, typed something in, then said, "You're on the list. Doors open at ten. You'll fight your first round at eleven."

6. ROUND ONE

When we got back that night at ten thirty, the small parking lot was already filled, with a young man directing people to a second one. Although it was just as well hidden, I suspected people living along the road couldn't help but notice the increased traffic. I supposed, as long as the brothers kept things quiet, neighbors were willing to look the other way.

And the Gallantes did keep things quiet. A couple more young men in the yard directed patrons, making sure they quickly got into the barn. While the Gallantes hadn't spent a fortune on the gym, they'd obviously splurged on soundproofing. I could barely hear a murmur as we approached the barn.

When we stepped into the bouncer's room and gave our names to Rico, I could make out cheers and boos from within, along with the occasional dull thump of fist hitting flesh. But it wasn't until we opened the inner door that the full cacophony hit us, shouts, grunts, and groans punctuating the thump of the blows.

There were two fighters in the ring. Both young men. That went for most of the combatants milling around the staging area. The clientele was older, averaging fifty, most of them male. The women there seemed attached to a man, and while a few avidly watched the match, more were avidly checking their watches.

Heads turned when we walked in. Then more heads, as people nudged their neighbors. Patrons leaned over to ask Ethan who we were, while the fighters asked Shane in the staging area. Their gazes swung to Savannah as the brothers presumably said she was fighting tonight. After they checked Savannah out, they asked another question—*whom* was she fighting? When they got the answer, they streamed to the betting window.

"Now that's a rousing show of support," Savannah said. "One look at me, and they're betting their life savings."

When I didn't answer, she rolled her eyes. "I know they aren't betting on *me*."

She'd made sure of that when she picked her outfit. It was still the same white blouse and chocolate-brown pants from earlier, but she'd bumped up the accessories: chunky necklace, bangle bracelets, and gold chain belt, plus boots with stiletto heels. She was better dressed than any of the girlfriends and wives here . . . and looked even less likely to step into the ring.

We were wandering around, scoping the place out, when another woman walked in, unaccompanied. She was about twenty-five, short and stocky, her broad face set in a permanent "don't fuck with me" scowl.

"I do believe my competition is here," Savannah said. "As for supernatural type, I'm betting dwarf." She caught my look. "Yes, I know there's no such thing."

"Not what I was going to say."

She sighed. "Fine, I'll be kind. Short people have their uses." She set her water bottle on my head. "They make great tables. Good footstools, too, once you knock them down, which is exactly what I plan to do with that one."

"Don't get cocky."

The other fighter walked over to Ethan and leaned in to say something to him. He waved Savannah over.

"Georgia? I'd like you to meet Mel. Mel, Georgia. Your opponent tonight."

Savannah extended a hand. Ignoring it, Mel looked Savannah up and down, then turned to Ethan.

"You're kidding, right?"

"Don't worry," Savannah said. "I can fight on my knees."

"I bet you can do a lot on your knees."

"Oooh, trash-talking already. This is going to be so cool!"

"Who's that?" Mel said, gesturing at me. "Your girlfriend?"

"Manager. I'm hetero." Savannah bent down to Mel and mock-whispered. "Sorry. You are kinda cute, though."

Mel grabbed Ethan's arm and marched him off. "I thought we talked about this. I want real opponents, not pretty girls . . ."

Savannah watched her go. "I know, I know. Don't get cocky. She's obviously not an amateur."

"Correct. Now, let's mingle."

Mingling wasn't difficult. The problem was getting away from the men so Savannah could prep for her match. As she changed, I tried to ignore the two guys hitting on me and concentrate on Mel, who was warming up in the staging area. That warm-up included hand exercises and a lot of muttering under her breath. When Savannah emerged, I excused myself from the men and hurried over to her.

"I know Mel's supernatural type," I said.

"Witch. I know. I asked the guy getting changed next to me, who was distracted enough to forget he's not supposed to tell a new fighter. Any last-minute lectures?"

I shook my head.

Her eyes widened in exaggerated surprise. "Seriously?"

"I could tell you to be careful, but you'd only roll your eyes and say you aren't stupid. I could tell you to not overdo it, but you already know that. I could give you a dozen strategies, but you'd only ignore them all and do it your way. So all I can say is, good luck."

She gave me a one-armed hug. "Thanks." She bent to my ear. "And I will be careful. Not that you're worried or anything."

I was, and she knew it. I also knew better than to show it. I'm not her mother. That's always seemed too strange a role to take with Savannah when I'm only ten years older. It also seemed disrespectful to her real mother, Eve, who's still around, in spirit if not in body. I see myself more as a big sister. Like a big sister, I can worry, but I'm not supposed to show it too much.

I had reason to worry, too. Even at twenty-one, Savannah is a more powerful spell-caster than Lucas or I can ever hope to be. Her mother was a dark witch and her father was a sorcerer, making her equally proficient at both kinds of magic. Eve was also the daughter of a lord demon, and while Savannah didn't inherit any of those abilities, the demon blood acted as a power boost for a girl who really didn't need it.

When Savannah walked into the staging area, every guy turned to look at her—even the one sparring with Mel, who snapped off a left hook to his jaw for the lapse. Mel stopped and gave Savannah another once-over, slower now, but ending with the same dismissive sniff. She'd made up her mind about her opponent: if Savannah was in decent physical condition, it was only from too many hours on a treadmill at some overpriced health club.

I hadn't been watching the match in progress, but I think one of the fighters caught a glimpse of Savannah and was just as distracted as Mel's partner. The next thing I knew, the ref was calling the match and Shane was striding over to escort Savannah and Mel into the ring.

The bell had barely rung before Mel was on Savannah, hitting her hard and fast, as if determined to make a fool of her with a short match. Savannah dodged and ducked but didn't throw a single punch, infuriating Mel until she resorted to magic—a knockback spell, then an energy bolt, then another knockback. Savannah easily evaded each before dodging behind Mel. She caught Mel's wrists and held them as the woman twisted and snorted like an enraged bull.

"What?" Savannah said. "I'm only holding your hands. That means you can't cast sorcerer magic. But you aren't a sorcerer.

You're a witch. Don't need your hands for that." She leaned around Mel. "You do *know* witch magic, don't you?"

With a snarl, Mel pulled free and wheeled on Savannah, fist flying. Before it could land, Savannah nailed her with a right hook that sent her reeling, probably more from surprise than force. She bounced back, her fingers flying up as the first tentative cheers rang out.

"You really like knockbacks, don't you?" Savannah said. "Fine, then. I'll let you have it."

Mel hesitated, fingers raised.

"Go on," Savannah said. "I won't even move. Hit me with your best shot."

The knockback struck Savannah in the shoulder, spinning her into the ropes.

"You call that a knockback?" she said as she recovered. "*This* is a knockback."

Mel was already running at her. She tried to dodge the spell's path, but Savannah hit her with a knockback that hurled her against the ropes. The tentative cheers turned to a collective whoop.

Mel cast one scowl around the room, then barreled down on Savannah. Halfway there, she stopped dead, frozen in place.

"Binding spell," Savannah said. "In case you were wondering." She glanced at Ethan. "I suppose that's illegal?"

He looked at Shane, who shrugged helplessly.

"Don't get many witches in here, do you?" Savannah said. "Not ones who know their own magic well enough to cast a binding spell, at least. Still, I'd make it illegal. Otherwise, I could just run over and knock her down, which would be terribly unfair."

She released the spell. Caught off guard, Mel toppled over. Savannah launched a fireball, whipping it toward Mel's head, making the other woman shriek and duck.

"Damn," Savannah said. "She screams like a little girl. Who'd have thought? Witch magic again. Fireball. Minor burns only—no worse than an energy bolt, which is legal. Well, unless you cast them like this."

Savannah whipped an energy bolt at her opponent. It didn't get within five feet of Mel, but it still made her scream and cover her head. The bolt hit the top rope. It snapped, both ends sizzling and jumping like a live wire, onlookers scrambling out of the way.

"Deadly," Savannah said. "Which is why I'll stick to the basic version."

She turned on Mel, who gamely leapt up, fingers out to cast an energy bolt of her own.

"Knockback," Savannah said.

Her cast sent Mel to the mat.

"Fireball."

Savannah singed the ends of Mel's spiky hair, then sent the fireball whipping around her, locking her in place as effectively as any binding spell.

"Minor energy bolt."

Sparks flew from her fingers, and hit Mel like an electric shock.

"And, just because it makes a cool special effect: fog."

She enveloped Mel in silvery mist, but her lips kept moving, and from within the fog Mel gave an agonized shriek. She crawled out, coughing and sputtering, then collapsed on the mat.

Savannah won.

7. BLACK MAGIC WOMAN

*A*s Savannah retreated to her corner, I whispered, "What did you use?"

"Energy bolt," she said.

"After that, I mean. The last spell."

"Fog?"

When I shook my head, she shrugged. "That's the last one I used."

It wasn't. But I knew I wouldn't get the answer I wanted.

Savannah has a secret stash of dark magic spells. She thinks Lucas and I don't know about them. I wish she'd realize that we understand there's a dark sliver inside her, and that we trust her to use it judiciously. That sometimes she'll use spells we won't necessarily approve of, and we're okay with that.

Elena says it's like when Savannah started having sex. She'd lie about spending the night at a friend's place and hide her stash of condoms. Lucas and I knew what she was doing, and we knew she was responsible enough to handle it. It was the subterfuge we didn't like. If she thought she had to hide it from us, it made us feel like we hadn't raised her properly.

I suppose she thought it might change our opinion of her. Or that she'd be subjected to "discussions" she didn't need. I'm not sure using dark magic is quite the same as being sexually active, but the basic analogy fits. I only hope that someday she'll trust me enough to talk about it.

The main thing was that Mel wasn't seriously injured. Just seriously pissed off. She was still shouting for a rematch when Shane hustled her out of the gym. No one paid any attention. All eyes were on Savannah as people crowded around, congratulating her, trying to talk to her, trying to set up matches.

She heard none of it. She was on the phone, lost in a call.

After taking the towel from me after she'd climbed out of the ring, she'd asked if I'd placed a bet.

"No, but Adam did."

"Betting against me? The bastard."

"Do you seriously think he'd bet *against* you?" I'd lifted her iPhone. "He even had me record the match, though I don't think we should tell the Gallantes that. Definitely against house rules."

She'd snatched the phone and called him, and everyone around might have been a ghost for all the attention she paid them, laughing and teasing and trading quips with Adam. If she did share her dark magic secrets with anyone, it would be him. I hoped she did.

Finally, I got her attention and motioned that she needed to get off the phone. We'd come for information, and now that she was the center of attention, we needed to take advantage of it.

"Witch versus sorcerer," the balding man, a fight promoter, was saying. "The match of the century."

Actually, the match of the past *few* centuries, and a rivalry I'd be happy to see die a quiet death. The man continued expounding on his idea for setting Savannah up in a special event. Ethan was listening, but I could see he wasn't interested. Too gimmicky for his tastes.

"They'd each use their own magic, of course," the promoter continued. "The ultimate showdown. Prove once and for all who has the better magic."

"It's not a matter of *better*," I said. "It's different, and if you restrict a witch to her own spells, you're seriously handicapping her in the ring. While we have minor offensive magic, such as the fireball, most of ours is defensive, like that binding spell. If we have to use our own, you'd have a witch fending off a sorcerer but doing very little damage, which only lends credence to the stereotype of witches."

"Run, little witch-mouse, run," Savannah muttered. "Hide from the big bad sorcerer."

Ethan nodded. He got it, but the bald promoter looked as if he'd tuned out halfway through my explanation.

"If you *were* to have a witch-versus-sorcerer match," I tried again, "it would make more sense to let them use any magic they know."

Savannah grinned. "Which would benefit the witch. Most of us learn sorcerer magic, too. Sorcerers don't bother with ours. If that puts them at a disadvantage, it's their own fault. Not like they *can't* learn it."

The conversation wasn't going anywhere useful—not for our investigation's purposes, anyway. I looked around for Shane and spotted him arguing with a man in the back corner.

No, *arguing* was too strong a word. Shane didn't look angry, just annoyed. The man was clearly trying to talk to him about something, and Shane didn't want to listen, shaking his head, arms crossed, gaze traveling the room.

I backed up for a better look at the situation. The other man was in his fifties. Heavyset. A former fighter? A badly set nose said yes. The cut of his suit, though, insisted he was no has-been. Another promoter? An agent?

Whatever he was trying to tell Shane, he really wanted him to hear it, gesturing and leaning forward. The younger man just leaned back and kept shaking his head. Then Shane went still. He turned to the old fighter, giving him his full attention.

The man said something. Shane blinked. His gaze flitted around the room and landed on his brother. He put a hand on the older man's upper arm, guided him into the office, and shut the door behind them.

I was about to excuse myself from the conversation—and see if I could overhear Shane's—when the next match was announced. Both were return fighters, so their supernatural types weren't a secret. When they announced that one was an Evanidus half-demon, I stopped.

Here was my chance to get some information on Ava and her brother. And yet . . . My gaze slid to the office. As interesting as that conversation looked, it was unlikely to have anything to do with Brody Cookson.

I turned to Savannah. "Did you hear that? A teleporting half-demon? That's got to be tough to beat."

"Hell, yeah," she said. "He can just zip away every time his opponent throws a punch. I'm surprised you allow them, Ethan. Is it even possible to beat one?"

The bald guy chuckled. "Oh, yeah, it's possible." He nudged Ethan. "Remember that girl a few months ago?"

Ethan rolled his eyes.

"You should have seen her," the promoter said. "Only a Tripudio, but still able to teleport far enough to avoid a blow. Really pretty girl. All dressed up nice, like you were. Only with her, it wasn't a show."

"Never done more than bitch-slap another girl?" Savannah said.

"I doubt she'd even done that."

"Why would a chick like that even bother showing up?"

Ethan shrugged. "With her powers, I suppose she thought it would be easy money."

The promoter laughed. "Easy money for everyone who bet *against* her. Even the guy she came with did."

"Huh," I said. "Sounds like maybe she threw the fight."

I glanced at Ethan, but his expression was blank—intentionally blank, I thought.

"I bet she did," Savannah said. "How'd she react when she found out her friend bet against her? No, let me guess. She was furious. Stormed out. Put on a helluva show."

"You got it." The promoter nodded sagely, as if he'd known it was an act, but I could tell the possibility hadn't occurred to him.

Ethan gave no reaction. This *wasn't* a revelation to him. He obviously wasn't a dumb hustler, easily conned.

Ava *hadn't* set them up, but it would have looked as if she had. Then she roared off in her brother's car, leaving him stranded with the club owners, who thought he'd cheated them. A week later, his body washes up on the nearby shore.

According to our file, the Gallantes had a reputation for running a fair operation. How far would they go to protect it?

"—how you have to do it," the promoter was saying. He was pointing at the ring, where the Evanidus half-demon was using his power not only to escape blows but to land them.

Savannah nodded. "If you're a good fighter already, it's a useful power. Otherwise, you're just going to wear yourself out dodging blows."

The half-demon's opponent—a sorcerer—hit him with a knock-back. The half-demon staggered against the ropes.

"The sorcerer isn't trying to hide his hand gestures," Savannah said. "He's telegraphing his moves. The half-demon should have been able to zip out of the way easily."

"He should have," the promoter said. "Now watch."

The half-demon righted himself, shaking it off, dazed. The sorcerer smiled, lifted his fingers for a stronger spell—and got grabbed in a headlock as the half-demon teleported behind him.

The promoter shook his head. "How many times has Davy used that move?"

"Often enough that Leo's an idiot for not seeing it coming," Ethan said as the referee counted down.

The match ended. The half-demon—Davy—left the ring, grinning and accepting high fives as he went. He headed toward Shane, and I realized I'd been so caught up in the fight that I hadn't seen Shane leave the office, which meant I hadn't seen his expression when he did. Now he was grinning at Davy, and the guy who'd taken him aside was nowhere to be seen. Damn.

"Now, Davy would make a good matchup for you, Georgia," Ethan murmured as the young man walked over to Shane. "Some of our boys would be an ass about fighting a woman, but Davy's a good guy. Still, it might be a little too much of a challenge so early in your career."

"Maybe," Savannah said. "Something to work up to."

Ethan nodded approvingly, as if he'd been testing whether her ego outweighed her common sense. He'd value the latter, and Savannah was adroit enough to realize that.

"Perhaps Shane, then. He's a better fighter than Davy, but if we let you use your powers, it would be an even match. A good exhibition event. Introduce you to a bigger crowd. Work up some excitement in the circuit." He started toward his brother, and waved for us to follow.

Davy was still pushing through the throng as he made his way toward Shane. When he disappeared, Savannah laughed.

"Taking the express route," she said. "Damn, that's a sweet power."

We watched for Davy to reappear beside Shane. Instead, a cry went up from the crowd. A few people dropped to their knees. Someone shouted for a doctor.

Ethan lunged forward and in his face I saw not worry but fear. He raced over. Davy lay facedown on the floor. Someone reached out to turn him over.

"No!" Ethan said. "Don't touch him. His neck may have been injured in the fight."

"Is he breathing?" someone asked.

"Of course," Ethan said. "He's just unconscious."

"He doesn't look like he's—"

"Out," Shane said. "Everyone out. I'm calling Dr. Phillips. Rico!"

The bouncer appeared from the cloakroom.

"Get the boys and clear this place. Have Pete wait in the parking lot for the doctor."

I squeezed in beside Ethan. "I know first aid. I—"

"I'm a paramedic." Ethan exhaled and leaned back on his heels. "Sorry. I don't mean to snap. I just need everyone out of here so I can take a closer look."

I nodded. As I rose, I took a closer look of my own. Then the employees from the parking lot swarmed in, shooing everyone out of the gym. I kept out of their way and lingered as long as I could.

The promoter cornered Savannah, saying he wanted to talk about that sorcerer–witch match, and if Ethan wasn't interested, he knew another fight club that would be. She tried to shake him. He wasn't budging, and soon we were swept along with the others, out the door and through the field to our rental.

When we reached the lot, Savannah finally brushed off the guy by taking his card and promising to call and "talk about it."

Then one of the guards swooped down and bustled us along until we were in our car and lining up to leave the lot.

"Really eager to get us out of here, aren't they?" Savannah said. When I didn't answer, she glanced at me. "And you know why, don't you?"

"That fighter wasn't unconscious. He was dead."

8. TAKING CARE OF BUSINESS

When the line of cars from the fight club turned right toward Santa Cruz, Savannah turned left. She circled back down the next road until we came out on the other side of the club. We parked, and walked through a copse of trees.

The secondary lot was empty. Even the primary lot had only three cars in it—the Mercedes and the pickup from earlier, plus a silver BMW.

"Ethan, Shane, and the doctor," Savannah whispered. "They've gotten rid of everyone else. Even the staff."

A crashing in the undergrowth had us launching cover spells. It was a man, tramping through the field to the small lot. He couldn't have been much over forty, but he heaved and puffed like a locomotive, jowls and belly quivering as he walked. The doctor, I presumed, and not one who heeded his own advice about healthy living. As he drew closer, I could see the medical bag in one hand and an envelope in the other. He climbed into his car and roared off.

We released our cover spells.

"Paid him off and sent him on his way," Savannah said. "But why call him in at all, if the guy was already dead?"

"Covering their butts. The staff saw the doctor arrive, and if anyone asks the doctor later, he'll say Davy was fine."

"All that to cover up one death? It didn't even happen in the ring. No offense, but maybe you're wrong and the guy really is fine."

I waved toward the barn. "One way to find out."

That top-notch soundproofing job really didn't help when we wanted to eavesdrop. We couldn't even hear the murmur of voices. They'd locked the door, too. An unlock spell solved that.

We slid in under blur spells. The voices came clear then—Ethan and Shane, arguing.

"Do you think I *want* to do this?" Ethan was saying. "If you've got a better idea, please let me know, because this is a shitty thing to do to a good kid like Davy."

"Maybe it wouldn't be so bad," Shane said, "if we just . . ."

"Told the truth?"

"Yeah."

"Admitted we've had two fighters *die* in the last six months? One more who would have died if I didn't keep an EpiPen in the back room? We run a clean game here, Shane. That's always been our goal—*both* of ours—and it's the only reason these kids come to us instead of flocking to the Warners. They get a whiff of this and we're through."

Silence.

"Do you have a better idea?" Ethan asked.

Shane sighed. "No, you're right. I'll take care of it."

"Thank you."

We never did find out exactly what "taking care of it" meant, because right after that, they started preparing to move Davy's body, and we didn't dare stick around. We hoped to follow them in the car, but they were gone before we made it back to the rental.

We drove to our hotel in silence. I was busy thinking and Savannah didn't interrupt me. As we walked through the hotel parking lot, I turned my cell on and checked for messages.

"How many times did Lucas call?" she said.

"None."

"Seriously? Better check your phone, 'cause I'm pretty sure your battery's dead."

"It isn't."

"Huh." She pushed the door open for me. "Must be busy fending off Ava, then. Probably praying *you'll* call and rescue him."

I smiled. "Probably."

I phoned Lucas from the elevator. It rang through to voice mail. I left a message.

"So, do I get your theory now?" Savannah said as we walked into our room. "Or can I give you mine first?"

I tugged off my shoes and sat on the edge of my bed. "Go for it."

"Okay, so apparently Ava and her brother weren't as discreet as they thought. Big surprise there. The Gallante brothers suspected they'd cheated. After Brody leaves, they go after him, kill him, toss his body in the bay. One guy dies, no big deal. But then a second guy has an allergic reaction or something and almost dies at the club. And now a third guy really *does* die, and the Gallantes realize they're in deep shit—with Davy dead, someone might find out about Brody and link them to his murder. So they need to hide Davy's body."

"One problem. They said the first death was a fighter."

"Maybe Brody *did* fight. After he won some of the money he owed, he figured it would be an easy way to get the rest. Shane fights, so obviously they accept fighters without powers."

"Possible . . ."

"But you doubt it."

I tugged pins from my hair. "First, I don't think Brody would jump into the ring so fast, not when he made easy money from betting. Second, if the Gallantes killed him, it was accidental. Neither strikes me as a cold-blooded murderer. Shane could have been roughing him up to teach him a lesson and he died of his injuries. But that doesn't explain them saying a *fighter* died." I set the pins on the nightstand. "So either you're right about Brody fighting . . ."

"Or we have two completely separate cases here."

❦

We were getting ready for bed when Savannah caught me checking my phone.

"You know why he isn't calling, right?"

My stomach did a strange little clench. "No."

She flopped onto the bed and grinned. "Maybe I shouldn't tell you. Spoil the surprise." When I gave her a blank look, she sighed. "My God, Paige, you'd think after eight years with the guy you'd have this figured out by now. He's in San Francisco, right? Only an hour away? He's coming over. Probably has a room reserved already, champagne chilling. A nice romantic getaway. Plus an excuse to bolt from Airhead Ava, which has got to be a huge bonus."

"Did he say he was coming?"

"No."

"Did you tell him where we were staying?"

That gave her pause. "Well, no, but . . . Okay, maybe he isn't coming tonight, but he will tomorrow, after he casually asks where we're staying."

I glanced at my phone.

"For God's sake, Paige. Just call him already. It's not like he's avoiding you. He's probably just trapped."

I nodded and called. On the second ring, someone picked up. Only it wasn't Lucas.

"Lucas Cortez's phone," Ava chirped. "How may I direct your call?"

She sounded drunk. Music boomed in the background. Annoyance darted through me. I felt . . . I wasn't sure what I felt, but there was an extra snap to my voice when I asked to speak to Lucas. She passed the phone over, giggling as Lucas said something I didn't catch.

"Hello?"

"It's me."

"Paige." He sounded relieved. "Just a moment."

He murmured something to Ava. She twittered a response and then giggled that she'd get him a refill. The music receded as he presumably moved into a hallway.

"You sound like you're in a bar."

"Hmm."

His tone suggested it wasn't by choice. He went on to say he'd gotten my message and had been trying to get away to return my call before I went to bed.

We talked about the case. He agreed with my theories. His own leads weren't nearly as promising.

"The fight club certainly seems far more intriguing," he said. "Chasing gambling debts is rather mundane, particularly when they don't seem to be leading anywhere."

"I bet."

There was a pause. Probably looking around, wondering when Ava was going to show up. I waited. After a moment, he cleared his throat and said, "I suppose that any lead should be followed to its end."

"Unfortunately." I remembered what Savannah had said. "And if we don't finish ours tomorrow, I could always swing by there. It's not much of a drive."

"To San Francisco, no. To LA, yes."

"LA?"

"It appears that's where the loan sharks are based. Apparently, I'll need to go to Los Angeles tomorrow, which means notifying Sean, so he can let his family know I'm in town."

Sean Nast was Savannah's half brother. While he'd personally be happy to see Lucas, the notification wasn't to give him a chance to arrange a welcoming party. Sean was heir to the Nast Cabal, based in Los Angeles. Now that Lucas officially did some work for the Cortezes, he needed to notify other Cabals when he'd be in their territory.

"Travel has gotten a whole lot more complicated, hasn't it?" I said.

"Among other things." A pause, then he sighed. "So, while I would love to see you tomorrow night, it won't work out, I'm afraid."

"Oh."

I let the silence hang. He could come here tonight. There was still time. Just ask where I was staying . . . I shook off the thought. That was silly. Selfish, too. He had leads and couldn't spend half the night commuting to see me.

We talked for another minute, then I hung up. When I looked over at Savannah, she was watching me. She said nothing until I crawled into bed, then, "Are you guys okay?"

"Sure." I must not have sounded convincing enough, because worry clouded her eyes. "We're fine, Savannah."

She watched me for a few more seconds and then turned off the light.

I was disappointed that Lucas wasn't coming, but I had to be careful around Savannah. Even a hint of trouble between Lucas and me brought out a side of her we didn't see very often. A vulnerable side, a little girl who hadn't known her father and lost her beloved mother, and ended up with something she thought she'd never get—a family. When Lucas and I argued, we threatened her family. Or so it seemed, no matter how often we'd told her, when she was younger, that our little spats meant nothing, and they certainly *were* nothing compared with the knock-down, blow-out fights some of our friends had. But she felt threatened, and she got nervous, even now.

But Lucas and I were fine. Just fine.

I rolled onto my stomach, crossed my arms under my chin, and stared at the headboard.

We were fine, weren't we?

I was fine. Well, not exactly—the issues with the Cabal were gnawing holes in my self-esteem. But I was being careful not to let that spill into my relationship with Lucas. As painful as the decision had been, he was right to help his father. I believed in that and I believed in him, and I wanted to fully support him, which meant keeping my problems to myself.

Whatever external issues I was dealing with, I was fine with Lucas. But was *he* fine with *me*?

Sneaking down here for a romantic surprise was just the kind of thing he used to do. Before his brothers died. Before the Cabal moved into our lives.

He would have called, too. Texted me, at least, ostensibly to get updates on the case, but really just to connect. Why hadn't he done that today?

When was the last time he *had* done that?

Had he really been trapped with Ava, unable to return my call? Or had I moved to the bottom of the priority list? Just his wife. He'd call me back when he could. After he was done having a few drinks with a beautiful young blonde with a damsel-in-distress complex.

I silently laughed at the thought. Um, no. Some guys, sure. Not Lucas. And yet, while I knew no young blonde could tempt him to stray, I could see how the "damsel-in-distress" part might appeal to a deeper need. Lucas liked saving people. That's how we'd met. He'd come to rescue Savannah and me from the Nast Cabal, and found two very unappreciative damsels. As clients, that had been less than satisfactory. As a lover, it was exactly what he wanted—a woman who could look after herself, and was more interested in rescuing than in being rescued.

And yet, maybe what he needed eight years ago wasn't what he needed today. Maybe *I* wasn't what he needed today.

So what he needed was a ditzy girl barely older than Savannah? Someone to make him feel big and strong?

I shook my head and thumped my face onto the pillow. Now I was being stupid. And insulting to Lucas. If he felt the need to offset the ethical challenges of working for a Cabal, he'd get his confidence boost through work, not pretty girls.

Still, there was an issue here I'd been ignoring. He *was* struggling to find his balance. We both were, but I'd been focused on my own fight.

I was feeling put out because he hadn't planned any romantic interludes in a while? Why did *he* need to plan them all? That was incredibly sexist of me.

I crept out of bed, opened my laptop, and started exploring a few ideas of my own.

9. UNDER NEW MANAGEMENT

The next morning, Savannah fired me and made an appointment to interview my replacement. I'd be a lot more hurt about that if it hadn't been my idea. Still, I will admit to being a little miffed at how quickly the real ones had swooped down after her match, whispering—in front of me, and not very quietly—that she seemed to be in need of better management.

Over breakfast, we went through the half-dozen business cards and compared recollections of those who'd slipped them into her pocket. When we reached the last, I took one look at the name and slapped it onto the table, brushing the others aside.

"This one," I said. "Call it a hunch."

"Right. The day you or Lucas act on a hunch is the day I give up spell-casting." She lifted the card and peered at it. "Travis Nichols. Say, isn't that—"

"The manager of the young man who died last night. Davy."

"Well, he definitely needs a new fighter. He just doesn't realize it yet."

As we headed up to our room after breakfast, I suggested ways I could be in on the interview, without actually being there.

"We should have brought that new spy camera the Cabal tech lab gave Lucas," I said. "I've been dying to try it out."

"Geeks and their tech toys," Savannah said. "Let's keep this simple, shall we? You want to be in on the interview? Come along."

"Right. Help you find a new manager after you fired me."

"I didn't fire you. You quit. Just when my career starts to take off, and I need you more than ever. Ungrateful bitch." She opened the hotel room door. "But just to show there's no hard feelings, I'm going to let you come with me."

"You're too kind."

When Travis Nichols opened the door and saw both of us, he stood there gaping, then snapped his jaw shut and waved us in with a smile as phony as his hair weave.

"Come in, come in. So happy to see you. *Both* of you." He cleared his throat. "Georgia, could I speak to you for a moment? If you'll excuse us, Miss . . . Sorry, I didn't catch your name."

"Manager," I said. "Ms. Ex Manager."

He stumbled and stammered about misunderstandings, and how he hoped he hadn't stepped on any toes, and he didn't realize Georgia was already represented or he'd never . . .

"It's okay," I said. "You were right. She needs someone else. Someone with experience."

I followed Savannah into the living room, turning to wave the startled Nichols through as if he were the guest.

I continued. "I'm not a professional manager. Just a friend looking out for Georgia. Now that she's won her first club bout, I'm happy to step aside. But, being a friend, I'm not going to just walk away. I'm here to hear what you have to offer and help her make a decision."

That put him at ease, and he laid out his offer. I had to nudge Savannah a couple of times to remind her to at least appear interested. She was restless, shifting and squirming and trying to hurry his pitch along so we could get to our part.

When he was done, I asked him some questions. Savannah didn't. I doubted she'd been paying enough attention to know what to ask.

Then, as we relaxed with coffee and slid into the "getting to know you" part of the interview, I asked, "So, were you at the club last night on business? Do you represent one of the fighters?"

"Davy Jones." He laughed. "And yes, that's his real name, poor kid." His smile faded and he reached for his cell phone, checking it. "I couldn't stick around last night, but I've left him a few messages. That was a bad fall he took."

"I saw. What happened?"

"Lousy refereeing, that's what. Believe me, I'm going to have a talk with Ethan about that. Leo must have cast one of those knockback spells right at Davy's head, and that's against the rules. He's just lucky my boy didn't get a concussion or I'd have his ass kicked off the circuit."

"Is the refereeing there always so bad?" Savannah asked. "Ethan was talking about setting me up in a match against Shane, but maybe it's not the best place for me to start a career."

"You against Shane?" Nichols's eyes glittered. "That's gold, girl. Doesn't matter if you win or lose, it'd get your name traveling through the circuit. Shane's good. Damn good. Too good for . . ." He stopped, shrugged. "Well, you know."

"He's professionally trained, isn't he?" I said.

"Hell, yeah. State champion in high school, and that's just boxing. He racked up medals in wrestling, too. Everyone expected him to hit the pro circuit after graduating. But Ethan wanted him to go to college. Nothing wrong with that, of course. Ethan only wanted the best for his little brother. He didn't get to finish college himself. Their folks died when he was in his first year, and Shane was only a kid and . . . Well, I'm sure you don't want to hear this."

"Actually, we do," I said. "If Georgia's going to fight at the Gallantes' club, I'd appreciate a little background. So Ethan raised Shane, I take it?"

"Right. He sent him off to college. Can't remember what he majored in. Didn't matter, really, because everyone knew he'd get back into fighting. Only he didn't. Not on the pro circuit, anyway. He got a job working at a gym downtown, and that was it."

"What happened?" I asked. "Was he injured?"

"No, it's just . . ." Nichols rubbed his mouth. "Word is, Ethan didn't want him going pro. Didn't think he had what it took and didn't want him wasting his time on it."

"Nice brother," Savannah muttered.

"What did Ethan do?" I asked.

Nichols shrugged. "Just talked him out of it, I guess. I don't know the whole story. That's just the rumor. Anyway, I'm sure Ethan thought it was best for Shane. Few years later, they opened the club together, and I think that was Ethan's way of making it up to his brother. Shane sure as hell doesn't bear him any ill will. Those two are as close as ever. Still live in the same house where they grew up."

"Okay," Savannah said. "So obviously, with Shane's rep, a bout with him would be sweet. But if the club is badly managed . . ."

"Hell, no, it's one of the best around. The ref missed a call. It happens. Shit, even I didn't see Leo cast that knockback or whatever he must have done to make Davy collapse after the fight. I'll talk to Ethan and, sure, I'll give him hell for it, but that's just me, watching out for my boys, like I always do. Just last year, one of them . . ."

He launched into an anecdote to prove to Savannah he'd make a good manager. I kept her from interrupting, but as soon as he finished she said, "So the Gallantes are good? Fair? That's what I've heard, but you never know."

"I run my boys up and down all the fight clubs in this state. Even over to Texas when the money's right. But all other things being equal, you'll find them fighting for Ethan and Shane. Now, some folks will say the Gallantes are too clean to run a fight club. I say bullshit. Those boys have carved out a nice little niche in the market for those who prefer a fair fight to a bloodbath."

"But there's a point where you can be *too* fair, overly cautious," Savannah said. "Like not wanting to call out a cheater in case you're wrong."

"Uh-uh. Believe me, with the Gallantes, fair means no cheating. They catch you, you're banned for life. Lost one of my own boys that way. He was in a slump, started taking something for it, they caught him, and he was out. Out of my stable, too."

"Sure, but what about throwing games? I heard there was an incident just a few months ago, with another teleporting half-demon. They suspect she threw the fight so her friend could cash in. If the Gallantes knew it and they let them go . . ."

He laughed. "Oh, they didn't let them go. Don't you worry about that. Sure, the girl got away, but she left her friend stranded. And when that boy finally did leave, Shane followed."

10. THE ART OF BLACKMAIL

*M*an, that Ethan's a piece of work," Savannah said when we got into the car. "Can you believe what he did to his brother? Deciding he's not good enough to turn pro? Shane should have taken *him* into the ring years ago."

I gazed out the window and said nothing. There'd been a time when Savannah had dreamed of a career as an artist, and while I'd never have outright denied her the chance to go to art school, part of me had wondered if encouraging her wholeheartedly was really the right thing to do.

Savannah had talent, but no more than thousands of other kids who dreamed of their first gallery opening. We'd subtly tried to steer her toward graphic design or another use for her skills so she could make a living while pursuing art on the side. She wasn't interested in that. She wanted to be an artist.

In the end, it was Savannah herself who changed her mind. As high school had progressed, her interest in art had waned. These days, it was only a hobby. She'd found her passion in her job. Well, not her actual job as admin assistant. What she loved were these forays into the field that she hoped would get her out of the receptionist's chair for good. And they would, as soon as she'd matured a little more.

If Savannah had been hell-bent on art school, would I have found a way to persuade her not to go? No. I couldn't do what Ethan had done. But I'd have been tempted.

I had to admit, though, that it was different with Shane. Being state champ meant he did have the talent to go pro. He might not have become a star, but he could have made a living at it for a while. Was that what Ethan feared? A short-lived career? Retiring young, bitter, and disillusioned, with nothing to fall back on? Had he set Shane on a different path to spare him that fate? As someone in a similar position—raising a younger "sibling"—I could understand that urge to protect. I just wasn't sure I agreed with it.

Thinking of retired fighters reminded me of the scene I'd witnessed at the ring, Shane talking to that former boxer. Had the man been trying to lure Shane into a bigger arena? What had he said that had alarmed Shane? Made him look over at Ethan and move the conversation to the office?

"Okay, you're thinking something," Savannah said. "What's the plan, boss?"

"We need to speak to the Gallante brothers again. Separately this time."

Finding an address for the Gallantes was easy enough. Nichols said they'd lived in the same place all their lives. A simple property search gave us a location on the other side of Santa Cruz.

While Savannah drove, I worked on theories. From Nichols, we'd confirmed that Brody hadn't fought in the ring the night he died, which meant that when the Gallantes talked about another fighter's death, they didn't mean him. Which left us with a problem.

I could see Shane Gallante going after Brody and beating the crap out of him. I'd spent enough time around werewolves to understand that in some subcultures, violence was the language everyone understood. As even-tempered as Shane seemed, he *was* a fighter. Considering what Ethan had done to him, there might be a deep well of rage and resentment there, just waiting to be tapped by a kid like Brody Cookson.

So Shane beats up Brody, who accidentally dies. Then they have a fighter who also accidentally dies, another who accidentally *almost* dies, and another who dies last night . . . again, accidentally.

"Either these guys aren't nearly as clean as they seem," Savannah said, "or I really hope all their insurance is paid up, because someone's put one hell of a curse on them."

We found the house—a small, Southwestern-style ranch in an older neighborhood. The Mercedes was under a carport, but there was no sign of the truck.

"Ethan's in; Shane's out," Savannah said. "Good enough?"

I nodded.

We parked a couple of doors down and were walking toward the house when the front door swung open. I cast a quick cover spell. Savannah did the same.

It was Ethan grabbing the mail, shirt untucked and half buttoned, feet bare. He stepped halfway out, and propped the door open with his back. Then he stayed there, flipping through the mail with his back to us. I broke my spell and motioned that we'd continue our approach.

We were close enough to call a greeting when Ethan's cell phone rang. He answered, still sorting mail. Then he stopped.

"Who is this?" he said, voice loud and harsh enough to reach us.

We vanished under fresh cover spells.

"Either you give me a name or—" Pause. "Absolutely not. Anything you have to say to me, say it in the next thirty seconds or—" Pause. His shoulders went rigid, then he spat, "Fine," and hung up.

He tossed the mail inside and tucked in his shirt as he stepped in after it. The door didn't even get a chance to close before he was striding out again, shoes and keys in hand. Seconds later, the Mercedes roared from the drive.

"Follow?" Savannah said as she broke her spell.

"Absolutely."

Ethan went straight to the club, fast enough that I was glad I'd let Savannah take the wheel. We parked where we had after last night's match and then cut through the woods again. Ethan's car was there, alongside an old Camaro, complete with an eagle on the hood and big-breasted girls on the mud flaps.

"Classy," Savannah said. "Love the mud flaps. I didn't think they still made those."

"No hit on the plate," I said as I finished searching it on my phone. "Either it's fake or stolen, and removed from the system."

"Like I said, a classy guy. Since we don't have a name, I vote for Guido." She caught my look. "Yeah, yeah, I'm sure there are perfectly nice guys named Guido. In some universe."

We made our way inside the barn. Ethan and his guest—no, I wasn't calling him Guido—were in the office. We zipped into the main room under blur spells. In the silence, the voices came clearly through the closed office door.

Ethan was talking. "—listened to what you have to say. Now I'd like you to leave."

"I'm only trying to help," the other man whined.

"No, you're trying to blackmail me. I suspect you're new to it, so let me give you some advice. In order to effect a successful blackmail scheme, you need to know something blackmail-worthy. Something important to your victim."

"Important? Your brother is trying to sabotage your operation here and—"

"The second piece of advice? Do your research. Make sure your information is reliable. If you're going to try passing off lies, at least be sure the lie will work. Know who you're dealing with."

"I know who I'm dealing with. A guy who gave up his *life* to look after a kid brother who's now—"

"Turning on him. Ruining the business. After I devoted my life to raising him. After I built this club for him. Is this where I start ranting? Swear vengeance? As I said, *sir*, do your research. You've cast me in a very poorly fitting role. You can bring me all the evidence you want; my answer will remain the same. I trust my brother."

"Then you're a fool."

"Perhaps I am. Now, if you'll excuse me, I have work to do."

We zipped out ahead of Ethan and his visitor. The other man left. We followed and got a few pictures of him. Then we went back to the barn.

Ethan was still in his office.

"Hey," Savannah said. "I hope it's okay coming by like this—"

He turned in his chair, the squeak cutting Savannah short.

"Hello, Georgia," he said. "Or do you prefer Savannah?"

Before I could find my voice, Ethan continued. "You woke me up in the middle of the night, you know. I suddenly remembered where I knew you from. Well, not you. Your mother. I met her once. I was sixteen, just starting to see ghosts. My father had heard that Eve Levine knew a spell that would fix that."

"Fix it?"

"Take away my powers. Or at least make them more manageable. Necromancy drove my grandmother mad. An old story. My father didn't want that for me, so he took me to your mother. Turned out the rumor was false. There is no such spell. She was nice enough about it, given her reputation. Gave us some vervain to help me banish ghosts and told us where to buy more."

"Okay, you got me." She extended a hand. "Savannah Levine. And, yes, since you know my mother's rep, you know why I used a fake name. No one's going into a ring against Eve Levine's daughter."

"True, but that's not the side of the family you're trying to hide. I didn't know much about you, so I contacted a few sources this morning. Information is still trickling in, but I did hear one interesting tidbit. The identity of your father. Clever of the Nasts, sending a witch as a spy. We wouldn't see that one coming."

He stepped up to her. "Tell your family that Santa Cruz isn't LA. I don't need to pay them a protection fee or whatever the hell they want to call it. If they insist on sending spies and blackmailers, I'll file a complaint with the interracial council. I hear they're actually getting off their asses and doing something about issues like this."

"We're trying," I said.

Ethan turned to me, as if he'd forgotten I was there.

"If you want to complain to the council, that'd be her," Savannah said. "Alternatively, you could hire Lucas Cortez to defend you. That'd also be her. If you want to send a message to the Nasts, that wouldn't be me. I could try, but I think they have special spells on their LA office now, just to make sure I don't get past the front door."

I stepped forward and extended my hand. "Paige Winterbourne. I'm—"

"Head of the interracial council," Ethan finished. "And wife to Lucas Cortez."

It'd been a long time since I'd been identified in that order. "Right on both counts. But I'm not here representing the council or the Cabal. I'm investigating the death of Brody Cookson—the young man who bet against his teleporting half-demon sister. Can we talk?"

11. BROTHERLY LOVE

*W*e settled into chairs in Ethan's tiny office, and I explained the situation. As investigative techniques went, this was far from ideal. But he'd thrown us a curveball, recognizing Savannah, and coming clean seemed our only option.

When I finished, Ethan took a moment to gather his thoughts, calmly, seemingly unconcerned that it might make him appear to be concocting a story. As he paused, I looked around the office. It was barely more than a closet, but as tidy as my own. No personal mementos here, though. A sterile and efficient workspace . . . with one exception. On a shelf, amid binders and books, were a half dozen boxing and wrestling trophies.

Shane's awards, not displayed in the main room as advertising, but here, kept by Ethan. Odd that he'd do that if he'd dissuaded Shane from a professional career.

"If this young man is dead, we know nothing about it," he said at last. "Yes, we thought he cheated. Yes, Shane discussed it with him. And by *discussed*, I don't mean he took him for a beer and gave him betting advice. Shane is our enforcer, however uncomfortable he is in the role. He followed the boy and demanded our money back. The boy resisted. According to Shane, he didn't resist past a few blows. He gave Shane the cash, and my brother left him walking and talking."

"This is what Shane *told* you," Savannah said.

"Which means it's the truth. But I don't expect you to believe that, so please feel free to ask him yourself."

"A blow to the head could still do it," I said. "Like that fighter who collapsed last night. Brody might have walked away, then later became disoriented from a concussion and ended up in the bay."

Ethan shook his head. "Shane is very careful about that. He hits fast and hard, but never to the head. It's an attack designed to scare, not seriously injure."

"Maybe that's his usual way of handling things," Savannah said. "But that's not how this one went down. The kid smart-mouthed Shane. Or your brother's adrenaline was running high from the club. Things got out of hand."

"Not Shane."

"You keep saying that. We heard you saying it to that black-mailer, too. Protesting a little much, don't you think?"

Ethan's cool gaze met hers. "Not protesting at all. Simply stating facts."

"He accused Shane of betraying you," I said. "Trying to shut down the business. He said he had evidence."

"Manufactured evidence."

"You sound damned sure of that," Savannah said.

"I am."

"What did he accuse Shane of?" I asked.

Now those cool eyes turned my way. "A matter unrelated to this boy's death. A matter that is being taken care of and that, I can assure you, has nothing to do with my brother."

A matter of murder, the death of two fighters. A matter that someone thought was related to Shane Gallante. I wasn't sure I disagreed.

We tried to get more from Ethan, but the only thing he'd provide was a location for his brother. To be honest, I was surprised he gave us that, but I suppose he knew we'd track him down sooner or later, and he didn't want to start trouble with the council.

Shane was at a gym in Santa Cruz, where he worked part-time, as Ethan did as a paramedic, providing a legitimate source of income for the authorities.

The gym was what I'd expect—shabby but clean, a place for local fighters to train and a place for neighborhood kids to learn the basics.

"And look who teaches the kiddies," Savannah said, rapping her knuckle against a dog-eared poster. It promised free after-school lessons, taught by former state champion Shane Gallante.

"I bet he does it for free, too." She shook her head. "Some people, huh? Raising a kid who isn't their own. Running a squeaky-clean business. Finding time for community work. There's good, and then there's too good."

"I'm not sure how good you can be if you're running an illegal gambling operation."

She looked at me. "You're running an illegal gambling operation?"

"I thought we were talking about the Gallantes."

"Oh, right. Damn." She looked down at me. "Do you think we *could* run an illegal gambling operation?"

I pushed her toward the doors. She swung them open and breezed through, and for perhaps the first time since she'd turned sixteen Savannah walked into a room full of young men and not one glanced her way. That may have had something to do with the drama playing out ringside.

A hulking young man was leaning over the ropes, sweat dripping from his bald head. Behind him, his opponent staggered toward his corner, blood trailing in his wake.

"Now will you fight me, you arrogant son of a bitch?" the bald fighter shouted to someone ringside.

The reply came so softly I barely heard it. "No, and it doesn't matter how many bouts you win, Max, I'm not ever going to fight you."

With a snarl of rage, the fighter leapt over the ropes and flew at his unseen target. Two guys rushed in to the other man's defense, but he only rose from the bench, waving them off. As he did, I saw his face. Shane Gallante.

Shane stood his ground as the bald fighter loomed over him.

"I'm not fighting you, Max, and that's not an insult. I'm just not interested."

The fighter grabbed Shane by the shirtfront.

"Uh-oh," Savannah murmured. "That's not smart."

Shane didn't throw a punch. He just let the younger fighter put him up against the wall, then calmly said, "Okay, you got me. If you want, you can throw me down and tell everyone you beat me, and I won't argue. Is that what you want, Max?"

"I want you in the ring, Gallante."

"Well, it's not happening. I concede to your superior skills. Now, if you'll excuse me, a couple of pretty girls just walked in, and I really hope they're looking for me."

Max dropped Shane hard enough to make him stagger. He recovered his balance, then flashed us a big smile and strolled over as if nothing had happened.

"Hey, ladies," he said. "Ethan said you were coming to see me. Paige and Savannah, right?"

"That's right," I said, extending a hand.

We did proper introductions, but I was sure his brother had already told him who we were and why we were there. He took us into an empty office and ran through his encounter with Brody. He gave more details, but in essence it matched his brother's story.

"So, you're the club enforcer," Savannah said when he finished. "You like doing that?"

He looked from her to me, then sighed. "Okay, what did Ethan say? No, let me guess. He told you I hate it."

"You don't?"

Shane's nose wrinkled. "Mmm, it's not my favorite part of the job. But it *is* my job. It's a bit of an ongoing dispute between me and my brother. He knows I don't like it, so he wants to have one of our boys take over. How would that reflect on me as a fighter? No, I need to play the heavy, even if it's not my favorite role."

"We saw that," I said, nodding toward the ring.

Shane shifted. "Yeah, well, that's how it goes. You're the lead fighter, everyone wants a piece of you. In the club, we can control it. Here? I don't have time for guys like Max."

"You handled it well," I said. "Not many fighters could step down like that. This sport runs on adrenaline."

He slid off the desk and waved us to the window overlooking the ring. Inside, Max was pummeling another opponent. "You look at his face, what do you see? Adrenaline?"

"No, I see rage." I turned to him. "And that's what you don't have. It's why you're not comfortable being the club's enforcer."

"And it's why Ethan stopped you from going pro," Savannah said.

Shane laughed. "Heard that story, have you? My evil older brother squashing my dreams? Yes, he was concerned. Yes, I'm sure he wanted to discourage me. But he never did."

He crossed to a poster on the wall, advertising a bout between him and another former school champion. "*This* is what I'm good at. High school matches, where technique is what counts. When I tried a few pro bouts, I discovered I was missing something most fighters have. Drive."

He sat on the desk again. "Not the drive to win, but the drive to pummel a stranger into hamburger. A guy fights me in the ring, I'm going to give it everything I've got, then I'm going to ask him out for a beer after. It's just a game to me. When you hit the pro stage, it's not like that anymore. You're up against guys who are mad at the world, like Max."

"But you still can't escape your reputation," I said. "It's not just other fighters like Max who pester you, is it?" I mentioned the man I'd seen him talking to the night before.

"Promoter. They don't come after me that often anymore, but

this guy heard . . ." He trailed off and shrugged. "Stupid rumor about the club. Nothing to it."

Were people figuring out that the Gallantes seemed a little accident-prone?

Savannah missed the cue and barreled forward. "So Ethan didn't make you go to college. But he couldn't resist using you to open a club."

This time, Shane's laugh boomed through the room. "Using me. Right. That Ethan, it's all about him." He shook his head. "The club was my idea, too. Ethan fully supported it. Even took out a mortgage on our parents' home to set it up. Yeah, maybe there's a little guilt there—he wonders if I chose college to make him happy—but if anyone did the manipulating, it was me." He grinned. "That's the power of being a little brother."

"Okay, I've solved the case," Savannah said as we walked out of the club. "Well, not our case, because I have no flipping idea who killed Brody Cookson, and frankly, I don't care. He sounds like a little snot."

I sighed.

"What? You're thinking the same thing. You just can't say it because that would be wrong. Forget Brody for now. I know who's killing the fighters. The same brother who wants the club shut down. Only it isn't Shane."

"Ethan?"

"Obviously. Yeah, I know Shane was teasing about manipulating him, but there's truth there, too. Ethan raises the kid. Maybe expects it to pay off when Shane goes pro. Only he wimps out and goes to college—"

"I'd hardly say that's wimping out."

"Whatever. Point is, Ethan lost his ticket to the high life. Probably got stuck with the tuition bill to boot. Then Shane guilts him into opening the club. It's more hassle than Ethan wants. He's risking jail time for a business that might barely turn a profit. He's spent twenty years taking care of his brother. The guy hasn't even moved out of the house yet, for God's sake. Now Ethan's had enough. Time to make the club dream go poof."

She rounded the corner, striding to our car and glowering at two school-age kids checking it out. When one reached for the door handle, she zapped him with a small energy bolt. He fell back with a yelp and they took off.

She clicked the fob to open our doors. "People have caught wind of the deaths. First that promoter, then the blackmailer. He has evidence that a brother is involved, and has heard the rumor that Ethan forced Shane out of the biz. So the blackmailer presumes Shane's behind it. But who's more likely to have found a way to kill these guys from across the room? The fighter? Or the paramedic?"

I climbed into the car. When I still hadn't said anything and we were pulling from the lot, Savannah glanced over. "You disagree."

"Let's just say I'm not convinced. I think it's a little coincidental that a fighter died last night, when we were there, and that Ethan got a blackmail call just as we're walking toward his house."

"You think Ethan isn't the only one who made us?"

"I think Lucas isn't the only one reaching the stage where he needs to presume most supernaturals know who he is."

12. FOLLOW THE MONEY

*A*s we headed to the hotel, my phone beeped, reminding me I had a message. It'd come in while we were with Shane, but I'd forgotten to check. Now I read Lucas's text.

"Well, I'm pretty sure the Gallantes had nothing to do with Brody's death," I said.

"What?"

I motioned for Savannah to keep driving, as I sent back a response and a question. The answer came in seconds.

"Lucas is on his way to LA, but he just got a callback from one of Brody's friends. The last time he saw Brody was the day *after* Brody left the fight club."

"Maybe Shane hadn't found him yet."

"No, he had. Brody was trying to reduce the swelling from a black eye and complaining about a loose tooth."

"So he was fine after the beating. But maybe he went back to the club looking for revenge."

"Possible. Yet according to the friend, Brody was more frightened than angry. Something—or someone—had him very scared. I think I know what it was."

I started a reply to Lucas.

"Care to share?" Savannah said as I texted.

"Why did Shane go after Brody?"

"To teach the brat a lesson."

"No. Not really."

As she turned a corner, she checked her mirrors for anyone

tailing us. "To get back the money. Which he did. Meaning Brody had nothing left to pay off his debts."

"Exactly."

At the hotel, I took a good hard look at Ethan and Shane Gallante, harder than I had earlier, when I thought they were just a step along the path in retracing Brody's final days. I conducted the kind of background check that disputed Savannah's assertion about our business methods being squeaky-clean. What we run is an *effective* business, and sometimes that takes creative and ethically question-able applications of my computer skills.

"The club is profitable," I said after I'd done my research. "The brothers paid off the mortgage a year after taking it out. Shane bought his truck last year without taking a loan. The Mercedes is older, but no loans there, either. No lines of credit at all. These guys even pay off their cards every month. They aren't multimil-lionaires, but they certainly aren't in debt."

"Okay, so no financial motivation to shut down the club. Maybe Ethan just wants out. Get his own life. Leave California. Marry, have kids. Only he's tied to his brother through an illegal business. Shane's not going to let him leave easily. Christ, the guy still lives with him. As someone who has an adult ward still leaving tooth-paste globs in her sink, you've got to know how that feels. Imagine how you'd feel if I was still doing it a decade from now."

"Shane hasn't always lived at home. He went to college in Texas."

"Okay, so he moved out for a couple of years—"

"Then came back to Santa Cruz and rented an apartment, where he lived until he got married and bought a condo with his wife."

"Wife?"

"Soon to be ex-wife." I tapped the computer screen. "The divorce is almost final. After they filed, Shane moved in with Ethan while his wife stayed in the condo. We know Shane's not a fighter at heart. My guess? Ethan insisted he move back in until the divorce was done, to avoid putting him through the hassle of bickering over the condo."

"Damn. Blows my theory out of the water. What about the wife, then? Could she be sabotaging the business?"

"If she wanted revenge, it would be a lot easier just to notify the authorities."

"True. Okay, so if it's not Ethan and it's not Shane, who the hell is it?"

"I think it's time to ask them that."

The Gallantes weren't at the club when we arrived, so we parked down the road and waited. They arrived later in the afternoon. We gave them time to get in and settled, then followed, and found them right where they'd been the day before—Ethan on his laptop and Shane doing push-ups.

Shane rose as we entered. "I'm hoping you're here to talk about that bout Ethan suggested. You and me. Make a helluva fight. But I have a feeling that's not it."

Ethan stepped out of his office. "Shane didn't kill that boy. Neither of us did."

"We're not here to talk about Brody's death," Savannah said. "We're here to talk about Davy's."

I said, "I've seen enough dead bodies to know there's no way, short of necromancy, that Davy Jones walked out of here last night. If you insist otherwise, then I'd like to speak to him. Refuse, and I'll get in touch with your friend, Dr. Phillips."

I pulled a chair from the office and sat. "Did you know we have a file on Phillips? Seems there's a reason he needs that extra cash. A daughter up on drug charges in Orlando. I wonder what he'd say if we offered him a deal? He tells the truth about Davy and the fighter who died a few months ago, and Lucas will represent his daughter for free."

"We didn't kill anyone," Ethan said.

"Never said you did. But two fighters *are* dead."

A pause so long I was ready to repeat my threat when Ethan finally said, "Yes. Davy died last night."

"And you dumped the body," Savannah said.

"No, we moved him to Dr. Phillips's office, where he can conduct an autopsy. As you said, this isn't the first time it's happened. In six months, we've had two deaths and one near fatality. The first time, we thought it was a fluke. It does happen, as hard as you try to avoid it. The fighter collapsed in the ring. We cleared the place out, as we did last night. Then we took him to his hotel."

"And made it look like he'd died in his sleep," I said. "Possibly from injuries sustained at the club. But with the doctor confirming he'd walked out, no one would blame you. You chalked it up to a freak accident."

"Until it happened again," Savannah said. "And then again."

"The second time, the fighter *did* walk out okay, and he's still walking around. But if I hadn't had an EpiPen here, he'd be dead. Everyone knew he was allergic to nuts, so they figured that's what it was."

"You disagreed because he was in the ring, fighting, not sitting down to a meal that accidentally had nuts in it."

When Ethan didn't answer, I said, "You think someone's killing your fighters. The obvious reason is cheating. Poison or magic to defeat an opponent, only occasionally the results are lethal."

Shane shook his head. "It's been a different opponent each time, and with two, the victor would have taken the match anyway. No reason to cheat."

"So what do you think the problem is?" I asked.

Silence. Savannah waited five seconds this time, then stood. "Fine. You want us to figure it out for ourselves, we—"

"It's the Warners," Shane said.

"We *suspect* it's the Warners," Ethan said. "They run—"

"A chain of fight clubs," Savannah said. "We've done our research."

The Warners owned a club in San Francisco and a half dozen others, ranging from here to northern Florida. They were a family of sorcerers who had once headed a Cabal before being squeezed out by the big four. Now, having shed their corporate cloak, they ran everything from fight clubs to drug rings to brothels, all aimed at the supernatural market.

"When we first opened, they were fine with us," Ethan said. "We were far enough from San Fran, and our place is a dive compared to theirs. They even sent patrons and fighters our way."

"Yeah," Shane snorted. "The ones they didn't want. That's why they were fine with us. We were their garbage pit. Send the cheaters and the losers to us. Only we wouldn't take them, and eventually our place was cleaner than theirs. A lot cleaner."

"So you started attracting the better patrons and fighters," Savannah said. "Which is when they decided they weren't as happy having you here."

Ethan nodded. "They've offered to buy us out. Six months ago, they stopped offering . . . and we started having accidents."

13. HOMEWARD BOUND

*W*hile we were with the Gallantes, Lucas had texted to say he suspected my theory was correct. Brody had hoped to use the money he'd made at the club for a down payment on his gambling debt. Only Shane took the money, so his creditors added to his beatings. I doubt they'd meant to kill him—a corpse can't pay back anything—but the results had been fatal.

I left that investigation to Lucas. I had a new case to work. The Gallantes had hired me to investigate the deaths at their club. I'd start by getting a better, unbiased view of the situation with the Warners. Eventually, that would require a trip to San Francisco. First, we needed to do a lot of reading through files and putting out calls to contacts. The boring part, as Savannah called it.

Yet she volunteered. Savannah knew that private investigation wasn't all fights and break-ins and tailing suspects, and she was determined to pull her weight.

There was, however, another reason she'd volunteer—she had contacts far more suited to researching black-market types like the Warners. Savannah cultivated a network of contacts who'd never work with me or Lucas. Former associates of her mother, they hoped to woo Savannah as an ally. Like her dark magic spells, she thinks we don't know about them. Like those spells, I hate maintaining the fiction that we don't know, but for now, it seems best.

So Savannah headed home to do her part. I stayed in Santa Cruz but made plans for a trip of my own—to Los Angeles. Time to pay a surprise visit to my husband.

Unfortunately, I had no idea where Lucas was staying. Savannah tried to help by calling him and hinting for details, but he didn't bite. I ran a credit card check, but there were no transactions in the last day. Ava must have been footing the bill for his hotel room, which was odd. We usually charge expenses. If she'd insisted on paying up front, though, he wouldn't have argued—less paperwork.

Before Savannah left, she said, "Forget surprising him. Just tell him you're coming." So I called and told him Savannah was researching the Warners.

"So while she handles that, I'm free."

I paused, expecting him to ask me to join him. When he didn't respond, I said, "That means I could come there. Help you out."

"Ah."

Ah? "Is that a no? Okay. I, uh, guess you're close to wrapping this up anyway."

"No, I wouldn't say that. Unfortunately."

There was a pause before the last word, as if he'd had to remind himself to say it. He hurried on, listing all the tasks he still needed to accomplish and insisting, regretfully, that he probably wouldn't be home for a few days.

Lucas was an expert liar, but I'd learned to recognize when he was prevaricating.

"You're going home, then, I take it?" he said. "Today?"

"I guess so."

"Good. There should be a flight back later this afternoon. Take that, go home, and rest. No need to rush off after the Warners."

I smiled as I realized where this was heading. "I don't know. If I get in early, I really should head to the office. Get caught up. Help Savannah."

"Absolutely not. You deserve a rest. Go home."

"Should I call you when I get in?"

A pause. "You can try, but I suspect I'll be out. I have several leads to follow that can only be done at night, and I may have my phone turned off."

He lied about the case being almost done. Made sure I was going home. Warned me not to expect to hear from him. Someone was planning a surprise visit of his own.

"All right, then," I said. "I'll take the evening off. Savannah was planning to go back to Adam's place and hang out." She'd said no such thing, but I was sure I could convince her easily enough. "She'll probably just crash there."

"Excellent. You'll get a decent rest, then."

I smiled. Oh, I wasn't planning on doing much resting tonight.

I managed to get a seat on a flight heading home, barely squeaking through security in time. Savannah had taken my car from the airport lot, so I caught a cab and made a pit stop at my favorite lingerie store.

I bought champagne and strawberries, plus everything I'd need for breakfast in bed. I grabbed a few more things, too—a travel book, sunscreen, and a Hawaiian shirt. Then I went home and printed off pages for Maui sell-off vacations I'd bookmarked the night before. I didn't dare to actually book a vacation for us—too risky with our schedules—but this would do. I tucked the pages into a suitcase with the book, sunscreen, and shirt, and hid it in our room, where I could pull it out while we were catching our breath.

Final step—change into my new bustier, panties, and garters, then put on the low-cut green silk dress I usually saved for romantic dinners. After that . . . well, after that there wasn't much else to do but wait.

Savannah had e-mailed me pages on the Warners, and I was just settling in to read those when my phone blipped with a text. I smiled and grabbed it, only to find a message from Ava, wanting me to call her ASAP.

Lucas must have left already. She was probably trying to get in touch with him before he got on the plane, tell him she urgently needed him back, only to find he'd turned off his phone early.

I considered not calling her back, but that would be petty. Worse, it was acting like I'd "won," which implied I'd seen her as a threat. I should thank her. She'd highlighted hairline fractures in our marriage, which I was going to repair before the stability of the whole was in danger.

When I called, her line was busy. Had she gotten hold of Lucas? I hoped not. If she made up a plausible enough story, he'd feel obligated to go back.

I texted her and returned to reading the files. Nearly an hour later, she texted to say she was busy right now, but could I phone her in an hour? Lucas had left a message and wanted to be sure I got it.

Call in an hour? A message from Lucas? If my husband wanted to speak to me, he was quite capable of using either text or e-mail. Ava Cookson was up to something.

Savannah texted me at eleven to say she had a lead on someone who owed the Warners a lot of cash. She was investigating now and we'd discuss it in the morning. I considered calling her back, but I needed to find out what Ava was up to first. Lucas could be in a cab heading home right now, so I wanted to get this over with.

When Ava didn't answer after three rings, I almost hung up and called Savannah back. Then the line clicked and her sleepy voice said, "Hello?"

"It's Paige Winterbourne. You asked me to call."

She swore and bedsprings creaked, as if she was sitting up fast. "Oh my God, I'm so sorry. I completely forgot."

"That's fine. If it's urgent, have Lucas—"

A faint clatter cut me short. It was a sound I knew so well I could visualize it. Lucas waking, half asleep, reaching for his glasses on the nightstand . . .

"Who is it?" asked a voice, and I struggled to breathe, praying I wouldn't hear—

"Your wife," came the reply, muffled, as if Ava had covered the phone.

A soft curse, then the sound of someone scrambling out of bed.

Someone? *Someone? You know who's climbing out of her bed.*

A murmur, words indistinguishable. Footsteps padded across the floor. A door clicked shut.

"Sorry," Ava said, coming back. "I'm not alone, which explains why I totally forgot you were calling. Totally forgot *everything.*" She giggled.

I hung up.

14. WAKING NIGHTMARE

I sat on the sofa. Just sat there, unable to think, unable to form a thought. When I could, all I could think were two words. Not possible. *Not possible.*

I was dreaming. I'd fallen asleep while I was waiting to call Ava, and I would wake up soon with Lucas's hand on my shoulder, his warm breath on my cheek, the faint smell of his shaving lotion . . .

Tears burned my eyes. I blinked them back. There had to be another explanation. He'd been in her hotel room, discussing the case. They'd fallen asleep.

On the bed? *Together?*

Maybe it wasn't a bed. They were on a couch and he'd been getting his glasses from the side table and the creak of springs had been sofa springs.

That wasn't what it had sounded like.

I called Lucas's number. As it rang, I pictured him listening to my ring tone, seeing my picture on the screen, just sitting there, waiting for voice mail—

"Hello." His voice was hesitant, as if he already regretted answering, and my insides knotted. The first tears trickled down my cheeks. I wiped them away.

"Hey, you *are* answering." I tried to sound casual. "I thought you were out."

"I am, unfortunately." His voice had an odd echo. In a bathroom? *Her* bathroom, where he'd retreated after I called? "I really shouldn't talk."

Couldn't talk. That's what he meant. Wasn't ready for me. Wasn't sure if I'd heard him with her. Wasn't ready with an excuse.

"Ava called," I said. "She had a message from you, but I never did get it, so I thought I'd go straight to you."

"Message?"

A pause, and I knew there'd been no message. Of course there hadn't. She'd texted and told me to call back in an hour because she knew by then they'd be dozing, and I'd call and she'd nudge him, accidentally, of course. He'd wake and I'd hear him and I'd know.

"Perhaps she misunderstood," he went on. "There wasn't a message, so no need to worry."

Someone spoke in the background. A young woman. Lucas quickly covered the phone and murmured to her.

"Who's that?" I said.

"Just the contact I was meeting. I really should go. I'll call you in the morning."

I said goodbye, but he'd already disconnected.

No "I love you." No "Sleep well." No "I can't wait to be home." Nothing.

I sat there, phone still in my hand, tears streaming down. Then I collapsed back on the sofa and sobbed until I couldn't breathe.

I gasped, wiping my face, struggling to get a grip, make a plan.

Make a *plan*? I couldn't even form a coherent thought.

Lucas had cheated on me.

Everything inside me screamed I was wrong. I had to be wrong. This was Lucas. *Lucas.*

When someone knocked, I blinked, then turned toward the front door and checked my watch. Who'd be here at this hour?

A second knock, and I realized it came from the back. A key clicked in the lock.

"Paige?" Adam called. "I need to grab a file from your home office."

When I didn't answer, he called my name again. Then his

footsteps sounded in the kitchen. I held still, praying he'd think I'd gone to bed and slip past, find the file, and leave. He came into the living room and saw me on the sofa.

"Paige?"

I faked a yawn. "Sorry, just dozing. What's up?"

He flicked on the light before I could stop him. I tried to turn away, but he strode over, saying, "Paige? What happened?" Then he looked at the phone still in my hand and stopped dead. "Shit. It's not— Is everything okay?"

I couldn't answer.

"It's not Lucas, is it?"

Fresh tears filled my eyes. I blinked them back, but not fast enough, and he crouched in front of me.

"Is he hurt?"

I shook my head. "He . . . he slept with her. Ava."

I waited for his laugh. Not just a chuckle, but a tremendous burst of laughter that would tell me I was nuts, that there was another explanation.

Only he didn't laugh. He didn't say anything. He just sat there, looking at me, and the expression on his face wasn't shock or disbelief. It was pain.

"I'm sorry," he said.

My heart thudded against my ribs. No, this wasn't right. Adam should laugh. He should tease about me getting into the champagne early or falling asleep and having a bad dream, because clearly—*clearly*—Lucas had not cheated on me.

My mouth opened, but I couldn't say anything. He hovered there, as if trying to decide something, then lowered himself beside me. He leaned forward, elbows on his knees, silent for a moment, then he twisted to meet my gaze.

"A few months ago, when you were out of town, I . . ." He took a deep breath. "I caught him. With someone. It wasn't anything . . . Well, it wasn't completely incriminating, just . . ."

He hesitated, then shook his head as if deciding I didn't need details.

I was misunderstanding. I had to be. Or he'd misunderstood what he'd seen. Not Lucas. *Never* Lucas.

Adam went on. "He fell over himself insisting it wasn't what it looked like, that he was just under a lot of stress because of the Cabal stuff, and with you away, and he'd had a few drinks . . ." He rubbed his chin. "I believed him. I figured he was just flirting, and me catching him was all he needed to realize how close he'd come to completely fucking up his life."

"But . . . Ava," I managed. "You knew she—"

"—had the hots for him. Yeah. I figured this was the best test I could give Lucas. If he didn't give in to temptation, then everything was okay. And if he did . . . ?"

Adam clenched his fists and I could feel the heat radiating from them.

"Don't," I whispered.

"He doesn't deserve you, Paige. He never did. When you hooked up with him, I wondered what the hell you were thinking. But you were happy, so I didn't say anything. Then you bought this house, and he moved in, and next thing you know, you're marrying the guy. He barely earned enough to cover his expenses, jetted all over the country playing crusader while you slaved at home and raised Savannah."

"It wasn't like that."

"Yeah, it was. But then he bought the office with his trust fund, so you guys had a place to work together, and I figured he was finally manning up. Then a few years later, what happens? He joins the Cabal. The *Cabal*."

"It's not like—"

"Not like that? Listen to yourself. You spent years supporting him. Then years helping build his business. And what does he do? Joins forces with the bad guys and screws around on you. Don't defend him."

I kept my mouth shut, but inside I was still thinking, *It's not like that*, because it wasn't. I'd been the one who insisted Lucas take pro bono jobs instead of paying ones. I'd seen how much it hurt him to watch me working while he chased his dream. I'd known how hard it was to dip into his hated trust fund, but I'd known it was important, too, for him to buy the business so we could pursue that dream together. I understood why he helped with the Cabal and how much he struggled with that choice.

"We should have seen this coming," Adam went on. "As soon as he joined the Cabal. Screwing around on your wife is just part of the culture there. Hell, his own mother was Benicio's mistress, and the guy saw nothing wrong with making his bastard son the heir. A complete lack of respect for his wife."

Again, I wanted to say it wasn't like that. Benicio had made a political marriage, and ended up with a vicious woman who threatened to ruin his business if he divorced her. They hadn't lived together for decades.

Adam knew all that. He'd never had a problem with it before. Never had a problem with *Lucas* before, and certainly never said he thought I was being mistreated.

Adam was my oldest friend. Whenever he'd had issues with my boyfriends, he'd said so, which meant he was backfilling now, reshaping history to make me feel better. Only I didn't want him to tell me what an asshole Lucas was. I wanted sympathy and support until I'd calmed down enough to make a decision.

Adam shifted closer and put his arm around my waist. I tensed, then leaned against him, closed my eyes, and let the tears fall again.

"Lucas has changed," Adam said after a few minutes. "He's not the guy you fell in love with. You know that. You've known that for a while." His arm tightened around me. "You've grown apart. We've all seen that. He's becoming the Cabal heir, and you're becoming the heir's wife. Not his business partner. Not his confidante. Not his lover. Just his wife. You're trying to be everything he needs, but *you* haven't changed, Paige. It's all him. He's not the same guy, and you know it."

But he was. Even now, knowing what Lucas had done, I couldn't find comfort in that excuse—that he'd changed—because he hadn't. His life had changed. His work had changed. But as I'd watched the Cabal sucking him in, I'd watched for any sign that it was changing him. It wasn't. He was still the guy who wanted to save the world. He'd just come to realize that it might not happen quite the way he'd thought it would. He'd learned to be flexible. He'd grown up.

I wasn't making excuses for him. None of that changed what he'd done. I'd need to deal with that, but I couldn't just say, "He's changed into a selfish jerk." Whatever had happened to us, it was more complicated than that.

Adam brushed my hair from my shoulders and held me as I cried. When he kissed the top of my head, I stiffened, but only for a second, before relaxing back against him.

"He doesn't deserve you," he said, putting his hand under my chin. He lifted my face until our eyes met. "He never did."

Adam leaned forward. His lips touched mine, and I jerked back so fast I tumbled to the floor.

He gave a wry smile. "Not that scary, is it?"

He bent to help me up. I scrambled out of his way and shot to my feet. Then I looked at him, staring at me like a twelve-year-old who's had his heart trampled by his first crush.

I was having a nightmare. There was no doubt about it now. First Lucas sleeping with Ava. Then finding out it might not be the first time he'd cheated. And now Adam—*Adam*—making a pass at me.

Adam had never hit on me. Well, okay, once when he was thirteen, he'd tried to cop a feel, but considering our ages and my early development, I'd have been surprised if he hadn't tried that at least once. And once was all it had been.

There was no way my oldest friend just happened to be nursing a deep, unrequited love for me and had managed to hide it while working and socializing with me for years.

"Is it really that big a shock?" he said finally.

"Um, yes. Yes, it is. I'm . . . I'm going to go back to sleep now, and when I wake up, Lucas will be here and you'll be flirting with Savannah and everything will be back to normal."

"Flirting with Savannah?" His brows shot up. "She's a kid, Paige. We hang out. That's it. You're the one I—"

"No, I'm not. Trust me, I'm not, and we both know it."

He stepped toward me. I backed up—and smacked into the wall. He kept coming. I held up my hands.

"Stop right there, Adam. Do you remember what happened when we were kids and you tried to feel me up?"

He smiled. "How could I forget?"

"I zapped you with an energy bolt and you felt it for weeks."

The smile grew, his eyes crinkling. "Some days I think I'm still feeling it."

"And do you remember what I said? That if you ever tried something like that again, I'd aim lower."

He laughed. "I remember, and I get the hint." He stepped back. "I'll give you your space, but we need to talk—"

A binding spell stopped him mid-sentence. I strode over and looked up at him, frozen in place.

"I didn't hit you with an energy bolt. I calmly moved your hand away, and you got the message. We never said a word about it. No spells. No threats. I don't know who you are, but you're not Adam Vasic."

His eyes blazed copper. He lunged, and the spell snapped. I stumbled out of the way. When he kept coming, I hit him with a knock-back spell. He fell back against a lamp, and it crashed to the floor.

"Remember that lamp?" I said. "Remember where we bought it?"

"You honestly think I remember buying a stupid lamp?"

"No, because you aren't Adam. If you were, you couldn't have snapped that binding spell."

A humorless smile. "Face it, your spells aren't that good, babe. Especially when you're as stressed-out as you are right now, which also explains why you're pulling this shit. I'm making my big confession here, laying my heart on the line, and—"

"You aren't Adam."

"No? What's the explanation, then? Glamour spell? That only works if you were expecting to see him tonight, which you weren't."

"Demonic possession."

"Right, like any low-level fiend would dare possess a demon lord's son."

No matter what he said, there was no doubt that the thing talking to me wasn't Adam. He wasn't even bothering to try now, throwing off Adam's tone, his personality, his mannerisms.

I had to be sure what was going on, though, before I could do anything about it. I knew a spell that would reveal a possessing demon, but it came with a dangerous side effect. Definitely a last resort.

"Okay, if you are Adam, tell me this. When—"

"I'm not playing that game anymore, Paige." The phone started to ring. He snatched it up and threw it across the room. "Do you know how much this hurts? We've been friends—"

"Since when?" I said. "When did we first meet? How? Who was—?"

He dove at me. I tried to swing out of the way, but he caught my arm and wrenched it, and I hit the floor, pain screaming through my shoulder.

"I don't want to hurt you," he said, coming at me again. "I just need you to sit down so I can talk—"

I caught him in another binding spell. His eyes glowed and he broke free with a snarl. I lifted my hands to launch a knockback, but he grabbed my arm, red-hot fingers searing into me. I howled in agony and he let go. I stared down at my arm, blistered and raw.

Then I slammed him with an energy bolt that knocked him off his feet, and he hit the floor, convulsing.

I cast the demon reveal spell, and Adam's form shimmered. His eyes blazed pure white and when they turned my way, I knew I was seeing a demon. A very pissed-off demon.

He struggled to his feet. I tried to smack him down with a knockback, but nothing happened. That was the side effect: reveal the demon and your spells react as they would on a demon, which means not at all.

15. DRAGON'S BLOOD AND BUCKTHORN

I raced upstairs. Once in the bathroom, I slammed and locked the door. Then I went through the door leading into our room and locked it behind me, hoping he'd think I'd barricaded myself in the bathroom.

As the demon thumped up the stairs, the phone rang again. I thought of veering for it, but he was too close.

I snuck into our walk-in closet and eased the door shut. Then I used a spell to unlock a second door, this one leading to a cupboard barely big enough for me to squeeze into. A decent hiding place. But what I wanted was what we kept in this hidden cubby: our ritual materials.

I'd only tried demon exorcism once. Lucas was more adept at it, but even he couldn't always manage the tricky ritual.

At the thought of Lucas, I hesitated. If Adam was possessed, could Lucas be, too? No, he drank a weekly potion to guard against it. So did I. Adam was supposed to, but he swore the brew gave him a headache, reacting with his demon blood. Besides, as Adam argued, they rarely possessed the children of lords. Too many political implications.

But even if Lucas *wasn't* possessed, maybe this was still connected and he hadn't really—

A thud as the demon pounded on the bathroom door. "Come out, you little bitch! I made a bargain and I'm damned well going to keep my end of it."

I started gathering everything I'd need. Dragon's blood, buckthorn—I pulled the box for buckthorn off the shelf. It was empty.

Empty? Who the hell would leave—

Savannah.

Goddamn it! Taking the last piece of bread and not putting it on the grocery list was bad enough. We were going to have a talk about this. Right after I had a talk about Adam not drinking his anti-possession brew.

"Do you think I can't break this door down? You have three seconds to come out, or that's not all I'm breaking!"

Okay, forget Savannah and Adam. First, I had to survive long enough to chew them out.

I grabbed more boxes from the shelves, ripping off lids, praying Savannah had just misplaced the buckthorn.

"Three, two, one . . ." A crash as he kicked in the bathroom door.

Face it, I wasn't finding the buckthorn. Not in time, anyway. What other ritual could I use? Would rituals work against him if my spells didn't? What if—?

"Where the hell are you hiding, witch?"

His footsteps thundered down the hall.

I grabbed vervain from the shelf. It was for banishing ghosts, but maybe it could weaken the demon enough for my spells to work.

My hands trembled as I poured the dried herbs into a censer. As the demon thumped into the bedroom, I lit the censer. He went straight for the closet and ripped open the door.

A grunt, as if he could sense me inside but couldn't figure out where I was hiding. Hangers clicked as he searched. Then, with another grunt, he found the inner door. He kicked it in. Splinters rained down on me as I blew hard on the vervain, sending a cloud of smoke into his face.

The demon coughed and swatted at it. The yellow glow in his eyes dimmed.

"Vervain?" he said. "Do you think I'm some lowly shade to be banished with—"

I hit him with a knockback. He barely teetered, but his eyes widened as he realized I'd weakened his immunity.

I hit him with an energy bolt, then a knockback, then another bolt, and he stumbled back, dazed. I hit him again—this time with my hands—and dodged past him into the bedroom.

"You're only going to piss me off, witch," he yelled as he came after me. "And that's not something you want—"

He stopped. Still running, I glanced back to see him frozen in place. Then I smacked into Savannah as she rounded the top of the stairs.

"That isn't—" I began.

"Adam. Yeah, I know. He was acting weird at the office. Avoiding me, which is weird for Adam. I knew something was up, but when I went to confront him, I found myself trapped. Bastard jammed a chair under the doorknob. Unlock spells don't really work well on that. I tried calling you, in case he was coming here, but I guess he'd already arrived." She glanced over at me. "He hasn't been taking his anti-possession brew, has he?"

"Apparently not. I cast a demon reveal, thinking I could get into the storeroom and whip up the exorcism potion. Seems we're out of buckthorn."

She winced. "Sorry. It's downstairs in the kitchen cupboard."

"Why would you—?" I shook my head. "Fine. Let's tie this guy up, and I'll get the buckthorn."

Savannah had put the herbs in the tea cupboard, reasoning that they looked enough like tea leaves not to concern human guests. As for why she'd needed it in the kitchen at all, I wasn't going to ask.

I headed upstairs. All was silent up there, meaning the demon was still locked in Savannah's binding spell.

I was starting down the hall when the stairs creaked behind me. Before I could turn, something cold went around my neck. I grabbed it and spun, lashing out with a knockback spell that sent my attacker slamming into the wall.

"Lucas?"

"Your defensive reaction has improved. Apparently, sneaking up to deliver a gift is no longer such a wise idea."

"Gift?" I looked down at my hand. What I'd grabbed was a necklace with an engraved red stone for a pendant.

"A carnelian amulet of Hamiah," he said. "I know you've been looking for one."

I stared at it and my first thought was: *It's an apology. He thinks he can buy me off with baubles.* But then I looked up at him, and he smiled, and I knew whatever I'd heard on the phone had been an illusion. Counterfeit magic to convince me my husband had been unfaithful.

I lifted onto my tiptoes and kissed him. He kissed me back with no hesitation, no surprise, no sign that I'd have any reason *not* to welcome him home.

"Oh my God!"

Savannah's voice made us jump apart. She strode down the hall, gaze fixed on Lucas's shirt. I followed it to see a spreading crimson stain. He looked down and touched it.

"You're hurt," I said. "How—?"

He cut me off by pressing his stained fingers to my lips. Sweet and fruity.

"Strawberry jam?" I said.

"Spread, actually. Another gift. Your knockback must have broken the jar in my pocket."

"Strawberry spread?" Savannah said. "Why would you—?" She stopped and lifted her hands. "Dumb question, and I don't want to hear the answer."

"Nor was I going to provide it. So—"

A muffled sound from the bedroom cut him off.

"Shit," Savannah said. "Binding spell broke."

She hurried in to recast it. Before I could explain, Lucas strode to the bedroom door. He looked at what appeared to be Adam, bound, gagged, and sitting on our bed.

"Ah," Lucas said. "Seems I interrupted something. My apologies."

Savannah laughed. "Only you would walk in on this and apologize. It's not what it looks like."

"It's not demonic possession?"

She shook her head. "And only you would jump to that conclusion."

"Yes, it's possession," I said. "Someone sent him here to seduce me—"

Savannah made choking noises.

"It didn't work," I said.

"Well, duh. I just mean . . . eww. Adam is not going to live this one down."

"I'm sure he won't. But before we bring him back, we need to find out who sent the demon."

"Someone who's not very bright," Savannah said. "Sending *anyone* to seduce you would be a waste of time. But Adam?" She shook her head. "Time to get some answers."

16. CONTRACT NEGOTIATIONS

*S*avannah walked over and yanked the gag off the demon. "Okay, who's the dumbass who sent you to possess Adam and seduce Paige?"

The demon pressed his lips together and glowered at us.

"I asked you a question," Savannah said.

"Let's forget who for now," I said. "*Why* did someone want you to seduce me?"

Again, he didn't answer. Savannah lifted her hands, as if to hit him with a spell, and then quickly lowered them, as if she'd remembered it was Adam's body she was about to blast.

"We should begin the exorcism," Lucas said. "Clearly, he isn't going to reveal his employer's identity."

"Employer?" the demon said.

"My apologies. A poor choice of words, as you are not receiving financial compensation. Whoever holds the chit against you, I mean. Whomever you fear if you break this obligation."

"I fear no one. And I answer to no one."

As Lucas kept baiting him, I looked at the stain on his shirt. He'd come home early to surprise me. There was no way he'd even been in Los Angeles when I'd called Ava.

I cast a privacy spell so I could speak to him without being overheard. "How did you get back so fast? I talked to you less than an hour ago."

I'm sure he wondered why I was interrupting to ask this, but I had a feeling the answers might help us get some from the demon.

He cast his own privacy spell. "My father was in LA for meetings with the Nasts, so . . ." He gave a faint smile. "I borrowed the keys to his jet. I was almost here when you called."

That explained the hollow sound—he'd been on a plane. It also explained the young woman talking in the background—the flight attendant.

Ava hadn't sent those messages hoping I'd catch her in bed with Lucas. She'd known that wasn't happening. She'd sent them so I'd catch her in bed with someone who'd impersonate Lucas.

I turned to the demon. "It was Ava Cookson, wasn't it? She wanted me to think Lucas had cheated and then you'd come over to console me."

"She thought she could convince you that Lucas had screwed around?" Savannah snorted. "She's even dumber than she looked."

I felt Lucas's gaze on me. He knew I'd fallen for it. Shame washed over me, and I looked away.

"I don't doubt Ava's involved," Lucas said. "But not as the mastermind. She's simply a pawn. Like him." A dismissive wave at the demon.

The demon's eyes blazed yellow. "I'm nobody's pawn."

"No? Then if you don't fear repercussions, tell me who summoned you."

"You're supposed to be a genius," the demon said. "You figure it out."

That's what he wanted. Us to figure it out. Otherwise, he could have left Adam's body the minute Savannah bound it.

He wanted to negotiate, but the contract that bound him forbade him from revealing who'd made it.

"We know that Ava's brother did die," I said. "That was a matter of public record. And we know he was at the Gallantes' fight club, although I doubt they killed him."

"They didn't," Lucas said. "As you suspected, he was killed by his human debtors. I verified that today, and I believe Ava knew it all along. However, her case did have potential supernatural overtones. It was an excuse to hire me and put the plan in action."

"So the plan was to make Paige think Lucas had been unfaithful," Savannah said. "And then drive her into the arms of her sexy guy friend. But why?"

"Ava was chosen for a reason, wasn't she?" I said to the demon. "Whoever hired you chose Ava because he wanted us investigating the Gallantes' fight club. He wanted us there the night a fighter died."

"Seems the little woman is a better detective than you," the demon said to Lucas.

"No," I said. "I'm just better at thinking out loud."

"Clearly, your assumption is correct, then," Lucas said. "Someone wanted Adam to seduce you *and* wanted us investigating the Gallantes. I fail to see how the first part ties into the second, but if the Warners are orchestrating the deaths to put the Gallantes out of business, then they would be the obvious suspects."

"Or someone who owes the Warners a whole lot of money," Savannah said. "Who might do this for them in return for his debt."

"Possibly," Lucas said. "However—"

"Remember that message I sent you?" Savannah said to me. "I know who owes the Warners. Someone with the clout to call a demon. Someone who'd love to see Lucas suffer as a bonus. Someone who's nasty as hell, but not quite bright enough to pull this off."

"My brother," Lucas said. "Carlos."

Savannah nodded. She turned to the demon. "Blink twice for no. Once for yes."

He blinked once.

We had to strike a deal with the demon to get him to fill in the blanks. Ten years ago, I'd have been horrified at the suggestion. But Lucas wasn't the only one who'd learned to be flexible. Demons could be bargained with, if you knew what you were doing. Lucas did.

The agreement was simple. He'd tell us the details and in return we agreed to stand as his defense and character witnesses, should Carlos accuse him of breaking his bargain. We'd support his claim that Carlos had sent him on an impossible mission. Sounded silly, but demons are like any other contract worker: if they break a deal, no one's going to call them back.

Once we agreed, the demon told his story. Carlos owed the Warners for debts rung up at their fight clubs. They came to him with an offer—put the Gallantes out of business and they'd forgive the debt. I'm sure they figured he'd use his Cabal clout to do that, but he couldn't, given the Gallantes' club was in Nast territory. So he hired someone to inject fighters with poison during a pregame backslap from a supporter.

It would have worked eventually, but Carlos was impatient. Besides, he had another, more irritating thorn in his side to worry about. Then, while he was in LA on business, he had a one-night stand with a half-demon who told him about her own experience with the Gallantes. With that, Carlos saw the solution to both problems. Hire Ava—that half-demon—to get us on the case and pretend to seduce Lucas.

Yes, *pretend* to seduce him. Carlos knew his half brother wouldn't actually cheat on me. The point was simply to send me into Adam's arms. Lucas would be crushed and would blame himself, thinking his involvement in the Cabal had driven me away. To keep me, he'd leave the Cabal. Carlos was sure of it.

After the demon finished his story, we returned Adam to his body. I decided to let Savannah explain what had happened. It was a little too embarrassing coming from me. Lucas and I went downstairs and he insisted on tending to my burned arm. As he bandaged it, I fingered the amulet now around my neck.

"Thank you," I said after a few minutes. "For this."

He nodded and finished binding my arm before he said, "Did you really think I'd been unfaithful?"

"No, but the proof seemed to be there and I . . . I guess I didn't want to be one of those women who sees the signs and pretends she doesn't. Anyway, Carlos's plan didn't work. That demon didn't get anywhere with me."

"Of course not."

I know he didn't mean for those words—spoken with such certainty—to sting. But they did. Even Carlos—never known for his brains—was astute enough to realize Lucas wouldn't cheat. Yet he believed he could convince me he had, and he'd been right.

I thought about Ethan Gallante and remembered what he'd told his blackmailer: "You can bring me all the evidence you want; my answer will remain the same. I trust my brother." I thought I'd have said the same thing about my husband. But I'd let my problems with the Cabal wear down my confidence and my trust, and the shame of that burned.

"I'm sorry," I said as Lucas sat beside me on the couch.

"Don't be. If you thought there was a possibility, then we have a problem. I've known that for a while."

"There's no problem," I said. "Sure, things are tough, but you and I are—"

He twisted to face me. "Paige, please. Don't keep saying everything's all right. Don't keep acting like it is. I can't address the problem when you won't admit there is one."

"I—"

"You're struggling. You're feeling left behind and left out. But you don't want to upset me, and you want to handle it on your own. You think if you keep working at it, the Cabal will realize you're a valuable asset."

Nailed it on the first try.

His voice softened. "That's not going to happen, Paige. I thought it would. I hoped it would. But it's not."

"And it won't. I'm a woman, I'm a witch, and I'm married to the guy they'd rather not have as part of the company at all."

The demon had tried to seduce me by insisting Lucas was no longer the man I'd married. Part of me did grieve for the life we'd lost when his brothers died. I understood why Lucas needed to be part of the Cabal, but I still grieved.

Yet even when I'd wanted to hate Lucas, I'd recognized the demon's lies for what they were. My life had changed; my husband hadn't.

Our marriage *was* in trouble. Pretending it wasn't would only make things worse.

"I'm leaving the Cabal," Lucas said.

I shook my head. "We can handle Carlos. I have some ideas. He won't try anything like this—"

"Carlos has nothing to do with it. It's not working out. I need to make a choice. Maybe I'm being selfish, but I choose you." He leaned over, lips brushing mine as he whispered, "I always choose you."

Only, he couldn't. As strong as Benicio was for his age, the stress of preparing a new heir to fight Carlos would be too much. In the meantime, his search would leave the Cabal vulnerable. The Nasts, sensing weakness, would strike.

The supernatural world needed the Cortez Cabal to balance the Nasts and St. Clouds. The Cortez Cabal needed Benicio. Benicio needed Lucas. Wishing it wasn't so wouldn't change that.

"You can't," I said.

He squared his shoulders. "Yes, I can, and I—"

"No, you can't. The ball is in my court on this one. You're right, I need to stop pretending nothing's wrong. And stop pretending it's going to change."

"You shouldn't—"

"But I will. Suck it up and deal. That's what I have to do." I looked over at him. "When I was in Miami this week, after the meeting, one of the employees talked to me. She'd just been promoted to management and was having a problem. The other managers hold weekly meetings at a strip club, which means she's missing out. She wanted my advice. I told her she had two choices. One, take it over their heads and insist they move the meetings. Two, go to the meetings anyway. I suggested the latter."

Lucas chuckled. "They'd probably be so embarrassed that they'd change the venue."

"Maybe. But whether they did or not, the point is she wouldn't miss the meetings. She agreed and thanked me. She said there wasn't anyone else for her to talk to. I've been butting my head against their damned glass ceiling, determined to make a difference. But I *did* make a difference on that trip. I was just too focused on the big win to celebrate the small one. That's where I can do some good. Helping anyone who feels like an outsider, who wants to talk to someone who isn't a Cortez, isn't a sorcerer."

"You're right that the Cabal could use you as an ombudsman for employees who feel disenfranchised, but I don't want you to feel you're settling—"

"I never settle. I just lower my oversized expectations. I've always aimed too high, first with the Coven, then the council, now with this. I've only ever set my sights on the best once and gotten it." I kissed him. "Can't expect to get that lucky ever again."

He pulled me to him, and we sank into the cushions. Then Adam's and Savannah's voices sounded in the hall.

I said, "They're going to want to know what we plan to do about Carlos. Like I said, I have an idea . . ."

17. MAINTAINING THE CHARADE

*L*ucas and I went to Miami. It had been months since we'd worked together. I'd told myself with recent cases that it made more sense for us to split our resources. A lie. Smarting from the Cabal's rejection, my confidence had needed the boost of succeeding on my own.

I realized my mistake now. Working without Lucas hadn't bolstered my confidence; it only hammered a wedge between us. So we flew to Miami together, even if I didn't need to be there.

While I stayed at the hotel, Lucas went into the office early, taking our new spy camera so I could watch my plan unfold. He spoke to his father first. He didn't tell him what had happened. Lucas had never tattled on his half brothers, even when they'd tormented him as a boy. He just said he'd come to do some work. And was Benicio free for lunch? He'd like to discuss that offer to buy him a condo in Miami.

Flying halfway across the country to "do some work"? Wanting to discuss the condo, after refusing to consider it for years? It was odd. Very odd, and I'm sure Benicio wondered what was up . . . which was exactly the point.

One of Carlos's sycophants would be quick to tell him that Lucas was in the office, and had met with their father. Carlos would go straight to Benicio, find out what Lucas had said, and then . . .

Lucas's office door banged open, his admin assistant fluttering in behind Carlos, motioning that he'd barged past her. I watched the scene through the camera.

Carlos parked himself in front of Lucas's desk. The first time I met Carlos, I had to admit he was the most attractive of the Cortez brothers. Over the years, his looks had faded—too many drugs, too much alcohol, too many other habits I preferred not to think about. Since his brothers' deaths, he'd cleaned up the dope and booze, but those were really the least of his sins, and that dissolute look had hardened into something a lot more dangerous.

"What the hell are you doing here?" Carlos said.

"Working."

Carlos peered at him. While Lucas looked perfectly presentable, he wasn't his usual pressed and polished self. His chin bore shaving nicks. His hair looked unwashed. His clothing was rumpled.

Carlos smiled. "You're not having lunch with Dad to talk about the condo. You only said that so he wouldn't worry. You're going to tell him you're leaving."

"Leaving?"

"The Cabal. You're here to clean out your desk." He tried to look thoughtful. "It's Paige, isn't it? Something happened with Paige."

Lucas blinked in feigned surprise and then shuffled papers. "I prefer not to discuss it."

"Ah, so I'm right. Problems at home, huh? Not like we didn't all see this coming. So you're telling Dad that you're leaving—"

"Staying."

Now it was Carlos's turn to blink.

Lucas straightened the papers. "I'm here to tell him that I'm staying. My marriage is over, so I see no reason to maintain this charade."

After a moment, Carlos managed a strangled, "What?"

"The Cabal needs me. You can't be expected to cover both Hector's and William's jobs. I'm fooling myself taking on minor assignments and thinking that helps. It doesn't. I need to be here, and the only thing holding me back was Paige. She hated me working for the Cabal. Now that my marriage has ended . . ." His jaw tightened, eyes cooling. "It appears to be time for a fresh start. I'll be accepting my role as heir."

"Wh-what happened?" A split-second pause. "Did she find someone else? Because if she did, I'm sure it's not what you think. Just a one-time thing. It happens. No need to—"

"Paige has not been unfaithful. Apparently, she thinks I have been. She kicked me out."

I swore I could hear Carlos's sigh of relief. His plan had gone awry, but this could be fixed.

"I'm sure it's a misunderstand—"

"It's an excuse," Lucas cut in. "She's been unhappy for months. I've tried to fix the problem, but obviously she doesn't want it fixed, so she's concocted this wild story—"

"Are you sure she concocted it? What does she think happened?"

"I have no idea. The conversation never went that far."

Carlos strode over to the coatrack and picked up Lucas's jacket and bag. "Some gold-digger slut has set you up. Happens to me all the time."

"I don't think—"

"Just go home. Talk to her. You'll work this out. You don't really want to be here."

Lucas looked around, undecided, and in the silence that followed, I knew what Carlos was thinking. He'd made a fatal miscalculation. If Lucas lost me, he wouldn't fall apart. He'd grieve in his own way . . . by throwing himself into work.

Without me to remind Lucas of his goals, he'd fulfill Benicio's greatest dream and Carlos's greatest nightmare. He'd become a true heir.

Bullshit, of course. Lucas didn't need me to keep him straight. But as Lucas hesitated, it only confirmed Carlos's fears.

"Go on," Carlos said. "You owe your marriage that much. Hear her out. See if it can be saved. You still love her, right?"

Lucas hesitated so long I swore I could hear Carlos's heart pound. Then he said, "All right," and took his coat.

After Carlos left, Lucas called me.

"Well played," I said.

"It was your script," he said. "Somehow, I don't think we'll need to worry about Carlos trying to break us up again."

"I hope not. So the next step is to foil his plan with the Gallantes."

"That will be a simple matter of exposing it. We'll head to Santa Cruz later. In the meantime, I suspect I can't wriggle out of lunch with my father."

"You shouldn't. And you might want to take his condo offer. I know we've discussed it. Go ahead and accept. That'll keep Carlos on his toes, thinking you're planning for a possible marriage failure."

"Agreed. Lunch, however, isn't for a few hours. Any thoughts on how we might fill them?"

"Oh, I have a few ideas."

"I'll be right there."

I smiled and hung up the phone. Things weren't back to normal yet. That would take work. But we'd get through it. I'd make sure of that, starting with a little Hawaiian getaway for two.

Also available from #1 *New York Times* bestselling author
Kelley Armstrong

The Otherworld Series

978-0-452-29664-0

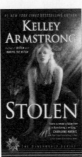

978-0-452-29666-4

978-0-452-29722-7

978-0-452-29799-9

978-0-14-219674-8

www.kelleyarmstrong.com

PLUME
An imprint of Penguin Random House LLC
www.penguin.com

Also from #1 *New York Times* bestselling
author Kelley Armstrong

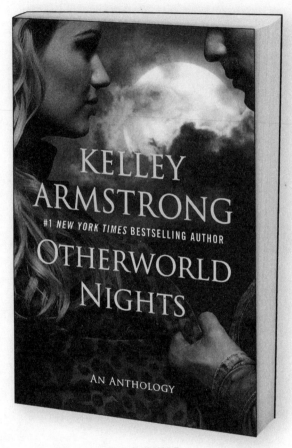

978-0-45-229834-7

PLUME
An imprint of Penguin Random House LLC
www.penguin.com